THE FLIGHT OF THE SPELLBOUND

THE FLIGHT OF THE SPELLBOUND

A ROMANTIC FANTASY ADVENTURE

THE KARNEESIA CHRONICLES
BOOK TWO

CLAIRE TRELLA HILL

This book is a work of fiction. Names, characters, places, and incidents are the product of the author's imagination or are used fictitiously and are not to be construed as real. Any resemblance to actual events, locales, or persons, living or dead, is coincidental.

THE FLIGHT OF THE SPELLBOUND

Copyright © 2025 by Claire Trella Hill

Cover Illustration by Kay Fine

Cover Text and Formatting by MIBLArt

Copyedited by Amy McNulty

Paperback ISBN: 979-8-9883463-4-0

All rights reserved.

For all those who fear their prayers go unheard.
Please keep knocking.

How long, Lord? Will you forget me forever?
How long will you hide your face from me?
How long must I wrestle with my thoughts
and day after day have sorrow in my heart?
How long will my enemy triumph over me?

— PSALM 13:1-2

…My heart in hiding
Stirred for a bird…

— "THE WINDHOVER," GERARD MANLEY HOPKINS

PROLOGUE

GUIDATH, DAMASLAR'S CAPITAL CITY—THIRTEEN
YEARS AGO

The tavernkeeper shook the boy hard on the steps of the fine mansion, making his small head jolt back and forth, rattling his teeth. "Now, you listen to me," he said, spittle flying from his lips as he tried to form the words correctly, drunk as he was. "Listen. Don't you come back. Nothing for you there now."

The boy twisted but couldn't free himself from the fingers clamped on his shoulders. Even drunk, the man had a grip of iron.

The tavernkeeper rang the bell of the grand house, and a lone chime echoed inside. "And keep your mouth shut. Else you'll end up jus' like her. They don' want your kind. You hear?"

The boy looked up. Fear poured off the balding man along with the sweat plastering his remaining hair to his head. The tavernkeeper eyed him sidelong, and the boy heard the word as clear as day, though the man's lips didn't move.

"Unnatural."

The boy clenched his teeth.

The door creaked open cautiously, and a thin man with a beaky nose looked out dubiously in the dusk light at the drunk and an odd-looking redheaded boy in his grasp.

"May I help you?" the servant asked, clearly hoping he couldn't.

"Here to see the High Wizard," the tavernkeeper said, pushing the boy into the light that spilled from the doorway. "Got his bastard."

The boy vainly tried to scrub away the tear tracks on his face.

The servant gave the boy a long, slow look. "Follow me," he finally said.

He stowed them in a small parlor with a fire crackling in the grate and left. After a time, the servant returned with a tall, dark-haired man with narrowed blue eyes and a few threads of gray in his beard. His rich green-and-gold robes swept the floor.

The wizard looked the boy in the face, and the boy looked back. He knew what the man saw—red hair, blue eyes, and pointed ears, the elongated tips a clear indicator of faefolk blood somewhere in his line.

"I don't know this child," the wizard said.

The boy saw the truth in the eyes the same shade as his own.

"Liar." The word popped out before he could stop himself.

Those ice cold eyes bored into him. The boy shivered.

The wizard turned to the tavernkeeper. "Why have you brought him here?"

The tavernkeeper cleared his throat. "Beggin' your pardon, m'lord—"

"Your Grace," the man corrected smoothly, a thread of iron in his voice.

"Yer Grace," the tavernkeeper went on uncertainly. "Him and his mother worked at my tavern until yesterday—The Crane and Cup. You remember. The mother's dead. Down a well by mob rule. They would've taken the lad as well, 'cept I hid him when they came lookin'. But he can't stay. I got customers to think of. They don't much like being served by sommat could witch 'em."

The boy gave one shuddering gasp and then was quiet.

"I see." With a long, assessing stare at the boy, the wizard glanced at his servant. "Give this man something for his trouble, Yoast, and see him out."

The fat man glistened appreciatively, and then the boy was alone with the wizard.

"Well, what are you called?" the wizard finally said, breaking the silence of the crackling fire.

"Fee," the boy whispered.

"What?"

"Fee. Feonar," he said, voice stronger. "Yaldson," he added pointedly.

"Well, Feonar, while you are a bastard and do not bear my name, I am your father." The wizard's gaze swept him again, and Fee clenched his hands at his sides to resist covering his ears. The pointed ears that marked him as different. Something other.

"*Can* you 'witch them'?" his father asked, his voice full of bored curiosity.

Fee stared at the man who had sired him and did not respond. This night had taught him the value of silence.

The wizard's voice slithered into the boy's head, coldly assessing: *"Perhaps this boy may be of use to me after all."*

SOUTHERN DAMASLAR—NINE YEARS AGO

The snatchers hauled the girl out of the wagon with the rest of the crying children, all chained together in a line. The black stone tower loomed over her, hiding the sun and throwing them all into shadow. An old man with white hair and black eyes emerged from the tower, carrying a tall, carved staff. Behind him, a dark-haired woman, thin and pale, stared at the line of children, her eyes watering.

"For a batch of ten, that's ten gold apiece," the snatcher in charge said, his voice thick with phlegm. He hurked the mucus up and spat it into the dirt.

The old man barked, "You know I don't want them all."

"Do yer test, then." The snatcher shrugged. "The ones you don't want, I can sell down in Darikar and the Wastes."

The girl shivered, trying not to rattle her chains. The winter was cold, even here in the south, and she was barefoot, wearing only her flannel shift and smallclothes, those now dirty and stained from weeks of travel. But Darikar was even farther from home.

The staff in the old man's hand made her uneasy. It was covered in glyphs, runes she didn't understand. They weren't the common printing, or the complicated script that nobles and royalty used. That left only the wizards' script.

Magic.

The old man sneered. He traced one of the symbols and muttered a few words.

The hair stood up on the back of her neck. She stared wide-eyed down the line of children as, above a select few, tongues of fire appeared. Of the ten children, three sported flames flickering weakly above them.

Then she tilted her head back, and her eyes rounded. Above her head hovered what was comparatively a signal fire, flaring nearly a foot in height.

The old man rubbed his hands together. "I'll take these four."

The snatchers moved quickly, uncoupling the chosen from the line. The other three began to wail in earnest as they were shoved towards the door at the tower's base.

At the end of the line, the girl dug her heels in. "No! I don't want to go in there!"

A clout from a heavy hand made her eyes water and her ears ring. "Shut up."

"No! No—"

He walloped her again.

The sad-eyed woman ducked her head and counted out coin

to the snatchers with shaking hands. One pinched the woman's bottom and laughed. Her face blanched, her hair sweeping forward like a curtain to hide behind. The men returned to the horses, pulling the unwanted children behind them.

The girl grabbed on to the doorframe and hung on grimly. Something inside her warned of the danger inside. She shrieked, "I'm not supposed to be here! I was stolen! I'm—"

"*You* forget *who you are*," the voice in her memory said. "*Forget even your name. Only then can you stay alive.*"

And then a cudgel came down on her hands with bruising force.

Her grip released. She was pulled through the great, gaping door into the dark.

SHE CAME TO CONSCIOUSNESS LATER, gasping on the cold, stone floor as the old man cackled. "It finally worked!" he crowed to the younger woman, his hands flying, moving quickly to form unknown shapes. "This proves that my theory is correct!" He sat down at a great desk and began to write frantically, his quill flying across the page. "Those fools will have to lift my banishment now!"

The girl tried to push herself up, but her bones felt like melted wax and she could barely move. The woman knelt beside her, holding a cup. She barely sipped from it before falling back to the cool ground.

The woman carefully gathered her small body into her arms, ignoring the dirt and the smell of dried urine. She walked out of the big, circular room and down a flight of stairs. They came to a small room with a bed, a small washstand, and a clothespress in it.

"What..." The girl coughed, her whole body shaking. "What happened to me?"

Flashes came back to her—a ring of glyphs on the floor. Trapped inside that circle. Blinding pain.

Bodies, off to the side. Discarded.

The woman did not reply as she set her on the bed. She reached for her hem.

"No!" The girl scooted back on the bed, searching for something to throw.

The woman held up her hands in a gentle, pacifying gesture. She picked up a cloth, dunked it in the washbasin, wrung it out, and offered it.

The girl stared at it a moment before snatching it from the woman's hand. As the girl rubbed it over her face, the woman pulled a clean shift from the clothespress and set it on the bed beside the girl. She mimed disrobing and washing before pointing to the shift.

At the farthest point on the bed from the woman, the girl shed her ruined clothes and pulled on the shift as fast as possible. It was far too big—one of the woman's, possibly. She washed with the cloth once she had the shift over her head to cover herself and then pulled her arms through it.

The woman pointed to the bed, patting it.

"Don't you talk?" the girl asked, frowning.

The woman tapped her mouth and her ears, shaking her head. She rapidly moved her hands.

The girl stared, confused.

The woman sat on the edge of the bed and traced a letter from the common alphabet on the wall with her finger. She leaned toward the girl hopefully, her eyebrows raised.

"T," the girl whispered.

The woman smiled and traced three more letters. A, L, A. Then she pointed to herself.

"Tala?"

The woman nodded and moved her hand. A hand in a fist, her thumb between her pointer and middle fingers. Fist, thumb at the side. Fist with pointer and thumb extended in an—

"L," the girl said. "T-a-l—"

Tala made the fist with the thumb at the side again, smiling. "*TALA.*" Then she gestured to the girl.

The girl reached out a hesitating hand to the wall.

"*You can't trust anyone,*" her memory insisted. "*Tell and you're dead.*"

She pressed her lips together. Then, slowly, she traced the letters. E, Y, L.

The woman showed her the hand signs for the letters and smiled. "*EYL.*"

She nodded and gave the woman her own tremulous smile. Maybe she could trust her. Maybe she could escape—return home—

But that hope died at the break of day, when the old man's magic did its work and all her bones broke in unison.

CHAPTER

ONE

EYL

As the sun met the edge of the western horizon, painting the sky vibrant shades of orange and pink, Eyl felt the familiar tingle in her wings.

Banking sharply to catch an updraft, she flew higher over the wood and screamed, the sound echoing through the air. Her keen eyes could see the faint outline of the waxing moon to the east, rising above the trees. Eyl screamed again as the tingling became stronger, spreading down to her talons. The need came over her, as it did every night, to return to the lonely stone tower that jutted through the sparse treetops to the south, but she kept her gaze stubbornly away, fighting the urge as long as possible.

Eyl's golden eyes swept the landscape. She spied a flash of movement on the winding road that led through the wood. Hunter's instincts triggered, she dove.

Impressions rushed in at her as she plummeted. A dark horse. A rider, cloaked. The head tilted back—

Blue eyes.

The tingling in her body became a burn, burrowing into her skull, overriding her will.

Screeching her displeasure, she jerked up sharply and banked, heading back to the tower, back to prison of the worst sort.

Her powerful wings closed the distance as the last burning beams of dying light flared across the sky. She dove through the skylight in the top of the tower, her body prickling with sensation. She had barely made it back in time.

She fluttered behind the long, dingy curtain in the corner, her one shroud of privacy, and landed on the cold stone floor. More pins and needles spread through her body. Eyl braced in horrified anticipation, even though it was the worst thing she could do.

It was always the same. There was no escape.

Less than a minute later, all her bones snapped.

Pain exploded behind Eyl's eyes. Instinctively squeezing them shut, she shrieked and thrashed. Her whole body throbbed—and shifted. It seemed an eternity while her bones ground together and her limbs elongated. Feathers receded. Skin ached. Her brain felt as though it had been stirred with a red-hot poker.

Finally, the pain eased. Eyl opened her eyes and stared at her human fingers splayed out on the floor. Coughing, she shook hair so pale, it was nearly white out of her eyes and sat up, flexing her hands. She sometimes needed reminding of what she was—a girl or a bird.

She held back a shudder, remembering the few times her change had gotten stuck halfway. She'd lain there in agony, wishing to die. She always made it through, but she held a secret horror that what if this time would be the time she wouldn't complete the transition, if she'd stay like that forever—neither one thing nor the other, trapped in hell.

Eyl tasted the tang of iron. She had bitten her tongue. She drank greedily from the flask of water that sat beside her rolled-up pallet and her clothes, the only things in the world she really had a claim to.

Once she had drunk the flask dry, she pulled on her leggings and tunic. Straightening the tunic, she padded around the curtain and into the tower room proper, blinking as her eyes adjusted to the firelight.

Bookshelves and racks of scrolls crowded the large, round

workroom. Cabinets stuffed with bottles and jars filled most nooks and crannies, save for her small, curtained alcove. Worktables and a few armchairs ate up most of the floor space. On the other side of the room, the large fireplace burned merrily, eagerly snapping up the fresh wood Imani laid on the fire.

The girl turned to look at Eyl and straightened. Her dark skin glowed in the firelight. The same eternal embers flickered red-gold behind her eyes. Strange that a girl from Cadruissau, a country made up of ocean and islands, had gained power over fire.

Nodding at Eyl and smiling faintly, Imani returned to her post by the old man as he muttered and paged through a tome in his overstuffed chair.

"How was he today?" Eyl signed.

Imani flicked her fingers furtively. *"All right."*

Eyl scanned the worktables. Not many new notes. The old man's arthritis was probably hurting him. That wasn't good. He got testy when he was in pain, and when he was testy, he forgot more.

When it came to his studies, his research of magic and spells, his brain was as sharp as ever. But his body was weakening. The staff he'd once used for magic now doubled as a cane, and his gaunt frame showed none of the hearty meals they cooked for him. Worst yet, his memory was going. That, more than the tether runes on their bodies, served as a cage that grew tighter around them every night.

Memory rose again. Two blue eyes.

Eyl would have to speak to Kai about the person on the road.

"I'll be right back," she signed to Imani, shielding her flicking fingers so the old man wouldn't see.

Imani nodded, her eyes flaring with light.

Careful to keep out of the old man's line of sight, Eyl hurried down the long, circular stair that ran the height of the tower. Halfway down, she bumped into Kai on his way to take over the old man's duty. He always sat with him while she and Imani got supper ready. He was a dependable boy, and she hoped he knew how much she relied on him, since she couldn't bring herself to say it.

"I saw someone on horseback," she told him, "heading this way."

Kai nodded once and went back down the stairs. Eyl followed hard on his heels. They emerged in the kitchen, and she waited by the door as he stepped out into the darkening twilight, peering at the road.

She could not pass over the threshold as a human. The rune on her foot saw to that. Wouldn't want the precious experiment to escape. Imani could go as far as the clearing's edge, but only Kai could go as far as the village a few miles down the road. Thank goodness for that, or they'd all starve.

"Which direction?" Kai asked. A thin, emerald-green garter snake slid from between Kai's lips. Its forked tongue flickered, tasting the air. Kai pulled it free of his mouth and dropped it gently in the grass.

"From the north." Eyl pointed, and he strode away to investigate.

They had all been irrevocably changed by the old man's magics. She was forced to be a gyrfalcon during daylight. Imani could control fire. Kai spat up bugs and all manner of creepy crawlies when he spoke. Outside the tower, that was. The tower was spelled against vermin, and Kai hated coughing up dead things even more than live things. Luckily, they all knew hand signs, courtesy of Tala.

The familiar ache came again at the thought of Tala, gone for almost three years now. The only one who had cared.

Kai came back, a frown on his face. "There was no one in either direction."

"What? Are you sure? Could they have passed by, or stopped to camp?" Eyl leaned as close to the doorway as she could and peered down the dark road's long expanse.

Kai shook his head. "Only if they were on horseback."

"They were!"

"But I saw no tracks." He stared down at her. He and Imani both had surpassed her in height. She hadn't grown much in any direction after the old man's magic had its hooks in her. Another thing to blame him for.

Eyl stared up at him, her eyes narrowed. "So what are you saying?"

"Are you sure you saw someone?" he asked quietly, then he spat out two moths. They fluttered towards the light shining out of the doorway, but when the first reached the threshold, it shriveled and fell to the ground. Kai flinched and looked away.

Eyl bit her lip, leaning against the doorframe. *Had* she imagined it? Two chips of blue in a face. They had seemed so real…. She swallowed back the bile that rose up in her throat. Were the moorings between her and the falcon beginning to unravel? She had read of such things in the old man's tomes, shape changers and others with a beast nature losing themselves to the animals within. Some night hence, would her body change without her mind intact?

But would she have imagined the *horse*?

"I'm going to start supper," Eyl finally said.

"I'll spell Imani and send her down to help." Kai pulled the wriggling lizard from his mouth and set it on the tower's outer wall, away from the doorway. Then he stepped inside and headed for the old man's workroom.

Eyl hung the kettle on the hook over the fire, listening to his footfalls fading away. Then she sagged against the wall. "I can't be going mad," she whispered, squeezing her eyes shut. "Not now. You owe me that. You *owe* me." She pinched the bridge of her nose. "But thank you for Kai."

She and God had a contentious relationship, but she made a point to acknowledge the small mercies, for fear even they would disappear. And Kai was a mercy.

He had arrived here at eleven years old, but even at that age, he had shouldered more responsibility than necessary. Before that,

Tala had been the one to deal with her father and his needs, helping him wash and dress, getting him in and out of bed, because even then he had started to slow down. Kai had insisted on taking over those chores.

When Tala had died and the old man had gotten more unmanageable, Eyl had tried to help Kai, but the boy wouldn't hear of it. No woman ever attended a man to whom she was not related in Sarkan'ande culture. Not in Eyl's, either, but the sorcerer was old, and he'd never seen them as people at all, so Eyl doubted it would ever occur to him to be improper to his experiments. But Kai had stood firm, and she loved that boy for it. She couldn't be prouder if he were her own brother.

Brother.

She fumbled the cutlery as the memory threatened to overwhelm her.

"There you go, Eyl. Can't go riding on adventures without a sword, can you? Once you get the hang of a wooden one, I'll get you a real blade. Here, let me show you the first position."

Eyl tried to breathe through the unexpected slice of agony and threw the mental door shut.

"It will sign your death warrant," whispered the specter of the past.

Imani padded down the steps, her voice preceding her. "I made bread while the old man was napping today," she said cheerily, stepping into the kitchen. The younger girl's eyes danced, sparks lighting within them. "We can have it with the meat pie."

"Good." Eyl squeezed the girl's shoulder and gave her a crooked smile. "I'll slice it. Is the rabbit for the pie cooked?" She had dropped off what she had caught earlier in the day.

"Yes. What did you want to talk to Kai about?"

The knife in her hand trembled. "I thought I saw something from the sky. I was…." *Seeing things.* "It was nothing."

As Eyl sliced the bread, Imani stretched her hands over the fire in the hearth, and the flames leapt up to meet her, like loyal dogs eager for a master's praise. The hearth burned brighter, and Imani added a few more logs to feed the flames. She had turned out the best of the old man's experiments. What he had done to her had actually worked instead of corrupting her.

Eyl shoved away the thread of bitterness. She was alive, wasn't she? The scores of graves beyond the tower were testament to how much worse it could have been. She had no call to hold something against a thirteen-year-old that she had had no control over. No, she held it against the old man, who had bought children to experiment on. He was the one to blame.

Eyl's hand clenched around the knife. *We will be free,* she promised herself. *Even if it takes forever. There must be a way. If I just keep searching, I'll find it.*

"After the old man goes to sleep," Imani said. "Can we practice?"

"Yes," Eyl promised. She had taught Kai his letters and to read when he'd arrived, hidden from the old man and Tala. Now she was teaching Imani. It was hard though. Unless the old man was sleeping, one of them had to be with him at all times. And she didn't want him to know any of them could read. She had had to learn to keep secrets when she'd been sold, but she had learned well.

And she had kept her secrets—from the snatchers, from Tala, and even from Kai and Imani.

It was safer that way.

Imani beamed. "I'm getting better—I know I am. My hand doesn't shake and wobble as much when I make the letters. I practiced in the flour when I made the bread."

Eyl smiled. "Good for you."

"Kai arranged for the deliveries tomorrow, and he brought the mail and newsletters back from the village today."

The newsletters the old man ordered from Guidath, Damaslar's capital, were their one link to the outside world. They contained news on Damaslar's neighbors, politics, economics, and the war. Tala had always held them back for a day before she gave them to her father, and Eyl did the same—he would never share what the letters contained otherwise. "We'll read them after practice, then," Eyl promised. "See what you can pick out."

When the meat pie had finished cooking, she and Imani carried their dinners up on trays, and Kai silently served the old man.

His arthritis was definitely paining him today. His rheumy eyes glared at her over his plate. "Well, girl?" he finally said, his voice rasping like a sawblade. "What did you see today? How far did those wings take you before you came back?"

He enjoyed taunting her, knowing very well that his magics ensured she had to come back to the tower every night. The freedom in her wings was an illusion, but he would not take the few scant hours she had to herself. Eyl put the meat pie in her mouth and chewed deliberately without answering.

"You open your mouth and speak to your master, you little beast."

She swallowed. "You didn't make me a beast; you made me a bird."

Imani hunched her shoulders.

"You answer me, girl." He threw power behind the words.

Eyl rocked hard and ground her teeth together as the lance of pain found its mark. She knew better than to needle him when he had his staff in his hand. "I flew to the village and back," she snarled. "To Stagfell. That's all." She wasn't about to tell him she'd flown north as far as she could before the tether had pulled her back.

The old man sneered. "I wanted a nightingale, you chit, for Tala's voice. Not some growling monstrosity."

Then you've got only yourself to blame for the results, Eyl thought.

The old man glanced around the room, eyes narrowing when he did not find what he wanted. "Where is Tala?"

Eyl paused mid-bite. Kai's jaw tightened so hard, she thought it might break.

"Master," Imani whispered. "Tala's gone. Don't you remember?"

"She can't leave," the old man said flatly. "The tether rune forbids it. None of you can ever leave me, especially not my own daughter. Now where is she?"

There was no way this could end well. Eyl tried to swallow the food in her mouth, now as dense as lead.

The old man banged his staff on the ground. "Tala? Tala!"

Kai raised his hands to sign, but Eyl opened her mouth first. "She died three years ago."

The old man's wild eyebrows shot up his forehead before drawing low over his eyes. "No. No, I don't believe you. You're lying! Tala, get out here!"

Kai snapped to get the old man's attention and signed, *"It is the truth—"*

"I won't have you lie to me!" the old man raged. He drew his fingers along the carved staff, tracing a symbol on the wood.

Eyl tried to dodge—though even after all this time, she had no clear idea if that was even possible with a spell; *could* you move or deflect it, as if it were an arrow?—but she felt the magic hit her like an acid splash.

Pain laced through her limbs. But she didn't cry. This was nothing compared to what she endured every day.

"Speak, girl! Where is my daughter?"

The spell pulled the truth from her like a hooked fish on a line. "She's under the oak tree," Eyl panted. "With the children. Dead three years in autumn."

His face went slack. The spell assured him her words were true. But then a blaze of fury filled his eyes, and he swung the staff at her, striking her across the eye socket and temple. Stars exploded. Eyl heard Imani gasp in horror, followed by a sharp scrape of a chair on stone.

Good, Eyl thought as her head rang like a bell. *Kai pulled Imani out of the way.*

The staff walloped her across the shoulders, and then on the knee. "Damn you," the old man panted. "Damn you, damn beast...."

Did you really love her, or are you just angry she's gone? Eyl wondered through the haze of pain. She curled up in a ball to protect her head and torso. She knew better than to ask. He might really kill her then, and as tempting as that escape was, Kai and Imani needed her.

TWO

EYL

Eyl dabbed at the split, bruising skin around her eye with a cold cloth. The old man's anger had lasted a long time, even with Kai there to try to take some of the rage. He had finally gone feeble and trembling and demanded to be taken to his bed—Kai's duty. Luckily, Kai had only gotten a few glancing blows and could still take the old man's weight.

Eyl peered through her swollen eye. Blurry. "I don't know that I can read the news tonight," Eyl told Imani with regret.

"Oh." Imani sighed, her shoulders sagging. There went not only the newsletters, their one connection to the world, but her story for tonight. Kai and Imani could both read printing—she'd taught them—but had not graduated to script, and both the letters and storybook were all rolling script and curlicues.

Kai came up the stairs and signed, *"He's asleep."*

"Eyl doesn't think she can read," Imani announced.

Eyl touched her eye, wincing from pain both physical and emotional. They had so little they looked forward to. She hated disappointing Imani. "Well, I haven't tried. Heat the letters open and let me try. And why don't we open the gingerbread tin while we're at it?"

Imani beamed and dashed downstairs.

The old man ordered the newsletters, the avvisi, from the capital; besides political, military, and economic news, they contained a surfeit of gossip about people with whom they were unfamiliar. It was sometimes puzzling, but often like another story, told in installments, about people they would never see. Kai slid a heated knife under the seal and opened the envelopes, handing her the contents as Imani returned bearing the gingerbread tin. Eyl baked and kept a variety of treats on hand that they never shared with the old man. They were solely theirs, to be a treat and a pick-me-up when everything became a bit too much to bear.

Mouth full, Eyl stared at the elaborately written sheets. If she closed her swollen eye and squinted with the other, she could focus.

Scanning quickly, she swallowed and said, "'The war rages on. Damaslar troops were pushed back from the Lliore River to the Trellester border by Altesian troops, newly arrived to aid Trellester. The Damaslar armies are regrouping at the border.'" Bold of them to assume Altesia wouldn't come to an ally's aid. "There are some casualty estimates, probably wrong so that the proud people of Damaslar can keep believing the war will be over soon. Hmm. Let's see." She turned the page. "A detachment of infantry sent to the front has gone missing and the writer speculates that Blackthorn Forest has eaten them up."

Kai smiled. *"The ghost forest strikes again."*

Eyl shared his smile. The Damaskmen did love their haunts and ghoul stories just as much as their fussy chivalric odes. She combed quickly through the other pertinent Damaslar information and came to the gossip section, which Imani loved. The letter writers had the ability to make the people in the high society circles of Damaslar come alive on the page. "'Lady W— appeared this week before the court in a blue, brocade gown the exact shade as Lady M—'s and they greeted each other with a cool indifference.' Which in men's terms would mean they have called each other out for a duel."

Imani flopped back on the floor. "Lady W *always* does this!"

"The Lord P— is delivered of a son and heir by his wife, the Lady P—," Eyl continued, "And Miss O— seems to be starting a fashion trend with fans from Swiana...."

She skimmed the rest of it and then arrived at the foreign section. "Here we go. 'Cadruissau: The Royal Library is nearly finished. Renowned sculptor Marellus Carbey has installed statues of the seven virtues to grace the library's architecture. The new fleet was christened by the king and sent forth to patrol the islands.'" Cadruissau was a country comprised of a long strip of mainland and an island chain, boasting of religious orders, inventors, scholars, and explorers who ventured far out into the ocean.

Imani sighed, hugging her knees to her chest. "I've never seen the capital. Our village was small," she whispered. Imani had been aboard her parents' fishing vessel when a storm had caught them and flung them miles south of where they were supposed to have been. Her whole family had perished except her. Snatchers had pulled her from the wreckage and sold her.

"*You will see it one day,*" Kai told her emphatically. She flashed a watery smile at him.

Eyl turned another page. No news from the Sarkan. Damaskmen thought the Sarkan'ande reclusive barbarians, so it wasn't often that they were featured. She wished she could give Kai any news from home, though. She found the next heading.

"'Altesia—'"

She coughed. Tried again. "'Altesia still has no official heir. The queen has not recognized her dead husband's son as her heir nor chosen between several distant cousins. Ever since the princess died ten years ago, the country has been uneasy as to its future. Rumors persist that the Lost Princess, as she has been coined, will return to take up the throne. Whether she will return from the dead, this author could not say.'"

"Oh!" Imani sat up straight. "Returning from the dead! It's just like in a story! What else does it say?"

"There's nothing more about that," Eyl said, ignoring Imani's disappointed face. She did not read the next line aloud: "*However,*" *the queen has named her husband's son as official Altesian ambassador, so is this merely a testing ground for a would-be heir? We shall report further developments as the ambassador acclimates to his new position."*

Eyl's stomach churned.

"Oh." Imani slumped. "Anything else interesting?"

"Not really." She handed the pages back to Kai and closed her eyes with a sigh. "My head aches. I think I'm going to go to sleep, if that's all right."

"We can save the rest for tomorrow before we steam them shut again," Imani said. "Thank you."

Eyl carefully turned away from them on the pallet, resting her aching head onto the thin pillow. She put a new cold cloth over her eyes.

Imani obligingly snuffed the lamp with a wave of her hand, and the room dimmed except for the hearth fire.

Eyl let herself sink into the ache of her bruises and her heart.

So Ev was in line for the throne, was he? She could feel his mother's machinations in that.

She must feel proud. Nine long years' worth of work finally bearing fruit.

Eyl's fingers curled into a fist.

SHE WOKE IN THE DARK, the fire burned down to coals. She sat up on her pallet and peered around with the one eye that worked. Imani snored softly on her back, her curls in disarray around her face in sleep. She had forgotten to wrap her hair. Kai slept on his stomach, one arm under his head, the other fist pressed against his mouth.

Eyl was accustomed to little sleep. For years, she had wanted to remain awake in the night, to savor her humanity as much as possible and not waste it in sleep. Now it was difficult to sleep a full night through. Doubly so with this awful throbbing in her cheek.

She got up and walked down the stairs, feeling her way in the pitch black. The kitchen fire was nearly burned to ash, with only a few coals left in the grate. She set out another log and poked it up a bit, then moved to the tower door and lifted the bar and to swing it wide.

The night whispered to her, the quiet drone of insects and soft brush of grass welcome. She leaned into the doorway, wishing she could step over the threshold and feel the soil under feet and run under the moonlight. Freedom was so close. Some nights, she stretched herself out on the ground as far as she could go before the glyph clamped its invisible grip on her ankle, her head out the tower door to stare at the stars that peeped around the tower roof above.

For the thousandth time, she recalled where they kept the axe.

If it had been just her, she would do it. She would chop off her foot without a second thought like an animal gnawing off its leg in a trap for the chance to be free, even it was the merest sliver of a chance. She could taste the desperation in the back of her throat, that bitter tang of every hope and what-if she harbored. If it had been just her. But not all tether runes were so handily placed. An arm could be taken off at the elbow in Imani's case, but Kai's was solidly on his neck and collarbone. No cutting that off.

And who's to say, she thought, leaning forward to rest her head on her knees, *that it would even work?* No magical text she had read indicated that runes were localized to where they were performed. Why should it be the case for marks placed on the body?

"This is intolerable," she whispered. "We can't keep living like this."

And she *did* want to live. She wanted it with every fiber of her being.

But that meant continuing, one day after another, with no hope that she could see.

How could she?

How could she not?

She stoked the oven's fire and began to mix the ingredients for bread. She used the nighttime to help Imani with baking bread, as well as doing the prep work for the other meals, and most nights, to slip into the old man's library and continue reading all of his tomes she could understand. She was hunting for ways for them to escape, to break the enchantments that bound them to the tower and to the old man's will, but her efforts had borne very little fruit. Almost all of his books were thick, dense volumes of magical theory she did not understand, and almost half of them were filled with the magical glyphs she could not read. He had little-to-no primers in magic for beginners, no dictionaries to explain how to read the glyphs. It was maddening, to think the tools for her escape might be so close but barred to her.

So many times, she had cried out to God in the darkness to show her the right book, send her a helper, give her the gift of tongues.

He had stayed silent.

No wonder she thought she was going mad.

The one useful thing she had learned was that breaking a glyph or enchantment was possible through enough brute force but would result in backlash for the one who did the breaking. Backlash being, as far as she could tell, a magical blowback or explosion. It could kill them if the magic released was strong enough. It would also let the old man know that someone was tampering with his magic, since an explosion was not exactly subtle.

Some days, she toyed with that option just as much as the axe. But the will to live won—if only by inches.

She spread flour onto the table and dropped the bread dough down, giving it a solid smack. "You know I already felt mad, what with this pull to always fly north. I can't decide if it's just a longing for home or something else gone horribly wrong. But seeing things that aren't there? No. You can't do that to me. My mind's the only thing I have left. You can't take that too." Her throat tightened, and she dug her fingers into the dough. "Please. They need me."

Eyl kneaded the dough slowly, keeping her eyes on the open doorway. Only a few feet away. But she couldn't cross over.

"Yes, it's me again, the girl who yells at God in the middle of the night, when every other sane person is asleep." She kept her talks with—at—God to when she was alone. Imani prayed with a devout faith still, hoping for rescue. As jaded as Eyl was, she didn't want to take that from her. But it also meant she couldn't talk to Imani about her struggles. She didn't know what Kai believed or what rituals he observed—whatever he did, he did on his own, when he was alone. He was private about so many things.

But then, so was she.

She laughed, but the sound was discordant. "I'm going to keep yelling until I get an answer! I'm going to keep banging on your metaphorical door until you turn and *listen* to me." She thumped the dough into the tabletop. "Answer me. Smite me with lightning. Do *something*!"

She angrily swiped at the tear that ran down her cheek.

"You get us out of here," she hissed. "Or I'll never speak to you again."

But she would. Of course she would.

Only with God could she truly be honest. Because only He knew her, whole and entire.

THREE

EYL

Eyl woke in pre-dawn light to rain. She raked up the coals in the grate and set it to blaze again and started on breakfast as Imani came downstairs yawning. They worked in companionable silence until Kai stumbled down, rubbing his eyes.

Eyl was able to eat most of her breakfast before dawn broke. Imani and Kai looked away as she went behind the large butcher block table, threw off her clothes, and screamed as her flesh compressed, bones shrinking down and hollowing into a bird's fragile skeleton.

Kai swung the bar up and opened the tower door.

Feathers flashed, and she dove into the downpour. After two long rotations around the clearing, she flew back through the door and shook off her wings irritably. No long flights for her today. It would delay the delivery, too, with wet roads.

She hopped up onto her perch and the day ground on.

The old man stayed in bed much of the morning, the weather playing havoc with his bones. At least he knew a fraction of what her pain felt like. But after lunch, he rallied enough to take lunch in the book room. Eyl watched with a gimlet eye—the one that wasn't throbbing—as Kai and Imani fed him and gave him pen and ink. The old man probably felt her gaze, because aside from a few caustic grumbles, he scribbled in silence, only barking at Imani twice to stoke the fire and draw the blankets further over his scrawny legs.

Somewhere in that fading mind lingered the memory of a gyrfalcon's bite when he had raised a hand against Imani. The scar certainly lingered on his finger. He had, of course, dashed Eyl against the wall for it, but it had only dazed her. Imani had cried anyway, trails of fire down her face, prompting Kai to renew his plea to poison the old man. But would that trap them here for life, tethered with no hope of escape? They weren't sure.

Around the time of the old man's nap, the rain stopped, and the cart full of deliveries arrived from the village. Eyl sat on Kai's shoulder and gave Unger, the cart driver, her unsettling stare as he resentfully unloaded their sacks of flour, sugar, and salt and casks of oil and meat.

"All the way here in the driving rain," he muttered, slopping a barrel into a puddle. "Now all the way back in the muggy air, through mud. Like to sicken from it." He glared, wiping his forehead.

"Thank you for making the drive," Imani said politely. Kai crossed his arms over his chest.

"Owe me a half crown more for it," Unger announced. "Only fair."

Kai gave a sharp, decisive shake of his head.

"No one else will deliver out to you." Unger spat, looking up at the tower. "Cursed place, this is. With that devil man up there, doing his magics."

Well, there they agreed.

"If I wasn't to come, you'd all starve. You'll pay me a half crown more, regular like."

Imani bit her lip, looking at Kai.

Kai's lip curled. He signed, *Tell him no. I paid for goods and delivery. We will deal with him next month.*

"He says no," Imani said, fisting her hands in her skirt.

"Then I'll take all this back, shall I?" he said nastily.

"You can't!" she exclaimed. "That's stealing!"

"And who'll care?" he shot back. "No one cares what the monster's servants say. I can help myself to what I like." His face twisted, and he reached out to Imani. "In fact—"

Kai stepped in front of Imani, knocking his arm away.

Unger sneered at Kai. "Don't you wave your hands at me, sandscut—"

Eyl flapped her wings and screamed in his face. As he jumped backwards, she shot out and clamped her beak onto his nose. No one touched her children if she could help it.

"Ahh!" he screamed. "Get it off me! Get it off!!" He fell backwards into the mud, Eyl still attached to his face.

Kai and Imani didn't move.

With a last yank, Eyl fluttered back to her perch on Kai's shoulder, clacking her beak in a satisfied manner, making sure the tacky blood was visible.

Unger looked up at them from the mud, his face pale, blood streaming from the deep gashes in his nose. "Devil children!" He gasped.

Kai leaned over him and scowled, signing with hard gestures. Imani translated, "Stay down." They unloaded the rest of the load without his help as Eyl clung to the cart and watched Unger. When it was empty, Eyl moved to Imani's shoulder and let her stroke her still-ruffled feathers.

Unger stumbled to his feet and ran to the cart. "You can kiss your deliveries goodbye," he managed to snarl. "Never coming out here again, not for all the gold in Damaslar!"

They watched him go until he passed the bend in the road.

"Good job, Eyl," Kai murmured, and she restrained herself from snapping up the gecko he spat out. It upset him when she ate what he summoned.

As Imani and Kai sorted the foodstuffs, Eyl lifted into the air, finally free to soar. She flapped to gain altitude, rising to the tops of the trees. As she did, something flashed in the shadows. Like light shining on a bridle or a buckle.

She dove, streaking down to stop her flight just below the ground. Flapping frantically, she scanned the trees.

Nothing was there.

She searched for some minutes but couldn't find anything to account for the flash.

Mad, she thought, setting her sights determinedly on the clouds as she rose. *Mad.*

SHE FLEW THROUGH THE SKYLIGHT.

Her bones broke.

The magic shaped her back into a human. Weary to the bone, Eyl tugged on her clothes and padded around the curtain. The niggling urge had pulled her north again, past the village and up towards the open land, home only to the wildlife and the birds and the few wanderers not afeard of the haunted forest. *It must be inconvenient for Damaslar to have a haunted forest right in the middle of their country. People have to go around it all the time,* she thought as she took the dusting cloth from Imani and finished the task before going downstairs to start supper.

Kai met her on the way up, and one corner of his mouth turned up. *"You've got a little something...."* he signed, pointing to his mouth.

She snorted and rolled her eyes. "Get on with you."

His small smirk grew into a true smile as he passed her.

She let him ascend the bend in the tower before she swiped the back of her hand across her mouth. Just in case.

In the kitchen, she got supper started, the cool night air from the open tower door wafting into the kitchen to offset the fire's heat. Imani had begun filling their bins with the supplies Unger had brought but obviously had gotten distracted partway through. She'd finish that once the food was cooking, and then—

On the stout doorframe, someone rapped three times.

Eyl shrieked and whirled. Her breath strangled in her throat.

In the open doorway stood a tall stranger in a dark cloak.

She snatched up the carving knife, automatically adjusting her grip and stance so she held it like she would a short sword, warding him off. All those lessons had been good for something, at least. "Who are you? What do you want?"

He couldn't get to her. The tower wards kept out anyone who didn't belong. But what was he doing here? Was he from the village? Had Unger sent him? Did—

The stranger drew back his hood. The lamps illuminated a young man with bright-red hair that curled over his ears. A violent scar sliced down the side of his face from his hairline to his jaw, missing his left eye by the merest sliver. He was so tall, it gave her neck a crick to look at him, but he did not look much older than her.

He stared down at her with eyes the blue of icy mountain lakes.

"I did see you," she whispered, the knife trembling in her hand. "I'm not mad."

A shiver of relief ran down her spine.

FOUR

FEE

At last, Fee thought, *the third inhabitant of the tower.*

Fee had waited a day before approaching—partly from caution, but partly to recover from his mad dash on horseback. He could ride, but he was not used to continuous days spent on the back of a horse at as fast a pace as he dared. He could hardly stir a step by the end of his journey. Even now, after performing what little healing magic he could on himself, he still ached.

But it will be worth it, he thought grimly. If they believed him, this would all be worth it.

The pale girl before him was short—nearly miniscule. He'd have been surprised if her head reached his collarbones. Her hair stood out around her face like a dandelion puff, white and wispy and short, but her dark brows drew low over her eyes in a scowl. One socket was swollen, and a greenish-purple bruise darkened her eye and temple.

When he pulled back his hood, instead of flinching at the sight of his horrible scar, she sagged, the knife trembling in her hand. "I did see you. I'm not mad."

When had she seen him? He had cloaked himself in every "don't notice" spell he knew during his journey. But he could ask later. He had to explain, before she shouted the tower down or gutted him with that knife.

However, when he opened his mouth, instead of his rehearsed explanations, what came out was, "What happened to your face?"

It was clearly not what she had been expecting, either. "My face?" she repeated blankly. She automatically lifted her hand—not the one threatening him with the sharp carving knife—and then seemed to realize what he meant. Her eyes narrowed. "What's it to you? What happened to *your* face?"

My half-brothers tried to mutilate me. But no good ever came from the truth. He had learned that lesson well. Fee automatically dropped his eyes. "I apologize." He bowed. "Allow me to start over."

"Talk fast," she snapped, adjusting her grip on the knife. "What's your business here?"

He cleared his throat. "My name is Feonar Yaldson. Fee. I'm here to help you."

"I seriously doubt it. Try again, Feonar Yaldson. You have two more chances." Her eyes, silvery like mirrors, sharpened.

"This is the tower of Aedelbras the Sorcerer, correct?"

She lunged forward, catching his cloak in her fist and dragging his head down to her level. "How do you know that name?" she demanded. "How did you hear it?"

He braced himself on the doorframe so he wouldn't faceplant into the tower's wards. The knife was uncomfortably close to his throat. Closer still when he swallowed. Fee tried to focus on the girl's left ear, but she yanked harder on his collar. "Answer the question!"

He never looked anyone directly in the eyes if he could help it. He hated seeing through the window of their souls to all the mean and petty thoughts, jealous hatreds, fears and worries that consumed them. But his gaze swung to hers, pulled like a lodestone by the force of her will. Also by the knife.

He met her silvery eyes in terrible anticipation.

Fee sensed wind, the brush of feathers, a cold bite of frost, and fear.

But no specifics. No awful memories, no thoughts not his own. Just fleeting impressions. He blinked and then stared down at her in a dawning, amazed half-hope.

"Well?" she demanded, poking him with the knife he had completely forgotten about.

"Will you allow me to reach into my cloak?"

"No funny business," she said, easing up only incrementally.

He brought the sheaf of letters out of the inner pocket of his cloak. He pulled the most recent one free, then hesitated. "Can you read?"

"Yes," she said testily, snatching the letter from him before he knew what she was about. Then she hesitated, probably trying to decide how she'd hold the knife on him and read the letter at the same time.

He very deliberately crossed his arms over his chest where she could see them and leaned against the tower doorframe. "You don't have to be afraid," he said. "This door feels strongly warded to keep out intruders." He could feel its energy licking at him, ready to thrust him back should he attempt to enter.

Her eyes narrowed to slits. Obviously, that wasn't as reassuring as he had intended. Ah, well. However, she did put down the knife to read the letter.

Her whole body stilled.

He knew what she read. He had read it over and over on his journey south.

To the Most Excellent High Wizard of Damaslar,

Greetings. I hope this missive finds you well, and that the war effort continues to be fruitful. I have written you about an opportunity I feel may be most beneficial to Damaslar's cause. As you know, most magic used at the front is for defense and protection, the usual wizardry not suited to offensive measures. However, in my work, I have experimented with Wild Magic, infusing subjects with certain magical traits. These traits are used at will and take no time or preparation, which could be of great use at the front. Three such experiments were successful, and I believe I have perfected my process. I am willing to donate my experiments to the war effort, as well as my process to create new subjects, if the High Wizard will see fit to lift my banishment and return me to my rightful place in the capital and the Concordium….

"This is the old man's hand," she muttered. Then she swore.

"That puss-filled, maggot-ridden, stony-hearted snake! Craven-hearted…. Mountain snow take his sight!" She looked up and shook the letter at Fee. "How did you get this letter?"

"A week ago, I was at the front as a part of the wizard regiment. All registered wizards of a certain age and status are drafted." His mouth twisted, pulling at his scar. "I found these letters in the High Wizard's correspondence." He met her eyes once again, a strange, swooping feeling in his chest. He only felt the light brush of feathers, and the scent of pine.

"He was drafting an acceptance."

She stared at him blankly. "The old man writes letters. Kai takes them to Stagfell every month. We never thought to read them. No one's ever written *back*." Her voice cracked on the last word.

"Do you want to sit down?" he asked, straightening in concern. "You've had a shock—"

"Give me those," she demanded, holding out her hand for the rest of the letters.

He handed them over without protest.

She scanned them, opening a few. They all followed in a similar vein, crawling obeisance mingled with delusions of grandeur, asking to be returned to former glory.

"This last letter is the only one where he mentions experiments, and their benefit to the war effort," Fee said. "Possibly because the war has dragged on longer than expected." He swallowed back the bile in his mouth.

"Yes, the good ol' three-month war," she sneered. One small, savage smile crept across her face. "If they think *this* is long," she said, "just wait until winter."

She's Altesian, Fee realized with a start, listening to her voice. He hadn't realized. All that short pale hair—Altesians typically wore their hair as long as they could grow it. Damaskmen made rude jokes about horse tails when in their cups.The only notable exceptions were the soldiers because hair was heavy and a convenient handhold, so slightly impractical.

And the spies.

He shoved that thought—those memories—away as hard as he could.

"I take it that you are one of the experiments."

The girl drew herself up and raised one haughty eyebrow. That look was designed to flay off skin. Now, why did it make Fee want to laugh? He bit his tongue to try to suppress the wholly surprising and unruly emotion.

"The letter mentions three experiments. I kept watch on this tower before I approached. You and the girl and boy are the only people I've seen, unless the sorcerer has a secret dungeon in there." He nodded past the doorway.

"So you spied on us."

"Well, I didn't want to waltz up to the tower and immediately alert the sorcerer to my presence, did I?" He also had slept far longer than he'd meant to once his hell-for-leather ride had been over. He kicked himself mentally for the lost time.

Fee tilted his head back to stare up at the tower. "How much of a problem is he likely to be?"

"We'll get to that in a minute," she said darkly. "How did you find these letters, exactly?" She shook the damning evidence at him. "You're a Damask wizard, and you were in the army. You admitted it yourself. What are you doing here? Betraying your country?"

"Given the choice between betraying my country and saving you from my fate?" Fee shrugged. "I'd choose betrayal every time."

FIVE

EYL

Before Eyl could pry more out of the tall, scarred stranger, Imani came downstairs. "Eyl, I'm sorry I didn't finish putting up the supplies—oh!" Imani gasped, staring at the stranger from the safety of the stairwell.

"It's all right," Eyl said automatically, even though she still had strong doubts. "This is…Fee."

"What's he doing here?" Imani whispered, her eyes huge in her face.

"We'll discuss it after dinner," Eyl said briskly, stuffing the letters into a cabinet with the assistance of a stepstool. They'd have to get a move on with dinner, or the old man would suspect something. The old man who wanted to hand them over to Damaslar's army for his own profit.

Her hands clenched. Well, she'd known he didn't think of them as people already. This was just the final confirmation.

"We'll be able to talk once the old man has gone to bed," she told Fee. "I want us all to hear it from the beginning."

He nodded. "I have to look after my horse. I'll return then." He paused. "May I know your name?"

A horse! There *had* been a horse! She wanted to cheer. Wanted to cry. "I'm Eyl."

Fee bowed to her and Imani, a very correct, courtly gesture. "Very well, Eyl." He said it the Altesian way—*Ale*. Then he melted back into the darkness.

"Say nothing to the old man," she told Imani, whose mouth was open to immediately interrogate her.

"Well, of course," Imani said as they threw themselves into dinner preparations. "But what I want to know is—"

Eyl clambered onto the counter. "We'll discuss it *after dinner*."

Imani's mouth shut in a mulish line. "You know, *I* can get into that cabinet without a stepstool."

"Don't rub it in," Eyl snapped. "I just want everyone to hear the same story. And we'll wait to tell Kai," she added.

"He'll be angry you didn't tell him right away."

"He'll want to rush out and interrogate the stranger," Eyl said. "I'd like Fee to be in one piece when he gives us his tale."

Suffering through dinner would be interminable. They quickly prepared a repast of leftovers and a salad of greens from the garden.

Kai came down to help carry it up. *"He's quiet tonight,"* he signed. *"I gave him wine to dull the ache."*

Eyl nodded. "Go on up. I'll be there in a moment." Imani followed Kai with another tray, casting only one anxious look behind.

Eyl stuck her head out the tower door but saw nothing in the dark, no sign of their strange visitor. But he had been there, just the same. "I'm not mad," she whispered.

She could barely reckon with the fact that all her angry spiteful, desperate prayers had—been heard? Answered?

Suddenly, she could barely get enough air to breathe. She fought for control of her throat, swallowing down the tears. Finally, she hissed, "What *took* you so long?"

SIX

FEE

Fee returned to his makeshift camp. The bay gelding whickered at him, and Fee patted his neck and poured out a measure of oats to go along with the grass he was happily munching. Then Fee took him to the little stream a few hundred feet away and let him drink.

The horse was looking much better after two days' rest from the neck-or-nothing ride all the way from the front. Fee hated having pushed him so hard, but he had no way of knowing if or when someone would set out after him. But he hadn't seen any signs of pursuit, and his protection spells had never tripped, so no one had searched for him magically. Danger remained, but Fee felt a little more at ease. Once he'd warned them, he could go, disappear, make his own way….

But would he ever be free?

Fee shook his head to free himself from his woolgathering. One step at a time, he reminded himself. He led the horse back to his grassy patch before re-hobbling him. Fee pulled out some trail rations and munched on them halfheartedly. Lighting a fire so close to the tower was too risky—the glow might have been visible from a window. His protections only shrouded himself, and when he was riding it, the horse. But the night was chilly, and he would've done a lot for a hot meal. He made himself finish the food, though. With a last pat to its neck, he walked back to the tower.

When he had nearly cleared the trees, he stumbled over a stone in the dark and bit back a curse. The stone was overgrown, but what was it doing between these two trees? It wasn't a naturally rocky area.

Fee brushed the grass away from it and paused. His fingers found the grooves chiseled into the stone, tracing them. "TALA."

He went back to his camp and got a torch from his saddlebags.

On his return, he stared at the stone in the torchlight. It was clearly a headstone. And if one studied the earth and not the grass atop it, he could see it humped, just as it would have over a grave.

And not just by the stone.

He counted a dozen or so humps with the torch's light, and then age and time had smoothed away even that sign to a sliver. So he pulled out his notebook and wrote out a series of glyphs to detect human bones and called up enough magic to fulfill the spell.

Fee thought he might be sick.

"Two hundred thirty-three."

Fee cursed, instinctively striking out with the torch.

The boy jumped out of the way, and the Cadruissi girl held out a hand. The fire curved away from them, leaving the torch completely. It settled into her hand like a contented kitten.

Trying to get his breathing under control, Fee snapped, "What did you say?"

The Sarkan'ande boy, maybe in his mid-teens, stared at him with deeply suspicious eyes and a hard line of a mouth in the flickering firelight. "Two hundred and thirty-three failed experiments," the boy repeated. Then he spat out two small frogs.

The frogs derailed Fee's train of thought for a moment, but the horror would not keep at bay for long. "They're children."

Except for the grave with the headstone, the bones his spell had found deep in the earth were small, fragile—none older than the two children in front of him. Some of the bones were grouped together—three or four to a grave.

"Yes. Failed experiments. We're the only ones who survived." Three fireflies escaped his mouth, flitting up into the boughs above, tiny specks of light in the darkness. "Who are *you*?" A clear challenge rang in the words.

"I'm Feonar. I'm here to help."

"A Damaslar deserter." The boy raised a skeptical eyebrow.

Fee shrugged. It was as good a descriptor as any. "I think it shows my good sense, don't you? And you are?"

"This is Kai," Imani said. "When he speaks, um...."

"I summon insects and amphibians." The head of a garter snake slithered past Kai's lips, its lithe, green body slowly oozing down his chin. Kai and the snake both stared Fee dead in the eye.

Fee got the impressions of hot sands, hidden waters, and bone-deep determination. Nothing else. How was it possible? Was it something to do with their strange magic?

Regardless to say, Fee also got nothing from the reptile.

He reached out and plucked the snake free of Kai's mouth, another four or five inches emerging before it came free. Fee set the snake down gently on the gravestone. "Uncomfortable for the both of you."

Kai snorted, a grain of grudging respect in his eye.

"Where do they come from?"

Kai shrugged.

"Eyl thinks the sounds pull the bugs into his mouth," Imani offered. "Because they just appear and need to get out. She wants to talk to you, by the way. The old man is asleep."

"Why didn't she come herself?" Fee asked.

Imani gave him a look of surprise, and Fee felt the dual mixture of fire and sea water as she cuddled the ball of flame. "She can't. She's bound to the tower."

A{\small T THE ENTRANCE} to the tower, Fee peered at the glyph of runes on Eyl's foot. He admitted to himself that this escape endeavor might have become more complicated than he'd first expected.

"The tether runes don't let us leave," Imani said, pointing to the intricate black mark on her forearm. "They pull us back to the tower each night."

"But they have different boundaries," Fee said.

Imani nodded. "I can't go past the clearing, but I can tend the garden and feed the chickens. Kai can enter the village. But Eyl can't cross the tower threshold."

"As human, anyway," Eyl murmured.

Fee's head shot up. "What?"

"Imani controls fire. Kai's voice summons insects and creepy crawlies." Eyl shot him a flat stare. "I turn into a bird."

Bird? What bir—

His eyes widened. "The gyrfalcon?"

She glared. "And so what?"

He had seen it upon his arrival, wings flashing in the setting sun, and again in the rain today. At the sight, his heart had lifted for the first time in what had felt like months. And that had been *her*. It made the words fall out of him. "You're stunning."

For one moment, the antagonism dropped away. In her eyes Fee saw and felt deep, aching vulnerability—and deep wounds. On instinct, he dropped his eyes. Obfuscated or not, it wasn't something he had the right to see.

"I want to see these letters," Kai said in a hard voice.

Fee gestured. "I gave them to Eyl."

"I'll fetch them." Imani jumped up.

"And how did you come to possess them?" Kai pinned him with his stare.

"I stole them," Fee said honestly.

"From the High Wizard of Damaslar," Kai said.

"Yes."

"How did you know of them in the first place?"

"He leaves his correspondence and all of his things strewn

everywhere, frankly. He expects us to act the servant and clean up after him."

"Who is 'us'?"

"Army wizards."

"You are a magic user."

Fee nodded once.

"Where is your staff?" Kai's eyes narrowed.

"At my camp."

Since wizard magic was unsuited to fast casting, most wizards carved spells or simple runes into a staff to make things quicker. Just find the symbol and trace. Of course, that meant more mistakes, more chances for magic to go wrong, but most found the tradeoff worth it.

"You didn't think you'd need it?"

"I didn't think it prudent to show up at a sorcerer's tower and announce that I was also a magic user before I even got my name out. A good way to get my throat cut, I think." He glanced at Eyl with the ghost of a smile.

She lifted her chin, not a jot apologetic.

"And so," Kai said disdainfully, "you just saw these letters mentioning magic experiments and the war and decided to desert? A good Damask wizard like you?" His voice dipped into a sneer.

"I think we've already established I'm not a good Damask wizard," Fee said dryly. "I never wanted anything to do with this war. I wanted to be a healer. But I was forcibly drafted, and no one wants you to expend magic on healing. Only harm. Only pain." His voice cracked. "I hated every second, and I was plotting to get away. This discovery just made it happen faster."

"So you ran," Eyl said.

"Yes. I vowed I wouldn't let them do to you what they did to me."

"What?" Imani whispered.

"Douse me so thick in blood, I don't know if I'll ever be clean."

"How do we know this is the truth?" Kai demanded.

"You don't," Fee said flatly. "But here is what will happen if we do nothing. Someone, probably soldiers, will come here to take you all to the front, where the army wizards will do their best to make you into weapons. The sorcerer will turn over his work to the High Wizard, and they'll try to replicate it. More people will die, no matter what country they're from. You'll have to live with the blood, and the destruction, and the guilt, just like me. All for a stupid war to line Damaslar pockets and increase their borders."

His jaw tightened. "I can't live with that. I won't."

SEVEN

EYL

Fee looked terrifying, with that wicked scar slicing down his face, delivering pronouncements of doom unflinchingly. But his eyes were haunted.

"How?" Eyl said simply.

His gaze shot to hers. "What?"

"How?" she repeated. "We've wanted to escape from here for years. But we're bound." She gestured to her foot. "And the old man surely has a way to track his creations." Her mouth twisted.

"All wizard magic is, at its core, a detailed description of what you want the magic to do. No magic is irreversible. The trick is managing to find the right wording. If I add that to the glyph, the spell should release you."

"Can you do that?" Imani breathed.

"I'll certainly try," Fee said. "If I copy the different patterns down, I can start tonight."

"I can't cross this threshold," Eyl said dryly. "And neither can you."

"Is there a door spell? If you find wherever that is inscribed and copy it, I can do the same thing to it. If you copy the changes, it will release as well."

"It's just over the door!" Imani exclaimed. "On the lintel!"

"And then?" Eyl pressed.

"We run like rabbits and hope we can go far enough they won't catch us," Fee said. "I assume."

She raised a brow. "'Us'?"

He blinked. Then he flushed. "Metaphorically, us," he said. "Obviously, we won't be going in the same directions. It wouldn't be smart. Too easy to track a large group."

"Yes," she murmured.

"You can go wherever you like," he said.

Eyl just nodded. It wouldn't be that easy, she knew. The old man would have to be dealt with...one way or another. She was familiar with killing. He had made her so—a predator, a hunter. But hunting game in her falcon shape was different than killing a person.

But she said nothing as Fee copied down Imani's and Kai's glyphs into a notebook he carried. Then she sent them up to bed. "Much later than usual," she said. "And you'll have to be up early." They went with only a few grumbles because they knew it was true.

"Now you?" Fee asked, gesturing to her foot.

Eyl shrugged and sat on her side of the door, extending her bare foot until she felt the spell push back. Fee scooted close and began to copy.

"So, what's a good Altesian girl doing down here in this Damaslar hellhole, anyway?"

Eyl pursed her lips and shot him a cool look. "Who said I was good?"

A wry smile curled over Fee's lips, and he glanced up at her through his lashes before his gaze darted away. She had noticed him doing that—shooting her glances when he thought she wasn't looking. He looked at her like she was— what had he said? Stunning. He looked at her, even in her human form, too thin and short and ragged, like she was a wonder.

It made her feel funny. Sort of…tingly.

She cleared her throat. "What's a good Damaslar boy doing thinking for himself and deserting?"

"Fair enough. A question for a question, then."

She stared at her foot, concentrating on holding it still even as she tried to think of what to say. "I was stolen. Then sold. The snatchers brought me south, where they would get better prices. Altesians don't deal in indentures."

Indentures were the most common form of servitude in Damaslar, families who had to work their way out of debts. It was a system rife for exploitation, though. Conveniently lose the documents listing the time or amount owed, disappear family members or children in the dead of night, and what could they do about it? Indentured people had few legal rights. They in effect signed themselves away to pay off the money owed. Snatchers took those whose documents had "disappeared" and sold them on—to unsavory brothels or mine labor or private buyers.

Case in point.

"Is that why you kept your hair short?"

Eyl narrowed her eyes. "Partly." Most Altesians didn't cut their hair except when in deep mourning or for serious vengeance. Working people kept it around shoulder length, but not shorn, not like her. And so he knew she was Altesian. Fine. It wasn't exactly a secret. "That was two questions," she pointed out.

"All right. One more moment—I'm nearly done." She waited while he made the last few strokes in his notebook with his charcoal pencil and then straightened up, cracking his back. She flexed her foot and pulled it back underneath her.

Fee leaned back and stretched his legs out. "Ask your two questions, then."

She lifted her chin. "What happened to your face?"

He froze, his body full of tension. Then he stared into the

shadows. "My half-brothers didn't like having a bastard in the house." He traced the jag in the scar around his eye. "They were going for my eye, but I thrashed at the right moment and the knife slipped."

She pressed her lips together. "They hated you that much?"

"They were afraid," he said in a low voice.

"Afraid of what?"

"Is that your second question?" he asked in a low voice.

She hesitated. "Yes."

He slowly lifted his eyes to meet her gaze. His eyes were so bright, they nearly glowed—like blue lightning. She repressed a shiver. What did he see, with those eyes?

He let out a slow breath. "Well, don't say I didn't warn you." With that, he brushed his hair away from his ears and they— shimmered.

And changed.

Where round tops of human ears had been, Fee's now curved up into a pronounced, elongated point.

She jerked in surprise.

"Do you see now?"

"You're faefolk?" she whispered.

"Somewhere in the past, yes." He stared into the darkness broodingly. "The genes can manifest after staying dormant for several generations. When my father had an affair with my mother and I was born, he abandoned her. Horrified he had defiled his blood like that. He had nothing to do with me until she died and I was dumped on his doorstep."

Faefolk. The world's magical population, people and creatures who lived and breathed magic. Depended on it for survival. They had disappeared hundreds of years ago, though they had managed to mingle quite a bit with humans at some point. And because they were scarce and different—*and powerful,* Eyl reminded herself—people feared them—Damaskmen in particular, what with their bogey tales and melodramatic operas and legends centered on spook forests.

"You'd think they would've tried to cut off your ears, not your eyes," Eyl said, trying for levity.

Fee's expression eased somewhat. "You'd think." He smiled. "I believe it's my turn."

She swallowed. "Go right ahead." She pushed herself to her feet. "But first, hand me your notebook and pencil," she said, pulling a stool over. "I'll copy the door spell down for you."

He did as she'd asked, staying silent while she concentrated on getting the pattern exactly right. When she hopped down and passed it back to him, he said, "Oh, that looks pretty standard. I don't think it should be especially troublesome."

"Good." She wiped her suddenly sweaty hands on her tunic. "I'm going to start my nightly preparations. Would you like some tea?"

"Please."

Eyl felt him watching her as she pulled bowls and ingredients from their places around the kitchen. It made her itch. She should've realized that agreeing to an exchange of question and answer would require her to...well, answer. She had made it a practice to never say anything about her past. It was just better that way. She found his gaze...unsettling.

"What did the sorcerer wish to accomplish with his experiments?" Fee asked. "He was never very clear in his letters."

Her shoulders relaxed. Tala. She could talk about Tala.

"The old man had a daughter," she said, putting the kettle on to boil. "Her name was Tala."

"The name from the headstone," he said alertly.

"Yes. She died three years ago. She was a deaf-mute. He claimed his experiments with wild magic were to 'fix' her. But that's a lie. He was doing it for his own glory and ego."

"How do you know?"

"Tala didn't want to be fixed. She didn't think there was anything wrong with her. *He* was the one who treated her like a half-wit most of the time. And once I'd lived through the magic, he found out that his experiments only worked on children of certain ages—just about to enter adolescence."

"Ah. He exploited the potentiality to make a magical foothold."

Eyl stared at him. "…Sure."

He shook his head. "Ignore the wizard gobbledygook. So he knew it worked on certain ages…."

"Right." She frowned in thought. "Actually, he might've known it earlier. Tala told us he was exiled from the capital because he wanted to use child subjects." She made a face. "Human experimentation is apparently fine in Damaslar, but if they're children, it's suddenly a bridge too far."

"Obviously, he went ahead and did it anyway."

She nodded. "Anyone older than twelve the procedure just killed. Tala was an adult. It wouldn't have worked on her even when he had gotten it right." She put in the tea leaves to steep and started on the bread and biscuits for tomorrow.

Funny that when she'd arrived here at ten, she hadn't known how to do this. Hadn't known how to do anything, really. Tala had had to teach her so many things. But that wasn't surprising.

The past bubbled up again. *"Do not scream. Listen. She commanded me to kill you. Forget who you are."*

Eyl set her mouth in a grim line. As a child, she had had nightmares about that. Now she found it strange. She hadn't died, but that was what she'd dreamed about, not the snatchers who had found her hiding place and stolen her away.

But it was what he represented that she feared, that cut so deep and threatened her very sense of self. The betrayal. The broken promises.

"What are you thinking about?" Fee asked.

Her head shot up.

"Hmm?"

"The look on your face…." Fee trailed off, his eyes bright and keen.

She shivered. There was something about his eyes that drew her. Like he was the first person in years to really see her.

Well, stupid, that's because he literally is, she thought.

"Is that another question?" she countered.

"I guess not." The corner of his mouth curled up.

She poured the tea into mugs and carried his over to him, carefully extending it past the doorway. He couldn't cross the threshold, but she could—all but her foot, of course. "Good, because it's my turn. Are you sure the faefolk blood came from your mother?"

"Sure. He's—well, he's someone whose bloodline is unimpeachable. Family trees going back to time immemorial. That's why he tossed her aside when I was born. There was proof he'd been slumming it. The bastard faefolk get." He shot her a crooked grin.

"Why did you stay with them, if they were so horrible?"

The grin slid from his face. "Nowhere else to go. And it was a certain kind of protection. My mother died because—well, because a group of men got drunk in the tavern where we worked and thought I was some kind of devil child with the power to curse them. She interfered, tried to talk them down. They decided she was trying to bewitch them. She was very beautiful." He trailed off, staring into his mug. In a very different voice, he added, "She was trying to protect me. She told me to run and hide."

Eyl said nothing.

"They threw her down a well." Fee stuck a finger in his mug, stirring. He pulled his finger out and stared at it, red with heat. "Drowning is a slow death. I hope she hit her head and didn't suffer."

"I'm sorry," Eyl whispered.

He looked at her warily. "I think you've suffered rather more than I."

"Debatable," Eyl said. "But it's not a contest."

He smiled sadly into his mug.

After a moment, she hopped up to rummage in the cabinet. She pulled out the tin of gingerbread and offered it to him. "Here."

He peered inside. "What is it?"

"Gingerbread. We make it just for us. It's for…comfort." She swallowed down the ball of emotion in her throat and shook the tin at him. "Take one."

He did, and slowly bit into it. His expression cleared as he chewed. "This is delicious."

She took one, too. "They're Altesian."

"Thank you," he said.

She just nodded and bit into her piece.

"So," he said, savoring the treat and sipping at his tea, "What do you usually do at night?"

"Stay awake," Eyl said, happy to change the subject. "I do what I can for the next day's meals, clean, and pilfer the old man's library for anything that looks like it might be useful. I could never find anything helpful, though," she admitted. She still wasn't sure she *trusted* this young man yet…but she was weakening. "Only dire warnings about backlash."

"Good," Fee said. "They're not wrong about that. Backlash can blow you into next week, if not to smithereens."

"Still. Tempting." She took a sip from her own mug. "Where are you planning to go? After all this."

"You mean where am I escaping to?" Fee shrugged. "No idea. Anywhere I can disappear. Maybe I'll go to Cadruissau and find a boat, sail away. There's a lot of ocean out there."

"Pulling a Jonah," Eyl teased.

He blinked. "Huh?"

"Never mind," she murmured. Her mistake, for trying a church joke on a heathen Damaskman.

"What about you?" he countered. "Will you go home?"

Home. The ache under her breastbone gave a hard, determined throb. She shut her eyes.

"Is your family missing you?"

She shoved the rest of her cookie into her mouth and chewed determinedly. When she could put it off no longer, she swallowed. "I want to. Desperately. And I...hope they are. But...."

"What?" Fee asked.

She opened her eyes and looked at him. "I don't know if I can trust them."

"You think your family...." His voice trailed off.

She knew what he meant. It wasn't like that. But she let him think it. "Betrayed me. Yes."

He compressed his lips into a hard line. "I'm sorry."

Eyl shot him a twisted smile. "Maybe we'll tie for suffering, hmm?"

That pulled a reluctant laugh out of him. "Yes. I understand what it's like to not be able to trust your own blood."

Maybe he's one of the few people who really does. It was a strange intimacy, to be sure. They shared a commiserating glance.

Abruptly, Fee's smile dropped, and he cursed. He fished under the neck of his shirt and jerked a leather thong up, away from his skin.

She stared in amazement. It was strung with a series of metal and wooden disks that clanked dully against each other. The farthest disk on the string, a wooden one, had started to smoke. Unconsciously, she reached out a hand.

"No, don't!" He jerked the strand out of the way, swearing again as it connected with his chest. The disk was truly smolder-ing. "Don't touch it."

"Why is it on fire? Did it burn you?"

"It's part of the spell," he said tightly. "I didn't know it would actually burn."

"What's it for?"

Fee swallowed. "It means someone is looking for me."

Eyl locked her horrified eyes with his. The icy grimness had returned to his face. They both stared at the disk until it stopped burning, leaving the wood black and charred.

Fee tapped it, and it broke apart, pieces of charcoal falling to the ground.

"Well, I didn't expect that," he muttered. "Enid's *teeth*. Nine left."

"What does that mean, someone's looking for you? Is it still hot?" He hadn't let go of the strand yet.

"Someone's scrying me," he explained, touching the disks. "Looking for me magically. And no, it's not, but he's not going to give up that easily." He stared worriedly at the remaining disks.

"Why is he looking for you?" she asked, and then his wording sank in. "'He'? You know who it is?"

"I stole his letters and deserted, remember?" Fee stared gloomily at her and then jerked to attention as another disk sparked, hissing more emphatically than the first. It burned quicker, an actual flame licking around the wood before it dissolved into ash.

Eyl swallowed around the lump in her throat as he knocked the last flakes of ash free of the leather. "You mean to say it's the *High Wizard of Damaslar* who's looking for you? Personally?"

His mouth twisted. "I'm surprised it took him this long, really."

"But how does he know it was you who stole his letters? How could he have known? Couldn't it have been anyone?"

Fee shook his head slowly. "No, he knows. There are spells for that type of thing."

She swallowed. "Well, what will he do?"

"Come after me. Not himself," he corrected. "He'll send someone. But they'll act in his name, and they won't rest until he's got me."

"You're sure? He wants us that badly?"

Fee lifted one shoulder and dropped it. His head thumped back against stone as he stared at the stars.

Eyl drew in a shaky breath. "It's not just the letters, is it? It's you."

Fee didn't deny it.

"Why?"

He rolled his head to look at her, his face remote. "He's my father."

EIGHT

NICANOR

N icanor Beornraed pushed aside the flap of his tent and stepped out of the pouring rain. He pulled off his helmet and shook out sweat-soaked brown hair as the servants scurried to divest him of his armor and staff before drawing him a bath. The rose-scented water steamed in the cool air, and he stepped into the water with a groan, letting the heat soothe the aches that came from sitting astride a horse and spell casting through the whole day.

He scrubbed the perfumed soap over his body as the servants poured pitcher after pitcher of water over his head. After too short a time, he roused from his stupor to stand and wrap himself in the robe his valet held for him. Settling into a chair, he fell onto the meal at his table as the servants emptied the tub, his eye lingering on the curvaceous form of a dark-haired maid.

"Your Grace," his valet murmured, "the guardsman you sent to retrieve the, ah, package has returned. He is asking to see you."

Nicanor smoothed a hand over his dark beard and tore his eyes away from the feast before him. "The guardsman or the package?" If that boy was asking him to spare him a week in chains, he could think again. He had warned Fee the last time he'd tried this trick what he'd earn himself.

"The guardsman, Your Grace."

Nicanor nodded and poured himself another glass of wine. "Send him in."

When his trusted guardsman entered the tent, Nicanor said, "Did he manage to keep ahead of you the whole way, Marcus?"

Wordlessly, Marcus bowed. Nicanor had chosen him for his tenacity and ruthlessness. Now Marcus sported muddy clothes, a blue chin, and a deep scowl. He had not stopped to freshen up. "Your Grace. I must make my report."

Nicanor frowned, the corners of his mouth tightening. "What has happened?"

"I couldn't find him, Your Grace."

"Nonsense," Nicanor said flatly. Fee had run from the front before in the early days, and he had gone straight home to Beornraed and Kilmaren, Nicanor's ancestral estate and the small village it abutted. They had found him right where Nicanor had scryed him. It was the only place he could reasonably go, after the unpleasantness he had caused this time.

Where he had scryed him.

Nicanor's hand tightened on the wineglass.

"Your Grace," Marcus said, "I followed his trail the first day until it faded. I assumed it was from the busier roads farther away from the front. I kept expecting to see him 'round the next bend. I rode all the way to Kilmaren but could find neither hide nor hair of him. I spoke with the steward, and he said Feonar had not been to Beornraed. He must've doubled back to evade me. On my return, I looked for any signs, but...." Marcus scowled harder. "I'm sorry, Your Grace. I have failed you."

Nicanor held back the curses that threatened to escape. The boy had always been trouble, but this...this was outright rebellion. Downright *devious*.

It was a good thing Nicanor had not enlisted him as a true soldier, or he would have been killed for desertion, to say nothing of the previous infraction. Of course, he hadn't actually told the boy that. As it was, Fee was merely an acolyte wizard serving the war effort, and therefore under Nicanor's purview as High Wizard of Damaslar. A fit of pique about his magical duties had driven him home the previous time...or had it? Had it all been an elaborate plot to escape his responsibilities, his duty to his country?

For the thousandth time since the bastard's birth, Nicanor cursed bedding the achingly beautiful tavern wench with red-gold hair. He hadn't known about the faefolk blood in her veins, or he'd have steered well clear. Fee's gift was useful, but it came in a fractious package.

Nicanor made a face, smoothing back the long, brown hair from his face that only showed a few veins of gray. At least, he amended, he would have held off for a while longer, out of principle. He probably would have still bedded her. Lily had been so beautiful. He'd spent a good long time with her, until the baby and his faefolk blood had come along.

So where was the boy? Not at any usual haunts for a boy his age. *Nearly a man now.* But his bastard didn't gamble or carouse like the other wizards or soldiers. You'd never find him in some drinking den.

Nicanor downed the wine in his glass. Mindful of his guardsman's deep loyalty to the Beornraed family, Nicanor said, "No, the boy is wily. I will scry him, as I should have done at the first, and on the morrow, we will fetch him back." He allowed a private smile. "For now, seek your bed. Upon his return, you may assist in showing him the error of his ways." The thrashing of his life, more like.

Marcus bowed and made his exit.

"Bring me my scrying bowl and water," Nicanor commanded his valet.

TEN MINUTES LATER, Nicanor stared into his scrying bowl, displeased.

Idly, he rubbed the rune tattoo on his left shoulder, the one he had had inked into his skin after Fee had been born. No more children would he sire outside his lady wife's womb. Bastards were more trouble than they were worth.

Tracing the runes around the copper bowl's lip, he murmured again and cast his power into the bowl. The surface turned a milky white, rippled once, twice, thrice…and stilled, fading to clear water.

Nicanor's lip curled. The boy was *blocking* him. He didn't want to be found. Had he finally cracked? Didn't he know the duty he owed his family? His country? Was this all about that *wench*?

"Soft," Nicanor cursed under his breath. The boy was too bloody soft.

He scratched his beard in thought. Then he moved to his trunks and pulled out his spell books, paging through them until he found the incantation he wanted. On a sheet of parchment, he copied glyph after glyph. When he covered four lines, Nicanor waved the paper in the air to dry it and called power into the runes, infusing them with his magic. The runes shone gold, and he allowed himself a satisfied smile. If he couldn't find Fee now, he would see where he had been.

He looked up from the paper and watched the shimmering gold simulacrum coalesce. Just a see-through outline in the vague shape of a humanoid, the simulacrum would act out Feonar's last day in camp. Nicanor stood and prepared to follow it.

However, instead of walking out of Nicanor's tent to perhaps find Fee's barracks and start there, the gold form flowed to the back of the tent and rolled inside. The simulacrum moved to the washbasin and scrubbed for a long, long time.

After the business with the girl, then. It *had* been the trigger. Nicanor waited.

The form walked to the desk, sorted through a ghostly pile of books and papers, pocketed money and travel passes for soldiers. Then it paused, pulling forth a piece of phantom parchment from the haphazard stack where Nicanor kept his correspondence.

The simulacrum stood for a while, reading, and then stepped towards the oak trunk at the foot of Nicanor's cot. The simulacrum opened a phantom trunk lid and began to sort through the contents. Its hands found a shimmering, gold packet and sifted through it, looking at the contents a long time. It pocketed the lot of them. Then the simulacrum walked to the tent flap to step out into the rain.

Nicanor closed his fist, canceling the spell. He had seen what he needed to see. The simulacrum faded away.

With a hiss, he threw open his trunk lid and rifled through it, coming up empty. He didn't bother searching his desk. He slammed the trunk lid down with a growl of anger. The letters were gone. The banished sorcerer's correspondence, boasting of his accomplishments, how he could help further the war effort, was all missing.

And obviously, Nicanor's letter accepting the gifts had never been sent. He vaguely recalled missing the letter, but his valet often anticipated his needs regarding his correspondence. He had assumed, just like he had assumed Fee's original destination and motivation.

An awful oath burst out of his mouth, nearly searing the air. What was that boy planning?

Nicanor snapped his fingers, and his valet entered on silent feet. "Summon a squadron," he said in a clipped voice. "My personal guards, not army soldiers. Marcus will lead them after he's had a night's sleep. And trackers, the best you can find."

He wouldn't let the best opportunity he'd found during this war slip through his fingers due to his own thrice-cursed bastard.

CHAPTER

NINE

EYL

The quiet snap of the fire echoed. The whisper of wind outside the tower sounded as loud as a shout. Eyl watched dispassionately as Fee tugged his cloak closer about him. He was probably cold without the heat of the fire. She didn't care. Not at all.

"The High Wizard is your father?"

"Yes."

Her voice was cold. "And you didn't think that would be pertinent information to share?"

"No."

"Well, obviously, it *is*."

"In the great scheme of things, it doesn't matter," he said stubbornly. "And it's not something I really like to dwell on."

"Doesn't *matter*? Oh, just a little more incentive for the *High Wizard* of *Damaslar* to throw all his resources and all his magic into looking for you, because his son *defied* him, and you don't think it *matters*?"

"Bastard son," Fee muttered.

"You think that signifies?" Eyl said incredulously. "Whatever side of the blanket, you rebelled, ran away, and stole from him. He's not going to just shrug and go on his merry way, trying to smash Trellester and Altesia and the rest of the hill countries. He'll come after us!"

"You knew that when I told you I stole from the High Wizard!" Fee exploded. "You knew the danger. Is it really so surprising that I didn't want to admit what he was to me? I *just told you* that I understood not being able to trust your own family."

Eyl licked her lips and tried to get her anger under control. No, it wasn't surprising. He had told her that. "You still became a wizard, though," she pointed out stubbornly.

Fee glared at her, a blaze of true outrage, and then dropped his gaze to his fists, opening and closing his hands. "I wanted to be a healer," he said abruptly. "I wanted...." He blew out a sharp breath. "I hate his family. I ran away so many times in the early days. They tried to force lessons and manners into me while sneering at my birth in the same breath. The boys were never punished for what they did to my face." He turned and stared straight at her so she could get the full force of his scar. "I was forced into the wizard academy, but there, I found a modicum of freedom. I wanted to be a healer. I wanted to learn how to help instead of hurt. But then the war came, and I was pressed. And magic isn't wasted on healing. Only on tactics."

Eyl whispered, "They wanted you to harm instead."

"Yes. They killed a badly wounded soldier I tried to save. 'Stealing magic from the war effort.' That was the first time I ran from the front, but the only place I had to go was back to the estate, and I wasn't thinking clearly. They found me and brought me back." He gestured to the remaining disks on his necklace. "I planned better this time, waited for the right moment. But when —when I saw the letters, I knew I had to come here. I couldn't let it happen again."

Eyl opened her mouth—then shut it. She shoved the tin towards him. "Have another," she muttered.

He stared into it, then up at her curiously. "Is this how you apologize?"

"Just eat the stupid gingerbread," she said through gritted teeth.

He accepted two pieces. "I accept your apology," he said with a ghost of a smile, taking a bite. He groaned, closing his eyes. "Go ahead and yell at me some more. This is worth it."

Eyl made a face he couldn't see. Then she took another gingerbread for herself. "I shouldn't," she said. "Have yelled. Sorry. Having the High Wizard of Damaslar as your father is horrible luck."

"Don't I know it," Fee said.

She got to her feet to rummage in the kitchen. They had stocked up in burn ointment when they had realized what Imani could do, before she'd gotten her powers under control. They hadn't had to use it in a long time, but they still had a good supply—useful for other, more normal kitchen incidents. She found a jar in the back of a cabinet and brought it out, sniffing the oily stuff. It was pungent, but it would do the job.

She sat down and handed it to him. "For your neck."

Fee used two fingers to dab the ointment below his shirt.

"You know, in Altesia, the inheritance and family lines run through the mother. They're the ones who carry the children. Why should a man carry a family name?"

"You're right about that," Fee murmured, wiping the excess ointment onto his pants. "Sensible people, you mountain folk."

She grinned.

He looked up at her and blinked rapidly, then looked away and coughed. "We will have to be smart and stealthy in our plans, but that doesn't mean we can't succeed."

She smoothed her hair back behind her ears and nodded.

"After we get out of here, you'll need to keep a low profile," he continued. "But the good thing is, Aedelbras never included a description of you or what you could do in his letters. If we get far enough away and you find a place to blend in, you shouldn't have much trouble."

Eyl snorted. "He probably wanted to keep the High Wizard on

the hook by not revealing that two out of three experiments are useless."

Fee frowned. "You're not useless. You could scout as a falcon, then come back with accurate troop counts, report where lines are advancing, and spot any ambushes before they happen."

"And wait until dark to share that information?"

"What do you mean?"

"I mean I can't control when I shift. It's dawn and I'm a falcon. When the sun sets, I'm a girl. The magic forces it; I don't get a choice."

Fee stared at her blankly.

"Didn't we mention that before?"

"No, I don't believe you did," he said, sounding distant. "Is that what you meant by the sorcerer finally got his experiments right?"

She nodded. "Kai can't control what happens when he speaks, either."

"We'd better get to work planning, then, hadn't we?" Fee said.

Eyl heartily agreed.

TEN

FEE

Fee couldn't keep his eyes off of Eyl.

She moved from tasks to task with precision, cooking, cleaning, writing lists…she crossed the kitchen in determined strides, eating up the floorspace as fast as her legs would carry her. Her fast-moving feet were small and delicate, marred only by the black spiderwebbing glyph trapping her here.

Fee had been around few women at the wizard academy—only wealthy men who could pay the fees attended—and there were few women in his section in the army camp. Camp followers attached themselves to men whom they knew or who could provide for them—and that wasn't anyone of his station.

She moved to knead the bread dough. "Biscuits for breakfast," she said. "Does that sound good?"

"Wonderful."

She smiled, and he inhaled sharply. He couldn't stop looking at her. It was as if his ability slid off her like water or smoke. A miracle. He could watch her without fear or guilt.

But if she knew what he was, she'd never trust him.

It was a bitter pill, but he couldn't deny the truth. He could only pretend not to see it.

So he'd watch her and pretend a while longer, until they were free, and then he'd cherish this moment—for he'd never get another.

Eyl found several large satchels and began to fill them with supplies and food for the journey—if he worked out the solution to those glyphs, that was. They would be going nowhere if he couldn't find the key.

Fee shook his head and bent over his notebook. His tongue poked out of the corner of his mouth in concentration as he tried different combinations, searching for the pattern or wording that would release the spell.

He worked in silence for a time before Eyl said, "I've never understood how to read wizard runes. I've tried to read up on the old man's books, to see if there was a way to break the enchantment, but I could never find any sort of dictionary that would help me translate."

"It's not easy to learn," he said absently. "They're not individual letters. More words and concepts that get bits added to them depending on your meaning. But the other part is how they teach it. Nearly all rune instruction happens in the Damaslar Concordium." He looked up at her. "You don't find many lower-class wizards. It costs the earth, or very nearly, to go there. Only the cream of the crop." His mouth twisted. "And the by-blows, of course. One or two scholarship blokes who show an exceptional aptitude."

"And that's the only magic school?"

"I think there's one in Cadruissau, but then you have to get there. They love learning over there, or so I've heard." He sighed. "That must be nice." He glanced up. "What about Altesia?"

Eyl's nose wrinkled. "No magic schools. Not much call for wizards, actually. I never thought they were much good for practical things. Like philosophers."

Fee chuckled. "If more wizards were philosophers, we'd have less problems. As it is, most think like lawyers."

"How so?"

"Contracts. That's all magic is—in human terms, anyway. A

written contract stating what the magic you call up is supposed to do. How well it works depends on how ironclad the terms are. How clearly did you word what you wanted to happen? Poor enchantments come down to bad wording, and shoddy spells can be undone if someone didn't close all their loopholes. That's what I'm hoping for," he said, motioning to the notebook in his lap.

"How…incredibly boring."

"True."

"How does that work? What would happen if you didn't write it correctly? Healing someone, for instance? Why not just write 'And then the fever went away' or something?"

He raised an eyebrow. "Fevers go away when people die, too."

Eyl's eyes widened. "Not like *that*! You know what I mean."

"I do, but magic doesn't. It's always going to take the shortest, easiest route. To be a healer, you need to have a good idea of the underlying problem you're dealing with—is it an infection? Is it chicken pox? Pneumonia? Then you have to know what treatment would be given non-magically. You have to take into account any side effects. You have to word it just so."

"Ugh," Eyl said appreciatively.

"Yes. But healers are more concerned about consequences than most, and few aspire to that level of study. Most wizards only put in enough provisos to prevent the spell from collapsing."

"So they ignore exactly what they've been trained to do?"

He rolled his eyes. "Seems like it."

"What does Damaslar use wizards *for*? Besides war, I suppose."

"That's a question for the ages," Fee said bitterly. "I have no idea."

CHAPTER

ELEVEN

EYL

As she put the bread in the oven and set aside food that could be taken on their journey, Eyl thought and wrestled with the dilemma she had not yet voiced as well as her conscience. The trouble was, she didn't know what question she wrestled with. Was it necessary? Was it right?

Or did she have the courage?

Fee broke through her dark musings. "I think I've found the solution to Kai." He pointed to his notebook with a triumphant smile.

"Really?" she breathed.

"Yes. And Imani's glyph should be similar—yours is the one with lots of 'if-then' statements and clauses to it. But I'll get there." He splayed his hand over the pages. "I think I've got the rhythm of his spell working now."

"Good. That's good."

Something in her tone must have alerted him. "Eyl?"

She twisted her hands in her tunic. "I know when—when spells are broken, the caster can feel it. Backlash and such."

"If they're in proximity," Fee said. "I think if you broke a spell in Cadruissau, the caster might not notice if they were in Damaslar."

"What about when you release them?"

Fee stared at her blankly.

"What I mean is, will the old man feel us escaping and try to stop us?"

Fee licked his lips in thought. "Ordinarily, I would say *no*," he said slowly. "Because it's more like untying a knot than hacking through it. The rope being the magical power flow."

"But?" Eyl pressed.

"I suppose it would depend on how sensitive he is to his magic. Or how paranoid," Fee added.

Eyl clenched her fist. "Then we may have a problem."

"Paranoid?"

"Yes."

Fee's face turned grim as he stared at the far wall, considering.

"We'll have to kill him, won't we," Eyl said.

His gaze shot to hers, eyes wide. Then he wrenched them away again. "No. No, I wouldn't advise that at all. If he's as paranoid as you say, he may have death spells in place fit to wreak havoc should someone try to do him in."

Eyl paled. She had never considered that. "So...what do we do? And there's another problem."

"What?"

"Say we escape, but he's still here, alive. And the people the High Wizard is sending show up. He can tell them exactly what we look like. Maybe track us. Certainly explain his process, or notes...well, maybe not, since he is scrambled these days, but... we won't be able to just disappear."

Fee let out a long, slow breath. "You're right."

Eyl looked around the kitchen, knowing every knife placement, the location of the axe. She was a predator. Using a knife was no different than claws. She just had to keep freedom in the forefront of her mind, spells or no. She set her shoulders and stood.

"How paranoid is he, exactly?"

She looked over her shoulder. "I don't know. Is there some sort of sliding scale one uses to measure?"

He turned his charcoal pencil over in his hands. "Is he so paranoid that he tests his food for poison? Toxins, so forth?"

"Not that I've noticed," Eyl said slowly.

"It would either be tracing a spell on his staff, or writing something before eating or drinking, or touching an amulet or some other trinket to the food."

"No, I've never seen him do anything like that. I suppose he doesn't think he has to, since Tala used to do the bulk of the cooking."

Fee nodded slowly, watching the pencil rotate in his hand.

"Do you think we should poison him? Would that get around the death spells?" She cast her eyes around the kitchen, trying to picture what substances they had on hand that could kill a man.

"No, no, not at all," Fee said, stopping the pencil's movement. "Poison would certainly set off the death spells, if they exist. I imagine they're defined by unnatural death. But if he doesn't test his food, I can spell something—his wine, perhaps—to make him sleep. That will give us time to work all the unbindings." He gestured at the doorway. "Then when I can get in the tower, I can check for the spells on his person and on his staff. Dismantle what I can. Then—"

"I'll kill him," Eyl said.

He shook his head, a quick, decisive gesture. "No, it will be me."

"I'm the one he's held captive for nine years," Eyl objected.

"So, you deserve something better. Don't dirty your hands with his filth."

"It is my right," she insisted.

"No. It's no one's right to take a life. That's what makes it murder. I'll do it."

"Fee—"

He turned his blue eyes on her, icy as the Lady's Mirror in the dead of winter, and just as fathomless. "I said I'll do it."

Staring into his eyes, Eyl realized she wasn't the only predator in the room.

TWELVE

FEE

Eyl turned back to the oven, and Fee was glad. He didn't know what she'd seen in his face, but he knew she had seen *something*. He stared sightlessly at his notebook. Maybe he wasn't the only one who could catch a glimpse of the truth.

And the truth? He already had blood on his hands.

He had used his magic to attack the enemy, to trigger catapults, traps, create boggy ground, fire. But primarily, he had been forced to interrogate prisoners. He had stared into their eyes and seen their most intimate secrets and spoken them aloud. He had cracked prisoners open like oysters and stolen their safety from inside their own heads. He could see every one of their faces staring at him in horror and disgust as he'd pulled their secrets out.

But it was the spy who had broken him.

Fee swallowed, closing his eyes. He could still smell the stuffy air in that tent, the burning lamp oil. Hear the whispery timbre of her voice.

"There's been a mistake," she had whimpered. "Please."

"You're a spy," he had told her. He hadn't looked at her after Nicanor had thrust him into the tent, instructing him to pry her secrets out of her, but her wide, tear-filled eyes wouldn't leave his head.

"Please," she had said in a tearful voice. "My parents will be worried."

True. Fee closed his eyes against his gift.

"We got separated, and all I did was go the wrong direction—I'm not supposed to be here!"

"You're still a spy."

"What will they do to me?" Her voice wavered. "Kill me?"

He said nothing.

"They will, won't they?" She gasped. "Just because I blundered into the army lines."

"Damaslar lines," he said. "You're Altesian."

From the corner of his eye, he could see her face. Caught the subtle surprise she'd hidden remarkably well.

"Your hair. Freshly trimmed, all the same length, for all that it's dirty and you say you've been traveling a time."

"I'll give you anything." Her voice had changed from young and vulnerable to husky and seductive. Her blouse had slowly slipped down her shoulder "Anything at all."

He'd known what she'd been doing, even though nobody else had attempted it yet. But then, she'd been a spy, not a soldier. He didn't blame her for trying. She ought to do her very best to get out of this trap. But he couldn't help her.

"Does the deer beg the arrow to spare its life, or the hunter?" he'd asked. "You're confused, miss. I'm not the hunter. I'm the weapon."

She'd been still and quiet for a while. Then she'd said, "You're that one. The mage boy."

Fee had flinched. He remembered that. The bile had risen in his throat. He was known outside the army camp? What did they say of him? *"The devil boy bewitches all your secrets from you, just by staring in your eyes"?*

It had been too much.

"If you just tell me something and make it believable," he had whispered, "I'll pass it on."

"I'll still be dead," she'd said. "You can't let them kill me."

He had laughed—a little wildly, a little unhinged. "I told you. I have no power here. None at all."

"Please," she had whispered. "Please. You must help me. Don't let them kill us." And her hand had crept protectively over her stomach.

He'd known that this was another ploy to get him to help her —she had tried childlike, seductress, and now vulnerable mother. She'd been doing her utter best to manipulate him.

But *she'd been telling the truth*, even if she hadn't known it.

It had hit him in the chest so hard, he'd bent over, trying to breathe.

"What will they do if they know?" she'd whispered.

He'd been so tired. So, so tired. But he had tried. For the sake of her unknown truth. To have done one good thing in this war.

And it had all ended in mud and blood just the same.

"It happens to everyone with their first female spy, boy," Nicanor had drawled in his bored, condescending way. "I hope you at least got a good tumble out of it."

After that, there'd been nothing in him but rage and despair. So he'd stolen the letters. He'd run. He'd had nothing left to lose.

He had her blood on his hands, the blood of the first soldier he had tried to help. All those who had come before. He might as well add some blood on purpose for once. At least this time there would be a *point*.

A cork popped.

Fee pulled his focus from the abyss.

Eyl poured from a dusty bottle into two glasses. "Here."

"Gingerbread, and now wine?" Fee took the glass she offered.

"Whisky," she said, just as he swallowed.

It was like liquid fire running down his throat. He coughed and felt his hair stand on end.

"Good for what ails you," she said, sipping her glass placidly.

"Because you quickly forget it when that stuff is trying to kill you," he wheezed.

"Whisky is a good mountain drink. You've just been raised on weak Damaslar grapes."

"It's frankly shocking the bounty Damaslar vineyards actually produce. My father's ancestral estate has a vineyard attached to it. I can still recall the smell of the wine presses."

"Sacrificing quality for quantity, then." She swirled the liquid in the glass. "I agree that magicking the old man's subpar wine is a good idea. We'll table the other discussion for now. Don't mention it to Imani, though."

Fee raised an eyebrow. "But with Kai it's all right?"

"Kai is the one who suggested killing him years ago. We were just afraid none of his enchantments would end and we'd still be trapped like rats."

"Wise of you."

Eyl lifted her glass. "To wisdom."

"And successful schemes."

"'If the Lord's willing and the Gap's passable,'" she said as if by rote, and they drank.

Eyl didn't sleep during the night, but Fee did. He dropped off sometime in the early hours of the morning, leaning against the doorway, wrapped in his cloak.

She let him. He had found the solution to Kai's and Imani's glyphs as well as the tower spell. He couldn't keep thinking on fumes.

As the pre-dawn sky lightened to a blue gray, Eyl wondered if this would be the last night she spent trapped in this tower.

But she'd still never feel the sun on her face again.

"This had better work," she told the still morning. "You waited this long to help us. This had *better work.*"

She turned away from the door as Imani and Kai came downstairs, yawning and rubbing their eyes.

"We wanted to catch you before you turned," Imani said. "What's the plan?" She sent fire into the embers of the hearth and added more logs. The crackle of flame echoed loudly through the kitchen.

Fee inhaled sharply and blinked, straightening slowly from his curled-up position. "Good morning," he said, voice rough with sleep. "Or *is* it morning, yet?"

"Very nearly," Eyl said, swallowing. The rasp of his voice sent shivers through her. "Here's breakfast—hot biscuits and sausage, and if someone will find me some eggs, I'll fry a few."

"*I'll go*," Kai signed. He vaulted over Fee's legs and made for the henhouse.

Fee stood and cracked his back.

Eyl felt a jolt as she again realized just how tall he was. Sitting on the ground all night had made her forget.

"It smells fantastic," he said.

"There's coffee, too, if you like that. Kai insists he can't live without it, so we pay the earth for it when traders have it."

"Should I profess my undying love now or later?" Fee said with a slow smile, watching her from the corner of his eye. Her toes curled, and then she realized everyone could see them.

"Don't be silly," Eyl said briskly as Imani giggled.

"Might I beg a pail of water to wash in?"

Imani drew him a bucket of water from the tower's well, and he dunked his face in it. He came up whistling and hissing from the cold. "That's one way to wake up."

"Autumn's coming on; what did you expect?"

"Oh, I could've heated it, I'm sorry," Imani said. "I didn't think."

"No, I wanted to be clearheaded, and a good dunk is the best way," he assured her as Kai came back bearing a basket of eggs. "My thanks for the water."

Eyl cracked the eggs into the pan on the hearth. Fee took his place at the side of the doorframe, and Kai joined him so he could speak without signing. Though he probably wouldn't talk when he was trying to eat. There'd be a blockage in the pipeline that way.

Imani fetched the plates and jam from the pantry before clasping her hands and closing her eyes.

"Should I...?" Fee murmured, pausing in the act of taking a biscuit. Eyl waved him on. Imani finished praying and then poured everyone coffee. Kai commandeered the sausages and put everything on his biscuit, like a sandwich.

"Just explain the plan," Eyl said, passing him a plate.

"Nhow?" he mumbled, mouth full of biscuit.

"Before dawn." She dished up the eggs and glanced out the tower door. The sky was definitely lightening.

"Umm. Yhes." He worked to swallow, then said, "I'm nearly done finding a solution to the runes. Eyl has been packing provisions for you. Today, I'll work on the last glyph and hopefully crack it. Tonight, I'll spell the sorcerer's wine before you take up his dinner, so he'll sleep through our business. Then we'll work all the unbindings. After that, Imani and Kai will take all of the supplies out of the tower, so we'll be ready to leave."

"What about you?" Imani asked.

"Eyl and I will dismantle any"—he looked at Eyl. She did her best to nail him through the wall with her warning glare—"tracking magics the sorcerer might have active. Then we're free."

Imani beamed, the flames in her eyes dancing. "That's amazing, Fee!"

Eyl let them talk, focused on putting as much breakfast into her mouth as she could. Her fingers were tingling.

She had consumed about five sausages and four biscuits before the tingling became an ache that commanded her obedience. "Imani, everything from last night is on the hob," she said abruptly. "Don't forget to feed Fee during the day and remember to act normally in front of the old man. He's—"

Her voice shrieked up into a falcon's scream, and she clutched her head.

Dawn had come.

CHAPTER

FOURTEEN

FEE

"Don't look! It's awful." Imani said, throwing her apron over her head. Kai turned away, face grim.

But Fee couldn't tear his gaze away. Maybe it was Eyl's face, wracked with agony, or the fear that shone in her eyes, but he rose up to his knees so that someone would stand witness to her pain. So that she wouldn't be alone in the torment.

He held her silvery gaze as she screamed. The awful sounds of a body reshaping itself filled the air. "You're—I'm right here," he said strongly, changing what he meant to say. He knew there would be no platitudes she could stomach. "I'm here with you." He clenched his teeth in sympathy.

She stared at him like he was a lifeline, even as her screams made his ears ache and his skin crawl. Feathers sprouted from her skin, white and silvery. Her hands and face remade themselves into a beak and talons.

The shriek reached a horrible crescendo. Her body collapsed in on itself. Her tunic and leggings fell in a pile of cloth to the floor. Then there was an angry gyrfalcon trying to fight its way out of the cloth and failing.

"There, now," Fee said, making his voice soothing, the way

one talked to wild things. His fingers itched to help her, and he couldn't. Instead, he curled them tightly into fists. "Peace, Eyl. It's all right now. Imani, help her get free."

Imani turned hesitantly. "Oh, you got tangled." She pulled the tunic off the bird. "Usually, she undresses first. It makes it easier."

"My fault, then," Fee murmured, awed by the sheer size of her. His father's estate had had extensive mews, but he had never had much to do with it. He disliked the thought of wild things in fetters.

Eyl was a silver gyrfalcon in color, nearly two feet long. He didn't know how large her wingspan would be at full extension, but large. Very large.

She cocked her head and stared at him, and Fee's heart stirred, lifting in his chest. He had thought it long dead. Perhaps Nicanor had not managed to kill it, after all.

He saw little from the falcon-Eyl—only a longing, deep and unspoken, for something he could not name. Fee swallowed.

The movement must have caught her eye, for she blinked. Then with a powerful flap of her wings—which all three of them had to dodge—she launched herself out of the doorway and into the dawn. The brush strokes of sunrise dappled her wings, and the frantic wingbeats against the gold-vermillion light shone like the sharpest knife in his chest. A sight too grand for words.

Imani gathered up the discarded clothes and folded them, sniffing. Kai gathered up her abandoned breakfast plate without speaking. They both disappeared into the kitchen.

The gyrfalcon circled above the clearing, beating her wings.

Fee shaded his eyes with his hand, tracing her flight. He couldn't reconcile the horror and the wonder together in his mind. On the one hand, her change was agony—he could even see that from the one glimpse. And doing that every day—! But ah, the brutal beauty and pride that shone off the very silhouette of the gyrfalcon.

On instinct, he put up his arm, like a falconer might.

The gyrfalcon stopped circling and dove, pulling up sharply to land without issue on his outstretched hand and forearm. He belatedly braced himself for her weight, but she didn't weigh quite as much as he'd expected—the hollow bird bones, maybe. Even the structure of her bones needed to change, he thought, and he clenched his jaw.

Fee winced a little as she settled and adjusted her weight—the press and pinch of those talons made him remember why falconer's gloves existed—but then she turned and regarded him with one luminous, brilliant eye.

"Hello," he whispered.

She shifted her feet again.

"A better perch? Do you want to sit with me?" He lifted her to his shoulder, and she situated herself until she was facing the direction she desired.

Then she ran her beak through his hair, and he felt absurdly pleased.

A SUDDEN RATTLE and clang from the tower kitchen pulled Fee from his dazed stupor. He lifted his eyes from his notebook, rubbing the sand from them. "I think I've got it," he said incredulously.

After breakfast, he had gone to see about the horse. Eyl had accompanied him on his shoulder, as she'd seemed in no hurry to leave her perch. The horse had blown a bit and stamped as the sight of the scary bird who just might eat it—Fee had rolled his eyes—but after he'd spoken soothingly to the beast for a bit, the horse had settled enough to take a long drink from the stream and eat his grain. Fee had packed his meager belongings from his camp and tacked the horse up, under the assumption that it would be better to have the beast close by the tower for tonight.

In the tower clearing, Fee had hobbled the horse in a large patch of grass before unloading his burden. "Here you are," Fee had told the polished oak staff as he'd pulled it from its wrappings. It was not completely carved with runes, as he was not a master yet, but the areas one typically laid hands on were filled in. "What do you think?" he had asked Eyl.

Eyl had given it a cursory once-over and then tucked her head under her wing to sleep. She'd needed it, after staying up all night. So, hiding a smile, Fee had set the staff down and settled carefully under a tree to work on her glyph. In the shade he could feel the chill in the air as autumn closed in. It was a bit warmer here in the south, but the days were shortening and soon the chill would be inescapable. He had pulled his cloak around him carefully as he'd worked, wishing a little wistfully for a warm, feathery coat as well. But now, staring at his notebook, he didn't feel the cold at all.

Another resounding bang echoed in the clearing. A pot exited the tower door, propelled by Kai's foot. The pot rolled drunkenly on its side in large arcs until it came to a stop halfway to the henhouse.

Eyl woke with a start, fluttering her wings on consternation. She launched herself from Fee's shoulder—*yowch*—and fluttered above the pot, complaining loudly to all and sundry about its treatment.

Kai left the kitchen and glared up at her. "Yes, I know it's a good pot, but we're not bringing it with us. I'm allowed to dent it a little. Please shut up." Several cicadas buzzed out of his mouth. Eyl eyed them before Kai snapped to get her attention. "Stop."

Eyl landed on his outstretched hand in a huff.

Fee stood, cracking his neck. He was tired to the bone but grimly victorious. "I've found the key to the last glyph," he told Kai, and he held up his notebook.

"Wonderful. Imani is making lunch," Kai said shortly. Then he turned towards him, and Fee got a good look at his face.

Fee stiffened. Kai sported a bruise on his chin and a swelling lip, much the same as Eyl's fading bruises around her eye.

"What happened?"

Kai's jaw tightened and he looked away. "A fight over bathing."

"And he hit you?"

"He got me with his elbow." He managed a brittle half-smile. "You wouldn't think it, but they're very pointy. He's settled now, though, with his books and his papers. Thankfully this time he didn't use magic."

Fee pursed his lips. "This is a regular occurrence?"

"He's getting worse." Kai rubbed a hand down his face. "Sometimes he goes on and on for ages with complete clarity, and then he gets confused, forgetful. And then paranoid and suspicious, especially when he doesn't believe us when we tell him his daughter's dead, or that he's been here nearly fifteen years, or that he can't go to the capital. Last week, he couldn't think of the words he wanted to say. That was bad."

"How so?"

Kai shot him a look. "You know how magic works. A wizard who can't think of the right word he wants to use? Blasphemous. Most of the time, he can ignore any of the lapses because it's not his job to think about anything except his work. He's completely shut off from the outside world. We deal with that. But forgetting words…that frightened him. He was awful. We couldn't get near him because he kept swinging that staff."

Kai's eyes narrowed onto Fee. "Speaking of staffs. Don't you have one?"

"I do. It's with my pack and my horse." He hooked a thumb at his belongings and the horse, cropping placidly at the grass now that the extremely scary bird had stopped shrieking.

Eyl stretched out her neck and softly cried in Kai's face. "I am all right," he promised her.

Just to make sure, though, she rubbed her beak against his face. Then with a powerful shove, she shot up into the air, finding the wind currents she wanted, quickly shrinking to a speck above them.

"Where's she going?" Fee asked.

"Hunting. She gets restless without it." He glanced at the horse. "Should we begin to load him with supplies?"

"I don't like to burden him, since we won't be able to leave until nightfall. But we could leave supplies out here."

Kai nodded, squinting up at the sky. "If the clouds don't roll in."

Fee reached for his staff and traced a series of runes, infusing them with magic. His fingers tingled against the wood, and the knowledge came to him. "It's going to rain again, in the late afternoon."

"Does this change our plans?" Kai asked.

"It shouldn't." He reached for his notebook. "I can write a longer spell and find out."

Kai snorted. "Wizard magic is so foolish. So complicated, boiled down into action and consequence and measurements and specifics." He fished a lizard out of his mouth and glared at Fee.

"Is that why you hate me?" Fee ventured.

Kai shook his head forcefully. "I do not hate you. I dislike you. I dislike all wizards. Their selfishness ruined an entire race. You should understand *that*." He shot a sharp look at Fee.

"How so?" Fee said through stiff lips.

"The Sundering, of course."

"I don't understand."

Kai narrowed his eyes. "What do they teach you of the history of magic, in those foolish Damask wizard schools?"

"The Sundering was a great continental event that consolidated magic for human use."

Kai spat a swarm of midges. "Lies. Human wizards took what should be full of life and wonder and mystery and boiled it down to locks and keys and contracts, used only by a select few. They killed the natural flow of magic in the land and in the faefolk." Kai stuck his chin out stubbornly.

"How did they kill it?"

"As much as diverting a stream kills the fish and plants that lived there. The way building a dam hoards water for some but deprives those downstream. Faefolk use magic the way we use water or air, for survival. There was a time when the earth was full of it, freely given to all. But locking up magic deep within the earth, reducing it to a power source to be turned on and off at leisure, damned an entire race." He gestured around them. "Is it no wonder that faefolk have been disappearing from the earth? Did you never wonder where your heritage came from, and why?"

"It's seen as a shameful thing, in Damaslar," Fee said slowly.

"Damaslar is full of fearful idiots," Kai muttered.

"How do you know all this?" Fee questioned.

"My people remember," he said shortly. "We have not forgotten what the Damaskmen did, all those centuries ago, and I will not forgive them."

"I'm not sure I would, either," Fee said quietly. He fingered his ears, thought of his talent—what he had always privately viewed as a curse.

Maybe he could've used it for something good, if his magic hadn't been so confined. Limited by his blood and wizard runes. He could've done more to help the spy. The wounded soldiers.

Maybe—he swallowed.

Maybe, if he had been able to use magic freely, his mother would not have died.

***

Fee woke up from his post-lunch nap with a start, wincing and coughing as raindrops went up his nose. The sun had dipped low on the horizon behind a heavy curtain of gray clouds, and the sky had finally released a chilly downpour onto the wood. The soft, grassy space between two tree roots he had found to sleep in did not offer much shelter from the rain.

Yanking his waterproof cloak from his pack, he wrapped it

around himself and pulled the hood over his head, shivering under the deluge. He moved against the side of the tower to get what protection he could from the rain. Fee wiped the water from his face and grimaced.

Thunder rumbled, and Kai stuck his head out the tower door. "You all right?"

"Just wet," Fee said wryly, swiping away an errant drop of water that had found its way down the back of his neck. He held out his hands to the entrance, trying to make use of what warmth was available from the fire within.

"Thirty minutes till dusk and dinner, and then two hours until the old man goes to bed, give or take," Kai said. Three fireflies escaped his mouth. "Depending on how well your spell works."

"It'll work."

"It better."

Kai retreated back in the tower.

Imani passed him a steaming mug of coffee and murmured, "He's just nervous."

"I know." Fee blew on the coffee and sipped gingerly.

"Do you want dinner now? We usually eat with the old man. Have to encourage him to eat."

His eyebrows shot up. "Is it ready?"

"Yes." She beamed. "I don't have to worry about overcooking anything. I keep everything just the right temperature." She lifted her hand and fire flared to life in her palm, licking her fingers like a cat's tongue. She was not bothered by the heat nor burned.

"Then I'd love some."

Fee dug into the plate she brought him with enthusiasm. As he ate, he stared across the clearing, watching rivulets of water trickle down through the trees. Halfway through the meal, a streak of silver dropped out of the clouds and, shedding rain-drops, landed on his shoulder.

"Hello." Fee chuckled, wiping the water out of his face. He reached out a hand to stroke gently down her feathers. "Where have you been all afternoon?"

She chirped irritably and shuffled her feet, nosing under his hood.

"Wha—hey, stop it," he complained. "You're getting me all wet. You could go inside, you know."

She shot him a patently disgusted look.

He had wondered how much she knew or understood as a bird, but that look in and of itself cemented his belief that she was mostly herself. He could understand her not wishing to go inside the place where she was trapped as a human. A wild thing would seek freedom at all costs, whenever she could. "My mistake. Apologies."

Disgruntled, she stuck her head under her wing and sulked.

"Fine." He unclasped the cloak and, with some awkward maneuvering and at least two rivulets of water trickling under his collar, got the cloak and its voluminous hood over the gyrfalcon. "Don't say I never did anything for you."

Eyl carded her beak through his hair, then bit the pointed tip of his ear.

"Ow! Gently, please. I like all my bits attached to my body." He settled her by sacrificing a hand to stroke her feathers and finished the rest of his supper one-handed.

When light died in the west, Eyl hopped from his shoulder and walked awkwardly into the tower. Imani grabbed her folded clothes from the morning and set them down within reach.

Now Fee did turn away because she was going from bird to girl. He kept his eyes on the rain but talked to her as firmly and confidently as he could as the gyrfalcon began to shriek. Over the sounds of bones and groans that filled the air, he said, "It will be over soon, and you'll get to eat supper—it's good, Imani did a good job—and then we can begin. I've found all the solutions to the glyphs. We're almost there. You're almost free."

Finally, the sounds stopped. All he heard was panting and muttered curses.

"You can look now," Eyl said in a rasp.

He turned his head as she settled her tunic around her legs.

Kai signed something to her with his fingers crossed. Eyl nodded. "Good. We're ready." She ran a hand over her wild hair, like a dandelion puff, as Imani brought a goblet brimming with wine.

Fee stood and pulled his notebook out of its waterproof pouch. "Let's do this."

FIFTEEN

CORBETT

Corbett Gar was really looking forward to a quiet afternoon in a tavern with his brother and their best mate, dicing, drinking, and having a rest. They'd just come from a job on the border of Cadruissau apprehending illegal snatchers and had another lead on one to the southwest, but instead of camping on the road, they had found a relatively good inn, with *beds*, by God, and he wanted to enjoy it.

A tavern wench had even winked at them, and he had some hopes, since he was the most handsome of the lot. Rilen, the poor rascal, had that scar and no tongue to charm, and Nath was barely out of his stripling years. Thus, it was Corbett who would have the looks and quiet words to persuade her to join him later that night.

Alas, it was not to be.

"You the Gar brothers? The trackers?" someone behind them barked.

Corbett threw his dice. A one and a two. Mountain's bones. He stuck a finger in his ear, wiggled it around. "Did someone speak?"

The man came into his line of vision, clanking with chainmail and trail dust. Ignoring him, Corbett leaned back in his chair and asked his brother, "You hear anything?"

Rilen put his hands together and signed, *"Only a fart."* To emphasize the point, he puffed his cheeks and blew a sharp exhalation of air, smirking.

Nath gathered up the dice in his hand and rattled them, his teeth flashing white in his dark face. He threw.

Another poor toss. Mountain's bones, it just wasn't their night.

"You bloody well heard me," the man said furiously. "I have a summons here from the High Wizard of Damaslar! You are to come with me and attend him immediately."

Corbett smiled, his lips peeling back from his teeth.

When they had visited Nath's family in Cadruissau several months ago, his little sister had told Corbett his smile made him seem unhinged. Which was, of course, why he did it. It was actually the main reason why he stayed clean-shaven except in the direst circumstances.

"I sure didn't hear anyone say 'excuse me' or 'beggin' your pardon.'"

The guardsman ground his teeth together.

Corbett's voice lowered into a deep, dangerous rasp. "And I *sure* don't 'attend' anyone like a dog being called to heel."

"Excuse me," the guardsman forced through his teeth.

"Very handsome, but I *don't* excuse you, as it happens, so eat scree." Corbett turned back to the dice.

Rilen threw the dice. A three and a one. *"Did you jinx me?"* he demanded, squinting at Corbett suspiciously.

"Don't look at me; it was the guardsman if it was anyone," Corbett signed back.

Rilen grumbled with displeasure.

"He's not leaving." Nath nodded pointedly.

Hell's bells. "You're ruining our dice," Corbett said without turning.

"You cannot ignore a summons from the High Wizard! He has—"

"Shut up, Jorgen. You couldn't convince a pig to piss."

Another man entered Corbett's line of vision, jerking his head at the guardsman. "Out."

He turned and jutted his bristly chin in Corbett's direction. "My subordinate got off on the wrong foot. Allow me to apologize and introduce myself."

"You've got one minute," Corbett informed him, taking a swig of his grog.

"My name is Marcus Tooms, and I am the personal guardsman of the Damaslar High Wizard, Nicanor Beornraed. He would like to engage your services."

"We don't involve ourselves in the war," Corbett said in a bored voice. That was the agreement he and Rilen had come to when it had started. Even though they hadn't been home since that fateful day, they wouldn't oppose Altesia—but they wouldn't help, either. They would stay neutral for however long the conflict continued.

"This isn't about the war," Marcus said firmly. "The High Wizard wants you to find his bastard. The boy has run away."

Rilen scratched his beard, the dark hair parting for the twisted scar that stretched from the corner of his mouth up to his sunburnt cheekbone.

Corbett rolled his eyes. "Have you checked his treehouse? A clubhouse hideout, perhaps?"

Marcus's mouth turned down. "The boy is nineteen."

"How about the whorehouse?"

"We know where he is going roughly," Marcus said, ignoring that. "He stole correspondence from the High Wizard that indicates his destination. He is going to steal valuable items from Aedelbras the Sorcerer unless stopped."

"A *sorcerer* can't stop him?"

"The High Wizard would prefer his son not get that far."

"Even so." Corbett rattled the cup. "No dice."

"The High Wizard is willing to pay handsomely."

"How handsomely?" Nath asked, before Corbett could tell Marcus to stuff himself.

The guardsman named the sum.

Only extreme power of will kept Corbett's jaw from dropping.

"Maybe we should talk about this?" Nath whispered urgently. "That's not money to sneeze at. We might not see that much in a year. Maybe longer."

"We agreed not to do jobs that would interfere with the war, for better or worse," Corbett reminded him.

"This isn't for the war; it's find and retrieve," Nath insisted.

"One sad rich boy run off, boohoo," Corbett said. "Why should I care?"

"Don't care, then, just find him and earn us easy money."

"What do you think?" Corbett asked his brother. "You're the one who insisted on non-interference."

"This isn't for the war. It's a family squabble," Rilen pointed out, tilting his head to the side in consideration. *"Like this is becoming."*

Corbett made a quick, emphatic gesture.

Rilen's white teeth flashed in his beard as he laughed, the sound low and raspy.

"You know, I was really looking forward to a night of rest and recreation," Corbett grumbled. He turned back to Marcus, who waited impassively. "We'll do it."

"Good. We need to leave—"

"In the morning," Corbett said firmly. "We'll leave for the front at first light."

Marcus frowned. "The High Wizard—"

"Demanded, immediately, yes, yes. But if we rode all night and then had to strike out after this boy's trail right away, we wouldn't be fresh, would we?" He threw the dice.

One and one. Mountain's bones, hell, *blast*.

"Better get to bed, boys, we ride out at first light." Corbett cast a last regretful look at the buxom barmaid and sighed. It just wasn't his night.

CHAPTER

SIXTEEN

EYL

Just drink the wine, Eyl thought as hard as she could. *Drink. The. Wine.*

Alas, it was never that easy.

"And where did you go tonight, missy?" the old man asked, his head craning towards her on his wizened neck. It reminded Eyl of a vulture's beady-eyed stare.

"I stayed in the wood, master," she said, her voice level as Imani handed around the cornbread.

His eyes narrowed in suspicion and he huffed, picking at the food on his plate. "Every day, she flies as far as she can, and now she stays around the tower?"

"It rained, master. I took shelter." She had felt the pull—the ever-present tug, like a lodestone in her heart—towards the north, but Fee's presence, plus the rain, had kept her close. The promise of freedom, of escape, was so tangible, she could almost taste it in the food Imani served, smell it in the steam. And maybe the others could, too. It was a quiet meal, though most of them were, punctuated only by the old man's demands and complaints, but something crackled in the air about them. A new tension had sprung up.

Eyl worried that the old man could feel it. He was tetchier than usual, and his narrowed eyes kept flickering over them as if to spot something amiss, something wrong—so poor Imani, with the weakest poker face among them, kept her eyes averted towards the fire for much of the meal, though that was nothing out of the ordinary. Eyl carefully avoided looking at his goblet. Kai's face was planed clean of all emotion. Only his chewing movements betrayed anything he felt.

"Rain," the old man groused, like he thought that she was lying.

"It is still raining, master." She kept her mouth occupied with chewing so that she could not slip and sass him. They were so close. Then, once free, they'd deal with him.

His time is coming, she reminded herself. *Just hold on a few hours more. Then I will make him pay for Kai's lip, my eye, and all our years of suffering.*

"What cares a gyrfalcon for rain?" he demanded.

"All the prey takes shelter, master."

Kai gestured to the old man's bowl. *"Would you like more, master?"* He still hadn't picked through half his portion yet.

"I don't want this swill," the old man said, pushing it away. "Bring me something better." He lifted his wineglass and took a long swig, wiping his mouth with the back of his hand. Imani jumped up to fetch some of the fresh bread and butter.

They usually kept his alcohol intake to a minimum, so Eyl was hoping he'd take full advantage of the brimming glass. In the old days, when he'd still stood up straight, he'd drunk like a fish and his temper had worsened with drink. Only after would he become maudlin and bemoan his fate, exiled to some far-flung corner of the world away from learning and culture and influence.

Eyl never knew how such a miserable man had produced Tala.

Behind the old man's head, Kai signed, *"How long will it take?"*

Eyl raised one shoulder and dropped it. Surely, it would not be long. *Lord willing and the Gap passable.*

The old man chewed the bread, but after two bites complained the crust was too hard and hurt his teeth. He complained that it was too cold and demanded the fire be built up and the blanket wrapped tighter around his legs. Then he got too warm and Imani had to bank the fire until he was more comfortable. The lamp wasn't close enough to his book, he said, trying to eat and study at the same time. Then the glare was in his eyes. The text was small, but the magnifying glass was too cumbersome to use.

He was only halfway through his wine.

He went on and on with his complaints, though he yawned. Eyl hid an eyeroll.

"Would you be more comfortable in your chamber, master?" Kai asked solicitously, eyebrows raised.

Smart, Eyl thought. If he read in his room, he'd fall asleep for sure.

"There's a draft," the old man snapped. "I wake up chilled every morning."

"I'll stoke the fire in your rooms, master," Imani offered.

"And fill the rooms with smoke?" the old man growled. "No!"

"More food, master?" Eyl offered, gesturing carelessly to his plate.

"I'm finished." The old man pushed his plate aside and took another sip from the glass. Then he set it down.

Eyl checked furtively. A little less than half a glass left.

He persisted on in his reading for several more pages as they tidied the dishes and the room. Eyl nudged the glass closer to him as she wiped down the table, but he didn't pick it up again. He rubbed his face several times, yawned twice. The book shifted on his lap as his head nodded, losing his place twice before his scowl deepened.

"Here, boy," he called to Kai. "Help me to my rooms. I wish to retire. There's no use working longer tonight when conditions are so poor."

Kai nodded obediently and stood. Only Eyl could see his hand clenched into a fist behind his back.

Eyl and Imani finished up in the main room to give Kai time, and then they crept downstairs. Eyl swung back the bar on the door and opened it to reveal Fee waiting in the rain.

"Is he asleep?" Fee asked in a low voice, barely heard over the patter of raindrops. He tugged his hood further over his eyes.

"Not yet. Kai is getting him settled. He'll let us know when to start. But he only drank half the glass."

Fee's lips flattened into a line.

"Is that a problem?" she questioned, her heart rate spiking.

"As long as it takes effect...no." Fee frowned up at the dark sky as thunder rumbled in the distance. "But we'd best not waste time."

Eyl and Imani pulled the packs out of hiding and set them by the door.

"You've double-checked everything?" she asked Imani. "Food, blankets, clothes?"

"Yes."

"Money from the strongbox?"

Imani looked down. "Yes. Kai added it. But it's not ours...."

"He owes it to us," Eyl said firmly. "We've worked here for years. They're our rightful wages."

She left the 'he won't need it because he'll be dead' unsaid. She slid her sharpest carving knife into the back of her belt.

Before Eyl could answer, Kai slipped down the stairs like a ghost and signed, *"He's asleep. Snoring."*

"What did he say?" Fee asked.

"The old man's asleep." Eyl squared her shoulders. "We can begin."

SEVENTEEN

EYL

"Curse this rain," Fee muttered from under his cloak. "It's going to make this harder. The ink will run."

"We'll make it work," Eyl said firmly. "Who knows how long it will go on?" As if to confirm her words, thunder boomed in the distance. "We can hold a tarp over you. We have enough hands. What do you need?"

"A quill and ink. The charcoal I've used in my notebook won't do."

Kai fetched the quill and ink from the kitchen sideboard and wrapped a cloak around himself. He stepped into the rain and handed the items to Fee. "You really think you've found the solutions?"

"Yes," Fee replied. He sat in the grass as close to the door as he could get, hunching his shoulders and pulling his cloak tighter to his body. "Whom should I start with?"

"Imani," Eyl said decisively, rummaging for oilcloth in their packs. "She can't pass the clearing's boundary. That way, we can see for certain if it works." She directed Kai to take hold of a corner and she held the other, holding it above Fee through the doorway. It made the rain trickle into the kitchen in rivulets, but at this point, she didn't care.

Imani joined Fee under the oilcloth. The girl shyly offered him her arm, and he dipped the quill in ink, wiped it, and then began to draw additions to the tether rune, referencing his notes. Every few strokes on her skin, he would dab his work with a handkerchief so that the ink did not smear. He had to work slowly, careful not to make a wrong stroke.

At last, he made the final line. As they all watched, the runes all glowed a soft gold and melded together, the ink becoming a part of the previous etching. Then the glow faded.

"Did it work?" Imani asked reverently, her free hand pressed to her chest in hope.

"Let's see. Come back inside a moment." Imani scurried in, and Eyl helped her put a cloak on. Then she took two of the packs, stuffed with provisions and supplies, and handed them to Imani and Kai. "Both of you walk to the road like you're going to town."

Imani took her pack, biting her lip. Kai shouldered his own and took her hand, tugging her towards the path. The moon lit their way, glinting through the gray clouds as the rain pattered down through the trees, making silver rivers over the grass.

"They'll make it," Fee said fiercely. "They've got to."

Eyl shot him a sharp look. Maybe he was not as sure as he had made out. Fee kept his eyes trained on the two figures walking to the edge of the clearing and the path towards Stagfell.

Eyl held her breath and prayed as Imani hesitated at the edge of the clearing, her prison for the three years she had been at the tower. Kai squeezed her hand.

And then Imani stepped forward onto the path.

Eyl released her breath in a whoosh and leaned against the doorframe, her knees suddenly jelly.

Imani dumped her pack under a tree and threw herself into Kai's arms; the boy dropped his own pack just in time to catch her. Kai spun her around and around, throwing off a wide arc of raindrops that glinted silver in the moonlight. Then they ran back to the tower, breathless and amazed.

"You *did* it!" Imani shrieked, trapping Fee in a hug. As she clutched him, she suddenly burst into tears.

Fee rocked her back and forth, pulling a handkerchief from his pocket one-handed as little tongues of fire ran down her cheeks, sputtering and going out in the rain.

Her sob turned into giggles. "I'm sorry—I just never thought—"

"I know," he assured her, smiling. "Eyl?" Fee turned to her, gesturing for her foot.

"No," she said, her heart beating loud enough to wake the dead. "Do Kai first. Let's leave the tower wards for last."

He nodded. Kai tugged off his tunic and shirt and the process began again, that careful inking and blotting against his shoulder, as Imani and Eyl held the oilskin.

Freedom was such an elusive concept when it had been taken from you. And yet it was so close. The hope she had held so tightly for nine long, hard years—and Kai and Imani, too. She would make it true. She would see it done, come hell or high water. Lord willing and the Gap passable.

Lord, you'd better *make this work.*

Kai's rune flared gold and melded into his skin. Eyl breathed a sigh of relief. They couldn't test his, because his boundary extended farther. They'd have to trust that Fee knew his work.

"Now," Fee said, standing. "The protective wards."

Eyl lifted her eyes to the lintel. The aged wood of the door-frame sported a series of carvings she had copied down for Fee. "I'll get the stool."

He showed her the piece of parchment in his hand. "You'll have to carve the additions."

"I can—" Kai began.

"No, I'll do it," Eyl insisted. "I can reach it." She shot Kai a firm, mulish look. Being short didn't mean she was inept.

"Then I will steady the stool," he said with equal stubbornness, and he took hold of it.

Fee pulled a short, sharp stiletto from somewhere in his tunic and handed it to her. "It's for whittling," he said, misinterpreting her odd look. "It will do better with wood than a butcher's knife. Do you want me to hold the parchment for you?"

"Please. Thank you." Eyl clambered atop the stool, eyeing the paper he held up. And then she began to carve into the old, resistant wood.

"How deep must the cuts be, do you think?" she asked, digging the knife into the lintel. She grimaced. The oak felt more like teak.

"Matching the original if possible," Fee said. "I should be able to feel when the protections drop."

Eyl nodded and bore down, trying to make the cuts exact while still being deep. It was a slow process. Several times, she threw too much of her weight behind a cut and the stool wiggled. Then Kai grabbed the stool or her leg to steady her, making her jump. Then it started all over again.

Several minutes later, Eyl swiped an arm over her forehead, collecting the sweat there onto her shirt. Just one more cut, and then Fee could unbind her rune. She lowered her eyes to the parchment to make certain.

Fee met her eyes for a moment, and then his blue gaze slid past her into the tower.

His eyes widened in shock. "Eyl—"

"Thieves! Betrayers!"

Eyl jumped violently.

The knife slipped, skittering over the wood, and slashed through the rune.

A shockwave blew through the room.

Eyl slammed against the wall from the force of the blow, the knife clattering from her grasp.

Kai was thrown against the wall and landed badly.

Imani shrieked, blown backwards out the door into Fee.

Eyl twisted around on the stone floor. Her ears rang. She frantically blinked spots clear from her vision.

On the last few steps of the stair, the old man clutched his staff, reeling against the wall. He panted, as if he had just been forced to run a mile. Or been struck with a hammer.

Perhaps he has, she thought blankly. Backlash.

Something hot trickled down her face. She swiped her hand under her nose. It came away red. She pushed herself up on shaky arms and tried to find her bearings.

Chest heaving, the sorcerer bared his teeth, staring over them all out the tower door. "Thief! Think you I wouldn't notice you stealing from me? Do you think I'll let you take my life's work without a fight?"

His eyes were locked on Fee. He ignored the rest of them as though they weren't there. As if they were no threat.

Six feet away from the tower, Fee clambered to his feet in the rain, pushing Imani behind him. He clasped his staff.

Good, Eyl thought, trying to force her brain to act as if it weren't stuffed with wool. *If we need any weather divined, we're set.* She ground her teeth against the pain and forced herself to her knees. How had the old man woken from the enchantment? That stupid half-drunk wine. Not only that, how had he gotten all the way down the stairs?

It was no matter. He was here—and she was still trapped.

"Go!" she called to Fee in a voice she didn't recognize. "Get them out of here!"

She heaved Kai, who was coughing up bits of dead lizard, towards the door. He had yelled during the explosion.

"No, Eyl—" Kai said before his throat closed and he started hacking.

She tamped down concern. She had to make him safe. She used his coughing fit to shove him fully out of the doorway.

"Eyl!!" Imani cried.

"Go!" she screamed to Fee. He grabbed Kai by his collar and pulled him away.

She turned back and threw herself under the table just as the old man sent a blast of magic her way. Crockery shattered.

"So, it comes to this?" the old man demanded. "My own creation betrays me? I am your maker!"

"You didn't make me!" Eyl hurled a tankard at him, just barely missing his head. It glanced off his shoulder and clattered to the floor. Her arms were shaky from the blast.

"You didn't make any of us!" She grabbed another, threw it. Then she ducked back behind cover.

It crashed against the wall.

"I formed you from nothing! You owe your very being to me!"

"I existed long before you! You gave me nothing of value!" She hurled a platter. Ducked again.

The platter caught him in the chest, but the impact was minimal.

"Nothing of *value*?" the old man said incredulously, kicking the platter out of his way. "You went from rude, base humanity to magical creature! I unlocked the dormant heritage within you!"

"You gave me nothing but heartache and trauma when you *tortured* me, locked me up, stole my *freedom*—" The outrage nearly choked her.

She threw the heavy, wooden rolling pin. He knocked it away with his staff.

"You cursed me with this magic, trapped me in this tower—"

The old man clenched his boney fists. "I gave you wings! I am your god!"

She had run out of things to throw and was nearly out of cover. "You are *nothing* like a god, and you are *certainly* not mine!"

The old man raised his staff.

Eyl braced.

Someone grabbed her shoulder and shoved her out of the way, a staff held out to take the effect of whatever whistled towards her. The air rippled, the spell's effect countered.

"Sorry I took so long," Fee panted.

Eyl gaped at him. "You...you came back?"

"Of course," he said, pulling her farther back. His fingers traced of the runes of his staff.

"I told you to get Kai and Imani away!" she exclaimed.

"I did! That's what took so long!"

The old man threw fire at them, and then Fee was too busy to talk.

The air between the two wizards flooded with fire, light, and wind as spells and counter-spells flew too thick for Eyl to understand.

The air felt heavy, pungent. Charged with ill intent.

Fee blocked the blasts the old man sent, but just barely. "How is he so fast?" he panted. "He's not even tracing runes!" His finger moved faster and faster along the runes on his staff, but even Eyl could tell that Fee spent more time defending from the sorcerer's onslaught than attacking.

"You're going to make a run for it, all right?" Fee told her.

"Fee, I'm still stuck," she said. "My glyph. I can't leave!"

She caught up a stack of plates and hurled them at the old man to try to distract him, but a blast of magic caught them and blasted them into smithereens. The shards rained in all directions, nicking any exposed skin.

She cried out, covering her face with her arms.

They were at the doorway.

"Get ready," Fee said through stiff lips.

"What?"

"Get ready," he said again, and then he used both hands to trace a pattern on his staff.

Lightning crackled in the air between them. Then it flashed.

The old man reeled backwards.

Fee instantly dropped his staff and scooped up a long shard of crockery. He brought it down in a sharp slash on her tether rune.

Eyl screamed, but it was lost in the explosion's concussive roar.

They both went flying backwards out the doorway. Eyl landed hard on her shoulder and hip, skidding over the wet grass.

It felt like Fee had blown her foot off. Rain pattered down on her face as she struggled up to her elbows, staring frantically down.

Her foot was still there. Just with a bloody cut on it.

Out. She was—out.

He had *done* it!

"Fee," she gasped, breathless. She rolled over and froze.

He lay on the grass, white as bone, his scar standing out in sharp relief. He wasn't moving.

"Fee?" She shook his shoulder. "Fee, wake up."

Rain splashed on his face without rousing him, wetting his eyelashes and his hair.

Her heart leapt into her mouth. She held her hand over his lips.

Air huffed against her skin, and she breathed a huge sigh of relief. "Come on, get up." As she tried to grab him by the armpits to pull him, all her limbs shook like jelly. Fee was dead weight, and she couldn't shift him.

"You ungrateful golem."

She looked up through the rain, pushing hair out of her eyes.

"I made you—molded you—you exist by my hand," the old man said, clinging grimly to the doorframe, though blood ran down his temple. "I'll never let you go willingly."

He raised his staff.

Eyl threw herself protectively over Fee.

"No!" someone screamed.

A ribbon of fire flew through the air to hit the old man's staff. It flamed like a struck match.

Eyl looked over her shoulder to see Imani pointing at the old man, her face frozen in astonishment.

The old man screamed. His staff glowed, runes lighting from within. Then it splintered and broke. Fire spewed forth, catching on his robes and traveling back farther into the tower. He stumbled backwards, batting ineffectually at his robes, howling with rage.

Kai ran forward and grabbed Fee, hauling his dead weight backwards. "Come on, Eyl, run. Run!"

She staggered to her feet and tugged on Imani to get her moving. The tower doorway glowed an angry, reddish orange from within as the hungry fire devoured everything it could.

The old man's screams filled the air.

Then the tower blew up.

EIGHTEEN

"He's dead, isn't he," someone said.

"Certainly."

Fee frowned. He didn't think he was dead. Nearly everything hurt, and he didn't want to move for fear of it getting worse. But he didn't feel dead.

In fact, the ability to hear voices would be a strong point in the negative for dead.

"I killed him," the person whispered. Imani. It was Imani.

Eyl said flatly, "No, you didn't."

"Yes, I did!"

"The tower blew up. It's not the same," Kai said. The hum of some insect filled the air and then faded.

"I made the tower blow up, though."

"You set his staff on fire," Eyl corrected.

"It's the same thing."

"No. He could've dropped his staff or thrown it. He could have run out into the rain and put the fire out. He didn't. It's not your fault."

Imani was silent for a while. In the silence Fee could hear the splatter of rain all around them, as well as distant thunder. Actually, he felt quite a few of those raindrops, too. It was freezing. He tried to wiggle his toes. It worked, but they were stiff from cold and…what had happened?

Oh. He remembered. Backlash.

Finally, Imani said, "Is Fee going to die?"

"No. He's breathing. He'll be fine. Lord willing and the Gap passable," Eyl added with a mutter.

Fee coughed and pried open one eye. "What does that even mean?"

"Fee!" A blur flew through his limited vision to throw herself on him and cry. "You're alive!!"

"I just said that," Eyl said, peeved. "Let him breathe, Imani."

Imani pulled back, wiping her eyes as flames trickled down her face.

"Well, I think it was a near thing. Do you want my handkerchief?" he rasped, pushing himself up onto his elbows, even as his head swam. "I imagine it would be soaked, but…."

Imani shook her head as the fiery tears trailed away into puffs of smoke, extinguished by the rain. They just left smudge marks on her face.

"Here." Eyl grasped his hand and helped him sit up all the way.

Fee leaned against a tree and panted, cataloguing his aches. "So I'm assuming we made it? It worked?"

"It worked." Eyl pointed to a messy bandage around her foot. "And the old man's dead. The tower blew up."

"Blew *up*?" Fee stared. So much magic in place, so concentrated—it must have uncoupled the stone. "How did we survive?"

"Kai can lift very heavy loads. Turns out carrying heavy sacks from the village is worth something after all," Eyl said dryly.

"You saved me?"

"You saved us; fair is fair." Eyl handed him a waterskin. "We weren't going to leave you to get crushed. And it means 'we'll be able to do it if it's possible.'"

"Huh?"

She said, raising her voice, "Lord willing and—"

"I know what it means in context," Fee said irritably, holding a hand to his head as it throbbed. "What is the reference to 'gap passible'?"

"Taliesin's Gap is the major mountain pass in and out of Altesia. You could journey over the mountains another way, if it were just you. Maybe. But any major traders or caravans or groups of people going in and out of the Caleahanach Mountains enter and exit by Taliesin's Gap. And during winter, if there's been a particularly heavy snow, or an avalanche…." Eyl shrugged.

"Ah. So we are able to do this or that, if the Gap is passable." Fee nodded—carefully. "Who's Taliesin?"

"Legend says, Taliesin was the explorer who discovered the Cirondel Valley. His daughter was our first queen."

Her voice rang with pride. Fee wondered why. He had never cared about his own history or politics. *What must it be like, to like where you live?*

He stared around them at the darkened wood. Close by, a stream burbled under the sound of the rainfall. It might've been the general area where he had made camp. As close to cover as he could, Kai sorted through two packs and catalogued the contents.

"We've got a pack of food, and a pack of clothes and blankets," he announced, spitting out a cicada. "And the money from the strongbox is in my pockets. But everything else was still in the tower. Do you think you can walk?" he asked Fee. "Because we need to move now, before people come to see about the fire and the awful din the tower made when it fell."

"To say nothing of the dawn." Eyl folded her arms and cast a wary eye to the horizon.

Gritting his teeth, Fee got to his feet, confirming that everything worked, even if it hurt like the very devil. "I don't suppose my staff came with me," he murmured, looking around him.

Kai shook his head, fishing in his mouth for the amphibian going the wrong way. "Too fast. Not enough hands. Too likely to be crushed by falling rocks."

And no time to go back and hunt for it in the rubble. Fee flexed his hands. Then he groped for his notebook pouch in a panic. He had a recollection of shoving it—yes, there it was. He relaxed.

"Never mind, then," Fee said, even though the loss of so many ready spells stung. But not many traveled with rune-marked staffs—certainly not commoners—and it would keep them unnoticed. He'd have to rely on his own cunning for spells now.

Though the staff would've come in handy to keep him upright. Fee swayed on his feet before he caught his balance. "And the horse?"

"Bolted," Kai said glumly. "It would've been useful."

"Which way are we headed?" Imani asked.

Fee looked up. "*We?*"

"You can't walk without wobbling," Eyl said flatly. "And there are only two packs of supplies. I think we'd better stick together for at least the day—until we can find a village and resupply—"

"Not Stagfell," Kai said.

"No," she agreed. "Not there."

"What else is near?" Imani asked.

"Woeford," Fee said. "I passed it coming south. It's a little village a day's journey or so; I'm not exactly sure how much longer it will be on foot."

Eyl nodded hard. "Yes. North. Yes, let's go there."

Fee sighed as all his aches intensified at the thought of walking miles. But there was no help for it. "So we'll purchase supplies, and then—"

And then go their separate ways, and then he would be alone, never able to look at another soul. Again.

KAI AND EYL shouldered the packs—Eyl insisting she'd carry it till dawn, and she could pull her own weight. Imani and Fee fell in together. He cut himself a branch to use as a support until he got his feet under him. His head ached. They followed the stars while it was still dark as the rain tapered off.

When the sun came up, Eyl changed, and they were all shivering from the cold and blindingly tired. "We've got to sleep a little," Fee said as the bright sunlight made his head shriek with pain. "Eyl can keep watch."

Eyl nodded, and they all stripped out of their clothes and hung them to dry, wrapping up in the blankets in the driest spots they could find and falling asleep all in a huddle.

Before Fee drifted off, Imani whispered, "*Did* I kill him?"

"You did what you had to do," he said, eyes shut against the light. "A cruel man met his end, and all the lives at the edge of your clearing finally have justice. Let that be the end of it."

Eyl woke them when the sun was halfway up the sky, and they changed into dry clothing and set off again.

It was a hard day. Eyl, high above, set the direction and the pace, but she frequently had to look back to them and urge them on. Imani was unused to the strain of walking all day over rough terrain, and her shoes wouldn't hold up long against the onslaught. They all needed good boots, and more supplies. A good tent, or at least a tarpaulin, wouldn't go amiss, either. Fee allowed himself a five-minute mourning for the packs buried in the tower—and then was glad they still had supplies at all.

After ranging far ahead in the afternoon, Eyl came back and settled onto Fee's shoulder to put her head under her wing for her own nap.

Much of their long trek was silent, though they did take several breaks to spare everyone's feet. They made their way through woods and wild lands, but in late afternoon, as the sun dipped down towards the horizon, they came upon farmland, and all their spirits lifted. They'd managed aright and found the outskirts of Woeford.

They made camp near the outskirts of the village. Not so close that it would be noticed, though. Imani fell to the ground, moaning in relief, as Kai laid out Eyl's clothes and a blanket from a tree branch for a rude curtain. Then they all went about eating and making camp. Imani built the fire—the normal way, Fee noted, with flint and striker, though she did encourage the flame with her gifts to take hold of the wood and grow. They set out everything else that was still damp and waited.

Eyl changed back as the sun disappeared. Imani had fallen asleep halfway through her meal. Fee sat with his back against the tree and talked to Eyl through her change.

"You can stop," she finally said, pulling the blanket down from the tree. "I'm done."

"Good. Do you want to come into town with me?"

She stared at him suspiciously. "Town? I thought we'd go in the morning."

"Well, we will—I'm sure some shops and stalls won't be open after dark. But I thought you might want to go now. Since you'll be a falcon in the morning."

She stared at him in blank astonishment.

"I will stay with Imani and watch the camp," Kai said. He plucked the lizard from his mouth and set it down gently. "Go and see."

Fee bit his lip, hiding a smile. "So are you coming?"

NINETEEN

EYL

For the first time in nine years, Eyl walked into a village as a human.

The wave of humanity came back to her in intense memory—but many small things she had forgotten. The way villages smelled—a mix of food, animals, unwashed bodies, and herbs and rushes strewn to hide it. The smell of life. The way crowds talked, loud and boisterous or a quiet grousing.

Silence had been a large part of her existence for nine years. Being awake when others slept, being muzzled around the old man for fear he'd lash out, signing in solidarity to Tala and then later to Kai—so much of it had lent itself to silence. But humans were loud. They laughed and scolded and spoke in carrying voices. They dropped pots and babies fussed and their animals were loud, too.

Eyl stuck close to Fee. In a sea of newness, he grounded her.

The village had a few evening entertainments. The market was not quite closed down when they arrived, and they bought a few things. After some dickering, the cobbler, a man with graying hair concentrated below his ears, informed them he could have two pairs of boots finished in the morning for a higher price, and Fee nodded in agreement. He took the measure of Eyl's foot with only one word: "Tiny."

"For the other pair," Fee said, "double that."

Galling but true. Imani was going to be very tall, and she had the feet to prove it.

"Do I really need boots?" Eyl asked wryly. "Will we be doing much night walking?"

"You never know when you'll have to run," Fee said under his breath, then he assured the man they would pick them up in the morning.

"I should've been taller, you know," Eyl said as they moved farther along the street. "No one in my family could be called short."

"I imagine it was the magic." Fee shot her a sympathetic glance. "Changing every day and night isn't easy on you."

"No." She was realizing that more and more, seeing women pass by—women of all shapes and sizes, curved and toned, wispy and strong. By comparison, she looked starved, in spite of everything she ate.

"Here."

She lifted her head from her musings to find Fee presenting her with a large meat pie.

"I had dinner."

"I know. Now here's supper."

She opened her mouth to protest, but he said, "Do you want me to take a page from your book and say, 'shut up and eat the pie'?"

She shut up and ate the pie. It was delicious.

Fee haggled well—far better than she would've done. She had all of the theory and none of the practice. Kai had done all the bartering, buying, and selling, and before that, Tala had just paid what merchants had asked. And of course, Eyl had never had to purchase anything as a child. As he haggled, Fee looked off into the distance, or just above the seller, or down at the stall. Never right at the merchants.

As the seller pulled the tarpaulin from the stack and took their money, Eyl asked, "Why are you doing that?"

Fee hefted the tarp into his arms. "Huh?"

"You're always looking away." Come to think of it, he had done that when he had first arrived at the tower, too—like looking right at them made him flinch.

Fee paused, then said, "I don't want anyone to get a good look at me, in case our pursuers come through and ask."

"Should we be here at all, then?" Eyl asked, looking around.

"We need supplies; we can't avoid it. And the glamour will help." He motioned to his face. He had taken a moment to write a long and complicated series of runes in his notebook before they'd set out for the village, to cloak his pointed ears and mute his appearance. His red hair was dull, his scar negligible, and he appeared depressingly normal, with no standout features at all.

"You've got a cloak on and nobody knows to ask what you look like. You'll be fine." He moved onto the next stall, haggling for packs to carry their purchases in.

As the pair left the main square, a lone bell tolled. Fee frowned. "I wonder what that is."

She shifted the pack on her shoulders. "It's Vespers."

Fee stared at her, mystified.

Oh. She'd forgotten the Cadruissau missionaries were still not fully accepted on the plains. The country made up of a long, skinny strip of mainland and a wide island chain had brought the religion across the water at least a century ago, perhaps more. Damaslar as a whole had stayed indifferent to the church, while it had come to Altesia nearly a hundred years before and been well received. Odd in a land that was so much of a melting pot, but perhaps the doctrines of the church clashed with the deeply entrenched conflict that characterized so much of the plains.

She explained, "Vespers is the evening prayer service." Eyl lifted her head and searched for the source of the bell.

Sure enough, on the outskirts of the village, a steeple rose, jutting towards heaven. "I'll show you," Eyl said, tugging on his arm. Fee followed her, and when they got closer, she pointed out the simple design of the chapel, a mixture of wood and local stone only slightly bigger than the surrounding cottages. Figures emerged from the lit doorway, heading home after the service.

They stood to the side and watched the small number of worshipers trickle away. How funny it was, to find a church here. It was so familiar. Eyl could recall the songs, and the smell of the wax candles and incense, and the way the prayers had made her feel as a child, kneeling on a too-thin pillow, determined not to interrupt the service with an inopportune squeak because Ev would have teased her—privately, of course, once they'd been back in the nursery—

And abruptly, it stopped being funny, and more a bitterness welling up from deep down. A church, here. Only a very long day's walk from the tower. So close. So close to her imprisonment, to the misery, the *death*.

You couldn't stir yourself eight miles closer? she thought, suddenly furious.

A figure emerged onto the steps of the chapel with a broom. The dark-skinned woman wore a long, gray robe and a starched wimple around her face. Her rosary hung from the belt around her waist, clicking softly against the symbol of her order. Eyl couldn't make it out. After sweeping the stoop for a minute or two, the woman looked up and smiled gently directly at them. "You are welcome to come in."

Fee glanced at Eyl curiously. "Can we go see?"

She swallowed, staring at the chapel. "No."

"Is it not safe?" Fee murmured.

She cleared her throat. "Chapels and churches are sanctuaries." She heard how short her voice sounded and tried to dial back the biting anger. It wasn't Fee she was mad at, after all. "You just said you wanted to keep a low profile."

Judging by Fee's expression, it didn't work as well as she'd hoped. "I think this would be the last place they would look for us."

She still wanted to pull him away. She didn't want to make nice with God. The betrayal bled deeper than she realized.

But then she thought, *Why not?* Yes, they'd go in, and she'd finally have it out. She had a bone to pick with God. He'd hear her in here, surely. He'd hear her, or she'd know the reason why.

The nun smiled in welcome. "I'm Sister Jeanetta. Are you travelers? What brings you to Woeford?"

"Just passing through," Fee said firmly.

She nodded at them. "Traveling mercies to you, then. You're welcome to come in and look from the inside. We're very proud— our chapel is new, not even a year old yet. I'm just cleaning up." She smiled and disappeared inside, leaving the door ajar.

Eyl took the lead and stepped inside, pulling back her hood.

The floor was simple stone, the altar unadorned except for a meticulously embroidered cloth and a crucifix. Two long, embroidered tapestries hung from the walls, depicting creation and the flood. In three windows, stained glass glowed proudly. The other windows stood empty. At the back of the chapel, in what would have been the narthex in a larger building, a small, veiled statue greeted them with its fisted hands thrust down and to the side, chin raised.

"What is that?" Fee whispered.

"One of the virtues. The Cadruissi like to decorate everything with them, and they form the basis of the religious orders. Faith, charity, justice. That one looks like fortitude." Which was interesting. Usually, missionaries belonged to the Order of Charity.

"Until we can afford more stained glass, we must be content with tapestries to depict Bible stories. Though they will wear faster due to the elements and the moths," Sister Jeanetta said from the altar, closing shutters on the empty windows and using a candlesnuffer to put out high lanterns hung from hooks on the walls. "Of course, I am used to churches open to the rain and salt. But mosaics do not mold the way tapestries do." She chuckled and left two candelabras at the front lit as well as the lanterns at the back. "Please feel free to take a closer look if you like. We're very proud of them."

Fee wandered up to stare at the tapestries, but Eyl stayed where she was at the back of the church, breathing in the scents of beeswax and tallow and incense. Drawn like a moth to light, she stepped towards the closest stained-glass window. It tugged at something in her, whispering to things she had left buried for too long. It depicted tawny lions circling a lone man in the darkness, their jaws poised to snap. The small pieces of glass glowed in the candlelight, bits of red and yellow winking at her like jewels, the chips of glass that made up the fangs gleaming. She could only imagine what it looked like in full sunlight.

"Do you know the story?" Sister Jeanetta asked softly, coming up beside her.

"Yes," Eyl said, a little more curtly than she'd meant. She winced. It had been an honest question. She knew very well that reading was not a widespread ability among the lower classes in Damaslar. And stained glass in churches was a good teaching tool for worshipers who couldn't read. It was perfectly understandable that she should ask. Eyl cleared her throat. "Yes, I know it."

Sister Jeanetta raised an eyebrow. "Altesian, are you?"

Eyl nodded, bracing for questions.

But the sister only said, "Ah, then I shouldn't be surprised. We decided to depict this story rather than, mmm, other stories surrounding Sir Daniel." Her eyes twinkled. "Damask people do not respond well to dragons. My order thought a more neutral story would be best, and this is one of my favorites."

Eyl snorted before she could stop herself.

"You don't like it?" Sister Jeanetta inquired.

Eyl flushed. She shouldn't have been rude, not to a *nun*. But the homesick feelings and the bitterness had all rushed together in her chest. She hadn't come here to be deliberately insulting.

No, just to shout at God from the privacy of her heart.

Eyl stared at the lions, at their claws and fangs. "Wouldn't it have been better for Daniel to never have gone into the lion's den in the first place?" Eyl argued. "Shouldn't God have protected Daniel right from the first? Wouldn't that have been the action of a good God?"

"For Daniel?" Sister Jeanetta shrugged. "Perhaps. Wouldn't that be nice? A safe, comfortable life without any tragedy or strife." She turned to Eyl. "But what about the king? What about all the people?"

Eyl's heart lurched.

"God allows all men choices, for good or ill. And many, many people choose ill. Because we live in a broken world, and evil walks. We will never understand fully the mind of God. But we can be confident in this: What men intend for evil, God turns to good. Every time."

Eyl's throat closed, and she couldn't get away from the relentless hammering in her head. *Many people choose ill. Evil walks.*

Evil walks.

"It may take long time to see it. We may even never see it. But that is the nature of faith."

God turns it to good. Every time.

Sister Jeanetta touched her shoulder gently and moved to speak with Fee, sensing that she needed a moment. Eyl's throat was thick with too much feeling. It was overwhelming her.

She stared at the lions, the man surrounded by danger and the dark for a long, long time. Then she coughed hard and covered her face with her hands. "I'm still angry at you, you know," she mumbled. "Just because this is familiar doesn't mean...."

She dragged her hands down her face. "Just because—"

She couldn't even find the right words to pray anymore. She let her head fall back, her eyes closed.

What about the king? What about the people?

What was she supposed to do with that?

What had God been up to, these nine years? If he had heard every single one of her cries, seen every tear she had shed and all those that she hadn't. How was God turning this desperate ugliness to...good?

But Fee had come, hadn't he? Had that been God moving in the strangest of ways, to put their paths together just so?

She planted her hands on her hips. "So now what?" she asked. "What am I—*we*—supposed to do now?"

"Who are you talking to?" Fee asked.

Eyl winced and opened one eye. "What?"

"Just now." He raised an eyebrow. "Were you talking to me?"

She shook her head. "No. God."

Fee stared at her, blank-faced. Then he scanned the church.

Eyl hid a smile. He looked like he expected the incarnated Christ to pop out from behind a pillar any moment.

"Does he ever...talk back?"

"Not audibly." She pursed her lips.

"So, you hear him in your head?"

"Not like that."

Fee thought about this. Then, "Is he listening?"

'No' trembled on her lips, but it was a word drenched in bitterness, in nine years of torment. An untruth, and she knew it.

Perhaps the real truth was too much of her soul depended on her answer being yes, because all those years, even in anger, in sorrow, in torment, she had railed, begged, pleaded, and scolded God. If she hadn't...if she had been utterly alone...she would not have survived. She knew it as surely as she knew her own name.

Eyl swallowed. Opened her mouth, and then shut it again. She finally settled for, "He'd better be."

CHAPTER

TWENTY

FEE

On the walk back to camp, Fee wondered about the chapel. He had wanted to go in because of the oddness around it. Though oddness wasn't the word. The…something.

He had never sensed anything about a *building* before.

He hadn't been able to figure it out once they had gone in and inspected the windows and the tapestries. The closest he had gotten to figuring it out was when the nun had come over to him and asked him something, for the life of him, he couldn't remember what. But she had come up on such quiet feet, he had been surprised into looking at her face. Fee had nearly been poleaxed by the flood of compassion he had felt from her. *Poor, hurting children*, he had heard very clearly.

He had been so startled, in fact, that he had blurted out, "Please don't tell anyone we were here. If they ask. Which I hope they won't." He glanced down and away. He didn't think he could take another wave of kindness. It was too foreign.

"I will not. You have my word."

He saw her smile from the corner of his eye, but she was looking at him a little funny. He had a panic moment where he thought his glamour might have been slipping, but then her expression smoothed out and there was the push of empathy again. It was raw, unfiltered love.

The emotion had been so strong, he had had to glance away. That was when his eye had caught sight of the cross atop the altar and the brutalized figure on it. The look on the figure's face had been one of deep suffering, but his hand had been outstretched from his wounded side. Like some kind of offering. Or beckoning. It had startled Fee almost as much as the nun's compassion.

The only thing Fee could think of, as they said their goodbyes and disappeared back into the village, which had quieted as folk had gone home to their suppers and their beds, was that the compassion and the mercy of the nun as well as the chapel attendees might have seeped into the building, and that was what he had sensed.

There was another option, but that made him uncomfortable, so he didn't think about it. He didn't like to think of someone listening, watching. Because then Eyl's God had definitely seen every horrible action he had performed during the war. And it seemed like Eyl's God would take offense to that.

He had enough to worry about right now.

When they were close enough to catch sight of the campfire through the trees, Eyl said, "Thank you for inviting me to come with you. I—I needed that." She clasped her hands together tightly.

"I'm glad," he said, something in him coming loose. He had given her something good. He drank in her shadowed face, framed by her short hair that the moonlight had silvered, and enjoyed just looking at her without fear. He could look at her forever, given the opportunity. But all he'd get was tonight because in the morning, she'd be a bird, and then they'd go their separate ways.

He was unprepared for how painful that realization was.

Kai was awake and waiting when they stepped into the circle of firelight. "How did it go?" The moon moth that escaped his mouth spiraled in a purple arc above the fire and then disappeared into the dark.

They dumped their purchases and sat. "Well," Fee said as Eyl began to sort through the packages. "There are a few things I'll have to pick up in the morning, but I think we're set. And it didn't bankrupt us, either."

Kai nodded. "Good. Which stack is going to be yours?"

"We don't have to divide things until the morning," Eyl said.

"We do if you want a say; you'll be a gyrfalcon."

"Parcel out the supplies however you want," Fee said. "I'm just one person. I'm going to miss your cooking, though," he admitted in a low voice.

"Do we have to split up?"

They all jumped as Imani sat up from her pile of blankets.

"Did we wake you?" Eyl asked. "I'm sorry."

"I was awake," she said. Her orange eyes glittered in the sympathetic firelight. "Why can't we stay together? We can guard each other's backs, keep watch, share the load. Cover our tracks." She shrugged helplessly. "Why not?"

"Fee's got other places to go," Kai said.

"Does he?" Imani turned and looked at Fee. "You said you didn't know where you were going. Well, we don't know where we're going, either!"

"But is it practical to stay together?" Kai said. "Surely, it is easier to track a group of four than one."

"Fee can do magic," Imani argued. "He can hide tracks."

Their faces turned towards him.

"Obvious things, I can," he said. "Footprints, firepits, that kind of thing. Make it harder to follow. But I'm not a hunter, so I don't know every sign someone would look for, broken twigs or water on leaves or that sort of thing. I don't know a spell that would erase every trace of you from the environs."

"That's better than nothing," Eyl said.

"But don't you want to go home?" Fee asked, scanning them.

Imani's face closed, a stark contrast from her usual animation.

"My family died in a storm. Our fishing boat sank. There's nothing for me to return to."

He turned to Kai.

"My family believes I am dead. But I cannot go home until I have finished my oath to Imani and Eyl. I swore I would watch over them until they were safe. Then I will go home," he said firmly.

Eyl closed her eyes. "Kai—"

"I swore."

Eyl let out a strangled half laugh. "I don't even know—Kai, I turn into a bird. How can I go home like this?" She swallowed, passing a hand over her face. "But I have to, don't I?" she mumbled.

Kai and Imani exchanged a look. He clenched his jaw, and she pursed her lips.

A strange, sinking feeling started in Fee's stomach. "I know that you want to go home, Eyl, but since the army is in your way, why don't you all go south to Kai's family and wait the war out? Then you can go home."

"They'd suspect that, though, won't they? Running in the opposite direction of the war." Eyl licked her lips. "Why don't we just keep going north?"

He stared at her. "Keep going north."

She nodded emphatically. "It would be what they least suspect."

"Yes, well, there are a few problems," Fee said flatly. "First, there's a ghost forest directly north of us, and also the army along the border with the battle lines in a constant state of flux, so it's entirely possible you could walk right into a patrol without realizing. There's no guarantee that you could get there safely."

"That doesn't matter," she said in a low voice.

"Doesn't *matter*?" he repeated.

"You mean it's still there?" Imani whispered.

"What's 'it'?" Fee demanded.

"Yes. I've got to go north. I've got to."

The sinking feeling grew into full-on trepidation. "What do you mean, 'got to'?"

She glared at him. "You're going to think I'm crazy."

He spread his hands, a little helplessly. "Try me."

"There's a pull."

He waited.

"I don't remember when it started. But it grew stronger and stronger over time. I was bound to the tower at night, but during the day, all I'd want to do was fly north. It's like a—tug. Like I'm a fish on a line, being pulled in. If I hadn't been compelled to return to the tower every night, I'd have just gone. I don't know what it came from, or why. For ages, I just thought I was losing it, that being bound to the tower was driving the gyrfalcon to fly towards.... But now that I'm out of the tower, it's still there. And with nothing to hold me back…just sitting here is making me itch. I need to be going home. It's like a lodestone in my heart. For so long, I thought it was just longing, or something the old man had done. But he's dead, and we're unbound and I'm still being pulled. And it's stronger than ever." Eyl looked away, towards the fire.

"Can I try something?" Fee reached for his notebook.

She flapped a hand. "Go for it. What's a little more magic after all this time?"

He quickly sketched a few simple detection spells on the paper and focused.

"Well?" Eyl said after a moment.

He lifted his head. "I don't think you're crazy."

"What a relief," she said faintly.

Fee said, "It doesn't feel like the sorcerer's spell. It's coming from somewhere else. I can't sense much about it because it was cast somewhere else."

In the firelight, Eyl's face paled. "Can you break it?"

He slowly shook his head. "I don't think so. I don't know anything about what it's doing or why. I might be able to come up with something to block it, but that would take time, and I don't know how effective it would be."

"Is it bad?" Imani demanded.

"I don't know," Eyl bit out.

"What I'd assume," Fee said slowly, "is that someone is trying to find you." He watched her face carefully. "Is that good or bad?"

"I don't know," she whispered, crossing her arms over her body tightly. "But I can't ignore it. The pull." She closed her eyes. "Is this what you call good?" she whispered. "*Is* it?"

"What?"

"Not you. God," she muttered.

"So it's settled," Kai said, a blue beetle escaping his mouth. "We've got to go north for Eyl, for good or ill. She doesn't have a choice." He shot Fee a look. "You can do what you like."

He stared at the three of them—an undersized girl trapped as a bird in daylight, a boy trying to be a man who spat bugs when he spoke, and a tall but traumatized girl who could wield fire. How would they make it, all that way, through dangerous territory and dangerous people?

Trick question. They wouldn't.

He set his shoulders. "Then I'm coming with you."

Imani's face lit up. Kai glowered. Eyl eyed him warily. "You don't have to."

"You're going to have to travel one of only a few routes north, and I've covered at least one of those recently. Plus, later, you have to avoid the front and the patrols, and I'm the only one who can help you do that. Deserter, remember?"

"Fee—"

"I'm doing it. Imani was right. I didn't have a place to go, other than away. Altesia is away. Your chances are better with me than without me, and you know it."

Plus, maybe this would be a way for him to atone. For the spy, for the war and his part in it. Maybe getting Eyl and her brood safely home would help make it right with her God.

Eyl leaned back on one hand. "I can't guarantee what happens after we pass through the Gap, but once we do, you should be safe from your father and Damaslar, at least."

Fee nodded; their gazes locked in silent understanding. Perilous travel, but the hope of safety at the end. And more time surrounded by people he wasn't afraid to look in the eye. He'd brave a lot more for a chance like that.

In all honesty, he felt more alive than he had in years.

"It sounds like a pretty fair deal to me." Fee held out a hand, and she closed hers over his. He stared at their clasped hands and dared, at long last, to hope.

TWENTY-ONE

FEE

In the early morning, Fee returned to the village and picked up Imani's and Eyl's boots, as well as the rest of the food-stuffs he hadn't been able to buy in the evening. When he returned, Eyl was a gyrfalcon and impatient to be off.

"Is there a reason we have so much food?" Imani asked as they divided the rations between the packs. "We're not hibernating for the winter, surely."

Fee looked up. "Well, autumn is coming on, so foraging might become scarce. But I was also thinking about our route. If we go directly north, the way we have been today, we'll hit Blackthorn Forest and have to go around."

"The ghost wood."

"Yes, and if we do, we'll probably stop seeing villages at all. I thought it best to stock up before then."

"What do you mean, 'stop seeing villages'?"

"There isn't too much that lives so close to Blackthorn, so villages and chances to purchase supplies will be scarce. We'll be in no man's land and having to fend for ourselves, but we also won't run into many people. We'll talk about it, of course, but I thought it best to be prepared."

Eyl flapped impatiently from her perch in the tree's branches.

"Yes, nearly ready." Imani kicked out the fire and Fee cast the basic spell that would wipe their tracks and the signs of their fire clean.

"So much fuss over a forest." Kai hefted his pack, rolling his eyes.

"A forest that routinely takes lives every single year," Fee said defensively.

Two dragonflies fluttered past. "How do you know if no one ever goes into it?"

"They *do* go into it; no one ever comes out!"

Imani laughed. "Damaskmen really *are* superstitious."

"And Cadruissi aren't?"

"Only about the ocean," she said blithely.

"Large swaths of unknowable landscape tend to do that to a man," Fee said. He refrained from mentioning how many ships probably went down in the sea, considering Imani's family's fate.

"Not the desert," Kai said. "We're a very practical people. We know it could kill us. But we don't make up stupid stories about how." A butterfly winged its way free of his lips.

"Not according to the stories you told me," Imani protested.

"Spiritual is different than superstitious," Kai said firmly, and he set off after Eyl, who was done waiting around for them.

Imani fell in behind him, still arguing, and Fee brought up the rear.

Northbound it was.

TWENTY-TWO

EYL

The pile of rubble smokes. *Glowing, red-hot stones and ash: all that is left of the tower.*

In the blue-gray light of pre-dawn, the smoke stings Eyl's eyes. She rubs them, stumbling away from the heat of the ruin. Turns and chokes.

In the shadow of the trees, Tala waits, her skirts blowing in the breeze. Her eyes do not stream from smoke, nor is her hair dusted with ash. She looks as alive as she was three years ago—before the illness.

"Tala, we got out," Eyl signs. *Her voice is too hoarse from smoke and emotion to speak.* "We got out. I'm sorry—there was no other way."

Tala lifts her hands, her sleeves falling back to reveal the intricate rune on her forearm. Her own tether rune. "North," *she signs.* "You must go north." *Her hands are emphatic, her eyes wide and urgent.*

"We are. I am sorry we could not take you with us. I let you down. I should've done more. I'm sorry." *If she could do it differently—but what could they have done? There were no healers, no medicine they had access to. But it was Tala, the only person who had helped them survive during their years in the tower—and Eyl hadn't been able to do the same for her.*

"You must go north, Eyl," *Tala repeats insistently.* "You must not delay."

"We are doing what we can. They can only walk so fast—"

"North," *Tala signs over and over. She throws her whole body into the motion.* "North. Go north. Go north. Go—"

EYL SUCKED IN A HARD BREATH, sitting up in her bedroll. Her insistent pull thrummed in time to the phantom's echo. Go north. Go north. Go north.

"Eyl?" Fee whispered by the dying fire.

She rubbed a hand over her chest. "Just a dream," she choked out.

THEY GOT USED to the travel. The days settled into a rhythm as they developed blisters and callouses from walking. When they stopped for the night, Kai would gather wood, Imani would start the fire—still the traditional way, Eyl noted—Fee would set up the tarps, tents, and bedrolls, and Eyl would shift and do the cooking. Then they'd eat and sleep, and Eyl would stay up awhile making biscuits and food that could be eaten as they traveled the next day.

Sometimes as a bird she'd bring back something she had hunted—a pheasant, or squirrel or hare—and that would be a welcome source of meat to their diet. If that pheasant had a hidden nest, sometimes they had eggs, as well. They foraged as they walked, though much of the plant life was dying off as the nights got colder and colder. Fee had the most success because he was most familiar with Damaslar plant life.

At night, Eyl had to rein in the urge to get up and walk. Her feet were restless. They wanted to move ever north. She stretched, scratched, jogged in place, anything to rid herself of the itch. But it never left. She couldn't even escape it in sleep.

Fee noticed the dreams. Of course he did. It seemed he saw everything she tried to keep hidden. When she changed in the evenings, he was usually waiting with her clothes and a blanket, since the nights had grown colder. He kept her company while she cooked, dressing the game if she asked him to, since she preferred baking to most cookery, and turning the spit without complaint, though Imani did a good job of keeping the fire from burning their meals. But he didn't press for what troubled her.

If there was time before one of them fell into an exhausted sleep, sometimes they told stories—Imani always begged for something. Eyl suspected she had nightmares. She heard her twitching many times in the night, but Imani usually woke herself up before the thrashing got too bad. Eyl wasn't sure what to do about it, other than retell whatever stories she could. She told "The Miller and the Fishwife" and "The Harper of Thinquel" and "The Lay of the Dragon War," which were ones Imani particularly liked, though Kai always made rude noises as she recited the Lay.

Once those had been retold, Eyl had to dredge her memory for older tales—"Two Forest Cats for Sister Sera" and "Clever Reeny."

"I don't know that one," Fee admitted.

"It's an Altesian story," Eyl said quietly.

"Tell it, Eyl," Kai said as fireflies spiraled from his lips to join the stars above. "You haven't told it in a long time."

So she did.

"Once upon a time, there was a very clever girl who grew very beautiful as she got older, and her name was Reeny. She lived up on the lip of a valley and raised sheep, and her sheep's wool grew so thick and plentiful that everyone desired it, and she grew very wealthy. Her fame spread far and wide for her looks and cleverness and riches. Wealthy suitors knocked on her door daily, asking to be considered for her husband."

"I don't remember why that is," Imani murmured.

"Property and land flow through the female line in Altesia," Eyl said, then she cleared her throat and continued. "Even a prince from a far-off country came to her door, asking for her hand in marriage. But Reeny told her suitors, 'I will only marry one who can accomplish these three tasks: bring me a stag with the finest rack of antlers, a cloak spun from the softest wool, and a ring that demonstrates the wealth of his affection.'

"So, the suitors went out and got busy. The prince, for instance, sent his huntsmen out in search of the largest buck in his royal forest and shot it. He bought the softest, most expensive cloak from Damaslar, and the most ornate golden ring from Cadruissau inlaid with jewels from far Udresh. And the other wealthy suitors did similarly. But one young lad from the next village wished for Reeny's hand as well. The lad asked himself, 'How can I, a farming lad, compete with these lords and merchants and a prince for Reeny's hand?'"

Fee put in, "Is this the part where the faefolk godmother steps in? Or a wise woman at a well? Does she give him something magic?"

"No." Eyl scoffed. "No magic. The lad just sat down and thought about it for a while because he was sensible. Then he went and carded his own sheep's wool together with wool from Reeny's flock. He spun and wove and cut the cloak with his own two hands. Then the lad went out and stalked a deer in the forest that bordered their farms, but instead of shooting it, he caught and gentled the stag until it would eat from his hand. And for a ring, the lad fashioned a plain silver ring from the silver veins of the mountains, and all three things he brought with him on the appointed day.

"When all assembled in front of Reeny, she asked, 'Now who has understood me best?' All the suitors presented their racks of antlers and cloaks from far away and their gaudy jewels for her perusal. But the lad said, 'Here is the stag I gentled myself, because nothing is finer than a living, breathing beast that God has made. And here is a cloak that I spun myself as soft as I could make it, with wool from both of our flocks. And here is a silver ring from home without jewel or ornament because I had none. But here are some things you did not ask for—these two hands, to work with you by day and hold you by night. Two eyes to see you. A mouth to speak your name. And my whole heart, if you will have it.' And so clever Reeny chose the lad and proved her own cleverness."

"How did she prove her own cleverness?" Imani whispered.

"She knew that one who truly cared for her would not ask for her heart without exchanging his own," Eyl said.

"I thought you didn't like romance stories," Kai accused.

"Only when they're sappy and tragic," Eyl shot back, then she rolled over in her blankets and tried to sleep. Her dreams that night were of her mother's voice, retelling the same story when she'd been a child, and her hands carding through a younger Eyl's long, dark hair.

She woke at dawn with tears on her cheeks.

Their tramp settled into an exhausted tranquility, for the most part. They still worried about pursuers, but there was little they could do that they weren't already doing—spelling their tracks, keeping off well-traveled paths, avoiding contact with anyone who could describe them. Fee's scry disks went off twice more during their travels, which singed him pretty good, but Eyl had remembered to pack a jar of burn ointment, and it had made it into the satchels that had survived. They slathered it on and kept walking.

That exhausted tranquility lasted until they reached the river. Then it shattered like bad pottery in a kiln.

TWENTY-THREE

RILEN

A week's long, hard ride, and not even a tower to show for it.

Rilen Gar dismounted at the edge of the devastated clearing and nudged one of the fallen stones, disturbing a pile of ash. The wind picked it up and blew it in a low arc around his boots, whispering over the worn but well-cared-for leather before the ash settled down, feather light, on the scorched grass.

Corbett spat from atop his horse, his aim perfect even in his irritation. The spittle hit the stone dead-center. "Mountain's bones," Corbett ground out. "What happened here?"

Rilen picked his way forward, and Corbett swung off his horse and followed, earning them both an ugly look for not waiting for the rest of the High Wizard's guards.

For nearly seven years, it had just been Rilen and Corbett, taking bounties from whomever had been inclined to offer them. But in the last two years, they had been in demand enough to add another man to their band—Nath. They liked the smaller number and had learned to work well together, their skills interlocking. They didn't have to waste time jawing about the course to take.

Rilen cast a cautious look at his brother, who was scowling and ignoring that idiot Marcus's commands to his men. The long, hard days in the saddle had not been improved by a squad of soldiers at their heels. The travel had been full of uneasy tension. As the tracker, Corbett had been the one to map the route based on the faint traces. But it had been obvious that Marcus didn't like it, and he made his feelings known every time they made camp by directing his men on set up and tear down and watch schedules and basically making a nuisance of himself. Once he had tried to give Nath orders as well, but Corbett had shot him a look so black that he hadn't tried it again. Rilen could tell that the situation was eating at his brother.

Moving to Corbett's side, Rilen elbowed him and mouthed, "Fool," jerking his head towards Marcus.

Corbett smirked, though it looked more like a grimace. "Spread out. Find a trail or evidence of what happened here, or we end up deep in mage jakes. Make sure those bumblers keep out of our way." He jerked his head towards the guardsmen.

"I'll tell them," Nath said, loping off to speak with them.

Rilen shook his head. Nothing fazed that boy.

He breathed in deeply as he surveyed the rubble-filled clearing, coated with ash, and then narrowed his eyes at the untouched trees around the perimeter. It was obvious an extremely hot and violent fire had scored the earth here. How had the whole forest avoided being burned to the ground? Apart from that, what kind of force could bring down a whole tower?

The answer was clear but frustrating. Magic.

Rilen snapped his fingers and growled in the back of his throat at the wizard who had been sent along with the squad. A green boy of eighteen, he had just barely graduated from that highborn mage school. The boy turned to him and gulped, the spots on his face standing out in stark relief to his pale face.

Rilen motioned to the mounds of ash and scorched stones and then to the unburned trees outside of the clearing. *"What happened here?"* he signed. *"What spell contained the flames? How long ago did the fire rage?"*

The boy, whose name might have been Parthas or Parfan, wet his lips. "W-What's he doing?"

Rilen curled his lip and barely resisted rolling his eyes.

Corbett turned and raised an eyebrow. "I told you my brother had his tongue cut out," he said, his tone the cool grace of an adder ready to strike. "He speaks in signs."

Rilen resisted the urge to open his mouth and leer at the boy. The scar visible through his beard was proof enough. They had not been careful with their knives.

"I don't know what he means." Sweat popped out on the boy's head.

Corbett draped a hard, heavy arm around the boy's shoulder, squeezing it painfully. "Well, now, you'd best learn quick, because Rilen doesn't like being ignored. Now. Let's have it again." He looked at Rilen expectantly.

"You're a rogue," Rilen told him, hiding a smile. *"The kid's going to wet himself soon."*

Corbett dropped his arm and replied with a smirk, *"It's best to keep the young on their toes, I've found. What's up?"*

"Have the wizard look at what kept the fire from burning the whole forest down. If he can tell when everything burned, we'll have a timeline."

Corbett relayed this to the wizard. Parthas, or Pathos, scratched at his spots. "Um, well, I can do a divination spell—"

Corbett cut him off. "I don't want to know details; I want to know results. Just get it done."

Rilen turned away and began to search the clearing for traces of their quarry. Following the clearing's boundary line, he worked his way around until he came across a stone that did not look scorched. He brushed away the ash and frowned.

"What is it?"

Rilen looked over his shoulder. Corbett had followed him.

The Gar brothers looked remarkably similar, having been born just a year apart. Brown hair shorn close to the skull on both, though Corbett's lightened considerably in the sun, and tall, muscular builds. Corbett was the elder but rarely acted like it. Born in the slums to parents who had struggled to eke out a livable existence, Corbett had been content to escape into the woods as a hunter and tracker, but Rilen had dreamed of greater things.

More fool him, because that pursuit had ended up in ashes. Just like this clearing.

"It's a grave." Rilen pointed to the letters carved into the headstone and the rounded hillock below.

"Tala," Corbett pronounced. The corner of his mouth kicked up. "Pretty."

Stepping farther into the trees, Rilen kicked aside more burned stones to reveal another two hillocks, older. He snapped his fingers at Corbett. *"Two more graves. Unmarked."*

He moved along the ground, counting. Not all were obvious anymore, only a little difference in the grass color or texture of the ground. He got up to fifty before he stopped. *"Fifty unmarked graves or more,"* he told his brother, who spat.

"God's wounds," Corbett swore, "what was that twisty sorcerer up to?" He squinted up at the sky.

A shout rang out. "Bones! Burned bones!"

Rilen and Corbett both leapt for the source of the shout. They found Nath digging out a charred and broken skeleton with very little flesh left on it.

"Parthas!" Corbett roared. "Get over here!" They helped shift stones out from around the skeleton to try not to break the bones any further. Parthas came at a run, panting, Marcus and a few other guards behind him. The boy pushed his pale hair off his forehead and tried to catch his breath.

Soft, Rilen noticed dispassionately. Wizards had the tendency to cultivate the brain and let the body go.

"Can you tell who it was?" Corbett gestured to the bones. "Got to know whether we're chasing a flesh-and-blood bastard or his ghost." He grinned crookedly.

Parthas licked his lips. "That may not be possible. That would take a very specific, specialized spell—"

"Well, we know it's a man," Nath said, out of the blue.

They all turned to him. "We do?" Corbett asked sarcastically.

Nath blinked. "Sure. Narrow hips."

They all looked at the skeleton. "Doesn't say for sure," one soldier said, unconvinced. "'S not like we have a woman to compare it to." He grinned, the reprobate, and got a glare from his commander for his trouble.

Rilen elbowed Corbett. *"It's a good guess,"* he pointed out.

"And look at the teeth." Nath pointed to the skull. He crouched down and used a stick to open the jaw. "Some missing. Others ground down, pitted. This is an old man's mouth."

Corbett crouched and inspected the jaw himself, rubbing a hand over his chin. "All right," he said, "I believe you, Nath. So the sorcerer's dead, cause unknown."

"Fire might've had something to do with it," Rilen signed.

Corbett narrowed his eyes and made a rude gesture.

Rilen smirked. *"I know what you meant. This was no cooking fire. More like an inferno."* His hands indicated the great size.

Corbett nodded. *"Magic."* He stood and brushed the ash off his pants. "We're looking for the High Wizard's bastard and whatever he stole. Let's find those tracks! Parthas, twiddle those useless fingers and divine some answers, why don't you. They can't be too far ahead of us. We'll catch them soon enough."

The soldiers jumped automatically to obey his brother's voice. Marcus quickly bellowed the same orders, in a much louder volume, but the initial impulse to obey Corbett had still been there.

Hidden behind his beard, Rilen smiled. The journey was getting more interesting. Who knew what the coming days would bring?

TWENTY-FOUR

FEE

"No," Fee said flatly, staring at her over the flickering fire. "Absolutely not."

Eyl lifted her chin. "Why not?"

After several days of travel, Fee knew that look by now. She was spoiling for a fight. "No one comes out alive!" he exclaimed, aghast he even had to say it.

Her eyes narrowed. "Spurious nonsense."

"Fact," he bit out, furiously stoking their campfire, even though it needed no help from either him or Imani. He had to expend his frantic energy somehow. They were on the cusp of the river, only about a half day's walk straight east—and they'd have to go east to find a crossing or a ferry. There was nothing where they were, and there would be nothing farther north towards the forest.

Hence their disagreement.

Through tight lips, Fee said, "Every year, some doubters go into Blackthorn and wander hopelessly for a time, emerging exactly where they entered—and those are the lucky ones. A few souls never come out at all. Nothing lives there—no animals wander out of the trees, no birds fly over it, nothing. It's a cursed place."

"Trees live there," Imani pointed out.

"Grass. Moss." Kai spat out a moth. "Bugs, I'm sure."

"Have you seen the land?" Fee gestured, even though the dark of night didn't allow much outside their circle of firelight. But they knew; they'd been walking through it for near two days. "Have you seen a glut of birds or game or extraneous foliage recently?"

The lush farmland Damaslar was known for—the rumors that you could plant a gold coin and up would sprout a tree with gold leaves were *nearly* true—had devolved from plots of carefully tended acreage and patchwork farms with their rock walls and hedgerows to wild, untamed land with drying grass that nearly reached Eyl's waist and brambles of thorns and thistles and wild-flowers going to seed. The trees had slowly become smaller, thinner, and less frequent, dwindling into a near prairie. And off in the distance? A swelling, dark mass to the north. The impenetrable wall of Blackthorn Forest, a silent sentinel, warning all to *keep away*.

Fee had never seen it before until his mad journey south, where he had hugged it close enough to see its faint smudge on the horizon to his right, giving him, when he could find a minute to think as he endured the breakneck pace he and the horse had pushed, the creeps. He had not slept well then, and he knew without a doubt he would not sleep well tonight.

"The river," Eyl said, raising a supercilious eyebrow. "Surely, the forest doesn't kill the fish or eels that come through its environs. I'm sure we would've heard if the capital routinely received dead fish downriver. And don't salmon spawn upstream? So they would have to go the other direction—"

"We *cannot* go through Blackthorn Forest. It is a death sentence, and I don't have the mind to commit suicide."

"I don't believe that," Eyl ground out.

"You don't, but what about them?" Fee gestured to Kai and Imani. "You're willing to gamble with *their* lives?"

Eyl reared back like he had punched her, a wounded look

crossing her face. He gritted his teeth and refused to feel like a heel for it. He was *right,* by Enid's teeth.

Kai glared at him with murder in his eyes. "She gambles with no one's lives. We will choose where we go, and I choose to go with Eyl."

Imani rallied, though the distressed look didn't leave her face. "I'm not afraid," she said bravely.

Eyl hunched her shoulders. "Kai, that's sweet, but Fee has a point. I'm responsible for you—"

"We are not children." He glowered. "After our first week in the tower, none of us were children. We can choose our own paths."

"What if you two went with Fee—"

"No, Eyl, I don't want to leave you!" Imani threw herself into Eyl's arms. Eyl patted her back and shot Fee a glare over her head. When Imani let go, Eyl crossed her arms over her chest, her boney shoulders poking through her tunic in a way that Fee found he hated with a passion.

"We just go around; *everyone* does," Fee said, tendrils of desperation setting in. "We'll take the ferry crossing; there's a very well-traveled road. It won't take that many days—"

Imani raised her hand. "I don't want to cross the river."

"Why not?" Fee asked, exasperated.

"I'm afraid of water."

He opened his mouth, then closed it with a click.

"And it will *still* take too long!" Eyl insisted. "I *can't*—I've got to—" She rubbed the heel of her hand hard against her chest. "I've got to go straight on," she whispered. "I can't afford to go around."

Fee closed his mouth, torn. It was true; he knew it. She scarcely seemed able to rest. Even after flying all day, she'd be awake pacing restlessly inside the night's protective boundary when he woke to the crunch of leaves underfoot, or she'd be staring at the fire, twitching when the kindling popped. This—compulsion, or whatever it was—wore on her. She had dark circles under her eyes, and the slope of her shoulders spelled weariness.

"You don't have to come," she said tightly. "None of you. I can go alone. We can meet on the other side."

Fee dragged his fingers through his hair, resisting the urge to pull it out by the roots. He tipped his head back and stared at the stars overhead as the fire crackled. His jaw felt hard enough to chew granite. He worked it for a moment or two before he said, "Even if you make it through the forest, with no supplies, no clothes, no nothing. If whatever this is drives you hard enough that you don't think you can deviate from the path or take the time to go out of the way, do you think you'll be able to wait for us on the other side? You already have to fly back to us when we stop and make camp." *And just look what it's doing to her.*

Eyl met his eyes, misery in her gaze.

His hands itched to do something, anything, to comfort her. But he wasn't worthy to touch her. Not when everything he touched turned to black and ash, tarnished beyond redemption. There was only one thing he could do.

He swallowed. "Let's put it to a vote."

TWENTY-FIVE

EYL

Eyl plucked four long grass blades and made them the same length. "We'll all vote," she said. "If you vote for going through the forest, break your blade in half."

"Don't people usually do this when they *draw* straws?" Imani asked dubiously.

"This way, there will be no pressure like if we had a show of hands," Eyl said. "Just a vote. Your own opinion, that you decided without influence from others." Because she didn't want Kai or Imani choosing out of loyalty, or…. She stared down at the straws in her hands. It was all very well to joke about the ghost forest from safety, but it was another to be uncomfortably reminded of every story she'd ever heard about it when she was proposing leading three other souls into it.

And out the other side, she tried to remind herself. *And out the other side.*

It didn't help much.

She handed out the straws and then turned her back to split hers in half. She knew the truth in her bones. It was either split the straw in half or split herself in half. She couldn't even find words to describe the compulsion that took over her brain—more so as a bird than a human, but still—it was all-consuming. A tangible thing, tugging her, *hauling* her along. When would it stop? And what would she find then?

She shivered and couldn't answer.

"Ready?" she called.

"Yes," Fee said.

She turned around, straw in her fist. She opened her hand and showed them her shortened blade. Kai immediately opened his own hand and showed her his shorn grass blade. Two for. Fee made a sudden movement, but Imani straightened her shoulders and showed them her palm.

The grass blade was short.

"Three for," Eyl said. She looked at Fee. "You don't have to come—"

"I am," he said firmly. "Or what was the reason for the straws? We already said we'd stick together. And if we make it through, you'll need me." She couldn't decipher the look in his eye.

With that die cast, they rolled into their bedrolls and settled in for the night, their course set before them.

After ten minutes of Eyl staring at the fire, Fee murmured, "I know you're awake."

"Yes." She rolled over. "I can't sleep."

"Restless feet?" he murmured, turning his head to look at her.

"Something like that," she whispered. "I wouldn't blame you if you—"

"Stop," he said firmly. "Stop trying to convince me to abandon you."

"I just want you to be sure—"

"I am sure." And he handed her a blade of grass.

For a minute, she just stared at it. It was only the length of her pinky. What—

And then she knew.

"You said short, if you were for it," Fee said. "So I chose. And I made it short. I'm not abandoning you. I'm going to see this through."

Eyl tried to catch her breath and couldn't.

"But we need to be smart about it," he continued grimly. "The stories all have people wandering through the forest aimlessly and getting lost. So we should follow the river. It's hard to redirect an entire river. Not that I wouldn't put it past Blackthorn," he muttered, "but then at least we'd have a chance, since it runs more or less north-south—"

Eyl threw herself at Fee, wrapping her arms around his neck and squeezing hard. He caught her on reflex, steadying her so she wouldn't take them both down.

In alarm, he said, "Eyl—?"

"*Thank* you." She squeezed harder. "Fee. Thank you." What else was there to say?

He was at a loss for words, too. But he did find it in him to hug her back.

Eyl mumbled into his chest, "Don't worry. I'll protect you from the haunted forest."

Fee scoffed. "You'd better." But his lips rested lightly against her hair.

TWENTY-SIX

CORBETT

"Call him."

From his place around the campfire, Parthas started. "W-What?"

Corbett leaned back against his saddle, lazily stretching out one leg as he sharpened his knife. "The High Wizard. I know you do some sort of twiddly magic to send him reports every night. No one takes that long to piss." He smiled, the flash of teeth bright in the gloaming night. "Call him."

To his right, Rilen crossed his thick forearms and stared at the stripling.

Sweat popped on Parthas's forehead. "A-All right, but Lord Nicanor—"

"Will want to hear what we've discovered, won't he?" Corbett motioned. "Go on and do it. I'm sure the boys will like seeing some magic." Never mind that they'd watched Parthas do his scratchings and twiddling all afternoon around the tower clearing.

Parthas pulled out a sheet of parchment and a small, metal bowl and began to write. Then he filled the bowl with water and set it on top of the parchment. The water in the bowl rippled.

Rilen nudged him and signed, *"Wizards get less and less impressive every time I see them do something."*

Corbett bit back a laugh.

The water turned milky, and then it resolved into the irritated face of the High Wizard. "What?" he said, sounding lightly muffled.

"Well, well. Mountain's bones." Corbett pushed Parthas over so he could look into the bowl.

The High Wizard frowned. "Who are you?"

"I'm the tracker you hired. We've found the tower," he said without preamble, "but it's been burned and fallen down. Not more than five days ago, I reckon, since folk around here have said that's when it last rained. The sorcerer's dead. We found your boy's staff and a few tracks, but they vanish near a stream close by. We believe he's alive, though."

"How many tracks?" the High Wizard demanded.

"That's what's odd," Corbett said. "Your bastard must have some friends with him. There are four sets of tracks."

To his surprise, the High Wizard smiled, an expression that looked far too practiced on his face. "Good. The experiments are intact."

"Experiments," Corbett repeated, an unpleasant sensation snaking through his belly.

"Yes, the sorcerer's experiments. You must bring them back alive and undamaged. They are extremely valuable." The High Wizard rubbed his palms together. "Do you have a plan to pick up their tracks?"

Corbett clapped Parthas on the shoulder, who quaked. "Your boy Parthas here is going to search for signs that might be harder to hide magically, like campfires or latrines. But we'll spread out and search all directions. We won't miss them."

"Good, good," the High Wizard said. "Parthas can also scry for Fee; he knows what he looks like. He may still be protecting himself, but it's possible he thinks the danger is past. Call me when you have something else to go on." The bowl abruptly turned cloudy and then resumed being water.

"Well, look at that," Corbett said. "You're good for something after all, Parthas." Smacking the young wizard on the shoulder again, Corbett got to his feet and turned to face Rilen, whose face was set like stone.

"We need to talk," his brother signed.

"So, talk," Corbett signed back, walking with him into the shadows, where the moon cast just enough light to see each other's hands.

Rilen hooked a thumb at the cluster of men still gathered around the scrying dish. *"He said, 'experiments.'"*

"I heard," Corbett said grimly, pointing to his ear and then himself.

"I'm not going to hunt down captives." Rilen slapped his chest hard to emphasize his point.

Very likely that was what they were, Corbett knew. Most people didn't step up and volunteer for magical experiments. And that was a problem. Rilen harbored bitter enmity against any and all snatchers. He pushed to take the jobs that involved hunting down missing family members or rumored captives, even when there was little to no money in it for them. And when they found the snatchers? He gave no quarter.

Corbett humored him and took the jobs in between their more lucrative employment because he knew his brother harbored demons he didn't speak about. If this helped exorcise a few, he wouldn't stand in the way. Besides, Corbett held the same opinion; all snatchers were scum who preyed on the vulnerable stuck in a horrible situation to try to pay off generational debt.

But this definitely threw sand in his soup.

"I know how you feel, but this is Damaslar. They have different laws," Corbett signed back. You could take the man out of Altesia, but....

"We don't know that they're captives, or legal indentures, or what."

"This is too close to the line," Rilen argued, making a harsh,

chopping motion with his hand. *"He is too eager to have these experiments. I don't like this."* He pulled a revolted face.

"We agreed to neither hinder nor help the war effort," Corbett agreed. *"But this is a family squabble. If we bring back the boy, then the Wizard will be satisfied. We can always say we didn't find any experiments."*

"With his guardsmen along and his pet wizard watching our every step?" Rilen asked, his eyebrows raised.

"Maybe we can find a good excuse to split up," Corbett signed with a smile.

TWENTY-SEVEN

They made the forest's border by noon.

"Oh," Imani said under her breath as they approached. "It's...bigger than I thought. Like a sea of trees."

Kai took her hand without words.

Fee set his jaw as Eyl screamed overhead, as he was now intimately familiar with her "hurry up" noise. She had altered their route by a tad so that they would hit the intersection of the forest and the river. They could follow the river at a safe distance along the riverbank. The Lliore River was plenty wide, enough for several barges to traverse its length. But no one sent goods down it through Blackthorn; that was later, at Hiber, where caravans could load up goods and sail them down to the Cadruissau coast.

Fee squinted up against the glare of the sun to track the circles Eyl made in the air, growing inescapably closer towards the great expanse of forest. He pursed his lips and whistled a two-note sound, lifting the hand that he had reinforced with leather to form a crude falconer's glove days earlier. For a moment, he thought she'd ignore him. But then Eyl descended from her great height and plummeted to earth, landing on the glove for purchase, flapping her wings. Fee moved her to his shoulder, where she sat and surveyed her domain. He wanted her with them for whatever was about to happen.

The great expanse of trees remained an unsettling blot smack in the middle of the country. Fitting for Damaslar. The river, a smooth susurrus of sound off to their right, cut a dark-blue-green swath through the dark trees.

He tried not to think about the fact that the trees seemed to be waiting.

When they got within spitting distance of the forest, they saw the path.

Ahead of them, between two massive oaks, a path stretched into darkness. It was only wide enough for travelers to walk single file, only bare earth between two trees.

Fee stopped in his tracks. He could've *sworn* it hadn't been there ten minutes before.

His eyes had been trained on Blackthorn for the last two hours, making sure he could see if anything was...off. He didn't know what good his Sight would do, but he had Seen something about a building, so maybe he could see something about a ghost wood. It was the only resource he could put to use. And he had not seen the path.

It was as if it had just...appeared.

Could the others see it too? Was he making mountains out of a little bit of bare earth?

But I looked at it and thought, 'path.' Fee gulped.

"Oh, look, maybe travelers do pass through after all," Imani said. Eyl made a speculative noise.

"So, you can see it too?" Fee asked cautiously.

Imani gave him an odd look. "Of course."

They turned back to stare at the bare patch. "I definitely wouldn't say many people have traveled that. If any," Fee said, looking at it with a more critical eye.

"Is it an animal track?" she guessed.

Fee gave a swift, decisive shake of his head. Eyl shifted on his shoulder, rustling her wings before nibbling at his hair.

Imani twisted her skirt in her hands. "Well, we could always walk on the riverbank."

"Ignore a path at your peril," Kai said, breaking his customary traveling silence. Two dragonflies flew south, away from the forest. "My people know that well. A path may not go where you wish, but a way without a path leads to nowhere, and travelers become lost and rudderless, doomed to wander forever."

Eyl made a soft, derisive falcon noise.

"So. Do we trust it?" Imani chewed on her lower lip.

Fee exchanged a look with Kai. He was already as jumpy as a cat. This wasn't helping.

"If it veers off or gets too far away from the river, then we reevaluate," Kai said as a compromise.

"Fine." Fee gritted his teeth, steeling himself. Eyl's beak ran through his hair.

Then he stepped from sunlight into shadow.

Under the trees, the air carried a chill parted from the sun. They all collectively shivered. The forest smelled like a forest should, leaves and undergrowth and a hint of water close by. Imani and Kai took a few more steps farther in, and leaves crunched under their feet, but nothing else. No birds sang. No insects buzzed. He could hear the wind, blowing over the prairie no man's land, but he couldn't feel it, even when the grasses indicated it was blowing their direction.

They had entered a different place, separate. Cut off.

Fee rolled his shoulders to try to shake the feeling crawling up his spine. It made Eyl shift irritably.

"Do you feel that?" he asked. His voice sounded over-loud to him, so he repeated himself in a low whisper.

"Feel what?" Imani replied, matching his tone. She narrowed her eyes to stare around at their surroundings. But there were only trees, as far as the eye could see, as well as underbrush and grass and sedge. At a glance, he saw huge oaks and ash trees, with a few birch and thorn here and there. Over to their right, they could see the flashes of the river's progress through gaps in the tree trunks.

"Someone listening closely. Or someone watching us."

"Like what? The trees?"

Fee tipped his head back. The treetops seemed impossibly high, the boughs tightly woven together to block most of the sun. It turned the environment under them a kind of moody twilight, only broken by the rarest of sunbeams. He suddenly realized how close the trees felt, how quickly that sensation might turn oppressive. He clenched his jaw.

Imani turned in a slow circle, inspecting their surroundings with her hands on her hips. "No. It's just quiet. Let's go."

She started along the path before Kai overtook her with a stern look. "I go first." He set the small gecko from his mouth on a nearby leaf, and it scampered away.

"Fine," she said, making a shooing motion. "Go. We've got more miles to cover before nightfall."

Fee fell into step behind her. Eyl didn't move from his shoulder. He turned for one last look at sunlight before plunging forward into the ghost wood.

ONCE THE GROUP had walked past the initial throngs of massive oaks, the foliage changed.

Small patches of sun pooled here and there, illuminating surprising beauty in the silent, dark wood. They passed stands of silver birches, rowan, a grove of willows visible along the river, their long branches reaching down to trail in the water. Moss, a deep, rich emerald, covered the forest floor and sporadic tree trunks, as well as many colors of lichen. Bushes of sharp, saw-edged leaves with red berries—holly, Fee recognized with incredulity. Even several fir trees and a pine.

A silvery, gray moss hung down in hunks off some trees, like a lady's draperies in her dressing room. Fee remembered his mother tacking up silk and chiffon swatches in their small attic room when he'd been young, to make the place more inviting. They had fluttered on the breeze. This moss didn't flutter because there was no breeze.

They made camp directly beside the stand of firs the first night. The only warning that the day was drawing to a close was a flicker to the twilight before it blackened to darkness.

Eyl hopped off Fee's shoulder and began to shift. They all turned as Fee dug out her clothes from his pack.

Imani found the flint and lit a torch to illuminate the area. Fee made note of that to talk to Eyl about later as he waited through her agonized shrieks. Then he handed Eyl the clothes and forgot again.

"I can't believe there are firs this far south," Eyl panted when she had a voice again. "You can turn around now." She was tugging her tunic straight. "It's the wrong atmosphere. The wrong temperature entirely…." But she brushed the green, sharp-scented needles with reverence.

They carefully gathered what dried brush and fallen twigs and branches lay close to the path as they could, leery to leave it. "What if we never find it again?" Fee asked. Kai agreed with him, to his surprise. They lit the fire with the torch and Imani encouraged the fire to heat evenly as Eyl cooked supper. Talking was soft and stilted, abbreviated by the darkness and the silent pillars of trees surrounding them.

Imani and Kai rolled into their bedrolls and fell asleep relatively quickly. Kai would take second watch. But Fee kept his back to the fire and his eyes on the forest.

"You think something's going to pop out at us?" Eyl murmured from her bedroll.

"No," Fee said without conviction. The hair on his arms and at the back of his neck had been prickling all day. But he hadn't Seen anything out of the ordinary.

Which might've made it worse.

"What, then?"

"You're a predator," he said, shooting her a quick glance from under his lashes.

Her brilliant, silver eyes flashed. "And?"

"You know how it feels to hunt."

She nodded.

"You ever wonder how the prey feels?"

The corners of her mouth turned down.

"This feeling…it's only gotten stronger. You feel it, too."

She bit her lip. "Yes."

"I think we're being tracked," Fee said bluntly.

"By what? A ghost?"

He shot her a sarcastic look.

"Sorry," she mumbled.

"I don't think a ghost would have such a *solid* presence like this."

She sat up a little more and leaned back on the heels of her hands. "What else is supposed to live in a ghost forest? And why would they follow us?"

He didn't want to think about that. He shrugged. "Maybe they're just keeping an eye on us."

She squinted, thinking. "That makes an odd kind of sense. What do we do about it?"

"I don't know." Fee shook his head. "I don't think we *do* anything. Probably the worst thing we could do would be to strike out into the depths of the forest in an attempt to find whatever-it-is."

"So we mind our business and wait." Eyl worried her lip in between her teeth. "And it waits, too. For what?"

They shared a wary look as a log in the fire snapped.

TWENTY-EIGHT

CORBETT

Corbett leaned against his saddle horn. "And you're sure about the trail?"

Rilen nodded. *"It leads to the village. They would need supplies. If we can find someone who remembers them, it will firm up our timeline. We would also get descriptions."*

Corbett cracked his neck. "All right. Nath, you take a few soldiers and see if you can pick up their trail. Rilen and I will go into the village. We'll meet back here in an hour's time." Nath nodded and pointed to a few soldiers to follow him.

"We'll start with market stalls, foodstuffs, equipment," Marcus broke in. "Those will be the most likely vendors."

Corbett shot him a flat look. "Good. You can take point on that."

Marcus frowned. "Where are you going?"

"Plainsmen," Corbett muttered, hiding an eyeroll. He pointed. "You see that?"

Marcus followed his finger. "That long spike? So what?"

"That spike is a church steeple." And churches gave sanctuary. They might've holed up there for the night, perhaps even longer if they thought they could get away with it.

"They might not have realized they could take shelter there," Rilen pointed out.

"Then we'll quickly rule it out." Corbett clicked to his horse. "Let's go."

———

THE STONE CHAPEL WAS, apart from the steeple, outwardly unimpressive. When they entered the church, the soldiers—for Marcus had refused to let them go alone when he clearly did not trust the trackers—looked around with baffled or contemptuous eyes, but Corbett stepped forward with purpose and greeted the nun that looked up from replenishing incense. She introduced herself as Sister Jeanetta.

"Good morning, Sister. I wonder if I might pose some questions to you."

Her eyes took in the large group of men. "You may, but I'd ask your soldiers to wait outside. We prefer not to have arms in the chapel."

Corbett hooked his thumb, and most of the soldiers filed out without waiting for an order from their commander. Didn't *that* just twist Marcus's tail. Only Marcus and his stiff-necked second remained.

"We won't be here long," Corbett assured her.

She nodded. "Your questions?"

"We're searching for some runaways; they may have used your church for sanctuary at some point. Have you seen strangers pass through your village? Within the last week."

The Cadruissi nun blinked calmly at him, her dark eyes unreadable. "Our little church gets many curious visitors, but none have claimed sanctuary of me, sir. Most don't know that's something we offer."

"Well, you might've seen them, perhaps in town? Four strangers, most notably one with red hair and a scar on his face." Corbett traced the line from his forehead to chin.

Something flickered in her eyes. "And four children need so many armed men to retrieve them? For what end?"

Children, Corbett thought, clenching his teeth. Not just the wizard's son, then. Mountain's bones.

"We believe they are faeblooded and intent on wreaking mischief and mayhem in direct opposition to the war effort," Jorgen said stiffly, throwing out his chest. "If you have seen them, it is your duty to notify us."

Corbett clenched his jaw, fighting the urge to roll his eyes. They had just lost her. And who said they were *faeblooded*?

"I haven't seen four strange children," Sister Jeanetta said, lacing her fingers together. "But then, like I said, most Damaskmen don't know the church offers sanctuary."

Marcus ground his teeth together and turned on his heel. "Search the rest of the village. Ask in the shops; they would've needed supplies." He switched to Corbett. "Go and—"

"I'm not one of your soldiers," Corbett said, flashing his razor smile. "I'll meet you at the center of town."

Marcus opened his mouth to argue.

Corbett's smile grew in breadth and danger.

Marcus shut his mouth. "Ten minutes, and not a second more," he snapped before spinning on his heel and leaving the church.

Corbett slanted a resigned look at Rilen. His brother nodded emphatically.

Corbett pursed his lips, eyebrows raised. *"You sure?"*

Rilen nodded. *"Ask."*

He sighed and said, *"All right, but I don't know why you keep doing this."* Corbett turned back to Sister Jeanetta.

Her brows lifted slightly in confusion. "Yes?"

"Sister, do you hear confessions?"

She nodded.

Corbett motioned to Rilen. "My brother would like to be heard, but he cannot speak. Do you know hand signs?"

"I know enough to get by." She hesitated, her eyes flicking to

Rilen. "If I cannot understand you, do you wish your brother to—"

"*No,*" Rilen said firmly. "*Alone.*"

"As you wish," Sister Jeanetta said softly, and she led the way to the front of the church.

Corbett leaned against a pillar and cracked his neck, watching the morning light play through the stained glass.

"Hey." A soldier laughed, loitering by the doors. "You wonder what they're getting up to there, huh? Hey—urk!"

Corbett had him by the throat. He was the same bescumbered idiot from the tower. "Keep your filthy thoughts to yourself. Don't pollute the air I'm breathing. I might decide to do some spring cleaning."

"Fine, fine," the man choked out. He held up his hands in surrender. "Didn't mean anything by it."

"You did." Corbett glared. "Out."

"Marcus told me to stay behind to—"

"*Out.*"

He left.

Corbett resumed his position by the pillar, watching the sunbeams cross the stone floor. In a few minutes, Rilen reappeared, his face impassive.

"Feel better?" Corbett muttered. "Now that you're all forgiven and absolved?" *For the umpteenth time,* he added privately. Rilen did this every chance he got, at every chapel and church they came across. Asked for confession from the priest or nuns.

Rilen ignored him.

"I wish you'd tell me what you think is so bad that you have to confess it to every priest and nun you meet. Is this some kind of penance? Because I think you've already paid that twice over with your acts of service, plus your tongue. Permanent vow of silence and all that."

Rilen made a sharp, harsh motion. "*The tongue was not my choice.*"

Corbett swore. "*I know that.*" Corbett signed emphatically.

"That woman chewed you up and spat you out, threw you away like you were trash. But that's on her; *you don't owe her any kind of guilt over it!"* He missed his brother—the laughing, sweet kid he had been, a little naive and wet behind the ears for all his height and brawn. They'd stolen that from him, and Corbett would never forgive. Never.

"It is not about her."

"What, then?"

Rilen walked on without answering.

But it wasn't like Corbett expected one. They'd been having this argument, in different variations, for almost ten years. Slowly, Corbett nodded and turned back to the chapel.

The nun was refilling incense in the nave. On silent feet, Corbett came up behind her. "Now," he said as she gasped and turned, "are you going to tell me the truth?"

"I did not lie to you," she said firmly. "Get back."

Corbett grabbed her hand and squeezed her wrist in his grip. "But did you tell the truth?" He smiled, sharp like a knife.

Her eyes widened. "Do you think to threaten me here, in God's house?"

His smile grew. "You'll just have to forgive me afterwards, Sister." He set his knife at the base of her throat. "Now. I know they were here. Which ones?"

When she swallowed, the point of his knife nicked her skin, a bead of blood welling up red against her brown skin. But her stare was steady and hard. "I'll forgive you now. But I won't tell you what you want to know."

He pressed down harder. "Martyrdom, Sister? How noble." The bead turned into a trickle. "But I have *also* told you the truth. I'm being paid to find a runaway. When we find him, he will be returned to his proper place. I've no interest in any of the taga-longs. I don't hurt kids." He flicked a twist of hair that escaped from under her veil. "Adults are different."

"Hurting me will not profit you. I don't know where they came from or where they went."

"Tell me," he murmured, leaning in. "You know God hates liars. It was the boy, wasn't it? I saw your face when I mentioned the scar."

She leaned forward and breathed into his ear, "I do not fear pain or death because the hand of the Lord is upon me, and he has numbered my days as he sees fit. As he does yours." She set her hand over his. "The artery just here will serve your purpose better." She moved his suddenly nerveless fingers so that the blade found the proper place, holding his gaze the whole time.

A shudder tore through him.

A heavy hand came down on Corbett's shoulder, pulling the hand that held the knife carefully but forcibly away from Sister Jeanetta. Then a fist slammed into his gut.

Corbett wheezed but came up with bared teeth, snarling. But Rilen stepped between him and the nun and growled. The bass sound reverberated in the sanctuary.

Corbett stepped back and held his hands up.

Rilen pulled a handkerchief from his pocket and handed it to the nun. *"I apologize, Sister. My brother should not have frightened you. He has spent too many years among godless men. He forgets himself."*

Corbett slid the knife back into his sleeve.

Her eyes flashed as she pressed the cloth to the small nick. "These children you hunt. Be *very sure* of your purpose. Children are precious in the sight of the Lord—if you do them harm, be assured: the one who avenges blood remembers."

"'Vengeance is mine;' yes, I know," Corbett murmured, turning away. "Let's go."

Corbett walked out of the chapel, Rilen subvocal growling at him all the way. "We have a confirmed sighting now; what are you so mad about?" Corbett snarled.

Rilen grabbed him by the shoulder and spun him around. *"This isn't who we are,"* Rilen signed forcefully.

"This is exactly who we are! We hunt murderers, track down

dangerous fugitives and thieves! We have to be hard as nails to do that!"

"But we don't threaten the innocent."

Corbett opened his mouth to fire back a response and then paused. The look in Rilen's eyes—it was haunted, twisted and shattered. He had seen that look ten years ago, when Rilen had appeared on his doorstep, face cut up, tongue gone and cauterized, summarily dishonorably dismissed from his prestigious guard position. His little brother. Barely twenty at the time.

The old rage rose in Corbett again but turned inward this time. No faceless stranger had put the ghosts back in Rilen's eyes—this time, his own flesh and blood had done the deed.

Corbett cupped the back of Rilen's neck and pulled their foreheads together. "You're right. Of course you're right," he muttered. "I'm a bloody fool. Wait here."

Inside the inner door of the chapel, he pulled his money pouch from his pocket and poured it into the collection box.

The rattle of coins pinged against the wood at the bottom of the box, mingling in his memory with melted candles and incense, the taste of bread and wine. Sleeping in the vestry or on splintery benches with Rilen as children, in the periods when they'd had no roof over their heads. A refuge. He put his hand against the door, prepared to leave.

"What was that for?" Sister Jeanetta's voice rang out.

He lowered his head without turning. "A few more stained-glass windows, I suppose. And an *ave* or two, if you can spare it, Sister." He pushed against the door.

"Sir."

Against his will, he paused.

"I already told you. I have forgiven you."

He slowly turned. "I didn't ask for that."

Her voice was steely as one eyebrow arched. "Didn't you?"

Corbett held her eyes for a long moment. Then he nodded and ducked out the chapel door.

TWENTY-NINE

EYL

Eyl had initially laughed off Fee's concerns about a haunted forest. The Damask superstitious tales seemed far-fetched and ridiculous. Trees were just trees, right?

But she couldn't deny the feeling inside Blackthorn.

Even as a gyrfalcon, she noticed—perhaps even *more*. Fee was nervous to have her fly ahead and get too far from them. But she didn't really *want* to. She still felt the insistent tug, the pull to move north, north, ever north. But the wariness tempered it, and she spent most of the day on either Fee's or Kai's shoulder.

There was nothing else alive in this forest that she could sense. No small animals, no other birds. No insects or reptiles except for the ones Kai spoke forth, and those disappeared into the brush, never to be seen again.

EYL SOARS over the river as a bird, feeling the wind support her. The mountains shine in the sunlight, only the very tops dusted with snow yet. If she flies a little farther—a little faster—she'll be home.

The wave of homesickness crashes over her strong enough that it feels like a hammer to her chest. Eyl screams and beats her wings. North. She must fly north. Must fly home.

The wind carries whispers to her. They surround her in the air, clamoring to be heard. The gyrfalcon cocks its head. She knows the voices.

The words are lost in the wind, but she knows the tones. Ev, voice deep, speaking in calm, firm tones. It calms her too, until the broken whisper replies. The voice is soft and thin, like fraying thread.

No, Mother, stop, save your strength. I'm flying to you! I'm on my way. Mother —

Precise, cool tones break through the whispers. Hard and brittle, like glass, jarring and painful enough to make gyrfalcon-Eyl scream and dive —

PANTING AND COVERED IN SWEAT, Eyl sat up in her bedroll. The voice still rang in her ears. She pressed a hand to her chest, trying to get her hammering heart under control.

Eyl remembered playing with Ev in their nursery as a child. Once *she* had come to see him. Ev had run to her and thrown his arms around her. She had hugged him back, but over his head, she'd given Eyl *such* a look....

Eyl hadn't understood it then, but she did now.

It was pure hate.

Just a dream, she told herself through gritted teeth, pushing sweaty hair away from her forehead. *That's all. Nothing to fear.*

But the next nightmare arrived when she was fully awake.

THIRTY

The quiet was pervasive. Their words sank to whispers during the day—too much sound was too jarring. The bugs and amphibians Kai produced were tiny—flies, midges, mosquitoes, miniscule geckos. Soon, they stopped talking at all. It was too eerie.

Imani and Kai signed, and so did Eyl, in the evenings. Fee had to write what he wanted to say in his notebook. It was a hard and fast push to learn a number of basic signs, and they helped him practice as they journeyed.

No one denied the sensation of being watched anymore. The tension wound them all tighter than a spring, decreasing appetites and good sleep. *Maybe everyone who enters Blackthorn just slowly goes mad,* Fee thought morosely at the end of the third day. The river's trickle close by was the only companion to their feet, and even that grated on his nerves after a time.

As the light died, they looked for the best place along the path to spend the night, like always. Eyl drifted from his shoulder and landed on the path a few paces away. Fee busied himself with pulling her clothes from his pack, waiting for the inevitable sounds of pain before the process was over.

Fee hunched his shoulders against the inevitable snapping and cracking of bones. Eyl's groans turned into screams—and she kept screaming. On.

And on.

And on.

"She's stuck!" Imani shrieked, pointing with the torch she held.

Fee spun around. Eyl thrashed on the ground, human-sized and vaguely human-shaped, but covered in feathers. Her feet twisted into wicked bird's talons. Her arms morphed halfway between limbs and wings. She keened, a high bird's scream, as her misshapen wings thrashed against the ground. Her legs twisted around the wrong way to claw at the feathers on her torso, her face.

"No!" Fee leapt and got behind her, pulling her back against his chest. Wrapping his arms around her, he pinned her wings to her sides to restrain the appendages from thrashing. "Shh," he said frantically. "You'll be all right. Kai—"

But Kai was already holding down Eyl's legs so she couldn't hurt herself. The noise she made shredded Fee's eardrums. "Just relax," he said in her ear, over the screams. "Be human. Be Eyl. Listen to my voice. You can do it."

Feathers shivered, receded—and then came back with a vengeance as she thrashed in his arms. Tremors wracked her body, her flesh rippling with the effort. Her head snapped forward and back, wings buffeting him, a frightened animal trying to break free of imprisonment.

"Eyl, it's me, it's Fee, Kai's got your feet. Listen," Fee begged. "Breathe with me. Can you do that? In and out. One, two, three…."

She couldn't. Her falcon's scream rent the night, and he narrowly avoided a broken nose as she threw her head back again. He *felt* her bones move under his hands, straining for one shape or the other.

Imani sobbed, her hands pressed to her face, as the forest watched.

"You can change," Kai said, using his full body weight to keep her talons still; otherwise, they could've ripped them all open. He spat crickets, adding, "Eyl. Be calm. If you are calm—"

Eyl took a shuddering breath, and Fee felt some reason return to her, trying to fight past the blind fear and pain. Under his hands, her limbs grew smoother, the feathery down rippling to bare human skin.

But it didn't last. Feathers sprouted again with a vengeance. Her screams changed as her face distorted, becoming more avian. Her bones trembled in his grasp.

"Listen to my voice, Eyl! Listen!" If he could calm her—or help her change…Fee reached for the magic, readied to cast—then realized she'd bloody him if he tried to scrawl a rune. He couldn't even spare a finger. Her fear was too strong, the urge to free herself superseding all else.

Outside of their circle of fear and lament, silence flowed thickly, like treacle, nearly impenetrable. Fee couldn't stand it anymore.

"Help her!" Fee bellowed to the treetops. "Help her, by the ten stars of Mar! I know you're there. I know you're watching! Someone, help!"

His words rang with all the force of a struck bell.

Eyl's cries grew thin. Blood began to leak from her bulging eyes and misshapen mouth. It trailed down feathers and skin, staining both of them red.

Imani took up the cry, trickles of fire streaming down her face. "Help us! Please, please, please…." She spun in circles, appealing to the dark, impassive wood.

Fee had never felt so helpless, not even when his mother had died. "I'm here, I'm here. I won't leave you," he said, rocking Eyl in his arms. "I'll never leave you. Promise."

Her thrashing weakened. She started to choke, the foam coming out of her mouth tinged pink.

"Oh, dear," a light, musical voice said. "What a mess."

Imani gasped. Kai's eyes bugged and then narrowed to slits.

A brown hand settled onto Fee's shoulder, and its twin pressed down on Eyl's chest. "Breathe, child. Find your correct shape. Be at peace." The voice was smooth like honey, with the musical quality of chimes.

The hand on Eyl's chest glowed with a sweet, golden light. Eyl took a breath and slumped back against Fee. The feathers shivered and melted back into her skin, her talons molding back into feet, her arms taking their rightful shape. Her eyelids fluttered closed into unconsciousness, her face streaked with blood.

Fee registered that he was holding a naked girl, but he was too shocky to be embarrassed.

"There, now. Wrap her in this." A wine-colored velvet cloak settled over Eyl.

Fee used it to dab at her face, then wrapped Eyl tightly. "Thank you," he mumbled, finally looking up.

The stranger wore a gauzy, lavender gown that bared her forearms and swished along the moss like a whisper. Her dark skin reminded him of the bark of a tree, lined and whorled. She wore a crown of red and yellow flowers and greenery over a diaphanous gray veil, tucked closely about her face. From the weight, it looked as thin as a spider's web, but he couldn't see through it at all.

The woman inclined her head to him. "You're welcome." Fee saw her cheek curve underneath the veil. She was smiling. "Now, dear, put out your tears." She handed over a voluminous handkerchief to Imani, who took it wonderingly, blotting the flames.

"You, too." She held out another handkerchief. Fee stared at it without comprehension.

Clucking her tongue, she reached out and brushed away tears he hadn't known he'd cried. The fine linen caught around the puckered scar on his face. Here and there in the whorls of her skin veins of green shimmered, like iridescent moss. "Your hands, too," she said as she pressed the linen into his slack grip. He stared at the bloody streaks on his hands for a moment before scrubbing away the stains.

"Who are you?" Kai demanded, two bees buzzing angrily from his lips. "Where did you come from?"

"Well, the forest, of course," the woman said, gesturing to the trees around them. "The Heartwood is my home. My name is Marlaeda."

"Heartwood?" Imani whispered, inching forward, her eyes aglow.

Through the veil, they saw the curve of her smile once more. "That's the old name, of course, not what the humans call it. The Heartwood is a place of refuge for all faefolk. Now, pick up your friend and come with me." She strode resolutely away from the path into the darkness of the wood.

THIRTY-ONE

EYL

When Eyl opened her eyes, she thought was looking at a mirror and froze in abject horror.

Even though it didn't make sense, she couldn't shake the conviction that she was seeing a reflection of herself, and it was…wrong. The face above her own stared at her unblinkingly with bright-gold eyes set in a human-like face, but it was covered in down that grew into golden-brown feathers where a hairline would normally have been. Elongated, pointed ears twitched.

Then it blinked, assuring Eyl it was *not* her reflection.

Relief flowed into her so swiftly that she trembled. She wasn't stuck in the nightmare of *between* after all.

Then the thing opened its mouth.

"You're *sure* this is bird-kin?" it asked without taking its narrowed eyes off of Eyl. "Because it looks pretty human to *me*. Round ears and all."

"Well, no, not *sure*," a woman replied with a voice like a laughing brook. "But what else could she be?"

"Human," the bird-woman said morosely.

Eyl tried to lift her head. It felt like it weighed a hundred pounds. But she could turn it, enough to take a glance at the rest of the bird-woman and instantly regret it. She didn't seem to be wearing clothes. Her body was covered in a golden-brown feathery down.

The laughing brook voice said, "She shifted from a bird to a girl. How could a human do that?"

"You sure? Because she's lookin' more and more rattled by the minute," the bird-woman said, suspicion clear in her tone. She crossed her arms over her chest.

"She's *awake*? For shame, Uriakin. I told you to let me know the moment she woke!"

"And I did, didn't I?" Uriakin said, letting herself be shoved aside with a sharp nudge to the hip.

"You did not, and you know it." The stranger with the laughing voice took her place and leaned over Eyl. "Hello. My name is Marlaeda. Don't worry; you're safe and your friends are, too. You had a bit of a stressful experience." Her face was veiled by gray cloth, and on her brow sat a crown of yellow roses and red amaryllis, along with ivy leaves.

Eyl swallowed hard. She did not want to think of being stuck between. "Were you following us?"

"Not me," Marlaeda said cheerfully. "But I heard when you ran into difficulty." She patted Eyl with a hand the color—and texture—of walnuts.

"Who—what—are you?" Eyl demanded, steeling her muscles and pushing herself up onto her elbows. Her limbs shook, but she did it.

"Ugh, see." Uriakin waved a taloned hand at Eyl. "Just a useless, know-nothing human. Waste of time."

"There's no need for vitriolic name calling," Marlaeda said firmly. "And lending a helping hand is—oh, I don't know why I bother." She slipped a hand under Eyl's arm and helped her sit up all the way, bunching pillows behind her and tucking the blanket around her shoulders. And good thing, too—after her shift, Eyl wasn't wearing any more clothes than the bird-woman. Eyl flushed and clutched the covers around her chin.

"I'm a harpy," Uriakin said, planting a hand on her hip. "Vitriol is our natural state of being." Behind her, a pair of golden wings that sprouted from her shoulders twitched irritably. "Whereas your state of being is do-gooder. Whether it's orphaned fox kits, sparrows fallen from the nest, or fully grown humans wandering through the Heartwood, you can't help being a busybody."

"If I can't help it, you have had ample time to accustom your-self to the fact and resign yourself to it," Marlaeda said sweetly. "Now, collect her friends, will you, and we'll have supper."

Uriakin crossed her arms. "I'm not your errand-bird," she groused.

"You are if you want any of my seedcakes."

"You fight dirty." She went.

Marlaeda turned back to Eyl. "You mustn't be alarmed," she said softly. "Your friends are washing up at the river. You're quite safe."

"You're faefolk," Eyl said.

She nodded cheerfully. "Will you lift your arms for me?" She held up a dark-blue shift.

Bemused, Eyl did, and as her covers slid down to her waist, Marlaeda slid the shift over her head. The fabric settled into place, and Eyl tucked the skirt into place below the covers. Then she repeated the process with the sleeveless, silver overdress.

"There," Marlaeda said, evidently satisfied. "Now let me see about the supper things."

Eyl lay back against the pillows. Her momentary strength had departed, and it felt like her muscles had turned to water. As Marlaeda bustled around, Eyl gazed around the room—but it wasn't a room at all.

She lay on a pallet of blankets and pillows in a sort of pavilion, made up of eight enormous oaks spaced more or less evenly in a circle. They grew tall and straight, and the branches wove together high overhead, bending into a domed roof. She assumed they were tight enough—or fused together—to provide shelter from the elements. Between the oaks' trunks hung lengths of gold cloth that shimmered, reflecting the light from lanterns dangling at various heights from the bough ceiling. The enclosed area was large—as large or larger than the tower's circumference.

One of the golden drapes was thrown back with a careless flick. "Here they are," Uriakin said in a bored voice.

"Eyl!" Imani threw herself at the lush pallet. "You're all right!"

"Yes." Eyl hugged her. "What's happened?"

Imani said reverently, "Marlaeda came to help you. She led us here down a hollow way, and would you think that the forest looks completely different off that path? Plenty of moonlight and animal sounds and everything! Then they put you to bed. We sat with you for a long time, but Marlaeda finally told us to go wash off the travel dirt. Fee really didn't want to leave you."

He hadn't? Eyl remembered flashes—the blood and pain, being stretched without respite—and Fee's arms hard around her, clinging tightly.

I won't leave you.

She flushed and raised a hand to her hair, smoothing it down. Someone must've given her a cursory wash because she remembered the blood in her mouth.

Imani cast her an anxious look. "Are you sure you're okay?"

Kai and Fee entered the tent, also looking much cleaner and refreshed. Fee's tousled, red hair shone with moisture, and Eyl had the strangest urge to run her fingers through it and smooth it out.

"Are you feeling better?" he asked, coming right to her.

"Much." She laughed a little. "Thank you."

A look passed between them that she felt deep in her soul. He said, "Always."

"We were having a look at the river," Imani continued. "There's a *massive* bridge, and it's made out of roots!"

"A bridge? Why?" Eyl asked, slightly fuddled.

"Because we like to go places just as much as humans, and not all faefolk can fly." Uriakin rustled her feathers. "*Obviously.*"

"Do you mind?" Eyl snapped.

"Yes, very much. Are all humans as thick as you?"

"Keep needling me and find out," Eyl ground out.

"Little eyass has claws," Uriakin drawled. "How cute." Her eyes glinted with amusement.

Before Eyl could become incendiary at being called a baby falcon, and a little one, no less, Marlaeda intervened. "Peace, Uriakin. Can you keep from causing chaos for one hour? Let's eat. Imani, help Eyl up, would you?"

They gathered around a table heavily burdened by the amount of food on it. At a glance, Eyl could see sweet buns, sandwiches, fruits and nuts of all kinds, little cakes, a large cauldron of steaming, savory broth beside a stack of bowls, a loaf of warm bread, and a dish of honey butter. Her mouth watered. Their food at the tower had been limited to the supplies they could purchase and what their garden and culinary abilities could produce. Eyl had learned from Tala, and Imani from Eyl. Their dishes had been filling but simple. This feast hearkened back to Eyl's childhood, though the menu was different; variety, as much as you'd like, a delight to all the senses possible—taste, smell, sight.

Uriakin plunked herself down on a stool right in front of a platter of meat. "It's not bird, is it?" she asked Marlaeda suspiciously.

"It's glazed ham," Marlaeda said placidly. "You *do* know that you're a predator who hunts grouse and quail and who-knows-what on your own time, yes?"

"Of course I know," Uriakin said, piling the meat on her plate. "I just don't like it when other people serve it to me and titter and expect me to gasp or fall down in a faint when I find out what I've eaten."

They all sat on stools—somehow, Eyl ended up by Uriakin, horrors—with the boys on one side of the table and the girls on the other. Marlaeda sighed and poured from the massive, blue teapot, handing around cups. "I'll speak to them."

"Nothing I can't handle. Don't trouble yourself."

"Helping a friend isn't trouble."

"Do-gooder." Uriakin shook her head. "It's compulsive."

Marlaeda thumped the cup in front of her. "Drink your tea. Everyone, please help yourself. We pass to the right."

What followed was one of the oddest dinners Eyl had ever been to. Marlaeda and Uriakin carried on most of the initial conversation, as the rest of them were focused on eating. Eyl especially. Smelling the delicious food made her abruptly realize she was ravenous. She piled as much food as she could onto her plate, and as she ate, it still didn't feel like enough. She held on to manners by the skin of her teeth, but it was a near thing. Fee broke a lot of the passing laws by handing her platters directly across the table. She was too hungry to stop and say thank you but shot him several abjectly grateful looks, which he returned with smiles.

However, one place at the head of the table sat empty. The dishes and place setting were all there, and instead of a stool, a large, imposing chair with a back and arms waited for an occupant. On closer inspection, it all looked to be one piece of wood—not carved or assembled, but...perhaps grown.

Before Eyl could swallow and ask about it, Imani said tentatively, "Aren't you hungry?"

Marlaeda had unwound the base of her veil to sip from her teacup, but her plate was empty of food. "No, dear, I'll get something later," Marlaeda said easily.

"Where did all the food come from? Did you make it?"

Marlaeda laughed. "No, a feast of this size takes many hands."

Imani gazed around the pavilion warily. "So where are they?"

"Faefolk are private creatures, and we keep to ourselves most of the time. Some, if not most, are understandably wary with strangers. I hope you will not be offended."

Uriakin interjected. "What she means is, we mind our business except for the trooping faefolk, who are notorious busybodies, so Marlaeda told them to get stuffed."

"I most certainly did not," Marlaeda said with dignity. "I hinted that travelers ought to be afforded hospitality and discretion, and it would be wise to let you rest."

"Meddlesome snoops," Uriakin muttered into her teacup.

"So are there a lot of faefolk?" Imani ventured.

Marlaeda fiddled with her fork. "Well...no, dear. Not very many at all. Certainly not when compared to humans."

"Why?"

"The Sundering," Kai said abruptly. A firefly whirred up into the boughs, and he frowned deeply.

"Are you all right?" Eyl signed. Was he embarrassed to spew bugs in front of strangers?

"Fine." He picked up a roll and bit into it.

Marlaeda nodded. "Yes. Magic is something we need just as much as air or water, and after the Sundering, so much of the land's magic was barred from us. There are a few places in the world where magic still exists—rather like a puddle after a rainstorm has ceased. But even those places shrink, after a time. The Heartwood is one of those places. Or"—she laughed—"sometimes I tease and call it 'Hartwood.'"

Eyl exchanged a glance with Fee, puzzled.

Marlaeda finished, "It's the Last and Best Stronghold of the Faefolk."

The words had an odd weight to them, like a silent gong had been rung. They hung in the air, vibrating silently. A strong wind gusted through the pavilion's draperies, rustling the oak leaves and setting the lanterns to bobbing. They all came alert, except for Uriakin, who continued to demolish the cheese plate.

Marlaeda clasped her hands together. "Oh, good, he's finished his rounds. I had hoped he could join us for supper."

Eyl asked, "Who?"

Marlaeda tilted her head. "Oh, haven't I mentioned him? The Forest Guardian."

Fee tensed. "Forest Guardian?"

"Yes. I'm sure I told you."

Uriakin spoke around the brie in her mouth. "You didn't."

"Oh. My mistake. Well, you'll have the chance to meet him in person, then. Here he comes now." And Marlaeda turned, beaming, to the looming shape that pulled aside the long, golden drape.

CHAPTER

THIRTY-TWO

FEE

T he man bent low to duck under the drape—not because of his height, though he was tall, but because of the massive rack of antlers sprouting from his head. Fee counted at least twenty tines. When he straightened, solid and imposing, the man took up more space in the pavilion than he ought. The cloak draped about his shoulders was dusted with snow, as was the dark hair that curled around his shoulders.

Fee blinked rapidly. *Oh.* Hart-*wood.*

"Ciurin," Marlaeda said, the word full of throbbing joy. She held out her hand to him, her long fingers beckoning as she curled her wrist, an entrancing invitation. "You've finished your rounds? Come and have supper. But no spears at the table."

Fee jolted. He hadn't even noticed the wickedly sharp spear the man carried.

Frowning, Ciurin leaned the spear against one stout trunk before striding purposefully towards the table. Of course the empty chair was his—nothing else would have supported his frame…or been worthy of it.

"Visitors?" he asked in a low, bass tone. Keen eyes swept over the table. Fee worked hard not to react, though fear hummed in his veins. This man was dangerous.

Marlaeda rose from her place. She unclasped his cloak and drew it away, revealing his dark-green jerkin and leathers.

"Mmhmm. Were you up the mountain? It's quite early for snow, isn't it?" She reached up and dusted a few stray flakes of snow off of his antlers.

"Marlaeda." He stopped her fussing by catching her wrist with his hand.

She paused, looking up into his face. "They were on the path, and in a bit of difficulty, so I assisted and offered my hospitality."

"And how did you know they were in difficulty?" he rumbled.

"Serendipity," she said blithely.

He raised one heavy brow.

"Sit down and I'll make the introductions," she coaxed, draping his cloak over the back of his chair.

He folded himself into the chair, which no longer seemed imposing in the least, submitting utterly to the man who filled it. Marlaeda stood at his shoulder and handed him one foodstuff after another as she introduced Eyl, Fee, Kai, and Imani. Eyl squirmed when his amber eyes passed over her. Maybe she felt what Fee did. Then Ciurin turned his eyes on Fee. They narrowed to slits as they took in his face and scar, not missing his pointed ears.

Fee felt the heavy weight of ages fall over him, and deep-rooted power. His sight felt like falling down a long, dark tunnel. He wasn't *seeing* the Forest Guardian as much as the man was seeing *him*. And then the Guardian blinked and released Fee from the grip of his gaze. Fee gasped. He hadn't dared to breathe.

"Everyone, this is Ciurin, Forest Guardian of the Heartwood. Would someone pass the rolls?" Marlaeda asked brightly.

Instead of passing, Uriakin grabbed a roll from the basket and lobbed it.

Ciurin's hand shot out and grabbed it midair. "Don't try that with the butter," he warned as he broke open the roll and set it on his plate.

"Spoilsport," the harpy muttered.

Fee swallowed. This man was a power—and so was Marlaeda, though she was subtler about it. Fee had tried to use his magic to look at her on the path, and she had merely sent him a chiding smile. He could sense absolutely nothing about her at all.

Which was, frankly, terrifying.

"My plate is overflowing," Ciurin said pointedly to Marlaeda as she tried to give him another dish. "Why don't you sit down and explain your serendipitous assistance? Or would you like me to guess?"

She took her seat again. "Fee called to me, and so I answered."

Ciurin's eyes swung towards Fee once more.

Fee tensed. "I was just yelling. I don't remember what."

"Oh, it wasn't what you were yelling," Marlaeda assured him. "But *how* you called. You nearly deafened me with the force of your magic."

Fee's face went totally blank.

Eyl objected, "Fee couldn't use magic; he was holding me." Then she pulled up short and blushed.

Marlaeda said, "Oh, he did."

They all stared.

She continued, "Unsurprising in those of faefolk blood, though." Fee instinctually reached for his ears, but Marlaeda turned so that her smile encompassed the whole group.

"But...." Imani gulped as everyone pivoted to her. "But I don't have faefolk blood." She sat very still, with her hands clasped in her lap.

"Maybe not much," Marlaeda conceded, "but you do have some. All of you do. The Heartwood is a stronghold, a bastion of safety and magic for our kind. Only those with faefolk blood can enter safely. The sentinel trees showed you the path, didn't they?"

They all stared at her, astonished.

She nodded happily. "If you didn't have faefolk blood, you would not have seen the through-path—you *were* going straight through, were you not? If you had been seeking refuge, the path would've taken you in quite a different direction."

"Yes," Eyl rasped. "We were going straight through." She put a hand to her forehead.

Fee pushed the teapot her way. They—all of them—were like him. Maybe. He clutched hard at the thread of euphoria before it could grow too large.

Marlaeda paused in cutting apart a pan of sticky buns, as if realizing she had just imparted a revelation. She set her knife down. "Our people are not very clannish. When we band together in large groups, it usually results in a scrape or some other trouble with each other. So it's not so surprising that you should have wild magic in your line."

"It's not?" Eyl said weakly.

"No," Marlaeda said, like that explained all.

"I don't understand." Imani bit her lip.

"We like to be left unbothered, but we don't mind companionship. Some live among humans and take lovers. Some wander and leave a string of broken hearts. More so in times past, of course, when we were greater in number, and not as feared." She shrugged, her shoulders slumping a little. "And of course, our birth rate among our own people has declined more and more over the centuries. So you see, possessing traces of faefolk heritage—wild magic—is really more common than you'd think. The chance is low that it flares up so dramatically after such a long time," she said, casting an apologetic glance at Fee. "I'm sure it was not easy for you." She patted his shoulder gently before passing out the sticky buns. "Though I've never heard of one who could wield wizard magic and wild magic both."

Fee went cold. How could she know—could she *sense* his ability? "I don't know what you mean," he said through numb lips.

"Of course you do. You called to me, in the forest—quite strongly. And of course I came." She dimpled through the diaphanous veil. "I think that's why Ciurin's so upset with you."

Everyone's eyes slid back to the horned guardian. Ciurin's gaze grew even darker.

Fee gulped.

"I wish you wouldn't frown so," Marlaeda said absently, reaching out to smooth away the lines on Ciurin's brow with one finger. "I've spoken to you about it before."

Ciurin turned his head. His face softened, amber eyes warming. "So you have," he murmured, and his lips twitched in what might have been a smile.

"But do you listen?" Marlaeda asked in mock castigation. "Noooo...."

Uriakin heaved a put-upon sigh, her mouth full of the seed-cakes that her teeth were the wrong shape to chew. "Will you two give me a break and find a room already? It's enough to drive me to drink."

"You already drink," Ciurin said, narrowing his eyes at her.

The harpy dragged her talons through the turf, raking up the moss and grass. "But then I'll drink *more*, and goodness knows we don't want *that*."

"Decidedly not," Marlaeda agreed. "No one wants a repeat of Esme's name-day celebration. Eyl, dear, have some more sticky buns. Try a sausage roll. And the cheese, too. You're too thin. It worries me." She loaded Eyl's plate with a second helping of food.

"I just burn it off shifting," Eyl said glumly, but she took an enormous bite anyway.

"Dear, it really isn't healthy to change your shape so much," Marlaeda said. "It taxes your body and causes unnecessary strain. I meant to tell you. That's why you got stuck. You need to slow down or it will happen again."

"But she can't!" Imani exclaimed. "The spell won't let her."

THIRTY-THREE

EYL

The three faefolk looked up.

"Spell?" Ciurin rumbled.

"It's all right," Eyl said, exchanging a glance with Imani. "They'd find out at dawn anyway." She cleared her throat. "Until recently, we were all captives of Aedelbras the Sorcerer, who was experimenting with wild magic." She shrugged. "His results were...unpredictable. But Fee came and helped us escape."

Ciurin had become quieter and more unmoving through this revelation. The hand he had braced on one large knee tightened. "Is he dead?"

"Yes," Kai said, breaking his long silence. A large butterfly drifted onto the breeze. "After Imani set him on fire, the tower fell on him."

Uriakin arched a disbelieving eyebrow, but at Eyl's sharp look did not comment.

"Good," Ciurin declared in a deep rumble. "If he weren't, I would have dealt with him." The blatant threat in his voice was clear.

Kai turned to Eyl. "I'll bet that's what the old man was testing us for. He was looking for test subjects with traces of faefolk blood." He caught the two lizards that fell from his mouth and slid them into the grass.

"Why the magic worked and why it…didn't." Eyl stared at her hands. "Is that why we came out wrong?"

"Explain to me what 'wrong' means." Marlaeda came to Eyl and took Eyl's hand in her own, turning it over.

Eyl turned a beseeching glance on Fee. She didn't have the words to explain.

He understood. "The sorcerer wanted to channel wild magic for his own use, I think," Fee said, taking up the narrative. "He called up magic in the usual human way but then let it wreak havoc with no guidance on his test subjects, which all seem to have been children with faefolk blood. Eyl was the first to survive, right Eyl?"

She nodded, emotion pricking her eyes and the back of her throat.

"Eyl is a gyrfalcon by day and a girl by night. The change happens whether she wants it to or not. Imani can channel fire; she's the only one who can exert her will on her abilities. Whenever Kai speaks, he summons insects, amphibians, and reptiles from his throat."

"Oh. Gross," Uriakin said, fascinated.

Eyl drew herself up and glared at the harpy.

"Keep your feathers on, kid. Or off, as the case may be. Marlaeda, have you ever heard of anything like this?"

Marlaeda put a finger under Eyl's chin and tilted her head up. "No. The enchantment is strong and old. I know very little of wizard magic."

"It wasn't wizard magic; it was wild," Fee objected.

Marlaeda shook her head. "Only of a corrupted sort. No matter how uncontrolled, a wizard called the magic. It is bound in a fashion I cannot access. And since the Sundering, my power's virtue has waned. It took much to even ease your body into its rightful shape." She traced her fingers slowly over Eyl's forehead, down the sides of her face to her chin, then lifted her hands regretfully. "But this I do know—unless something is done, your changes will get worse. There is…a stressor on you. A pull."

Eyl's eyes widened. "Yes, yes. I have to go north. I don't know why."

"Someone has put a geas, a call on you, a power beyond this forest. I cannot gainsay that. You said you were held captive? Magically?"

Eyl nodded.

"Ah. The geas was kept at bay because of that, but now it is untrammeled, and this has unfortunately upset what balance your body has tried to find."

"So how do we break the geas?" Fee asked. "It doesn't originate with Eyl."

Marlaeda turned to look at him. "Gracious, why do you want to do that?"

"But if it's malicious—"

"Whatever made you think it was malicious?"

Eyl blinked. "I…isn't it?"

Marlaeda *hmmed* under her breath. "Well, a spell like that, so strong, over such distance…if the caster had evil in their purpose, I don't think it would've been able to find you, much less latch on and remain for so long. In these cases, if you didn't want to be found, it just—wouldn't work."

At Eyl's continuing look of confusion, Marlaeda went on. "Well, look at it this way. You're lost in a forest. Someone calls your name. What do you do?"

"Wait until I recognize the voice," Eyl said promptly.

Imani and Kai looked puzzled, but Marlaeda didn't react. "Assume you know it, but you're afraid. What then?"

"Run away. Hide."

"What if it's someone you knew or trusted?"

Eyl said warily, "Wait to see if they're alone."

Fee gave her a strange look.

"Assuming they are?"

"Go towards them to make sure it's really them. Call out to them once I'm sure."

Marlaeda smiled and nodded. "It's like that. In order to latch on so, to forge such a strong connection, something about your latent magic knows the voice and trusts it. They couldn't call and cling to you unless you were calling back."

Eyl licked her lips. "So...."

"Someone misses you rather badly," Marlaeda said quietly. "But what I was saying, dear, is that if you continue to change every day with the geas taxing your body and your strength, you will get stuck again. Your health will deteriorate rapidly. It could be disastrous."

"So there's nothing you can do?" Eyl swallowed. "No hope at all?"

"I can ease your body for a little while, give you some stores to build up your health, but the change will continue to erode your strength."

"We go north as quickly as possible," Fee said, meeting Eyl's eyes. "We can pick up our pace. Buy horses. Once we get where it wants you to be, it will be easier."

"Well, that is certainly one solution," Marlaeda said. "But I think you have another option."

They all turned to her. "We do?"

"There's nothing I can do, but I suspect someone else can."

"Who?"

"Fee."

THIRTY-FOUR

"I really wish you hadn't said that," Fee said, rubbing a hand over his scar before cracking his neck. He paced outside the pavilion in a nearby grove of thorn trees. After her epiphany, he had hurriedly begged a moment alone.

"Why not?" Marlaeda asked calmly.

"Because...they don't know." He cracked his knuckles. Cracked them again. He couldn't look at her. "They don't know I have wild magic."

"You haven't told them?"

"No! Of course not!"

"Why is that?"

He shot her an agonized glance, then looked away again hurriedly. "The only thing I can do with my talent is see secrets." He swallowed hard.

"The only thing you can do *right now*," she clarified. "With some practice, you should be able to do any number of things."

Fee forged ahead to the crux of the issue. He could hardly stop the words from spilling out. "How can I tell someone that I can see their deepest, darkest secrets at a glance? They'd never look at me the same. Nothing good has ever come of it. My mother *died*

—" His voice cracked. He pressed the heels of his hands against his eyes.

"Poor boy." Marlaeda's arms came around him in a hug. She smelled like tree sap and roses, and though she held him gently, he could sense the power in her, flowing through her like warm honey just under the surface. She rubbed his back comfortingly.

He shivered and then let his forehead drop to her shoulder. "How did you know?" he asked thickly.

"Dear, you're absolutely *stuffed* with power, and it spills out like a waterfall. Don't look like that," she said as he hastily raised his head. "It's not your fault you don't know how to use it." She squeezed his shoulders gently and then let go. "But it really is quite noticeable. We'll speak more in the morning. I think there might be a way to get it under control, and if you can do that, there may be a way to help your friend."

Help Eyl? He swallowed hard. "But what can I do that you can't?"

"If you learn to control your wild magic, you may very well be the first person I have heard of who can truly claim to be both a wizard and wild magic user. That may be the key to undoing your friends' entanglements."

Control. He'd never thought of his talent as something that could be controlled. It was simply 'active.' His eyes widened. "If I get my magic under control, can I make it stop? For good?"

"Why would you want to?"

He laughed hollowly. "You have to ask?"

"Talent is talent. Once understood and wielded correctly, it becomes neither good nor bad—just what you make of it."

"I can't think of a single good thing that has come from it."

"Can't you?" she asked vaguely. She turned to move away.

"My lady," he said hurriedly. "Please don't say more about this to—to the others." *I almost said Eyl,* he thought in horror. "My ability."

She regarded him through her veil, and he had to steel himself not to squirm. Was this how others felt around him? Far too exposed, hyper aware of all their vulnerable spots?

"Fee, dear, why don't you want them told?" she asked quietly.

"They won't look at me the same," he whispered. "These last two weeks have been—some of the best—" He swallowed hard. "I don't want that to change."

"But why should it?" she asked patiently.

"Everyone fears someone who can see their secrets."

"Yes, but you *can't* see theirs," Marlaeda said reasonably. "So why should it change?"

Fee opened his mouth—and stopped. "How did you know that?" he asked faintly. He wobbled on his feet.

She steadied him. "It stands to reason. Faefolk magic—wild magic—offers some passive protections against unaimed spells. It probably repels your seeking instinctively, even if your friends don't recognize it for what it is. I, however, being a much more experienced magic user, knew what you were doing." She patted his shoulder. "Now I must sleep, or I shall be as surly as a badger at breakfast. I will see you in the morning, and we'll talk more about how to get your magic under control." Then she departed, slipping through the trees out of sight.

You can't see theirs. Why should it change?

He ran a hand through his hair, tugging hard. Had being locked in fear for his whole life made him stupid?

Fee stared at the pavilion. He couldn't imagine going back there and putting his head down on his pillow. There was too much running through his head to sleep. He couldn't process.

He turned towards the burble of water. Maybe staring at the river for a while would make his mind finally slow.

THIRTY-FIVE

EYL

Someone is missing you rather badly. Eyl curled into her velvet covers and pressed her fist to her heart. Someone wanted her back. It was not malicious.

"Mama?" she whispered.

Who else would it have been?

Around her, Kai and Imani breathed slowly, wrapped in dreamless sleep on soft, down-filled coverlets and pillows. Ciurin and Uriakin had disappeared along with the supper things. Marlaeda had lowered the lantern lights with a wave of her hand before she and Fee had stepped outside the pavilion to talk. But Fee had never come back.

Can we trust the faefolk? she wondered. They had played the good Samaritan to be sure, but they were still strangers.

She rolled over again and punched the feather pillow. If they weren't trustworthy, it was going to be a problem, since the four of them were stuck in this semi-haunted, definitely magical forest. But if they were, if Marlaeda was right…then she had hope for the first time in ten years. Some surety that home was a place she could return to. A safe haven.

Hope was so dangerous.

She threw off the covers and padded out of the pavilion in her borrowed dress, wiggling her toes in the grass. She didn't know if she had that much vulnerability in her.

She stared around the moonlit clearing, repeatedly pulling her dress straight. She hadn't worn skirts in years. Where had Fee gone?

The burble of water led her through the trees to the river's edge. To her keen eyes, there seemed to be a faint path, even if it had only been trod by a few. She caught sight of Fee through the trees, silently staring at the water. "Can't sleep?"

He turned.

Eyl picked her way down the path to his side at the river's edge.

"What tipped you off?" he mumbled, lacing his fingers together behind his neck.

"Well, your absence in your bedroll was an indicator," she murmured.

He laughed a little, but it was an empty sound.

"What's wrong?"

He looked at her out of the corner of his eye—his bad eye, she noticed—and then glanced away.

"Was it something Marlaeda said? Something about me? Because I don't know if we can trust her. We don't have to do what she says—"

"What?" he exclaimed. "Of *course* we can trust her. She helped you. She...." He blinked, looking like someone had just thwacked him with a bandsaw. He swallowed. The words came slow and quiet, but they came. "We can trust her."

"Okay," she said. "So why are you staring at the river instead of sleeping?"

His hands dropped to his sides, dangling limply. The words came out in a quiet rush of exhalation. "I have wild magic, Eyl."

She wiggled her toes in the grass, shifting her weight. "Yes? I mean, I assumed?" She motioned to his ears. "Plus, you saw the path just like us—we've all got it, apparently."

"No. What I mean is, I knew before this. I've always known."

She wasn't sure what he was driving at. "Yes? You're a wizard."

"No. Wizard and wild magic are two different things."

"Ah." She bit her lip. "I don't understand. But I can tell that whatever it is, it's upset you."

He hesitated, then nodded. "Aren't you going to ask?"

"No. Not unless it's something you want to tell me." She stared out at the dark water slowly rippling past the bank. "We all have secrets."

Fee trembled like an animal trying to acclimate to a soft touch after a lifetime of abuse.

Eyl eyed his scar. If she ever got within a hundred feet of the High Wizard, he'd better watch his back. She'd claw his eyes out. She'd done that to a rabid dog once that had come up too close to the tower. Then Kai had shot it with a crossbow. It was a solid approach. Maybe she'd speak to Kai tomorrow night.

"I want to tell you," Fee said finally. "I need to. I'm just… afraid." He pressed his lips together, then squeezed his eyes shut. "I told you how my mother died."

"Yes."

"I didn't tell you it was my fault."

Eyl's mouth twisted and she lifted a shoulder. "I mean, you kind of did—"

"Not like that. Not because of this." He motioned to his ears. "Because—I looked at those men and told them what they were thinking. I looked into their eyes and heard their thoughts. Desires. Their secrets. One of them wanted to hurt my mother; I heard it as clear as day. And I blurted it out to his face." He raked a hand through his hair. "I had…known things before, when I looked at people, but not like this. I had never heard a secret so loud before. They thought I was reading their minds. And I was."

Eyl's heart dropped to her stomach.

"When they tried to kill me, my mother intervened, and they killed her instead. And I can't turn it off; it's been like this for my whole life…until I met you."

Her heart stuttered.

"I look at you and I don't see secrets or thoughts or the worst depths of a human heart. I just see you."

He lifted his head. "Well," he amended anxiously, "I get a bit of an impression of feathers. Wind. But that's it. I don't *want* to see anything, but Marlaeda said maybe there's a chance I can use it…." He trailed off, shoulders slumped.

Her breath left her in a *whoosh*. "*This* is what you've been so upset about?"

"I didn't want you to look at me differently," he whispered.

"No chance of that unless I grow another foot," she said wryly.

The barest glimmer of humor flickered over his face, along with a tiny spark of hope.

This explained his propensity to never look at anyone straight on. "Well, it's definitely strange to hear, and I think anyone would get a jolt wondering if they'd accidentally shown you something they shouldn't have." Her eyes flickered up to his. "But welcome to the odd and sometimes awful magical powers club." She smiled crookedly. "Now you're not the odd one out."

"You're not mad?"

She shook her head. Ecstatic he hadn't actually seen anything from her, yes. Mad? "No. Absolutely don't tell strangers you can read their minds. That's bad."

"Not everyone," he said. "Apparently, faefolk blood and wild magic provide a buffer."

"Good," she said firmly. "For *you*. I don't know if not being able to turn off your mind-reading powers is better or worse than not being able to turn off shapeshifting, but it sounds miserable." She reached for his hand and clasped it. "Don't ever be afraid to look at me."

He squeezed her hand, opened his mouth—

"*Ugh*," Uriakin scoffed, walking down the path. "Give me a break. If I have to see gooey eyes from you two, I'm gonna be sick."

They jumped apart. Fee stammered, "I—We weren't—"

Eyl planted her hands on her hips. "What is your problem?"

"Mushy stuff from two striplings barely old enough to molt is my problem. Do that somewhere else."

Fee tugged on Eyl's arm, pulling her back when she would've squared up to pummel Uriakin. "We're guests," he hissed in her ear. "No fighting or mutilations, please." He dragged her off as Uriakin smirked behind them.

"That—that—*harpy!*" she hissed, her whole head hot with rage.

"She was deliberately trying to get to you," Fee murmured, pulling her along. "I think that's just the way she is."

"Doesn't mean the next time I see her, I won't kick her teeth in," Eyl muttered. "Where are you going?"

"To cool off, hopefully. Let's take a closer look at that bridge."

THIRTY-SIX

EYL

Trees leaned over the wide river, creating a canopy that did its best to cover most of the water that traversed the river's breadth. In the moonlight, the water sparkled and burbled over the rocks and roots in the shallows in a musically pleasant mumble. Over the center of the river, from the west bank to the east, stretched a wide, arched bridge made of roots and trailing vines, much more like a living thing than a structure.

And it very well could have been. Eyl wasn't sure.

She and Fee had gone up it a little ways, high enough to throw twigs over the side and watch them wend their way under the bridge to the other side. Fee insisted that this was a game he had played as a child to see whose stick would win, but Eyl could never pick out the difference in the sticks in the dark. She suspected that he was cheating.

"On three," he said, and they cast their twigs over the wide.

"Do you think…." Eyl trailed off as they peered over the edge of the bridge into the dark current.

"What?"

She shrugged. "Nothing."

Fee turned and leaned against the railing, giving her his full attention. "No, what?"

"Do you think Marlaeda and Ciurin…?" She gave him a significant look.

He arched a brow, the one bisected by the scar. "Really?"

"Don't you think?"

He frowned. "What gave you that idea? You couldn't see her face, and his was like a stone wall."

"Because of the way she held out her hand to him."

"The way she held her *hand*?"

She made a face at him. "Yes. That kind of…welcome beckoning." She shook her head in frustration. "It's hard to explain."

"Take your time, then. I believe you, but I want to hear more about this beckoning."

Eyl tucked her chin into her chest and considered what she could and couldn't say. "My father. Before he married my mother, he had a lover. But the marriage to my mother would've been advantageous and well positioned and…all manner of things. So he married my mother. But he continued to see this other woman."

"How do you know?"

"My parents were married seven years before I was born, and I have a half-brother four years older than me."

"Ah." He pressed his lips together, staring at the water.

"As far as I know, my father always—" Eyl swallowed. "I'm not sure, but once, I saw them together, at the end of a long hallway, and she beckoned to him in a very similar way, a kind of"—she moved her hands—"sinuous movement. And the way he looked at her…. He never looked at my mother like that."

Even now, she could feel the phantom pain in her chest, her childlike confusion. How could he look at that woman like that? How could he not love her brave, proud, beautiful mother?

"I just don't understand how he could do that. To either of them," she mumbled to herself. "If he loved Ev's mother, why didn't he stay with her? If he agreed to marry my mother, why didn't he commit himself to her?"

"Ev. Is that your brother's name?"

Eyl froze. She had said too much.

After a long, awkward pause, Fee cleared his throat. "Some men think themselves above vows or honor. They answer only to themselves. My father's wife hated me, but I knew it was because the evidence of her husband's rampant infidelity was thrown in her face every day. He continued to be unfaithful—still is, I'm sure. I don't understand it, either."

The corner of Fee's mouth twitched. "But show me that hand motion again so I can watch for it tomorrow. Is it like this?" He crooked a finger, then snapped.

Eyl pursed her lips. "You know perfectly well I didn't summon you like a dog."

"Show it to me again and I'll get it."

She stretched her arm out and beckoned.

"Now do it without a sour look on your face," he advised.

She set a hand on her hip. "Well, you'd best look the part of a loving swain, then."

"Oh, I don't want to make it easy on you."

She arched an eyebrow and curled her wrist, beckoning.

"Very imperious."

She dropped her hand. "I'm doing it just like her!"

"Her who? Your father's mistress, or Marlaeda?"

Eyl stopped, arrested by the thought.

"Do it like Marlaeda."

Eyl focused on Fee's face and stared into his eyes. She took in a deep breath and thought about everything those blue eyes meant to her. Then she held out her hand, beckoned—and beamed at him.

He stared at her, wide-eyed.

"What?" She lowered her hand. "Did I do it wrong?"

Fee shook his head. "No, no! It looked great. Probably just like Marlaeda, if you had a veil on. Sadly, we'll never know."

She blew a raspberry at him. "No, really. Did I strike you dumb?"

"You…reminded me of something. It's strange."

"Yes, Marlaeda."

"Her…and the statue in the chapel."

Eyl stopped. "The virtue?"

"No, the figure on the cross. He was making the same gesture," Fee said awkwardly. "Or that was just what I thought of. Ignore me. I told you it was strange."

"Well, no. Not really," she whispered, and then coughed to clear the tickle in her throat. "Come on. It's late, even for me."

"Do you even remember how to get back to the pavilion?"

She scoffed, shaking off the goosebumps. "We went down one path; how hard can it be?"

Spoke too soon, she thought a minute later, pushing aside tree branches along the river's edge. In the dark, all the trees looked the same.

"Don't say I told you so," she muttered, following the murmuring river, hoping to come across the faint path back to the clearing.

"Who, me?"

Eyl stuck her tongue out at Fee over her shoulder and forged ahead. But soon, she realized that the murmuring they heard wasn't just the river.

Eyl cautiously stopped behind a stout tree trunk and peered through the gloom.

Uriakin perched on a low-hanging bough and bent down towards someone in the water. The man with a deep-olive tint to his skin and long hair that was probably greenish gold in the sunlight was naked to the waist. The water around him stirred, a fin breaking the surface.

Fee said in her ear, "Is that…?"

Eyl hushed him.

The river-man said something. The sharp-tongued harpy leaned closer. The merman reached up with webbed hands and gently cupped her cheek.

Eyl's shoulders hunched. They needed to get out of here. She elbowed Fee, nudging him backwards. They backed up a few steps, but he trod on a stick.

The snap echoed in the forest.

The merman slipped into the water faster than a wink, and Uriakin whirled around, fixing a furious expression on them. "What are you doing over here, little sneaks? Spying?"

"No," Fee said, holding his hands up in surrender. "We were just going back to the pavilion."

The harpy stalked up to them and poked one taloned finger hard against Fee's chest. "If you *ever* breathe a word about this, I will carve out your kidneys." Uriakin growled. Her eyes cut to Eyl. "*Both* of you."

"What do you mean by threatening us?" Eyl demanded. "We didn't do anything!"

"That's what I do to spies and sneaks," Uriakin hissed.

"Sneaks? What do *we* care about—"

Fee said quickly, "Just leave it, Eyl."

"And keep your mouths shut," Uriakin said again.

"We will. We were just going." Fee hurriedly dragged Eyl back along the path.

"Who would we tell, birdbrain?" Eyl said over her shoulder.

"Can you not pick a fight with her for five minutes?" he muttered. "Is this a bird thing?"

"Why did you just buckle under to her?" she demanded. "She had no call to threaten us like that. I—"

"Everybody has vulnerabilities," he said, cutting her off as they approached the pavilion. "She was obviously nasty earlier to get us to go away so she could have an assignation in peace, without anyone knowing. Then we blundered into it, and she got nasty again. I've found that poking someone where they're vulnerable ultimately hurts me just as much as them." He met her eyes. "People don't like it when you find out their secrets."

Eyl cast a glance over her shoulder, the weight of all the unsaid things inside her stirring. She admitted, "No, they don't."

THIRTY-SEVEN

In the morning when Eyl shifted, Fee's heart was in his mouth. It seemed to take forever.

Fee kept his eyes on Marlaeda, who had appeared, again veiled, with pre-dawn breakfast and promised to monitor the process. Her demeanor didn't give anything away—he couldn't see her face, after all.

But finally, Eyl finished, fully morphed into a gyrfalcon. She shook out her wings.

Fee held out his hand to her instinctively, the way he had done for nearly every morning now, but at the sound of a whistle, Eyl changed directions. She fluttered onto Ciurin's shoulder and he murmured something to her.

Vexed for reasons he couldn't explain, Fee settled for glowering in Ciurin's general direction.

"That's his job, to set things to rights within his domain," Uriakin said from behind Fee. "People, animals, plants—all of it. He's just checking on her."

Fee turned to watch her continue to put away an astonishing amount of bacon and eggs. She seemed to have no problem with eating eggs at all. He didn't have the nerve to ask her about it, though. His jaw still worked. "He still didn't have to call her like that. She's not a pet."

Uriakin tilted her head. "Did he? But maybe you're right. After all, he definitely didn't like it when you called Marlaeda." She smirked. "Turnabout is fair play, and all that."

Fee squeezed his hands into fists.

"Don't worry about it, little guy," Uriakin said, grinning with very sharp teeth.

"I am taller than you."

"Don't worry about it, you great gawp of a boy." She pushed away her empty plate and threw her head back. "Hey, Ciurin! You done having your gab? I'm going to take the bird girl for a *real* flight."

Ciurin raised one heavily disbelieving brow. Eyl flapped her wings and shrieked.

"Yeah, I said it, what are you gonna do about it?" Uriakin said belligerently.

Eyl shot into the air.

Uriakin stood and, with a powerful flap of her own massive wings, took off after Eyl, streaking into the air like a comet.

Fee dragged his hands down his face and went to join Kai and Imani, who were listening to Marlaeda identify the flowers and bushes and mushrooms in the clearing.

"Oh, there you are, Fee, dear," she said, straightening from inspecting a toadstool with a red-and-white cap.

"What you said last night, about wild magic?"

Marlaeda smiled at him. "Yes? Did you speak to Eyl?"

"I did. You were right," he admitted. "And I don't know if it will work, but I'd like to try to learn."

"Good. I know you'll do very well, Fee." She turned back to the mushroom.

"Oh—is now a bad time?"

"Oh, no," she assured him. "But the fact of the matter is, I can't teach you how to use wild magic."

Fee's stomach sank. "What do you mean?"

"Exactly what I said," Marlaeda responded placidly.

"You can't tell me I have the ability and not explain how to use it!"

She shook her head. "It's not a thing one explains."

"Everything is explainable."

Marlaeda snorted. "Is that so?"

"Of course! Everything has a cause, a process. You just have to learn it," Fee insisted. "I can learn wild magic, my lady. Please just give me the chance."

She regarded him patiently. "Explain to me how you breathe."

"The lungs pull in air—"

"Not how it works. How *you*, specifically, breathe."

He fumbled for words. "Well, I expand my chest to pull air in and then release it."

"You can expand your chest without breathing in," she pointed out.

"It's how you mostly do it," Fee said through gritted teeth

"How do you do it when you're sleeping?"

"It's automatic."

"So, you have no control."

"No. It's controllable when I think about it, but otherwise, it's automatic. I don't notice."

Marlaeda just looked at him.

He swallowed.

She nodded, satisfied. "It's not a matter of 'do this, do that.' It's not instructions to follow. It's a matter of taking note of your magical rhythms already in place—already active. Only then can you learn to interrupt and control them. Ciurin will take you on his rounds today."

Fee choked. *Ciurin*? His eyes darted to the Forest Guardian, who regarded him impassively.

Marlaeda gave Fee a stern look one he could feel even through the opaque veil. "Listen to what he says."

"Let's go, boy," Ciurin said, amber eyes glittering. He wrapped his cloak around his shoulders, taking up his spear as if it weighed nothing.

Fee tugged on his own cloak and followed him out of the clearing, his heart somewhere in the vicinity of his boots.

THIRTY-EIGHT

EYL

Eyl was a big gyrfalcon, but next to Uriakin's wingspan, she felt dwarfed, and that made her testy. Testier. And Uriakin knew it, because she cut her a look that was far too knowing when she caught up without a struggle. "If you bite me, little eyass, I'll bite you back," she informed Eyl before pulling forward with another powerful flap.

Stung—she was clearly a full-grown falcon, *stop saying that*— Eyl shot after her, avoiding the wind from Uriakin's wings. They unfurled and covered an impressive length from tip to tip. Then the wind currents distracted Eyl and she became wholly concerned with navigating the air.

Her sharp eyes covered the trees below her avidly, noting the hollows and hummocks in the land, the small clearings and peculiar twists and dips in the river. In a few clearings, she spotted structures built into the ground, like a mound, or in the treetops, one large, extended treehouse between several groves. She caught the swift flash of motion several times, but nothing concrete, and nothing that tempted her into a dive.

Crossing the twisting river, she noted the change—the trees were not so brightly green as those on the west side of the river as moss and mistletoe clung to the duller, mottled branches. The river water collected in small pools on the east bank, turning a significant portion of the land into bog. Once, Eyl caught sight of a small raft poled by a small, wizened figure, but it slipped silently under the sheltering boughs out of sight. Aside from a few slight whiffs of smoke on the breeze, she might not have guessed that any other living figures dwelt in the Heartwood aside from squirrels, harts, rabbits, birds, and assorted insect life.

But no, that was not true. Life hummed from the forest, a plucked string's subtle vibration. The scent of life, bubbling up from the ground. Perhaps that was why the path had seemed so alien and frightening. Stripped of that essential quality, that personhood, the Heartwood became...Blackthorn. A place of fear and terror.

But Eyl couldn't fully enjoy her perusal of the forest because Uriakin kept getting in her way. She tried to ignore her, but the harpy almost purposefully put herself in her path. After the third such encounter, Eyl realized Uriakin was *herding* her whenever she tried to fly too far north.

Eyl glared at her and then, out of spite, dropped through the treetops and alighted on the branch of a redwood. To her surprise, Uriakin followed, dropping down to the limb and folding her massive wings to a manageable size. "I know you're ruffled," Uriakin said conversationally, "but Marlaeda asked me to keep an eye on you. This is me, keeping an eye."

Eyl kept her head gazing steadily away.

It was silent for a time. The breeze rustled the leaves and squirrels chittered farther off, disconcerted by the presence of two predators. A long, flat body walked by far below—a badger, Eyl's sharp eyes identified.

"It's not because I'm ashamed of him," Uriakin said suddenly.

Eyl cocked her head.

"Last night. It's...it's not because I'm ashamed of him."

She laced her wicked-looking talons together and pursed her lips. "He'd be happy to tell everyone, even though the merfolk might kick up a huge fuss and ostracize him. He's not worried, even though there'd be no way for him to escape their scorn, bound as he is to the river." She looked down at her talons and scowled. "It's everyone else I can't stand. Because there'll be jokes." She snorted. "How can a bird love a fish? Where will you live? Or worse, when are you going to eat him?" She sneered. "It's none of their bloody business is what it is." And then, under her breath, she added, "I can't let him do that. Not for me."

Fee's words from the night before came back to her. *Everybody has vulnerabilities.* Eyl twitched her tail.

"This isn't an apology, just so you know," Uriakin said, side-eyeing Eyl.

Eyl shrugged.

"It also doesn't mean I like you."

Eyl shrugged again. She hadn't believed they'd be buddies all of a sudden.

Uriakin leaned forward, her mouth splitting into a wide grin. "So what was going on with you and the boy last night?"

Eyl reared back and screeched. What had happened to none of your business?

"Yes, but that was me," Uriakin said, waving a taloned hand. "I'm your elder and entitled to my privacy. Now we're talking about you. So? You and the beanpole. Dish! What's going on there?"

She shut her beak with a snap. Nothing had happened! Eyl chittered and turned away.

"What do you mean, nothing happened?" Uriakin said, outraged. "Eyl!"

But she was already flying away.

CHAPTER

THIRTY-NINE

FEE

Fee couldn't say why the Forest Guardian unsettled him. It was just obvious that the man was a power—physical and magical and who knew what else. He was dangerous, to be sure.

But Marlaeda was very similar in Fee's magical perception. He wasn't wary of *her*.

Ah, Fee realized. He had grown used to viewing dangerous men as threats—anyone with more power than he, in fact, but those were usually men. His father, his older brothers, the soldiers who had beaten him bloody when he'd run the first time.

He deliberately pulled his mind away from that. *No matter what your instincts say*, he told himself firmly, *it's highly unlikely Ciurin will…*what? Hurt him? He remembered the lashings with rulers and canes when he'd been slow learning to read, and later, to pick up wizard magic. He flinched.

Be cruel, he finally decided. *It's highly unlikely Ciurin will act out of cruelty.* He was called 'guardian' and 'protector,' after all.

Reassured but still cautious, Fee followed the Forest Guardian, weaving in between tree trunks. Ciurin led him down to a dip in the land between two rowan trees. Fee scrambled down the embankment after him.

They were either in a dry riverbed or a sunken lane. The walls of the deep trench were studded with moss and rocks and roots, and the byway was just wide enough for two people to walk side by side, if one of them didn't have a huge rack of antlers.

Fee prudently stayed just behind and to the right of the Forest Guardian as they walked, since he was tall enough for Ciurin's antlers to be a problem. The wind whistled down over the bank to them, cold and frosty, bearing the scent of snow. He tightened his cloak, and his eyes widened as flakes drifted down over them, lightly dusting their clothes. He stuck his tongue out, remembering the few winters with his mother as she'd taught him to catch snowflakes.

Then he remembered whom he was with and closed his mouth with a snap.

Ciurin looked back at him. "Catch all you like, boy."

Fee stared owl-eyed at his back. How had he known?

A snowflake landed on Fee's nose, and he licked it off. Then he tilted his head back and opened his mouth, catching two heavy flakes straight away. It had been a comfortable temperature a minute ago. Where was the snow coming from?

"Up here," Ciurin rumbled. He led them up a small path in the side of the sunken lane and into a frosted, pine-scented world. Snow crunched under Fee's boots and danced in the crisp air that burned his lungs as they walked uphill.

"Where are we?" Fee asked. "How have we come so far so fast?"

"We're on the mountain." Ciurin trudged on with no other explanation.

"Mountain? There's a *mountain* in the forest?"

Ciurin didn't answer, just kept on.

Fee followed the imprints the guardian's boots left in the snow. He'd almost expected Ciurin to leave no trail at all or to walk along the top of the snow like a snowshoe rabbit. As he looked about him, Fee spied a flash of black nose and eyes in the white. A white fox crouched under an evergreen, watching them pass by.

He unconsciously held his breath to prolong the wonder of the moment, watching the fox until he could no longer turn his head to see it.

He could not have said how long they walked, but soon Ciurin ducked in between two more rowans—standing out among firs and evergreen pine—and Fee scrambled down another path into a green sunken lane. He could not have said if it was the same one or not. He shook the snow off himself, and they continued on.

Fee cleared his throat. "Where were we? Where are we going?"

"We were up the mountain. I'm doing my rounds."

"I haven't seen a mountain peak in Bla—in the Heartwood."

"The forest is a big place."

Fee coughed. "Marlaeda said you would be—well, obviously, *teaching* isn't the right word, but—helping me understand wild magic."

"Aye."

"I don't know what I'm supposed to be doing."

"Must you always be doing, boy?"

"Huh?"

"Sometimes you should focus less on doing, and more on abiding. Are you watching?"

"Watching what?"

Ciurin rounded on him. "This is one of the last places in the world still saturated with magic. Are you looking for it?"

Fee opened his mouth, but nothing came out.

"Keep your eyes open, boy. That's your talent, isn't it? See. Then you'll understand."

Up the next offshoot from the hollow way, Fee stepped into a fragrant, interconnected world. At first, the scenery overwhelmed him—green vines wrapped around stout trunks and flowers, and plants of every color and shade. Everything was dotted with dew, filling the air with heady perfume, and underneath that, Fee could smell the earthy scent of dirt and decomposing plant matter. But soon he began to sort out how the trees and flowers drew nutrients from the underbrush and dead plants, how they supported one another in the tangle of root systems and vines and stems that crisscrossed the area.

"What do they draw from?" Ciurin rumbled.

"The earth. Water. Air."

"And?"

"And…." Fee stared, blinking hard at the scenes around him. All at once, it came to him.

"Magic. Wild magic," he said aloud.

Ciurin set a hand on Fee's shoulder. "Think about the mountain. What made you notice the fox?"

"How did you know—"

"I know. What made you notice it?"

"The black of its nose. The spark in its eyes," Fee whispered. "Amidst all the white, it stood out."

"The spark of life. In the Heartwood, magic sustains just as much as air or water. Faefolk *need* magic to live. Close your eyes."

Fee did, warily.

"You're tense. Breathe."

Fee tried, but with his eyes closed, the hand on his shoulder was suddenly too heavy, too close. He couldn't stop the slow crawl of his shoulders up to his ears. His breaths started to come faster.

"Fee?"

He forced through his teeth, "Your hand." In the deep and sudden silence, Fee opened his eyes and hurried to say, "It's not personal—"

Ciurin dropped his hand from Fee's shoulder. "I apologize."

Fee swallowed, his shoulders slumping. "It's okay—"

"No," Ciurin said firmly. "You are within your rights to set your own boundaries. I should not have trespassed."

Fee clenched his teeth and tried not to think of how much he would've given for an adult's hand on his shoulder as an eight-year-old, before he had flinched at every hand that came too close to him. "It's stupid," he ground out. "I should—"

"It isn't."

"I should be able to handle it," he continued miserably. But it was all too easy for a heavy hand to become a crushing grip, a cruel twist to his elongated ears, a clout to the head or the eye.

Ciurin bent his head until they were directly eye to eye. "It is not your fault," he pronounced. His amber eyes nearly glowed, they were so bright—seeing through him, illuminating all the muck and mire inside, the hell that was Fee's past. "Healing happens at its own pace, but it does happen. Rest assured of that."

Fee couldn't see his thoughts—but he could feel the guardian spoke the truth.

Healing felt like an utterly foreign concept right now, but he clung to the intangible hope Ciurin offered like it was a lifeline. Fee nodded, swallowing down the thickness in his throat.

"Close your eyes again and breathe. Listen to the world. Listen to all the life, fed by magic. Follow it. Heartwood, last bastion of magic, teems around you."

Fee breathed in and out, listening.

"Picture it. Connecting. Feeding. Moving. Now open your eyes."

Fee did, blinking against the light.

"Do you see?"

"No."

"You sure?"

Fee hesitated. "I...."

"Keep looking, then."

Ciurin led the way through the lush landscape into another sunken lane, and Fee scrambled on behind. They paced for a few minutes, and then arose in a temperate orchard filled with apple trees, glistening with water. The air smelled as if a light spring shower had just fallen, coating the earth and reinvigorating the plants. Leaves rustled; Fee lifted his head to see something rush through the branches and pluck an apple from the boughs before disappearing. He couldn't say if it had been animal or faefolk.

Ciurin leaned his spear against an apple tree and plucked an apple. It was as if the golden fruit had fallen into his hand. "Have you figured it out yet?"

Fee glanced around the orchard and had to admit, "No."

Ciurin chewed the apple meditatively. "What do you see, when you look at others?"

"Secrets. Thoughts."

"A scene? A voice?"

Fee shrugged one shoulder. "Both, or neither. Sometimes just an impression."

"What do you see when you look at me?"

"I can't see your thoughts."

"But what *can* you see? What do you *know*?"

"You're…I can tell you're powerful."

"How?"

Fee spread his hands helplessly, swallowing hard. Before, this was the point where the instructor would start the caning or the palm lashing….

"What other things in the forest have similar power?"

"You. Lady Marlaeda." He thought about it some more. "The great oak in the clearing. The pavilion lights, a bit. And something to do with the river." He slowly turned in a circle. "The sunken lane. And…." He blinked.

"Do you see?"

And suddenly, he did.

WHEN AT LAST they emerged from the sunken lane back at the pavilion, Fee had to shake himself to get reoriented. His head was buzzing from the sights and sounds he had taken in, the warp and weft of the integrity of the Heartwood. When Ciurin pushed aside the drape and motioned him inside, Fee stepped in with a sigh of relief, expecting a respite from the world of magic.

But each of the people inside the pavilion glowed with a

powerful, inner light. Marlaeda and Ciurin shone like solid, silver beacons. For Imani and Kai, tangled silver snarls wound through them, tied in horrible, malformed knots.

"I see it," Fee blurted out. "I see the magic!"

FORTY

RILEN

"*Their trail goes into the forest,*" Rilen told Corbett, slowing his horse with his legs and seat as he returned to the group from his initial scouting journey.

"Fabulous," Corbett ground out.

Blackthorn Forest, scourge of Damaslar children's nightmares, sprawled ahead of them, dark and intimidating and impenetrable. The trees confused and hypnotized the lucky wanderers who were brave enough—or foolhardy enough—to venture past its borders, spitting them out right where they entered.

The less lucky disappeared without a trace.

"What? What did he say?" Marcus demanded.

Rilen raised an eyebrow at him.

Corbett turned in the saddle. "He said, the trail goes into Blackthorn."

A collective murmur flowed through the soldiers. Their horses, sensing the sudden tension in the air, stamped and sidled underneath their suddenly panicked riders.

"I'm not going in there," a soldier declared as they all stared at the dark wood. It might as well have been the pit of hell. "You can't make me, by Enid's teeth. I'm not giving my soul over to no ghost."

Rilen rolled his eyes. *Save them from superstitious Damaskmen.*

Corbett bared his teeth. "It's never no mind to me, but the trail goes into the treeline, so we go."

Parthas coughed, very pale under his spots. "Um, actually—"

"Oh, God, save me from wizards and their 'actually's,'" Corbett muttered.

"It's been proven that no one can go into the ghost forest and live!"

"Just because no one ever found them again doesn't mean they died," Rilen signed, smirking devilishly.

"No, they just got stuck in the ghost forest forever," Corbett shot back.

"Good way to escape creditors or angry spouses."

But no matter what, the Damask soldiers would not budge. "I'm not going to die!" one shouted. "Not for that! I'll cut down any man who will face me with a sword, but I won't have no ghost or beastie steal my soul, eat me from toes to eyeballs! No!"

The rest of the men muttered loudly behind the first dissenter, clearly in agreement.

"Are we about to have a mutiny?" Corbett pondered.

"I thought that was only on ships," Rilen said, raising a brow.

Nath, the nautical one, signed, *"Mutiny is an all-purpose term usually used aboard ship or among a military force. This qualifies."*

"Hmm," Corbett muttered. "Also, you've gotten much more fluent."

Nath smiled beatifically. "I like to know what's going on. *Some* people haven't realized the virtue in that."

The fact that Marcus could not command the men to march onward clearly galled him, but he seemed to have enough sense to realize that if he forced the issue, he would have a bloody rebellion on his hands. He bawled to call his troops to order while the trackers conferred.

"There are only two options, according to the stories," Rilen signed to Corbett. *"Either travelers wander a while in the forest and emerge*

exactly where they went in, or they are never seen again. Yes?" He tilted his head.

"Do I look like I know the legends of spook hollow or whatever they call it?" Corbett asked.

Nath nodded rapidly. *"That's right. Exactly right."*

"All right." Rilen gestured. *"So, either they come out right here, and we just need to sit and wait, or they will die in there."*

"I don't believe that," Corbett said, his eyes trained on the darkness beneath the shadow of the trees. "The boy's Damask, isn't he? He'd know the consequences of going in there. He'd have been spoon-fed the spook tales from birth, right? So he'd have to have been pretty desperate to go in there."

Nath said, "The ford for the Lliore River is a day and a half travel to the east."

"And they couldn't take that much time, not even to go around," Corbett said slowly. "He knew someone was on his tail."

Rilen shaded his eyes with his hands, surveying the area. *"The river goes through the forest very close to here. If I were desperate,"* he signed, *"I might take a gamble on following the river, sticking as close to the bank as possible. Even a magical forest can't change the way a river runs."*

"So. Three options," Corbett said flatly, his hands on his hips. "They emerge right here. They die in the forest, and we kiss our payment goodbye. Or option three: They pop out on the other side, right as rain."

"But why would they follow the river when they could follow the path?" Nath said.

Rilen and Corbett exchanged a look, and then eyed Nath. "What?" Corbett said.

"That path." Nath motioned to the forest. "I mean, maybe it hugs the river, I'm not sure, but—"

Corbett edged Nath away from the main body of soldiers. "We're going to have another look, make sure we got all the signs," he declared to the soldiers before spurring his horse forward.

"Okay, Nath," he said, once they were far enough away. "*What path?*"

Nath stared at them both. "I thought that's what you were talking about. Their trail leads right to it. You can't see it?"

"No," Corbett said. "I wouldn't have asked if I could, would I?"

Rilen stared at the bulk of the forest ahead of them. Any space between the trees was filled with underbrush of the most unwelcoming kind. He was hard-pressed imagining a dog fitting through, much less a person. *"Point to it."*

Nath pointed. "It's just there, between those trees. To be fair, it isn't a very broad path, but it does look as if...." He trailed off, watching their blank faces. "You really can't see it?"

They both slowly shook their heads.

"Their trail leads directly to it," Nath said again, like they had just missed it.

Rilen rode closer to the forest and traced the faint trail they had followed for days directly to where it disappeared at the treeline. Well, it didn't *disappear*—it just ran directly into a holly bush.

"How about this—can you see that holly bush?"

"What holly bush?" Nath asked.

Rilen's eyebrows shot up.

Corbett leaned back in his saddle. "Huh. Some tricky witchery happening here. I believe you, Nath," he said when Nath opened his mouth to protest. "But the fact remains that neither of us can see it. And those Damask fools sure won't like the idea of following a path none of them can see. But I think you're right, Rilen. Those kids must've found the path."

And the likelihood of them living just went up. Paths led places. Rilen nodded. *"My money's on them making it through the forest."*

"You and me both."

"So now what?" Nath asked.

"You want to *what*?" Marcus bellowed.

"Go around," Corbett said again, slow and loud. "Getting up there in age, are you? Would you like an ear trumpet? I'm sure Nath could rustle one up—"

Rilen pretended to check his tack to hide his huge grin.

"I *heard* you the *first* time," Marcus ground out. "What do you mean by it?"

"I always bank on the most unlikely occurrence," Corbett said smoothly. "I think it's possible to make it through the forest."

"Not one of my men will set foot in Blackthorn," Marcus said disgustedly.

"They won't have to. We've confirmed the boy and his friends are on foot. If we ride hard and hug the forest's perimeter, then we can set up watch where the river emerges and wait."

"We risk losing them if they emerge here!"

"So we split your squad." Corbett shrugged.

Marcus appeared to consider this for a moment, hesitating. Then he said, with great declaration, "We only have one wizard!"

"So?"

"We would not be able to communicate with each other or His Grace."

"Actually," Nath said suddenly, "I think I could do the scry spell."

They all turned to look at Nath.

"That is, I watched Parthas do it several times. Doesn't look too hard," Nath said easily.

"You haven't the training for magic," Marcus said scornfully.

Corbett opened his mouth to snarl at the man, but Nath said apologetically, "Actually, I did two years of University in Cadruissau, and magical principles were one of the foundational basics they offered. I didn't take anything but the core principles because I wasn't interested."

Rilen grinned. That was their curious protégé. Doing whatever he liked simply because it caught his fancy.

"Let's see it, then," Marcus sneered.

Ten minutes later, the group stared into a flickering scrying dish, borrowed from Parthas's saddlebags.

"Well?" Marcus demanded of the wizard. "Did it work?"

Parthas gulped. "Uh, the High Wizard isn't answering…."

"I didn't call him," Nath said peaceably. "Didn't want to disturb him, since he doesn't know me. Instead of the two-way scry, I just did the traditional one-way perspective. I scryed Jorgen."

Marcus bent over the bowl. The image of his lieutenant coalesced. As they all watched, Jorgen dipped his hand into a saddlebag. Unfortunately for him, it wasn't one of his.

How very interesting, Rilen thought, stifling his smirk.

Marcus turned the air blue with curses.

"Well, this proves it." Corbett dusted his hands. "We split up."

As they left to set up camp a ways away from the soldiers, Corbett said, "Nath, how *did* you do that?"

"It wasn't that hard," Nath said. "I'm just good at noticing things."

Rilen signed, *"Like the path?"*

"Yep."

"Not hard, my arse," Corbett muttered with a grin. "We've got a budding magician on our hands."

Rilen was inclined to agree.

"Are you going to do anything else besides stare at me?" Imani worried at her lower lip.

It was early evening. She and Fee were seated outside the pavilion, and he had been studying the way the magic flowed around her for much of the afternoon. Because, though she and Kai both appeared to be a snarl of silver, Imani's magic functioned. Kai's did not.

"For now," Fee said. "I'm trying to understand what I'm seeing. What are you doing?"

Imani held up the ball of yarn and wooden hook. "Marlaeda showed me how to crochet." She frowned. "It's not going very well. I can't stop bunching it up."

"Because you skipped a stitch, dear," Marlaeda said calmly. She pointed out the mix-up and helped Imani unravel her work until she reached the missed stitch.

Fee rubbed his eyes. They ached from finding the knack of seeing the inherent magic in things—because the Heartwood was chock full of magic. Marlaeda and Ciurin glowed like stars. But he had to keep going. Now that he could see the magic patterns, he had the key to reversing what Aedelbras had done to them—if only he could discover how to turn it. He thought back to his and Ciurin's conversation that afternoon by the bank of a stream.

Ciurin picked up five smooth stones from the stream and dropped them back into the slow-moving water with small plops. "Do some magic," he said. "Wizard magic," he added, when Fee started to object.

Fee pulled his notebook out of his pocket. "What should I do?"

"Whatever you like. It doesn't matter. I want to watch."

After a short moment of thought, Fee sharpened his pencil and wrote down a relatively simple spell for finding a water source. He knew which way the spell would indicate; they were right by the brook. But he wrote down the runes and infused them with magic and watched as the rune on the rudimentary compass he drew glowed.

He looked up at Ciurin.

"Were you watching?" the guardian asked, amber eyes fixed on him.

"I thought you were going to watch."

"I saw what I needed to see. Did you?"

Fee looked down at his runes. "I feel like 'yes' is the wrong answer...."

"Do it again. Watch."

Fee took a deep breath and did it again.

It took three more tries before he finally caught what Ciurin wanted. When he wrote the runes, infused them with magic, he used his magic sight. And watched as magic from the environs around them was sucked into his spell to fuel it as the runes glowed. He cut the connection, and the magic fled.

He stared at the empty runes in his notebook blankly. Why did he feel like a thief?

"Wizard magic is not inherently evil," Ciurin said, startling him. "Neither is wild magic intrinsically good. Water is both life-giving and destructive. Much the same. But when you leave the Heartwood, you will see how empty the world is on a magical level. And you will see why you are so unique. A child who can use magic from both sides of his heritage."

Fee stared at him with wide eyes.

"I am old and strong, here in the heart of my power. But you cannot

teach me to do what you have just done." He motioned to the notebook. Then he picked up a twig from the ground and set it on his palm. Fee watched as magic flowed—not into the twig—but into him, and then into the twig. The twig slowly lifted off his palm, spun one, two, three rotations in the air, and then stopped, the tiny leaf on its end pointing the way towards the brook.

"I don't suppose asking you how you did that would be helpful," Fee said shakily.

"Wild magic depends on the amount of magic you can call to your aid and where your natural talents lie, as well your will to direct it. From the way your talents have tried to express, I'd say much of your talent lies with the mind. My area of expertise is this forest. It is why I was named Guardian." The twig fell back into Ciurin's palm. "Were you watching?"

"Yes."

"Then tell me the difference between human and faefolk magic."

Fee concentrated. "I...called the magic into my runes. You called magic into you and then put it in the twig."

"Yes. What else?"

Fee tried not to feel like a failure. "I'm not sure."

Ciurin lowered his head so that their eyes were at the same level. "You know. Think."

Fee stared into his eyes, wracking his brain. Then Kai's bitter words from days ago struck him like a rock: "Locking up magic deep within the earth, reducing it to a power source to be turned on and off at leisure, damned an entire race."

"The Sundering," he whispered.

Ciurin smiled, hard and bitter.

Fee dropped his eyes. "We did steal from you."

"Humans stole from the world, and one day, they will have to reap what they have sown," he said. "But you are a child of two worlds, even if you do not yet feel like you have a foot in both. But this is why you are unique: You can unlock the magic that human wizards have hidden away."

"You mean, all the magic that's been—dammed up?"

"Yes. The Sundering locked most of the world's magic away, but it also parted the connection between magic at large and faefolk. No faefolk creature can use magic like that." He pointed at Fee's notebook. "Even if you tried to teach us."

"Humans created their own runic language to handle magic," Fee said, turning his notebook over in his hands. "And when a human uses it, it's like a...a secret knock to open the door that holds magic at bay for everyone else."

Ciurin nodded. "Exactly."

Fee smiled. That nod of approval meant more to him than all the years in his father's house.

Watching Imani continue along her line of stitches, Fee sighed. "I have to keep going back and forth to just try to understand the mechanism of it, from the natural world to the faefolk to those spells, which are a part of you and yet not, and then between you and Kai...." Fee pulled on his ear, cracking his neck. "It's a lot."

"Here," Kai said. He handed Fee a sheet of parchment, with crudely drawn glyphs across it. "The symbols Aedelbras cast. It is as accurate as I can remember."

Dodging the three bees that came out of Kai's mouth, Fee scanned the sheet eagerly and bit back the thread of disappointment when it didn't reveal any secret mysteries. "Well, most of a binding spell is here, as well as calling up magic with no boundaries, so it's about what we thought," he said. "This confirms it. Thank you, Kai."

"That's not all."

"What?"

Kai held out a plate of food. "You were so buried in your own world, you didn't stop to eat."

"Oh." His stomach growled loudly as the food's aroma reached his nose. "You're right. Thank you." He rubbed his eyes and fell onto the food, trying not to shove it into his mouth all at once.

"You still think too much like a wizard."

Fee swallowed the bite in his mouth. "What do you mean?"

Kai motioned towards the notes he had made in his notebook. "Searching for your right words, loopholes. You seek to undo what has been done like Imani unknots her yarn." Flies buzzed from his mouth. "You think of the spell as a thing that functions. It doesn't. It's not something you can fix."

But I have to try, Fee thought as Kai walked away. *Otherwise, there's no chance for you and Eyl at all.*

When he was scraping the bottom of the bowl, Eyl and Uriakin fluttered down from the sky as the last lights of day disappeared. Fee watched the gyrfalcon's threads shift and writhe. *They move when she shifts*, Fee realized, rubbing his tired eyes. *Do they stretch? Morph?*

Uriakin bopped him upside the head. "No ogling, lover boy," she said, teeth bared in a grin, and he turned beet red.

CHAPTER

FORTY-TWO

EYL

"Hey, clothes right here," Uriakin called as Eyl emerged, two-legged and sweating from the shift. With a trembling hand, she took them and slid them on slowly, trying to control the shakes in her limbs. It had felt like forever—well, it always did, but this time, even more so as the change had happened. She had almost panicked, but the process had pulled her through to the other side.

How long before she got stuck again?

When she came around the tree trunk adjusting her tunic, Uriakin smirked and chanted under her breath, "Eyl and Fee, sittin' in a tree, k-i-s—"

Eyl elbowed her as hard as she could.

"*Oww!*" The harpy reeled, clutching her chest.

Eyl rubbed her elbow. "What happened to no teasing?"

"That was *then*—" Uriakin's talons lengthened as she raised a hand.

Eyl cocked a fist.

"Uriakin," Ciurin boomed from across the clearing. "Be civil while our guests remain with us."

The harpy made a face and lowered her hand. "All *right*." Uriakin's gold stare turned back to Eyl. "Truce, I suppose?"

"You keep your mouth shut about Fee; I'll keep *my* mouth shut." Eyl's significant glance towards the river indicated about what.

Uriakin nodded and looked away, but not before Eyl caught the glimmering of respect. "Fine. Little eyass."

Eyl just about spat fire.

"Eyl, come and eat," Imani said hurriedly. "Fee can see wild magic now, did you know?"

Eyl swiped a hand over her sweaty forehead. "What?"

"Ciurin took me around the forest through sunken lanes," Fee said, looking at her through his lashes, his pointed ears red. Yes, he had heard Uriakin, *ugh*. "I think they allow you to traverse different sections of the forest—although I think that would bend space-time, so I have no idea how the magic would work— wizards have been trying to come up with a workable teleportation spell for ages and nothing's ever succeeded that we know of."

"'That we know of'?" she repeated, inhaling two rolls and a slab of ham.

"Well, some have tested their ideas, but they've never reappeared. That we know of." He shrugged and smiled. "So, maybe it worked, maybe it didn't?"

Imani shuddered. "Ugh. That's horrible."

"That's why wizards are so careful about their terms and parameters and codicils in their spells—so many things can go wrong."

"Better to not interfere with forces they do not understand," Kai muttered.

"You went around with Ciurin," Eyl prompted, trying to rein in the conversation.

"Yes." Fee filled her in on his new findings and understanding, and what he had been trying to accomplish.

"Do you need to stare at me?" she said, draining the large mug of tea in front of her.

"I'm working on it. Still formulating ideas. I'll let you know if I need you to do anything special. Imani, can you call up fire so I can compare your magic to Kai's?"

Imani became uncharacteristically still. "I-I can't."

"Can't? What's the matter?"

She wrung her hands. "It just won't…it just…I can't make it work. I can't."

Eyl put a hand on her shoulder. "It's okay. Breathe. What about banking the fire? Can you do that?"

Imani nodded rapidly. "Yes. That works." She and Kai sat by Fee, and Eyl moved to Marlaeda, who was stacking dishes.

"Have seconds, dear," Marlaeda said. She pulled a cloth off the leftovers, and the scent of potatoes and gravy filled the air.

Eyl thanked her gratefully as she tucked in.

"Of course, I am sure you and Uriakin ate while exploring, but you need the nutrients."

Eyl glanced over her shoulder. "Lady Marlaeda, has something gone wrong with Imani? Is her magic…I don't know, degrading?"

"No, it isn't a magical problem," Marlaeda said. "It's a traumatic side effect. She told me what happened during your escape."

Eyl's stomach twisted. "We told her it wasn't her fault—"

Marlaeda nodded. "Yes. These things take time to sort out between body and mind. Don't push her. With time and distance, she will probably heal just fine on her own. But we can't rush it."

We can't rush anything, Eyl thought dismally, *except my shapeshifting and my need to go north. Those two things are powder kegs, and the match inches closer every day.*

FORTY-THREE

FEE

"Take a break," Eyl said softly.

Fee opened his eyes—he hadn't realized he'd closed them. "Don't have time for a break," he said around a thick tongue. Dawn would come soon.

"Sit there. I'll get you some water." Eyl stood up and moved back towards the pavilion, and Fee tried to pretend he hadn't seen the flicker of black despair in her eyes.

When everyone else had gone to bed, Eyl had suggested they go down to the river and sit while he worked. He had agreed, and there by the water, he thought he had found the end to her tangle of threads. He thought, with that end, he could untangle her spell. Eyl had given him permission to try. So he had looked at the threads, the way Ciurin had shown him, and, using a mix of wizard runes, fledgling wild magic, and instinct, had started to unpick the tangle of magic wrapped around Eyl. He could see her two forms when he looked at her just right, the gyrfalcon never far away, just resting beneath the skin, and the silver spell wound around them both like the thorniest snarl of twine. But his slow pluck and tug and pull barely made any difference over the hours, and it left him sweaty and breathless from the effort.

It wasn't enough. It wouldn't ever be enough. The strands

were fused in places, melted together with the weight of nine years and daily shapeshifting behind them. He probably could not even do better than a tiny faefolk child, unpicking the mess. His skill was not up to the task.

He hated to say it, but there seemed to be no way to uncouple her from the magic that had changed her so irrevocably in time.

"Here." Eyl handed him a flask of water. "What do you see?" she asked as he sipped. "When you look at me?"

"The threads are deeply entrenched. Soldered, even."

"Oh," she whispered. She flexed her fingers in her lap as the light above the eastern trees lightened from night velvet to dark indigo.

He rubbed gritty eyes. Had they really sat here all night?

"Too late, then. But maybe Kai, or Imani…." She trailed off, writing off her own hope with one short phrase.

Fee dropped his head into his hands. The taste of failure was bitter on his tongue. The defeat sat in his stomach like lead, making him faintly nauseous. The one thing he had wanted to give her, freedom, a day in the sun, dashed. No chance, no choice….

Fee blinked, then looked at her again.

He had tried to pick apart the snarl of magic around her, the great Gordian knot that gave her another form daily. But it was too massive, and probably even if he had managed, there would be no escape from some kind of side effect. One didn't undergo nine years of magic without some lingering trait.

But what if he didn't remove it?

Kai's words came back to him: *You think too much like a wizard.*

"Fee?" Eyl leaned forward, plucking the flask out of his hands. "Are you all right?"

He set his hands on her shoulders, gripping her. "Just…stay still." He closed his eyes again, reaching out with the nascent part of him that Saw. He had to do more than See now. He had to *act*.

I have wild magic.

I have power over the mind.

I can see her two natures.

Wild magic is all about talent and will. My will. Eyl's will.

I want her to be free to choose.

He opened his eyes to see her human self and her bird self. *I want to bridge the gap. I want her to use her own will and self-determination.*

Her magic.

Her change.

Her choice.

Fee ground his teeth together as his head ached with the strain, but he threw every bit of his will that he could muster into the stretch.

I want her to be able to choose.

With a snap, the magic released.

FORTY-FOUR

EYL

Eyl watched Fee's face crease in concentration. His hands on her shoulders gripped her tightly, hot points of connection in the cool, pre-dawn air.

She had the urge to bite her lip but didn't. That would be visible hope and she wasn't strong enough for that.

Why did you bring me all this way? she thought fiercely to the silence. *What was it* for?

She ground her teeth together instead, waiting for Fee to open his eyes and tell her that it was no use. That she had been entwined in the enchantment for too long.

But his hands grew hotter to the point of burning. She heard—or maybe *felt*—something pop, like a cork coming out of a bottle.

A wave of force blew them both backwards. Eyl rolled and fell as Ev had taught her, landing on a soft patch of moss. She picked herself up, scanning the area. Fee was on his hands and knees, blood flowing from his nose. "Fee! Fee, are you all right? What happened?" She gripped his shoulders, feeling him shake.

He coughed. "Well, that did it, I think."

She poured water from the flask onto her handkerchief and dabbed at the blood on his mouth and chin. "Did what?"

"I—Well, I'm not sure, but…."

Her hand faltered on his lips.

He took hold of her wrist and slowly pulled the handkerchief from her hand, mopping up the rest of his blood. Then he pinched his nose shut. "I tink dat stobbed it," he said thickly.

"The blood?"

He had the temerity to roll his eyes.

"Well, tell me exactly what you *do* mean, and you can go ahead and let go of your nose while you do it; I'm not going to try to guess what you're saying."

Fee let go of his nose and wiped another smear of blood from his face. "I couldn't fix his spell. But I think—I *hope*," he corrected himself, "I gave you a choice."

Eyl started to shake. "You think—really? You really, truly, think?"

"Hope." He pinched his nose again, but his free hand laced their fingers together. "I hope."

Eyl squeezed his hand tightly, turning without thought towards the lightening sky in the east. "Well, we'll know soon enough," she whispered.

Her hand curled around Fee's, needing an anchor in the world to hold fast to. His bloody nose finally stopped flowing, and he let go of his nose as the sky turned indigo, then cerulean, a robin's egg blue, then blue-gray, and finally burned with light along the horizon.

Hope was such an ephemeral, delicate thing, something she had hung on to by the tips of her fingernails. Eyl wasn't sure what she would do if it were crushed.

If you never heard me before, she prayed silently, *hear me now. Hear me now. Please.*

The sky washed with brilliant bands of orange, ink, and gold above the trees, the lining of clouds overhead catching flame. The seconds ticked by, and muscle memory made her twitch, demanding she throw off her clothes and take to the skies. She shuddered, closing her eyes.

"Let me stay," she chanted under her breath. "Let me stay me. Let me be a girl. Let me see the sun."

Fee put his other hand over both of hers. "You've got to open your eyes for that."

Swallowing twice past the lump in her throat, Eyl opened her eyes, wincing at the brightness as the sun crested fully. She got to her feet and stared around her at the light illuminating the river and the wildflowers on its bank in every shade, the trees so green above them, her own hands, pale as frost because they hadn't seen the sun in nine years. Then she looked at Fee, at the sun lighting his red hair ablaze as he bit his lip.

"I'm still me," Eyl whispered through hands pressed to her mouth. Then, louder, "I'm still me!" She shrieked and spun around, throwing her arms wide as the bobbing flowers accompanied her joy.

Eyl ran to Fee and clasped his hands. He barely got his feet moving before her tug pulled him in a circle, whirling. "I can't—I can barely believe it!" she said. "I'm fixed!"

"You can change back and forth at will now."

"No. I don't want to change ever again. It's sunny! It's morning! I'm here in the day and I'm never leaving again!" Eyl yelled gleefully. Then she threw her arms around Fee's neck—and abruptly found herself two inches from his lips.

She hesitated for a moment, but the wild euphoria in her blood took over. She pressed an enthusiastic, unpracticed kiss to his lips.

Fee froze with his arms around her.

After a second, Eyl pulled back, staring at his wide, blue eyes. "Was that all right? I'm sorry—"

"No." He shook his head. "Don't be sorry." He slowly brought his hands up to cup her face, staring at her like he had never seen her before. He leaned towards her, and then said, "Is *this*—?"

"Oh, for goodness's sake." She laughed and closed the distance. Their mouths came together in a warm caress. The blood in her veins fizzed and zipped, her head pounding so hard, she thought it might beat its way out of her chest.

"I like you so much," he breathed. "I love the way you chew me out. Your determination. Your grit. I can't think half the time around you."

Eyl burst out laughing, her smile so wide, it hurt. "You like me? Even after I threatened you with the knife?"

"That was something, all right. I liked it. And elbowing Uriakin for my honor, too."

"Oh, really?" She blushed and covered her face with a hand. "Not my finest moment—"

"Please," he said. "It was magnificent." Then he kissed her again, brushing his lips against hers deeper this time. The taste of him made her shiver.

"You know, this would be easier if I picked you up," he murmured against her lips.

"Hey," she objected, laughing and slapping his arm. "I draw the line at poking fun at my height."

"Not poking fun. I think you're the perfect size. Perfect in every way."

She shot him a look, her cheeks hot. "Maybe not just now. I'm hungry. And I want to tell Imani and Kai."

He smiled. "Let's go, then."

She led them back to the pavilion. He held her hand all the way.

FORTY-FIVE

EYL

Eyl burst into the pavilion and threw herself on Imani's pallet, laughing uncontrollably. Imani sat up, rubbing her eyes. "Huh? What—Eyl?"

"It's daylight!" Eyl shrieked. "Fee did it! I never have to be a bird again!"

Imani's eyes grew comically large and her mouth dropped open. "He did it?"

Eyl nodded vigorously, her hair flying. Imani screamed and threw her arms around Eyl, squeezing as hard as she could. Laughing, Eyl pulled a befuddled Kai into their hug. "Free, free," she chanted. "Free! And he can do it for you, too. Can't you, Fee?"

She looked over her shoulder at Fee, who hovered at the opening of the pavilion. She blushed again, remembering those kisses. His words. *Perfect in every way.* She shivered all over again. It was almost too much. Too much goodness at once. She was in overload.

"Yes, I think so, after I sleep a bi—ooof!" Fee let out a rush of breath as Imani launched herself at him. He caught her—barely. "You did it! You're a hero!" Imani exclaimed. "That's so amazing!"

"Goodness, don't deafen the poor boy," Marlaeda said wryly, appearing with a tray of food.

"Marlaeda, Fee did it!"

"I knew he could," Marlaeda said fondly, patting Fee's cheek, and then there was another round of wild hugging, which lasted until Uriakin and Ciurin's arrival. Then everyone settled down to breakfast.

"No more feathers, no more feathers," Eyl muttered to herself as she gorged herself on food. No more stick-thin body. No more broken bones. No more pain.

"You're still bird-kin, no matter your shape," Uriakin said matter-of-factly, plopping down beside Eyl.

"Really? *Now* I belong to the bird club?" Eyl said sarcastically.

"You know what makes you bird-kin? We all have claws, even if you can't see them. Don't forget about yours, little eyass."

Eyl didn't answer because she planned on doing exactly that as soon as she possibly could. She stretched her hands up to the golden sky and smiled. She was free.

"So what are we going to do now?" Imani asked.

"You don't have to do anything if you don't want to," Marlaeda said. "You are welcome to stay as long as you like."

Eyl's good mood depressed somewhat as the pull inside her reverberated like a plucked string. "I can't. I'd love to stay. It's so peaceful here. But I still feel the compulsion pulling me north." *I have to face my past.* "But everyone else—"

"I'm going with you," Fee said, his tone final.

"I can't ask you to come."

"I know. That's why I'm offering freely." He took her hand.

Her smile wobbled, but she returned the pressure.

"We're going with you too!" Imani insisted. "Kai and I talked it over yesterday."

"We will see the journey through to the end," Kai affirmed.

Ciurin said, "The Heartwood is a place of refuge and safety for all faefolk. You can always return here. The path will show you the way."

Imani cast a wistful look around at the pavilion. "That's nice. I'll miss this place."

Truth be told, Eyl would too. It was peaceful here. And her stomach churned at the unknown road ahead of her. She swallowed. "I bet it wouldn't hurt to stay one more day, would it?"

"If you can stand it, we can wait a day." Fee nodded.

Marlaeda beamed. "Yes. You both need to rest and eat and enjoy this day of freedom. Then you all can set off on your journey tomorrow morning."

Eyl said humbly, "Thank you."

"My dear. It is no hardship at all."

AFTER BREAKFAST, the exhaustion caught up with them, and Fee and Eyl crashed. He had been awake for nearly twenty-four hours, and she was about the same. Nine nocturnal years would not be overcome in a few days.

Eyl stumbled into the pavilion, yawning so hard, her jaw cracked. Fee followed her in. She picked up her quilt, hesitated, then came over to him. "Do you...?"

He scooted over on his pile of blankets and made room for her. She cuddled next to him, and he wrapped his arm around her, still amazed that she could do this with the sun up. That he would let her do it at all.

She cupped his face, touching his scar. "I always hoped, but I never believed. Now...it's like a dream has come to life and I don't know how to feel."

"About which part?"

"All of it," she admitted.

"That's okay," Fee mumbled. "All you have to do now is sleep."

She put her head on his shoulder. His hand stroked through her hair, soothing them both. "Are you going to grow your hair out now?"

Her hand clenched on his chest. Is your grieving or vengeance satisfied, he meant. "No. Not yet."

"S'okay," Fee whispered, brushing the short strands. "We have time."

***

"You move like a fish," Ev says appreciatively. "Good job!"

Eyl is small and dog-paddling around the ornamental pond in her chemise. Ev has stripped to his waist. If they're caught, they'll be in big *trouble, but it's so* hot.

"Can you swim a whole lap?" Ev asks.

Eyl isn't sure because that's far, but she's game to try. "Will you swim it with me?" she asks.

"Always! We'll start on three," Ev says. "One...two...." Then he throws himself into his strokes before he calls three.

"Ev!" Eyl objects, but she launches herself forward. She can catch him. Of course she can catch him. She—

Something under the water seizes her ankle and pulls her down, down into a dark void.

Eyl hears her *voice. Everything I do, I do for you, my son.*

It's all *for you.*

Eyl opens her mouth, inhales water the color of blood.

***

Eyl woke, her heart hammering in her chest. She stared at Fee's sleeping face and tried to get her breathing under control.

No, I can't grow my hair out yet. Not until the past is reckoned with.

FORTY-SIX

Nicanor resisted the urge to drag his hand down his face in exasperation. Instead, he stroked his beard and assumed a wise, pondering façade as the Damaslar generals surrounded the king, urging him to agree to the Altesians' demands.

The Altesians had a fresher army and the high ground, to be sure, but they didn't put much stock in wizards. This wouldn't even be a discussion if only his brat had stayed put—! Then he'd have all his magical assets and be able to crush the Altesians, fresh army or no. Nothing trumped magic for power.

"High Wizard," the king broke in, "what do you think, eh? Shall we turn and slink away or fight like men?"

His advisors all murmured hasty objections, like shepherds trying to herd one stupid sheep away from the edge.

It wasn't that His Majesty wasn't intelligent, Nicanor reminded himself dutifully, aware of the homage he owed to his liege lord. It was that the king was very…single-minded. An accomplished duelist and proclaimed fighter, the king would win any encounter he entered, Nicanor had no doubt. If only the other side would challenge him to single combat.

No, His Majesty Caldair, King of Damaslar and its

surrounding principalities, demesnes, and unincorporated city states, would trounce his opponent in an instant. But when armies collided, it was different. Two armies could not fight like duelists. Well, they could, but only if you wanted to lose great swaths of your fighters in one fell swoop. No, one needed tactics to conduct warfare and for that, the king needed generals. And Nicanor, of course.

He often wondered what sort of a king they would have had if His Majesty had had a brother. Damaslar custom dictated that the king had the prerogative to choose the next king to rule after him from among his heirs. Naturally, many brothers did not care for this, so there were frequently cases of fratricide among Damaslar princes. Murder, a trait that you could be hung for, was seen a little differently when one was royal. Also, one needed an heir, and usually, the fratricide offender ensured all other candidates were…not available.

Nicanor had no doubt that if King Caldair had possessed a brother, or even some bastard siblings, he would not be ruling now. The old king had died young of a wasting sickness with only Caldair to inherit the crown. And so far, Caldair had fathered only one boy among a great span of daughters. The crown prince stared across the table at his father, an ill-concealed look of frustration on his face.

If Caldair were wise, he would look out for patricide.

Or maybe he wouldn't, since he counted on his generals and advisors to be wise for him. And truth be told, they were getting a bit tired of Caldair, too.

"Your Majesty," Nicanor said smoothly, "I would suggest sending a delegation to the Altesians, inviting them to peace talks."

The king frowned. "Rather go down fighting."

Oh, we'd all rather, if it could be arranged for just you to die, Nicanor thought. *Unfortunately, we need the army.* "Your Majesty, right now, I am working on a plan to turn the situation to our advantage. I beg you will give me a little time before I reveal all.

Offer peace talks. Then I will explain my plan. Peace talks are only that: talks."

The king brightened. "Ah! Quite! I like that. Yes, by all means, send someone to arrange peace talks." He went out with his fighting men and generals as Nicanor slowly stacked his parchment in front of him. When would Marcus find the experiments? The last message he had received had been several days ago....

Nicanor found Crown Prince Reinald at his elbow, smiling. "Thank you for your wise words, High Wizard. Father only sees total victory or unconditional surrender, nothing in between."

"The king means well, Your Highness. But that is why one must have councilors who help see beyond your field of vision and expertise."

"Well, that's one way to put it." Reinald smirked. He was a fair youth, nearly eighteen, with strength in his arms and canny eyes. He crossed his arms over his chest, the large ring he wore on his finger catching the light. "He doesn't understand that there are subtler ways to go about things than letting two men bash themselves to death with swords. More advantageous ways."

"Subtler ways indeed, Your Highness."

Nicanor privately thought that the prince might have had more skill in subtlety as well if he had had a bevy of brothers upon whom to sharpen it. Then he would know not to wear a poisoner's ring quite so openly. The Damaslar court, while grown lax in recent years, still had minds that would recognize such items immediately.

Like Nicanor.

He decided to dangle some bait before the boy. "Even subtlety does not always get the job done. One wants a strategy that will accomplish one's goals and vanquish one's enemies all at the same time."

"Yes, exactly!" Prince Reinald exclaimed. "You are a man who understands strategy, Wizard Nicanor. When to employ bold attacks and when to use precision and discernment. Do you have a strategy in mind? You spoke of a plan...."

"Would Your Highness like to return with me to my tent? I can explain in more detail."

"Lead the way." The prince accompanied Nicanor as he left and walked through the encampment.

Nicanor pushed aside his tent flap and gestured the prince inside. Once the server had set out a flask of wine and had departed, Nicanor said, "Your Highness, very soon, I believe we will have a magical means to turn the tide of this war...as well as see a clearer path towards our...goals. I merely wait for confirmation that my soldiers have obtained it." *And they'd better hurry up, by bloody Perrin and the ten stars of Mar*, Nicanor thought.

"Magical means, you say?" The prince raised an eyebrow.

"Yes. I am a firm believer in magic. It is clean, traceless, leaves no trails or stains. And it always accomplishes its task."

"I would *love* to hear more." The prince lifted the wine flask and poured them both a cup of wine.

Nicanor kept his eyes fixed on Reinald's ring.

FORTY-SEVEN

EYL

"That's it?" Kai asked, touching his throat. No creature or insect spilled from his mouth.

"I think so," Fee said. After sleeping until lunchtime, Fee had woken and offered to give Kai the same choice. At least this time, he hadn't had a nosebleed. Eyl had been ready to thrust handkerchiefs and waterskins at him, but thankfully, there hadn't been a need this time.

Kai shuddered, his hands opening and closing. "I...I...."

Imani beamed. "It worked!"

Kai's eyes squeezed tightly shut. Then he threw his head back and let out a whooping laugh, screaming to the treetops with delight. And nothing happened.

"Like I told Eyl," Fee said, after Kai had finished hollering, "I didn't undo the spell, really. Just gave you control of the magic. If you wanted to conjure a swarm of wasps, you could."

"Really?" he said, intrigued. "So it is my will that controls the magic?"

"Yes, it—"

"Please, no more magical theory." Eyl groaned. Not on today, the best day of her life.

"What about something else?" Marlaeda suggested.

"Like what?" Imani asked.

"Wonderful! I'm glad you asked." Marlaeda beamed. She held out a basket from behind her back. "Let's go. Ciurin, get the hamper."

"Go where?" Fee glanced at Eyl. Her eyes widened in excitement.

"Come and see."

THE BASKETS WERE FOR BLACKBERRIES. Marlaeda led them to a meadow full of sunshine and summer breezes, and the thicket of blackberry bushes fairly burst with what were probably the last berries of the season. Though maybe seasons weren't as decided in the Heartwood as they were other places. Marlaeda handed out the baskets and let them loose on the blackberries after passing around a jar of ointment. "Smear that on your faces and ears and necks, dears, especially you, Eyl. The sun is not always kind. We don't want to roast you!"

Marlaeda followed her own advice and rubbed the cream onto her hands and arms. She also handed Eyl a scarf to shield her from the sun. Absently, Eyl took it and draped it over her shoulders. The rest of her was wholly absorbed in the blackberry meadow, humming with life.

The world was so *colorful.* To see the true beauty of the shades in nature, you needed sunlight. Bright, beautiful, golden sunlight. Not moonlight that bled all but the very barest of color from the flowers and plants all around. Eyl had such a hard time looking away from all the flowers, their blooms open and upturned towards the sun, glorious and splendid. She wanted to soak it all up, imbed it in her skin, her lungs. To hold the color there forever.

She had seen color as a gyrfalcon, of course, but birds' eyes were different. She had seen *more* as a bird, a whole schema of color and motion that had had reinforced how alien she had felt in her bird's form at first, how strange and frightening the world had become.

But today, the whole world was hovering on the last edge of summer, a perfect halcyon day of endless possibility. Winter would arrive—of course it would, it must, even in a magical wood —but for today, everything was perfect.

Eyl grinned up at Fee and his fair skin. She dipped her fingers in the jar. The salve smelled of roses. "Bend down and I'll do your ears."

Fee complied, bending down to her height and letting her smear the ointment over not just his ears, but his face and neck, too. "Now your turn."

Eyl handed the jar over and let him coat the back of her neck. He made sure to run a finger under the edge of her tunic's neck and get the backs of her ears as well. She bit her lip at the contact. "You didn't have to do that. I have the scarf."

"You still want the salve. I've had bad sunburns. They're awful." He handed the jar off to Kai, who proceeded to perform the same duty for Imani.

Eyl draped the scarf over her head in a light, airy hood and wrapped the ends around her neck. Then she took Fee's hand and they descended upon the blackberry thickets. Fee had to teach her how to find the ripe berries, and how to accept the occasional scratches from the thorns. She explained, "There weren't any bushes that bordered the tower clearing."

"None where you grew up, either?"

Her smile slipped a little. "Not really, no."

"Fair. My early years in the capital, it was a stretch to find anything green and growing."

"We're doing pretty well for a couple of blackberry novices." Eyl laughed.

"Pretty well," Fee agreed with a look at the growing pile in their basket.

Soon, all their baskets were full, even though a good portion of the berries had made it into their mouths. "You've got to make sure they're ripe," Fee insisted to Eyl when she mock-scolded him for popping every other berry between his teeth.

"What a marvelous bounty!" Marlaeda exclaimed when they brought the baskets back. She set one basket aside—"for eating"—and laid her hands briefly over the others.

"What's she doing?" Eyl whispered to Fee.

He focused on her hands and leaned forward. "There's a sheen on the baskets. When I lean forward, the air feels cooler. A protection or stasis spell, maybe? To keep them fresh?"

"Very handy!"

While the youths had been berry-picking, Ciurin and Marlaeda and Uriakin had unpacked the fairly massive hamper and spread a large blanket over the grass. Now they all settled down to a veritable feast—egg salad sandwiches on buttered bread, a salad with chicory, apples, nuts, cheese, and a few other greens and fruits Eyl didn't recognize, scones with cream and fresh blackberries, crisp and cool ginger beer, and what Marlaeda said was lemon meringue pie. Eyl said it was delicious.

Somehow still having room after snacking on berries, they served themselves with a minimum of bumped elbows and spills. Marlaeda again didn't eat, contenting herself with a glass of ginger beer. After they'd stuffed themselves on picnic fare, Fee lazed on the blanket in the sunlight. His red hair shone like fire in the sunlight. She lay down as well, her head on his chest.

"I'm going to go to sleep again right here," he said muzzily.

Eyl poked him. "No. Wake up. The world is bright and luminous and lovely. I just saw a butterfly."

He opened one eye. "Where?"

She pointed at the purple butterfly drifting on the breeze, its wings fluttering.

"That was me," Kai said, and a blue butterfly left his mouth this time.

Eyl sat up. "What are you doing?"

"I want to know how it works," Kai said firmly. "If I can choose when I summon insects and creatures, I want to be good at it. I want to control the magic, not let it control me." Four bumble-bees buzzed out of his lips. He frowned. "I was trying for a dragonfly."

"I'm never going to shift again," Eyl said, lying back down. "Never." She shivered as the phantom sensation swept over her, along with the memory of pain. Fee slipped an arm around her shoulders.

"You say that," Uriakin said, "but you can't deny yourself. Your gyrfalcon is a part of you. One day, you may even be glad of it." She picked at her teeth with one long talon. After complaining of the lack of crunch in the picnic lunch, she had sourced her own meat.

Eyl shook her head emphatically. "I'm never going through that kind of pain again."

"Stubborn eyass."

Eyl made a face.

Fee rubbed her shoulder, a reminder not to butt heads with the harpy.

She turned into him, her heart leaping a little at the way he smiled in daylight. "Maybe just a tiny nap," she whispered.

THEY ALL DOZED for some time after lunch. When Eyl woke, the sun had moved a little towards the west, and Kai had managed to summon a cloud of orange-and-black butterflies by whispering, "Tranquil" over and over again. "I'm not sure if it's the words that do it, or the sounds," he admitted.

They all watched in awe as the butterflies danced over the flowers in a mysterious choreography. There were one or two bees mixed up in the butterfly cloud as well. Eyl guessed his technique wasn't perfected yet.

Ciurin tracked the progress of Kai's bees with a meditative eye, and when they disappeared into the trees, he got up and followed. In a few minutes, he returned carrying something, a few bees hovering around him. "Who wants some honey?" he asked with a small smile.

Imani's eyes widened. He broke off a piece of the comb glistening with honey and gave it to her.

"Weren't the bees mad?" she asked.

"No. They were happy to share."

"They didn't sting you or anything?"

He shook his head, smiling in a satisfied way.

Eyl couldn't tell if Ciurin was stating the bees' natural inclinations or if Ciurin had done a little persuading to make the bees happy to share, but she grinned when Imani hesitantly licked her piece of comb and exclaimed, "It's so good!"

"Nothing better than honey from the comb." Ciurin handed around the pieces. Eyl and Fee accepted the sticky offerings and tasted the honey. Eyl smacked her lips while Fee closed his eyes, savoring the flavor. Ciurin offer his last piece of comb to Marlaeda. She shook her head, laughing, but he kept his hand extended. "Have some, Marlaeda," he said.

Their gazes held. Eyl elbowed Fee, who opened his eyes and she nodded surreptitiously towards the Forest Guardian and their mystery lady. She didn't know why Marlaeda didn't take off her veil—it was her business, and she certainly couldn't see her face— but Ciurin's face was intent, his eyes glowing hot.

"Oh, all right," Marlaeda murmured, unwrapping her veil around her neck. She lifted the free edges with her hand so the veil no longer clung to the lines of her face and took hold of his wrist, moving his hand under her veil.

Fee's ears turned red, and he glanced away to Eyl. She stared back with wide eyes as she licked honey off her fingers. "*I told you*," she signed, and she made a little beckoning motion with her hand.

"*Yes, you did*," he clumsily signed back.

Marlaeda was rewinding her veil. "Bees are the most magnificent artisans," she said dreamily. Ciurin said nothing, just put the rest of the comb into his mouth and chewed.

"I didn't know you could *eat* it," Kai said, interest piqued. He popped his own piece of comb into his mouth. "It's good!"

"Thank you, Ciurin," Imani said, wiping her sticky fingers on the handkerchief Kai handed her.

"My day is always brighter when I can share a bite of wild honeycomb," Ciurin said, and his gaze stayed on Marlaeda.

FORTY-EIGHT

EYL

"*N*o, silly, not like that," Ev says, adjusting her stance. "When you lunge, you don't want to fall over. Now try again."

In the new position, Eyl stabs her practice sword into the straw target and keeps her footing. Did Ev see?

She turns to him, but he's passing her by. "Mama!" he calls.

Eyl stares at the tall, blonde woman with hard, cold eyes. She stares over Ev's head, directly at Eyl.

The world darkens. She's no longer in the practice yard. It's cold.

There's blood on the snow. The straw mannequin in front of her collapses into a real dead body, staring straight at Eyl.

Terror seizes her by the throat.

Run, *the voice says.* Run far away—

Then Eyl is in a foul-smelling wagon, full of crying, dirty children. The looming shadow of the tower falls over her. Tala sits on her grave-stone, face gray and bloated in death. North. North. Go north, *she signs.*

Help me, *Eyl signs back, but she is shifting, her bones grinding together, blood pouring from her eyes and nose as the pain goes on and on and on and on—*

EYL SAT UP WITH A WHEEZE, struggling for air as her body shook. She had to clench her head in her hands and count her fingers and toes to make sure they were still there. Light was creeping in through the draperies.

I'm free of that. I will never change shape again, she tried to reassure herself. Even as the beat of her heart clamored, *North. North. Go north.*

"Eyl, what is it?" Fee asked, rousing from his blankets.

"I had a dream."

Fee sat up. "Of home?"

Yes. No. Both at once. She folded her shaking hands underneath her blankets. "It was a nightmare," she said in perfect truth.

IMANI GOT a little weepy when they took their leave of Marlaeda, Ciurin, and Uriakin.

Marlaeda wiped away the trickles of flame without fear. "There, now. No tears. It's time to face the road ahead of you without fear." She handed them a stuffed hamper of food. "Ciurin will lead you back to the path. I wish you safe travels."

Marlaeda turned to Fee and touched his cheek. "Don't forget that your gifts can bless as well as curse." He bowed his head and nodded.

Uriakin eyed Eyl. "Don't forget your talons, little eyass."

Eyl steeled her spine against the horror of her dream. "I don't have talons anymore."

"You will always have talons. You just have to choose whom they rake."

Eyl and company waved goodbye to Marlaeda and Uriakin and followed Ciurin over the bridge into the forest. They stepped through two trees that had grown into a natural archway and found themselves in the remote, silent portion of Blackthorn, with the path that led onward.

"Two or three days travel north," Ciurin said, "and you'll be out of the forest. Stick to the path and you won't go wrong."

"Wait. Fee said you could travel by magic—through sunken lanes," Imani said. "Why can't we leave that way?"

"None of the hollow ways go near the border," Ciurin said. "And besides—this is your road to walk. May you find what you seek at journey's end."

If only I knew what that was, Eyl thought.

IN ACTUALITY, the journey took more like four days because with a cessation to her shifts, plus a regular, healthy diet and sleep she could actually make use of, Eyl's body took full advantage.

By which she meant her courses started.

Tala had been the one to explain about babies and monthly courses to Eyl when they had initially begun, but she had never been regular. It was often many months between bleeding and never for more than a day or two of spotting. Eyl knew why—her body had been in such a state of stress, it couldn't manage even that basic function. But now it had started again and—oh, it was miserable.

"It's awful, isn't it?" Imani confided. She had grown out of her initial cramps, curse it.

"I want to die." Eyl groaned from her blankets, pulling the corner over her head. Her cramps and bloating were awful, and whenever she sat up, she felt dizzy.

"Do you want me to try a numbing spell?" Fee asked, pausing in the act of ripping up his extra shirts for her to use as rags. He had not batted an eye when Eyl had forced the need for more cloth through her teeth. It must have been Fee's healer tendencies.

"Please," Eyl said. "Let me be free of this agony."

"The problem is, it only lasts an hour at a time, and it numbs your whole body."

Eyl flipped the blanket back. "Why is that a *problem*?"

"Ever tried to walk when your feet are asleep?"

"Can't you modify it?"

"I don't have enough healer training on the body," Fee admitted, the corners of his mouth turning down. "If something goes wrong, it could seriously harm you. I could do something irreparable to your nerves. Who knows?"

"But Marlaeda fixed me when I was stuck," Eyl moaned. "She wasn't doing anything specific, was she? Just coaxing my body to be the right shape." She pressed her hands against her abdomen and cursed. Why did her body have to do this *now*? At least they were close to a goodly supply of water for washing.

Fee leaned back and thought about it, running a hand through the copper strands that hung in his eyes. "I suppose that using wild magic...there is an element of trust. I never understood that before. When I undid your spells, it was as much a feeling, a sense as it was a process. Faefolk trust magical processes. Wizards trust no one and nothing. They nail down every possibility, get magic in a stranglehold to bend it to their will...." He bit his lip. "I'm still shaky on trust."

She took his hand, squeezed. "I trust you."

He let out a shaky breath. "How can you? I'd understand if you'd never want anything to do with magic ever again."

"It's not magic I'm trusting. It's *you*. If your intentions and will are the things that matter, then I trust you. Because you'd never hurt me."

Fee went still, staring at their joined hands.

She squeezed, letting him reorient himself.

He let out a long, shaky breath. "Can you, uh, describe how it feels? So I know what to help...."

"Yes. Let me explain. It feels like a giant's fist is squeezing my abdomen. Everything from my waist to my tailbone aches. I want to eat bread. So much bread. But I can't eat because I feel nauseous and because I don't want to deplete our supplies. My guts are all unhappy."

"All of them?" Fee said, a ghost of a smile on his lips.

She glowered. "Every *single* one. Do not laugh. I will hurt you."

"Show me where it hurts," he coaxed.

Eyl rolled onto her side and took his hand. "Here." She put one hand on her abdomen, below her belly button but above her pelvis, and the other on her lower back. "There. Everything in there."

He closed his eyes, concentrating, and she stared at his long lashes as they swept down across his cheeks. Eyl was suddenly aware of his long-fingered hands spreading across her body, sending warmth through her—in more ways than one.

"Breathe," Fee said without opening his eyes. "I haven't done anything yet."

That's what you think, Eyl groused, but she breathed in and out obediently.

"All right. Let me try this."

Eyl waited for a zap or any other indicator that some magic was being performed. Nothing earth-shattering occurred, only a slight relaxing in her back muscles, a relief as cramps in her abdomen eased—not all the way, but enough that she was able to sit up instead of curling into a ball in her blankets like a roly-poly.

"How was that?" Fee asked.

"It's not completely gone, but definitely better." Eyl threw her arms around his neck. "*Thank* you." She kept other, more fervent pronouncements, to herself. She didn't want to announce her undying love because of the cessation of her cramps.

She'd save it for something spectacular.

"Lucky duck," Imani said. "What I would've given for something like that two years ago."

EYL WAS willing to keep pushing forward through the pain—in fact, the itching in her feet and in her mind pushed for continued travel, but Fee insisted she rest at regular intervals. "Your body is still finding its equilibrium. You need to give it the time it needs." So they loitered beside the river, taking frequent stops throughout the days before they made it to the edge of the forest.

"It was so lovely here," Imani sighed, staring out through the broad sentinel trees at the scrubby grassland beyond the Heartwood's border.

"I never imagined a place like this in all my life," Fee said.

Eyl shouldered her pack. "If we all have faefolk blood, then that means we can always find our way back, doesn't it?"

"I suppose it does," Fee said. "Where do we go from here?"

"North," Eyl said. "And...."

"What?" Fee asked.

Eyl stared at the group of people she knew better than anyone in the world, or very nearly. Imani and Kai because they had been through hell together, and Fee because...well, because he was Fee. She needed to tell them. Needed to explain what they could be walking into.

But it was hard to find the right words.

"I'll tell you tonight," she finally said. "It's a fireside sort of tale."

"All right," Fee said. "Shall we?"

"We shall." She took his hand and stepped forward.

Outside, the forest sounded different. It wasn't the quiet stillness they were used to. The grass crunched under their feet, and the air was full of a bitter chill. Right. Autumn was in full swing—none of the magical summer that the Heartwood had gifted them. They'd have to find shelter tonight from the elements. Was it cold enough that it would frost tonight? How long would their provisions last before they'd have to find a town to resupply? And where—

Fwwpt.

Two arrows flew through the air and struck Fee, one in the arm, and one in the leg.

Eyl screamed. "Fee!"

With a grunt of pain, Fee fell to the ground.

Eyl screamed again, this time without words as soldiers in Damaslar uniforms rose from the tall grass and advanced on them.

"Go," Fee ground out through gritted teeth. "Run." He snapped the arrow in his thigh and blanched.

"Not on your life!" Drawing her knife, Eyl put herself between Fee and the soldiers. Kai had done the same for Imani. If they could create some kind of barrier like a firebreak to cut off these enemies, maybe they could retreat to the forest. "Imani!" Eyl yelled, slicing at the first man within arm's reach. "You've got to use your magic!"

"I *can't!*" was the panicked reply.

Then Eyl was fighting too rapidly to see anything else. She had no illusions as to her skills. Anything she had learned was from nine years previous, and her only sporadic sparring partner in years since had been Kai. But she was small and fast, and the soldiers were slow and didn't seem to want to harm her. That put them at a disadvantage, she thought, teeth gritted, because she very much wanted to hurt them.

When a soldier tried to get behind her, Fee tripped him and kicked him in the groin with his good leg. "Run back to the Heartwood," he said, white-lipped as he tried to roll onto his hands and knees. "You'll be safe—go—" He slumped to the ground.

Eyl shrieked when a soldier lifted her off her feet, but she rammed her elbow into him. She kicked and thrashed and managed to switch hands so she could stab him in the gut. All she saw were gauntleted hands, reaching for Fee's still body. "Don't touch him! I'll kill you if you touch him!" she said frantically. Then a staggering blow met the side of her head, and all she knew was darkness.

FORTY-NINE

RILEN

Rilen could hear the scream from his hiding place in the tall grass.

They had ridden at a breakneck pace, first back to the Lliore River ferry crossing to the south and then straight north. They had stayed far too close to Blackthorn for the soldiers' comfort, but as much as an arsewipe Marcus might have been, he could sure push his men. They had left half the squad with his second-in-command to sit by the entrance to the forest, but Marcus had insisted on accompanying the party skirting the forest and dragging the wizard along. Probably because he had known, deep down, Corbett and Rilen were right, but he hadn't wanted to rely on Nath's magic. Though based on the quality of the wizard, Rilen thought Nath would've almost certainly been an improvement.

Knowing where to stop and wait for their quarry was like spitting in the dark, with only the mouth of the river as a general guide, but Nath came through again, claiming to find a path leading out of the forest that no one else could see. He swore up and down to the brothers that it was there. So Corbett had said, "This is it, then," and they had dug in.

And just in the nick of time, too.

Rilen stood in time to see the tall, redheaded boy fall, an arrow in his dominant arm and one leg. The towheaded, extremely pale girl screamed again, a loud, piercing noise that sliced across his eardrums as the soldiers advanced rapidly but cautiously towards them.

The gangly boy with copper skin pulled a knife and threw himself in front of the younger girl with dark skin. A string of bees and wasps flew out of his mouth as he yelled.

"Silence him!" Marcus roared to their wizard. Rilen didn't wait to see what result that would yield.

"Imani, you've got to use your magic!" the towheaded girl screamed, fighting any soldier who came close as she stood over the arrow-shot boy.

"I can't," the younger girl wailed, flexing her hands desperately in front of her. "It won't come!"

"Back to the forest! Run!" the insect summoner yelled, trying to hold off two men but losing ground.

"I won't leave you!" Imani cried.

"*Go!*" the summoner managed to yell before he gasped and went down, clutching at his throat, trying to breathe.

Parthas had better not kill him, Rilen thought harshly. He approached the young girl they had called Imani, pushing a soldier out of the way.

She was panting, almost hyperventilating, as she whirled around, trying to find an escape route. But the last few men had circled around and cut her off. She stumbled back from Rilen, gray with fear, and his stomach twisted.

He grabbed a soldier who would've gone for her forcefully and pulled him back, shaking his head emphatically. Better to take her quietly. Her fear was so palpable that it felt oily on his skin. He hated it. He gritted his teeth in revulsion and held up his hands in a non-combative but firm "calm down" motion.

"What the devil?" the soldier yelled, moving forward again. He got an elbow to the gut for his trouble.

"*Fool*," Rilen signed sharply, even though the man probably couldn't understand. *"There's no need to scare her witless, you idiot. Worthless sellsword."*

Imani gulped, arrested by the sight of his moving hands.

Rilen's ears rang with a scream of rage again. The blonde girl was holding off two men with a long knife. She held it like she knew what to do with a blade, but a third soldier got behind her and shifted the balance. He lifted her off her feet, holding on to the hand with the knife. She slammed her elbow back into his face and kicked his shins. As his grip slackened, she switched the knife to her other hand and stabbed him in the groin.

"I'll kill you," she screamed. "I'll kill you if you touch him!"

Then Corbett got close enough to club her on the side of the head. Her eyes rolled up and she went down. Corbett caught her, hoisting her up into his arms.

Rilen got his first good look at her face as Imani screamed, "Eyl!"

The name rang through his mind, echoing louder and louder each time.

No, Rilen thought. *No, it couldn't be.*

Her head lolled on Corbett's shoulder. Pale-blonde hair, cut short. Dark eyebrows. Her face shape…Her name….

"Eyl." Imani sobbed, her eyes leaking…flames?

Two soldiers hauled the groaning redheaded boy up and tied him before carrying him away, the arrow still in his arm.

Rilen took another step towards the younger girl. *"It's all right,"* he signed slowly. *"No harm. No harm."*

"Where are they taking them?" she signed insistently, to his great surprise. *"What do you want with us?"* She shrank away when the soldiers advanced, rope in hand.

Rilen growled at them, and they backed off. *"If you come with me quietly, I will not let them hurt you."*

She shot him a clearly disbelieving look but bit her lip at the sight of her friends being carried away. Rilen knew the moment her will collapsed. She stepped towards him, brushing the flames on her face into puffs of smoke. He gestured towards the direction of the camp, and they began to walk, her shoulders slumped in despair.

This was too familiar. His conscience clawed at him, as well as fear from the darkest part of his soul. The questions inside him would have to wait for now, but he had a feeling the answers would not be happy for anyone.

FIFTY

CORBETT

orbett set the unconscious girl down and bound her hands and feet before turning to the boy who was sweating and groaning, holding on to consciousness by the skin of his teeth. "I told you not to take the shot," he growled to Marcus, cursing the air blue. "The arm was enough. Leg wounds are tricky—you might've hit the artery there and then he would've died. You're not going to cost me part of my bounty."

"I couldn't take the chance that you'd miss," Marcus said stubbornly.

"I never miss," Corbett ground out. "Get your craven-hearted wizard over here." He drew his dagger and sliced through the bonds around the prisoner's wrists, making the boy wince again. "Hold still," Corbett instructed in a hard voice. "Don't fight me. We're going to get the arrows out."

The boy hissed something through his teeth. Corbett leaned closer.

"…'N the horse you rode in on…."

Corbett huffed a short laugh, surprising himself. "Nath, come here and hold him down." When Nath had a hold of him, Corbett broke off the second arrow as the boy growled again. "Here, bite on this." Corbett shoved the broken arrow shaft between the boy's teeth.

"He'll snap that in half in a second," Nath said. "I'll find something better."

The wizard arrived—pushed, very unhelpfully, by a soldier. "What do you want me for?" he bleated.

"Well, first you need to fix it so that he can't do magic," Corbett said, wishing he could bang his head against the wall. Why were wizards so stupid? "Then you need to heal him."

"What? I don't know how to do that!" Parthas exclaimed.

"God's *wounds*," Corbett bit out. "Then what's the *point* of you? I thought we had special chains for magic users."

"Oh. Yes!"

Nath came back with a large stick. "Here, this will work better."

Corbett removed the arrow shaft from the boy's mouth.

The boy spat and said, "At least make him numb my wounds."

Corbett raised an eyebrow. "Can you do that?"

Parthas tugged on his earlobe. "Uhhh…I'll, uh, go get those chains." Parthas dashed off with suspicious eagerness.

"You're more useless than a boil on my buttock, Parthas," Corbett muttered.

"I can do it myself," the boy said through clenched teeth.

"You're not going to do anything magical."

"Look," the boy said desperately. "Most of wizard magic is writing. I'll tell him what runes to use. I won't sneak in any hidden escape clauses. He can infuse them with his own magic. Please. If my wounds are numbed, then I can at least help you stitch me up better than if I were unconscious."

"Are you a healer?" Corbett asked skeptically.

"No, I never got that far in my training. They made sure of that," the boy mumbled. "But I know basic battlefield medicine."

"So do I," Corbett said. "If no arteries are nicked—and I don't think they are—it's a simple matter to stitch you up."

"And disinfect," the boy said hurriedly. "You must disinfect the wounds or there's a greater chance of festering. I know the spell for that. It's simple. You can have your wizard do that, too, if you don't trust me."

"Well, seems we'll be learning all matter of things today," Corbett said wryly.

Parthas wandered back over with the chains slung over his shoulder—long, silver links with cuffs inscribed with some of the wizard runes. Supposedly, they stopped the wearer from using magic. Personally, Corbett thought that a bag over the hands worked just as well, if a wizard had to write his spells.

"Here, Parthas, you listen to this boy and write down what he wants. Then we'll see if they're the spells he says they are." Corbett sat back on his heels, preparing water and cloths and sewing supplies while the boy told the wizard what to write down.

"That's the numbing spell. It'll last for an hour. The disinfectant spell will cover only the wounds, so make sure to clean the needle well," the boy said.

Corbett raised an eyebrow at Parthas. "So?"

"So what?" their namby-pamby spell spinner asked stupidly.

"Are the spells true?" Corbett demanded.

"Oh! Yes."

"Well, *activate* them, then." Then Corbett was able to send the wizard out of his sight and focus on the boy. He and Nath removed the arrowheads and flushed the wounds thoroughly, making sure there were no splinters or pieces of cloth left to cause fever or festering. Then they stitched him up. The boy watched him while he made neat stitches in his flesh, kind of strange, really. None of the men Corbett had sewn up had ever paid attention this raptly.

"That numbing spell really works, huh?" Corbett asked.

"Yes," the boy said. "It's just difficult to use for anything less than a serious wound. Because it numbs your whole body. I can't feel my other hand, for instance."

"Magic," Corbett said scornfully, tying off the thread. He wiped away the excess blood and wound the bandage around the boy's arm. "Is that numbing going to prevent you from riding?"

"Yes." The boy set his jaw mulishly.

"Hmm," Corbett muttered. "Convenient, that."

"I wouldn't have been able to ride if I were unconscious, either," the boy pointed out.

"We would've lashed you to the saddlebow. I suppose we still can," Corbett said, cheered. "Onward to the front we go."

"What is my father paying you to do?" the boy asked after a moment.

"Retrieve his wayward offspring and the magical experiments he absconded with," Corbett said. "Didn't mention that you all were ankle biters, though."

The boy stared at him, affronted. "I'm nineteen!"

"And you'll never know how young that is until you're thirty."

The boy glared at him. "Did he mention that the others will be forced to use their magic for Damaslar's warmongering? How do you feel about that?"

Not good, actually, Corbett thought. "You let me worry about me, boy."

The boy turned his head, craning his neck. "Where are they? What did you do to them?"

"They're over by the fire. I imagine they'll be waking up soon."

"Don't hurt them," Fee said. "They're just kids. They don't deserve this. They've been captured for years—trapped in that tower by the sorcerer. You know about the tower? The old man? All they want is to be free, but if my father gets to them—"

"Well, well, well, if it isn't Feonar Yaldson," Marcus said, coming up to them. "So nothing grievously injured, hmm?"

The boy's face screwed up into a terrifying glare. "If you lay one hand on them—"

"What?" Marcus held a hand up to his ear mockingly. "I can't hear you. What are you going to do? Oh, that's right. Nothing. Because you're going to get it this time. Your father isn't going to go easy on you now."

The boy spit, but it came just short of Marcus's boot, which Corbett found himself let down by. The guardsman drew back his boot with a curse.

Corbett snapped, "Until we deliver them to the High Wizard, they're *ours*, and we're responsible for their state! I'm not letting you put one more scratch on them. You're not going to lose me one crown I'm owed."

"Have it your way," Marcus growled in a low voice. "Your band is in charge of them, then." With a parting glare, he strode off.

"He hates me," the boy said in a low voice. "I suppose he was the one sent on the wild goose chase."

"Likely," Corbett said. "Now I'm going to put these cuffs on you. If you go quietly, then we'll wait here until your friends wake up so no one has to ride slung over a saddle."

"I might have to regardless," the boy said with a wince, looking at his leg. "There's going to be no good way to ride."

"We'll take it slow," Corbett said, plucking a blade of grass and sticking it in between his teeth, not caring about his bloody hands. "No rush."

"Don't you want to get paid?" the boy asked, casting a suspicious glance his way.

"We'll get paid," Corbett said. "There was no time limit on the bounty. So. No rush."

They exchanged looks, measured, assessing, testing resolves.

Corbett couldn't say who came out the victor.

Eyl came awake to the taste of blood in her mouth and a splitting pain in her head. When she tried to move, she realized her hands were bound. Then it all came flooding back.

"Eyl? Are you awake?" Imani whispered.

"Barely," Eyl muttered. "What's happening?"

"We've been captured," Imani whispered. "Damaslar soldiers."

Eyl's eyes shot wide open, and she rolled to sit up, even as her body protested and her head screamed at the movement. "Fee. Fee was shot. Where is he?"

"They're sewing him up. I think he'll be all right."

"Kai?"

"He's still out." Imani gulped and shifted on the ground.

Eyl followed her eyes to a huge man approaching with a waterskin. He had a dark beard that didn't wholly cover what must have been a mighty scar stretching across his face. He held out the waterskin to her.

Warily, Eyl took it. Her hands were bound in front of her, so she could bring it to her mouth. He watched her intently while she drank. She lowered the skin. "What? What is it? Does staring at your captives give you a thrill?"

"I don't think he can talk," Imani said under her breath. "He signed to me."

The man nodded, pointing to his mouth. *"How is your head?"* he signed, face concerned. He held eye contact and waited.

"What do you care?" Eyl snarled. "You took us prisoner."

Why did he look so wounded at her stating that fact?

"You will not be harmed," he said. *"My word on it."*

"And what is your word worth?" Eyl spat.

"Please," Imani broke in. "Can you tell us how Fee is?"

"He is not in any danger," he said. *"The arrows were clean strikes. They are tending to him. When he is fit to travel, we will go."*

"What about Kai? When will he wake up? What did your wizard do to him?" Eyl demanded.

"Soon." The man bent to check on Kai's condition and feel his pulse. *"It is a natural sleep. He will not suffer any harm."*

"They choked him," Imani said. "I saw. That's not natural."

He signed emphatically, *"Parthas was not authorized to do that. We did not mean to hurt you."*

"No, you've got to deliver the merchandise intact." Eyl sneered. "How noble of you."

To her great surprise, the big man flinched as if she had struck him. *"My word. You will come to no harm from me or mine. I swear it."*

"I've heard that before," she said in a low voice.

He jerked himself to his feet and staggered away.

Eyl stared after him with a frown, but then Kai groaned and twisted on the ground. She scooted towards him. "Kai, can you hear me?"

"Yes," he rasped. "Ugh." He put a hand to his throat, where a band of bruises, like prints from an invisible hand, were purpling to the surface. "What happened?"

"Rest your voice." Eyl helped him sit up and handed him the waterskin. "Drink."

"We're captured," Imani said. Her voice scared Eyl with its bleakness.

The dark-skinned tracker came up and held out a cloth gag. "No more stinging insects. But I'll let you drink your fill first if you don't try anything funny."

Kai bared his teeth but kept silent and drank.

"You're with me," he continued, carrying a Cadruissi intonation. "Name's Nath. The little one is with Rilen, and you're with Corbett." He nodded to Eyl.

"And Fee?" she couldn't help but ask.

"He's with that loon, Marcus." Nath shrugged. "Can't be helped." He slipped the gag over Kai's head and tightened it, but not viciously. "Time to mount up."

FIFTY-TWO

CORBETT

"New orders," Marcus said, pulling Corbett out of his daydream in which he broke this man's jaw. Repeatedly. "In the morning, we head northeast to the peace talks. The High Wizard wants the assets."

For peace talks? Corbett's thoughts grew dark and grim, but outwardly, he shrugged. "Makes no difference, as long as he has our payment." He returned to his place around the tracker fire. "Mountain's bones."

"What's up?" Nath asked, looking up from feeding more wood to the fire.

"Assets are wanted. At peace talks."

"What?" Nath's brow furrowed. "First I've heard of any peace negotiations. Thought Damaslar would dig in until the bitter end for the hillcountries."

"Nope. Altesia has come to negotiate with their allies." Corbett rubbed his chin, the bad feeling growing in his gut.

"Oh. Don't like that." Nath sat back.

"I've got a bad feeling about this."

He glanced over at his brother, but Rilen didn't give any sign he was paying attention. His gaze was fixed on the kids—targets

—*blast*, they were kids, even the runaway. Everything about this situation was going to hell, and he hated it.

"Rilen?"

Slowly, his brother blinked, shook his head, and slowly focused on Corbett. His gut sank further.

Something was the matter with Rilen. He knew his brother. Everything he felt, he felt deeply. He just didn't know how to show it on his face. It showed in his body, the tightly coiled tension pulled taut like one of Corbett's bowstrings. It was only a matter of time until the snap.

"Tell me," he said without preamble when the watch changed that night. They were a little ways from the fire, hidden in the shadows.

"We've broken the rule."

Corbett could barely make out his hands, but the moon was just bright enough to provide the illumination.

"Those bescumbered idiots withholding information broke the rule," he countered, but he didn't like it. Didn't like it at all. "What are we going to do about it? Walk away?"

"No." He signed the pinching motion violently as his eyes flashed.

Corbett raised an eyebrow. "No? Then we collect the bounty and go?"

"No."

"Then what? Make an enemy of the whole Damaslar army— no, the whole *country*—by helping fugitives escape?" He scoffed.

His brother shifted his weight, said nothing.

"Rilen," Corbett said, alarmed. "Rilen, don't be stupid. It's only the two of us. I don't think even Nath would throw in his lot with us to do something so foolhardy. That would only get us our heads chopped off. And if we escaped—a *big* if—we'd no longer be hunters, but wolf's heads. Don't ask me to do that."

Slowly, his brother signed, *"I did a bad thing. I've never told you, but I did a horrible thing, and I...."* Rilen shook his head, frowning deeply. *"I'm not going to do the wrong thing. Not again. If this is the price I have to pay to make it right, I will."*

"What are you talking about?"

But Rilen was already turning away.

He was watching her again. The mute one, with his fearsome visage. But Eyl wasn't fooled. He was big and strong, and the wicked scar didn't help, but the one she had to worry about was Marcus, who commanded the soldiers. He was the one sending looks of hate towards Fee.

They were at least valuable magical experiments. Fee was just a bastard son, and she could see Marcus making that mental calculation every time she looked at him, getting closer and closer to an answer each time.

And the worst part was Fee had had to ride with him. Eyl had ridden with the fox-faced tracker, who had only spoken to her to make it clear she could ride astride or slung over the saddle like baggage if she didn't behave.

Kai leaned over and poked her.

She started. "What?"

"Can you shift?" he signed, keeping his hands out of the soldiers' view, though by now, most were sleeping. When they had stopped for the night, they had cuffed them all in front so they could do menial things like eating and relieving themselves without as much issue.

"No!" she whispered.

"Have you tried?"

Eyl swallowed, bile coating her tongue.

The truth was, she hadn't. Whenever she'd thought about it, she'd felt pale and shaky, nauseous. The thought of inflicting that pain on herself *voluntarily....*

She pressed her lips together. "I'll try." She reached for the falcon, bracing herself for the pain. The first tingles sent a violent shudder through her, and she recoiled violently from the sensation. "No," she said, gasping. "No, I can't."

Kai's brows drew low over his eyes and he looked away. *"All right. I will think of something else."*

"What about Imani?"

"She is having a harder time than you."

"I could pull your gag off."

"I couldn't summon anything large enough or in enough quantities to make a difference. And they'll separate us if you try." The trackers had warned what would happen if they removed Kai's gag. They had watched like hawks when they'd passed supper plates out and had put it right back on again.

She reached out and gripped his hand. *"We* will think of something else."

Some of the chill wrapped around her heart lessened when he returned the pressure.

Movement flickered in her peripheral vision. Eyl's head jerked up as the big man—Rilen, he was called—moved towards them. She pulled her hand from Kai's. She wouldn't give them any information to use against her or her friends. She squared her shoulders and glared, lifting her chin. "What do you want?"

Without speaking, the big man untied the rope that held her to the tree and motioned for her to stand.

She shook her head. No way was she going anywhere with him.

"No harm," he signed.

"Unlikely," she muttered.

"Will you sit? Over there?" He motioned to a distant oak but still within sight of the fires. *"Please. We must speak."*

Warily, she stood and moved to the tree, sitting with her back to the trunk. He sat cross-legged in front of her, his back to the fire. She realized in this position, only she could see his hands.

"I must ask your forgiveness. Beg your forgiveness," Rilen signed. He ducked his head and hunched his shoulders.

"Forgive you?" she hissed. "You kidnapped me. Kidnapped my friends. You're the worst kind of scum—"

"Yes," he said. *"We are guilty of this, but I have sinned against you for far longer and for a much greater offense. Please. Forgive me. My princess."*

FIFTY-FOUR

EYL

The world stopped. Eyl couldn't hear the fire, or the wind, for the roaring in her ears. She couldn't even breathe.

He knows.

No one knows.

How does he know? *How—*

Abruptly, she fell back through time, through the walls she had built around her previous existence, that self before ten years of age she had tried so hard to bury, to that fateful day.

It was the first snowfall of winter, and she and her maid had gone wandering from their usual mountain picnic spot, leaving the guards by the carriage. Enchanted by the wonder of the snow and the crystalline world, they walked through the trees, carefree. Eyl was safe and happy in her firm belief that she was precious, beloved. That she was protected by the whole country.

Until a dagger sprouted from her maid's throat, and she went down in a spray of blood. Eyl could still feel the phantom pinpricks of heat, flecks of the lifeblood sprayed across her face.

Too surprised even to scream, she fell to her knees beside the older girl who had cared for her since babyhood. She pressed on the wound in a futile effort to try to keep the lifeblood inside her, even as her eyes went glassy with death. Then Eyl's hood was yanked back.

Eyes blown wide with terror, she met the dark gaze of a huge man with dark hair, knife poised to plunge through her heart. They stared at each other for the count of three heartbeats before the stark terror entered his eyes, too.

Clapping a hand over her mouth to contain her scream, he dropped the knife from his shaking hand and muttered, "The princess. The princess. She sent me to kill the princess."

"You." The word was barely a breath.

He nodded, his eyes full of anguish. *"Yes. I am sorry. Please, forgive me. I did not know."*

Eyl shook her head, befuddled, overwhelmed.

"They will kill me," he muttered, groaning like a wounded animal. "They will—but she—she will know I have failed and—" He swallowed, spinning this way and that as he thought frantically.

Eyl struggled a little. She tried to cry out, strained against his hold, but he was strong, a mountain of a man, and he would not let her go.

Seeming to finally come to a decision, he bent to look her in the eye, though he kept a hold of her mouth. "Listen to me," he rasped. "Do not scream. Listen. She commanded me to kill you. The king's mistress, Lady Petronella. She is jealous of you, deadly jealous. She wants your position for her son. She will kill to get it."

Eyl pulled at his hand. Slowly, he released her jaw. She had to try twice before she found the voice to ask her question. "Where are my guards? They will protect me, they—"

"Do you know how deep her hooks run?" the man demanded. "Do you know who is in her pay? She will try again if you go back. She wants you dead—and she will know that I did not complete the task she set for me...." He trailed off. "You don't know who supports her," he said harshly. "You think perhaps she has told her son that he will one day be king? Do you think the king would want his eldest child on the throne, rather than his youngest?"

Eyl swallowed, bile rising in her throat. No, not her father, not that. He was not often attentive to her, but he would not—would not—and not Ev, never Ev. Her brother, who taught her how to swordfight, held her on her pony so she would not fall, played with her every time she'd asked. He would not, surely—

"You must run, princess," the man said. "Run far, run swift. You go south. I know there are several charcoal burner camps down that way. And forget who you are when they ask. You are no one. You have no people, no name. I'll make it seem as though you have died here." He ripped the cloak from her shoulders, tore it, wiped it in her maid's blood and threw it into the snow. "Gown, too." He ripped it with aid from his knife, bloodied it as well. "A wolf attack, they'll say. Timberwolves mad for flesh. You forget who you are. Speak of it to no one. It will sign your death warrant. Go south. I will come and find you, and then—" He stopped speaking.

"And then?" she said, tears trickling down her face.

"And then we'll see. Evidence is needed to convince others of a crime."

"But you. She told you."

"I'm only a guard. My word against a lady's, the king's mistress is suspect. Not worth anything, especially against hers."

"Please don't leave me," Eyl begged.

"You must go." He shoved her—hard. "South! Follow the trees. Tell no one who you are. Forget even your name. Only then can you stay alive."

And so she had run, through the frigid forests, stumbling upon one of the charcoal burners' camps purely on luck and chance—just as snatchers from Damaslar had arrived on a raid. She'd been thrown without ceremony into one of the stinking carts full of crying children and adults and hauled out of the mountains, out of Altesia, her home, far from anyone who knew her. And she had held her tongue and done what he'd said— locked away even her name. To survive.

Because her father's mistress had wanted her son to be king.

The snatchers had cut her hair the first time. All other times, she had done it herself.

"Why now?" Eyl whispered, her voice cracking. "Why have you come back *now*? After nine years—" She pressed a hand to her mouth to stifle the sobs that suddenly broke over her, confronted with too much hurt, too much of the past agony. The tears sealed her eyes shut, but she couldn't stop crying.

She couldn't remember the last time she'd cried.

Rilen made quiet shushing sounds, and took one of her hands, pressing it to his lips. He mouthed the words 'I'm sorry' and 'forgive me' against her fingertips, the beard tickling her skin. The rough line of his scar caught on her callouses.

When she finally opened bleary eyes, the first thing she saw was a handkerchief offered to her. She took it and blew her nose, mopping her face. Then she straightened her shoulders. "Look at me," Eyl said, struggling to keep control of her voice. "Look at my face."

Rilen sat back on his heels and met her gaze.

"You spoke to me," she said. "Before. I remember that. What happened?"

He dropped his eyes.

She snapped twice and signed forcefully, *"You will tell me why."*

"She had my tongue cut out. So I would never be able to speak of what she had asked me to do," Rilen told her.

"Who," Eyl demanded, though she remembered. He had told her. He had been wearing her sigil that day. But she wanted to hear him say it again.

"The king's mistress. The Lady Petronella."

She shook her head, asked the question she had been wondering for nine years. "Why did you do it?"

"I was loyal to her, and more than a little in love with her," he said. *"We all were, in her guard. She picked me and said she had a task for me to complete. She asked if I would die for her, and I said yes. She asked if I would kill, and like a young, blind fool, I said yes, too. And then she told me what she wanted."*

Eyl stared at him, tried to subtract nine years from his age. The beard and scar made it difficult. But he could not have been too much older than she was right now. *"She wanted you to kill me. So Evander would be the only choice for heir."*

"Yes," he said. *"But she did not tell me my target was the princess. Only where to go at a certain time, and the cloaks my targets would wear."*

"So she ordered you to kill my maid as well?"

"Yes. She claimed you were both two ladies threatening her, trying to take her position, and if you succeeded, she would be cast out and forced to beg on the street...." He closed his eyes. *"There is no excuse for being a young idiot, but that is what I was."*

"Why did you kill my maid first? I have wondered that for years."

"She was taller. She was the greater threat, the larger target."

Eyl squeezed her hands into fists, feeling a strange amount of guilt for being ten and short. "Her name was Lissette."

"LISSETTE." He spelled the name back to her, looking for her confirmation. *"I have prayed for her soul every night. Now I will be able to add her name."*

Putting aside her old grief, Eyl tried to think rationally about his story. "All right. All that...I understand." Her eyes narrowed to slits. "But why the charcoal burners? Did you *know* the snatchers would come raiding?"

"No. I planned to come for you right away. As soon as I could. But when I told her I had completed my task, she had my tongue cut out. I stumbled to my brother's house, burning with fever. It festered. It was three days before I recovered enough to search for you. And by then, you were gone, the camp destroyed, no survivors.

"I could not stay in Altesia; the lady had cast me out of the kingdom and warned me if I ever came back, she would have my family killed." He pointed towards the other tracker who looked like him. *"But my family decided to come with me, even though I never told them what happened. I have searched for years for snatcher groups, against all hope, trying to find you. Even when I knew you would have been traded. We've tried to dismantle as many rings as possible...."* He spread his hands. *"I didn't know what else to do to make it right. Maybe I never can. I have blood on my hands."* His shoulders slumped.

"That you do," Eyl said. *"Now tell me why you didn't kill me when she wanted you to."*

He looked up into her face. *"It was a sin against heaven and against you. I was not going to knowingly betray my country."*

"Was my life worth more than Lissette's?"

"To the country? Yes. But in truth, it was simple chance. She was taller and I couldn't see her face. I saw yours. You were crying. You looked at me like I was the monster from your darkest nightmares come to life. And I know I am."

"How did you know me?" Eyl finally asked. "Nine years have passed."

"Your nickname, plus you look like the queen," he said simply. *"And I could never forget your eyes. My life is forfeit. It is yours, my lady. And I will do everything I can to help you."*

FIFTY-FIVE

CORBETT

"Rilen," Corbett said, growling, "we talked about this." He allowed his brother to tug him away to the remuda, where they wouldn't be overheard by any of the soldiers, with all the horses and pack animals. At least he managed to bring his drink with him. "As much as I don't like it, we haven't got a choice but to fulfill the contract. If you want, after we're paid, we can ride to the Altesian lines and let them know what's happened, even the scales a bit."

"No. We cannot bring them to the Damaslar army."

"So, what, we just pick up and leave? Abandon our contract? Write this whole escapade off to a loss of pay?"

Rilen rounded on him. *"We must help them."*

Corbett said flatly, "You're crazy."

"No, not now. Not anymore. But I was. Do you remember when this happened?" Rilen pointed to the scar that marred his face.

"Of course." The old, familiar anger burned in Corbett's blood.

"I never told you all. No matter how much you pressed. I was too ashamed. I hated myself."

"For days you were burning up with fever. Then once you were well enough to stand upright, you went tearing off. No one from your old guard unit would give me a straight answer. Tried to pawn me off with some story about attempted rape of that high and mighty woman you all toadied for. And I knew that was a lie —you were in puppy love with her and jumped when she said how high. Never mind that she had enough hidden knives about her person to make anyone she wanted eat scree. I hated all of them on your behalf. You only hated yourself."

"Here is the truth. I was too blinded by slavish devotion to the lady to deny her anything. She asked me to spy, I did. She asked me to vouch for her whereabouts, I lied for her."

"What are you saying?"

He continued resolutely, *"And when she asked me to kill a rival, I agreed. She told me when and where, not who, but described outfits, cloaks."*

Corbett felt the blood drain from his head, leaving him cold. "You...Rilen...."

"I went, waited. I stabbed the taller of the two. Bigger target, bigger threat. Then...." His brother scrubbed his face with his hands.

"Then?" Corbett said, his mouth filling with bile.

"Then I realized who the second girl was."

"The princess," Corbett muttered with numb lips.

The whole country had been thrown in uproar when the girl had died or disappeared or been stolen—no one had found any conclusive proof for a good explanation. Corbett had been too out of his mind with worry over his brother to think on it, even though trackers were employed to hunt the length and breadth of Altesia for her. Never in his mind had he connected the two events. Rilen had been a gentle giant at that age. He defended; it's what had made him a good bodyguard.

Unless he had been manipulated into acting as another's weapon.

"Yes." Rilen exchanged a glance full of misery with him. *"I panicked. My blinders shattered. I knew she had maneuvered me into committing treason. Already I was a murderer. But I could not betray my country. She was a child. I told her to run, south to the charcoal burner's camp you had told me of."*

He had, Corbett remembered. Over their weekly dinners, days off from Rilen's guard duty and his forester patrols.

Corbett scrubbed a hand down his face. "Well, that was stupid. Alone? At, what—ten?"

"I panicked," Rilen said. *"I went back to the lady, after setting the scene in the forest. I told her I had staged it as a wild beast attack, which was my original plan, and had dragged off and hidden the princess's body to make it believable. She seemed to believe me. Said she was very happy with me. Even kissed my cheek. Then her two lieutenants dragged me off and cut out my tongue. So I would never be able to speak of it. Then they threw me out. That's when you found me.*

"I went back to the charcoal burners camp as soon as the fever was gone, even though I was as weak as a kitten, but it was decimated. Hit by snatchers." He hung his head. *"I failed."*

"That's what you've been doing all these years," Corbett said slowly. "Every tracking case we've had involving snatchers, you insisted we take it. You were looking for her. The rumors—all the rumors that the princess was alive. They're true. God's *wounds.* Rilen."

"They're true. She's alive."

"After all this time? How do you know?"

"She's been riding pillion with you."

"She's—what?" He tried to focus through the ringing in his ears.

"I knew her face," Rilen said. *"Her hair is different, and she is older. But it is her. She goes by* Eyl, Corbett."

That short, gangly girl? The princess?

Hair cut short. Altesian accent. The name. Corbett didn't think he had it in him to be any more shocked, but apparently not. He set aside his cup and was abruptly and violently sick in the brush.

He was only vaguely aware of his brother holding his shoulders. But he took the canteen that was offered, rinsed, and spat. After nine years, how had it all come full circle like this? "I hit the Princess of Altesia over the head with a club. I could've killed her," he muttered. "Mountain's bones."

Rilen rumbled to catch his eye and signed, *"Do you hate me?"*

The words pulled Corbett up short. "What?" he sputtered. "No!"

"You should. It's my fault."

"Shut up and don't talk nonsense." Corbett growled. "Of course I don't hate you. I hate that scheming woman." He stared off into the darkness and brooded. "But you're right. We swore not to take sides in the war, but we're beyond that now. We're not leaving our princess to the Damaslar army." He was a lot of things, but treasonous wasn't one of them. What a blasted tangle! He stood. "We'll come up with a plan. Figure out a way to get them out of here. We'll have to decide where to go, how to hide—how to avoid pursuers, because we will be pursued." He shot Rilen a dark look. "Right now, I need to sleep. We'll have time tomorrow, especially as we ride."

He hesitated and then squeezed his brother's shoulder. "I'm glad you told me."

Rilen, his too-tall baby brother, bent down and rested his head on Corbett's shoulder.

"Everything's going to be all right," Corbett assured him roughly.

And it would have been…if the High Wizard of Damaslar hadn't ridden out to meet them.

CHAPTER

FIFTY-SIX

EYL

Eyl slept badly after Rilen's tumultuous revelations. Her chest ached as her body tried to absorb all the emotional punches she had pushed away over the years.

My father's mistress wanted me dead to put her son on the throne.

Had her father known? Surely not.

But Eyl would never know for sure now.

But what about Ev?

And the bogeyman she had feared for years, the stand-in for all her childhood trauma, was here. Rilen. And she hadn't even known him.

He was just another tool Lady Petronella had thought she could use.

But if Rilen spoke truth—and she thought he did—he would make his brother help them. He would ensure their escape. He wanted to atone.

I'm his princess, Eyl reminded herself. It had been so long since she had even dared to think the word.

Kai and Imani had wanted to know what Rilen had pulled her away for, but she had been too…too *everything* the night before to relay it all.

"He says he's going to help us," was all she could sign. *"We can*

trust him." And then she fell into her bedroll and had nightmare after nightmare about Lady Petronella, and Ev beside her, the mountains smoking, and blood covering the floors.

This morning, with soldiers chivvying them along, she could do little more than give Imani and Kai nods of assurance and try to catch Fee's eye across the camp before they were packed onto horseback again and set off.

Eyl rode in front of Corbett again, and she could feel the change in him. Whereas before, he'd been blank and ignored her, now he was full of tension. Had Rilen told him?

"You're spooking the horse," Eyl finally said between gritted teeth. "Relax."

He didn't say anything, but she felt his posture ease by degrees.

They rode for a time along the track before they heard a party approaching through the trees. Around the bend came an armed squad of soldiers and a covered wagon. The men at the front wore gleaming helms with resplendent plumes.

From behind her, Corbett swore.

Eyl froze.

Marcus rode forward and shouted a greeting. "Welcome, Your Grace. We've recovered them all."

"Right where Parthas said you'd be." The man removed his helm to reveal a graying head and beard, a mouth with lips that curved up in a cold smile—and ice-blue eyes.

Eyl couldn't draw breath.

This was Fee's father.

FIFTY-SEVEN

He was dead. That was all there was to it. Fee had suspected as much when they'd been captured, but now he knew. His father had ridden to collect his prizes personally and that could bode only ill for the one who had tried to keep them from him.

The High Wizard was accompanied by a group of armed men and a wagon. He pulled the horse to a stop in front of Marcus, who welcomed him. Frantically, Fee searched for Eyl seated behind Corbett. He had been separated from her and the others, to keep from making any schemes, apparently. At least the soldiers only blamed *him* for the escape. Marcus didn't seem to think magical experiments merited people status, and therefore, they couldn't possibly have instigated any escape plans.

Fee found Eyl staring at him in a panic. Sorrow washed over him. There were so many things he wanted to tell her, so much he wanted to say, and now there was no time for any of it. "I'm sorry," he mouthed. He prayed she could read his lips. He would've signed if the shackles hadn't bound his hands behind him.

Her brows drew down mulishly.

A fission of alarm tore through him. It would not go well with her if she pushed Nicanor. Fee started to shake his head, but then his father dismounted and turned to him.

"Here you are, Feonar," Nicanor drawled, tucking his helmet under his arm. "What do you have to say for yourself?"

Fee said nothing.

"You really thought you could steal from me?" His father spoke in a low, dangerous voice. "After all I've done for you, boy?"

"People aren't possessions. And children aren't weapons," Fee snarled.

"Morality falls to the wayside when I'm trying to win a war," Nicanor said. "Right and wrong lose their meaning. There's only winning and losing, and I intend for Damaslar to be the winner. But you never understood that."

"Even among thieves, there is honor. I suppose that puts you lower than them."

Fee didn't see the blow until his head snapped back from the force, reeling with pain and bloody from the gauntleted backhand.

"Leave him alone! Don't touch him!" Eyl shrieked.

Fee blinked the blood out of his eyes, trying to see straight.

"Ah." Nicanor chuckled. "Bring her over."

Fee's vision cleared in time to see a soldier frog march Eyl over, her eyes full of murder. When she was in range, she spat.

Fee flinched as Nicanor wiped the spittle off his cheek. "So you've tamed yourself a little wildcat, son?"

"I'm not your son."

"Oh, you are; I remember your conception distinctly." Nicanor smiled.

"Not in any way that holds meaning," Eyl said emphatically.

"Because Feonar is so much more honorable and decent, etcetera?" Nicanor sneered. His eyes slid over the pair of them. "So. You haven't told her, then."

Fee went cold.

"From your accent, you sound Altesian," Nicanor said conversationally. "You *do* know our Fee was attached to the Damaslar army?"

"Only under duress."

"Oh, yes. Duress. You make it sound like we chained him up and tortured him." Nicanor smiled. "It was the other way around. Fee was our interrogator."

Eyl's head jerked backwards like she had been struck.

Fee's stomach dropped. "Eyl—"

"And he was very good at it," Nicanor assured her.

"That's not true," Fee said furiously.

"Isn't it? Which part? That talent of yours is an impressive weapon."

Fee would have rather been arrow shot again than see Eyl pale like that.

"Tell her about the Altesian spy. Tell her what you did to her."

"I set her free," Fee said, tongue thick, hands clammy. "I freed her." Was this how it felt to all of his victims, to have their secrets dragged out into the light of day? Like your insides were being pulled out with a fishhook?

"Oh, did you?" His father smirked. "I thought you ferreted out every secret she had. You made her cry, beg, even. You were ruthless. It may as well have been torture."

Fee faltered, "That's not—it's not true and you know it."

"And you know all about that," his father drawled. "So tell her, then. I can see you haven't yet. In the spirit of *truthfulness*."

"I never tortured anyone," Fee insisted.

"Not with a knife," Nicanor gloated.

"They made me use my talent on her. Dig through her head for every scrap of detail. It hurts. To know someone is seeing all your secrets. And you can't hide or protect yourself from it." Fee's voice dwindled down. The weight of the shame pressed his head down.

"Wrenching it out of the captives. Laying their souls bare. Torture," his father gloated. "And the girl died in her escape attempt just the same."

Fee spun around, anger flaring. "If I was a knife, then you were the hand that wielded me! I never wanted to do any of that. You forced me to be your interrogator."

"What other use was there for you? I wasn't going to let you squander your talent in measly healing magic."

"It sounds like the person Fee needs to force to speak the truth is *you*," Eyl said in a low voice.

"Oh, be assured. Every word I have spoken is true. I made sure of that." Nicanor smiled. "Put them in the wagon. But gag them first."

CHAPTER

FIFTY-EIGHT

EYL

She landed in the wagon with a sharp exhalation of air, barely missing Imani. Kai and Fee were struggling to a sitting position. She wanted to scream. If they had just come a day later! Just *one* day! Rilen might have been able to convince his brother to help them escape.

And now they were captives—again. Of the Damaslar army, and the High Wizard in particular. Fee's father, who admitted that Fee had been an interrogator. He'd used his wild magic talent to pry secrets from Altesians, almost certainly giving Damaslar an edge in the war. So there *was* a reason they wanted him back.

Fee stared at her over his gag, anguish in his eyes.

Eyl went cold. Their secret seer, thrown together with the secret Altesian princess.

But Fee didn't know! He couldn't see much about her—he had told her so—only impressions—

I don't know that, she realized. *He can do more with his magic now.* He had fixed her, hadn't he? And he had used wild magic for her cramps. He had more control over it now. So it made sense that maybe he *could* see beyond the shield in her mind, if he tried.

If they force him....

He wouldn't tell his father, Eyl reasoned with herself. Even if he saw her darkest secret, he wouldn't tell. And anyway—how would they know there was anything to find?

But Corbett and Rilen knew. Imani and Kai didn't, but they had lived with her for years. They might know more via observation than was prudent. Might give away something inadvertently —like her insistence on going north, the pull she could not deny.

I should've told them, Eyl thought suddenly. *I should've trusted them. Forewarned is forearmed, and we were walking into danger the closer we got to my home.*

I was just so afraid—!

Eyl inwardly cursed herself. Freedom had been so close! If the wrong person even breathed a word, everything could be even *more* disastrous—politically catastrophic. What if they forced Fee to look, and speak what he knew? Her throat nearly closed from panic.

She forced herself to turn her gaze away from his.

She had to think. There had to be a way out of this. More was at stake now. There must be a solution.

Mustn't there?

Corbett glared at everything in his vicinity as he watched the High Wizard verbally rip his son to shreds. If they had gotten their orders direct from him, Corbett would have refused the commission. Sometimes one just didn't do business with scum.

Rilen put a hand on his arm and squeezed. *"We can't let them take them."*

Corbett ground out, "I thought we agreed you wouldn't do anything stupid or crazy."

"She cannot be taken. We must protect her. It is my duty."

"I know that, you great lump. I'm thinking."

"And the children, too. They wish to use the children against Altesia. We cannot allow that to happen."

"There's not a lot we can do about it right this second, is there?"

Rilen signed sharply, *"There is if you will listen to me. Insist that we must go with them to receive our payment. That we must deliver the assets to the army to fulfill our contract. I will explain everything later."*

Corbett tore his eyes away from where they were loading all the bound children into the wagon. "You want me to make an enemy of an entire country. That's what this boils down to, right?"

Rilen nodded.

Never let it be said his brother wouldn't take long odds or back down from a fight. Corbett groaned. "Let me talk to that blister Marcus, then."

MARCUS RAISED an unpleasant eyebrow as Corbett rode up beside him. "Suppose you're wanting your payment," he groused.

"No."

"No? Done all this for a lark?" Marcus laughed unpleasantly.

"No. We haven't fulfilled our contract yet. We were hired to retrieve and deliver to the Damaslar camp. We haven't reached the destination yet."

"We can take it from here," Marcus said, frowning.

Corbett smiled hard. "I wouldn't dream of leaving before our contract is fulfilled, whole and entire. And then we will collect our payment in *full*."

"Just what are you implying?" Marcus asked, ruffling up.

"Just what I said. We do not leave jobs until they are completed. When we reach the encampment, then you can pay us the agreed-upon sum." Corbett wheeled his horse and rode back to his brother as the larger procession began to move.

Corbett muttered to Rilen, "Can't believe I have to endure his presence more than necessary. So we get to the army. Then what? They'll be even more guarded."

Rilen guided his horse with his knees as he signed, *"We can't run now. We have no fresh horses and it's broad daylight. We wait for cover of darkness and then see what there is to accomplish."*

"What are we going to tell Nath? Do we bring him into this?" Corbett looked over his shoulder at their third tracker, silent and troubled several horse lengths back.

"He doesn't like this. They are children. He has strong feelings about it."

"Fine. I'll talk to him," Corbett said. "You be thinking how to perform miracles and spring four captives out from a whole army's nose."

"We will save them. Lord willing and the Gap passable."

Corbett shook his head at his brother's faith. He didn't see a way to do this. Not without getting their own throats cut.

CHAPTER

SIXTY

EYL

The journey was interminable. Every bounce and jolt in the back of the wagon sent another spike of agony through her bound limbs and her worried heart. Whenever the wagon missed the dry ruts in the road, the jolt was particularly rough, enough to bounce her a little off the wagon bed. And it was close and dusty under the tarpaulin, making it difficult to breathe. Or maybe that was her heart again.

It drizzled a few times on and off during the day, and that was the tarpaulin's only benefit—keeping them dry when all the riders got soaked. Many muttered curse words accompanied by shouts and the slaps of reins to their horses. Throughout it all, the tug in her chest grew stronger, thrumming like a plucked string that only swelled in volume.

When the wagon came to a stop, only belatedly did Eyl realize that the noise around them had gotten significantly louder. Before she had time to process this, the flap was shoved back and all four of them were unceremoniously yanked from the wagon.

She had the fleeting impression of tents as far as the eye could see, men in armor, and the sun sinking hazily towards the west before they were pushed into the opulent interior of a very spacious tent. She stumbled and barely managed to catch herself.

Fee, however, went down and did not get up. Blood stained the bandages around his leg and arm.

Her stomach twisted. She had been bounced into the wrong position to look at him during the day. How long had he been bleeding?

Kai was glaring like he might have been able to incinerate someone in the spot. Imani, who *could* do that, stood shivering in fear, making her chains clank. Eyl squeezed her shoulder.

The High Wizard swept into the tent, rolling his neck and snapping his fingers. Servants appeared as if from nowhere to pour wine, offer water for washing, and deliver other refreshments.

The four of them might have been invisible, or inanimate, in fact, until Fee growled, *"Father!"* through his gag as the High Wizard prepared to disrobe. When a servant pulled the gag free, Fee hissed, "There are ladies present."

The High Wizard's gaze finally focused. He hadn't given them a thought. He laughed but went behind a screen the servants snapped open.

As they were ungagged, Imani whispered, "Ugh."

Eyl concurred. That man could not care less about them. Another wizard who barely viewed their existence as sentient. Her stomach roiled.

The servants, taking their master's cues, did not speak to them and did not offer them anything. Not even a seat, not even water to moisten their parched lips. They sat as well as they could on the rug. Imani crawled to Fee. "Are you all right?" she whispered.

"Fine." He mustered up a weak smile for her and inched to a sitting position.

Nicanor finally came back freshly washed and in clean clothes. He sat down at his table and drank deeply from his wineglass and then surveyed the four of them. "What a motley crew." He drummed his fingers against the tabletop. "So, the boy, he spits spiders and snakes and other creepy crawlers. Interesting but not precisely useful at this point in time. Which girl is the firebug?"

Imani turned gray.

"Mmm, is it you, child?" He smiled. "And so, the other girl is the bird. Though I thought you were bird during the day."

"I no longer turn into a falcon," Eyl said stiffly. Her stomach sank even further. *Fee must not have found all the old man's letters.*

"Oh?" His brows lowered. "How did that happen?"

"Fee removed it," she snapped.

She wanted to pull the words back when his gaze turned dark and focused on his son. "I hope you know you just cost me a prime spy and scout," he said in a dangerous voice that promised violence.

"Even if I could still change, I never would've spied for your army," she spat, trying to turn his anger. "You're the worst sort of wizard, and I'll do absolutely nothing to help you."

"Oh, I can see the claws in you. The falcon's not entirely gone," he muttered. He turned to Imani. "According to Aedelbras's notes, you work the best out of all of them. Is that true?" Without waiting for the answer, he snapped his fingers again and a soldier appeared. "Unlock her chains."

Imani licked her lips over and over, breathing fast as the chains dropped from her wrists.

The wizard motioned to the paper on his desk. "Light that on fire."

Imani swallowed. Swallowed again. "I-I can't."

"Can't?" His eyebrows drew together.

Her hands fluttered uselessly. "I can't—I can't do that anymore."

"My soldiers told me a tale of a tower ravaged by fire," he said slowly. "Were they lying?"

"No," she said miserably. "But—"

"Then set the paper on fire. I'll wait."

Miserably, Imani stretched her hands out and closed her eyes. Her hands shook and sweat beaded on her temple. Eyl could tell she really was trying.

"Take it slow," she whispered. "Breathe."

But eventually, Imani dropped her hands and opened her eyes. "I can't," she said, voice shaking.

The wizard viewed her with hooded eyes. "Let's see if you can manipulate fire, then." He lit a candle, setting it on his desk. The he grabbed Kai's hand and stretched it over the flame.

"No!" Imani yelled. Kai hissed as the flame licked his skin.

"Father!" Fee exclaimed.

"Stop it," Eyl exclaimed, but the soldier, whom she hadn't seen leave, grabbed her arms in an unforgiving grip. Her fingers ached with memory of wicked, lethal talons long enough to gouge out eyes.

"Prove to me you can manipulate the fire," the wizard said, holding Kai in place with an iron grip that revealed no matter how indolent and pampered the man looked, he still was extremely magically and physically dangerous.

Kai growled deep in his throat at the pain.

Imani breathed rapidly, her hands shaking—and then the candle went out.

"Good." The wizard smiled, a slow, pleased grin. Then he used one hand to relight the taper. "Let's try it again."

***

AT THE END of that half hour, they were all dripping with sweat, and Kai had a series of burns along his forearm and had chewed his gag raw, but Imani had proven to the High Wizard's satisfaction she was able to extinguish, grow, shrink, and bend flame to her will—just not create it.

"That will have to do, I suppose," he said at last. "Now—"

"Bandages." Fee growled. "Ointment for burns, if you're not going to heal Kai. Food and water."

His father stared at him like he was a strange species of mammal that had just sat up and talked. "All right," he murmured, snapping his fingers at a servant. Within minutes, trays of food appeared as well as bandages and salve, for both Kai and Fee. Silent servitors tended to them and then disappeared. Imani ate the food with a look of relief, wrung out from her ordeal. The rest of them only drank water. The smell of burned flesh still lingered in the air.

"Now," Nicanor said, "let's discuss what will happen when you attack the peace talks and kill the king and the Altesian ambassador."

SIXTY-ONE

FEE

ee choked on nothing, his body spasming in shock and sending a jolt of pain through him. "*What?*" He gasped. "I thought you were going to use them to attack in battle!"

"While impressive, three magic users would hardly gain me much tactical advantage," Nicanor said calmly. "And since the peace talks have arrived so fortuitously, I want to strike while the iron is hot, and we have the element of surprise."

"Altesia has no king," Eyl said in a wooden voice that made Fee tense. "He died three years ago. A hunting accident."

Nicanor peered at her. "No, not Altesia's illustrious monarch, though I have heard strong rumors that the ambassador is the queen's secret heir. I mean, we will kill the King of Damaslar, Caldair."

All the blood in Fee's body froze.

"You would murder the one to whom you swore fealty?" Eyl's voice filled with dire portent. "Oath breaker."

"Do not judge us barbaric; the practice is customary and often done when the heir tires of his sire or competition. It ensures that our kings are strong and ruthless." He smiled thinly.

"What's wrong with the one you have now?" Imani whispered, ashen faced.

"He was an only child whose father died young." Nicanor's face twisted. "He lacks…vision."

Kai made a disgusted noise. "You mean he's not a bloodthirsty tyrant. I will not help you murder anyone." He made a dismissive motion with his bandaged arm. "No matter what you do."

"Well, my goodness," Nicanor drawled. "Isn't it a good thing I don't need a swarm of bees or locusts to attack the peace talks? Just a very large explosion." He turned to Imani, who gulped and looked as though the food she'd eaten might come back up.

Fee pushed himself to his feet and somehow stayed upright, though he swayed on his wounded leg. "No. Imani won't be a weapon. Not again. Never again."

Eyl jumped to her feet and steadied him. Fee could barely believe she wanted to touch him after what she knew, but he was pathetically grateful.

"You're a disgusting excuse for a father," she growled. "You use your own son as a private interrogator and now you wish to have a child do your dirty work. You're a wizard. Use your own filthy magic and let us be."

"Tools exist to be wielded. Otherwise, what use are they?" Nicanor gazed from her to Fee, lip curling. "A fine time for you to grow a spine, boy."

"I've always had a spine," Fee snapped. "It's just straight now without your boot on it."

Nicanor shot up from his seat and caught Fee by the throat. "Puling gutter scum," he snarled. "Just like your mother. I should've drowned you at birth."

"Let him go!" Eyl shrieked, scrabbling at Nicanor, and Fee's heart rose even as he gasped for air. She couldn't despise him if she was pleading for him, could she?

Nicanor casually backhanded Eyl into a guard, who caught her up and restrained her. His gaze turned from Fee to her, assessing and cold. "You have no magic," he mused. "Fee took it away, you said."

Fee froze in his struggles.

Eyl glared poisonously.

"Well, if you're telling the truth, that makes you useless. If you're lying…."

"I am not," she panted. "My magic is gone."

"We shall see." He called for soldiers and commanded, "Bring them!"

He hauled Fee out of his tent. "Don't think I didn't notice how you looked at her, the little waif."

Fee cursed as his leg tried to give out. He hopped along as best he could. Nicanor would just drag him along by his hair if he fell.

"Well, let's see how truthful your little lover is," Nicanor said as they cleared the tents to a little grove of trees and a crumbling circle of stones that framed a dark hole. "Bring a rope!" He shouted, dropping Fee.

Fee's tongue cleaved to the roof of his mouth, staring at the hole in the ground. His vision shrank. The past roared back, and he was a child again. Watching a mob seize his mother. Watching her scream.

"Now we'll see the truth," Nicanor said.

A burly, muscled soldier picked Eyl up even as she fought him with all her strength.

"No! Stop!" Fee shouted, the horror of his childhood flooding back to him. *Mother! No!*

"Last chance," his father said.

Fee stared at Eyl, beseeching.

Eyl shook her head, hard. What did that mean?

Fee's lips trembled with the truth that was right there. Eyl *could* shift, but—would she? "She can't shift, can't fly! Please!" he yelled. "She'll drown!"

"We'll see, won't we?" Nicanor smirked. Then he gave the order, and as Fee screamed, Eyl catapulted down the well.

Fee dug his fingers into the grass, thrashing against hands that held him back as he yelled to be heard over the roaring in his ears. *She's dead she's dead I killed her, I killed her again*, he thought. Imani and Kai were screaming as well.

Then Nicanor lifted a fist. A soldier stopped a coil of rope in his fist. It led down into the well.

Fee shook all over. They had slipped a rope around her. She wasn't dead. There was a rope. His mouth tasted like blood.

Nicanor ambled over to the lip of the well and peered over.

"Hmm," he said. "No wings. Disappointing. I supposed you were telling the truth, after all."

Fee panted, "Pull her up! Pull her up, by the ten stars of Mar!" She could swim, but for how long? Had he heard a splash?

"No, I don't think I will. It's a dry well," Nicanor added.

Fee shook, chilled from the sweat that poured off him. He was almost sick and dizzy with relief. He passed his hands over his face and tried to remember how to breathe slower than the rhythm of his pounding heart.

"Release the rope!"

The soldiers let the rope slither through their grasp until they reached the end. "Ran out of rope. She's still not at the bottom," the soldier said.

Fee's heart leapt into his mouth again.

Nicanor shrugged and said, "Cut it, I suppose."

"*No—!*"

A knife flashed. The rope disappeared into the well.

Fee gasped for air. How far had Eyl been from the bottom? Was she all right? What if she had hit her head? Or broken something?

"Now, she'll stay down there until after the peace talks, and if you refuse me, I'll have my wizards fill the well with water. Very slowly. I'll even let you watch," he told Fee. A layer of menace coated his words. "*Don't* refuse me."

Eyl screamed as the soldiers threw her in the well.

Then the rope about her waist jerked to a stop and she spun, suspended in air. This was *nothing* like flying. She retched as the rope cut into her waist. She snatched at it to stop spinning, clutching it so hard, the hemp cut into her hands. She was far too aware of the fathomless darkness below. She could hear yelling—crying—but the roaring in her ears made it unintelligible.

The rope began to lower her by jerks and starts into the dark. Every lurch lower made her heart skip beats and her stomach leap. She feared the open expanse of air for the first time in her life.

Eventually, the jerks stopped, and she hung, spinning slowly.

She looked up.

A figure looked over the lip of the well. She could not tell who it was, silhouetted against the circle of light above.

"Ran out of rope," they said.

And then the rope went slack, and she was falling—screaming, wishing for wings for the first time in her life—before she fell into soft muck with a splat. Eyl lay there and gasped, trying to pull the air back into her lungs as the other end of the rope plopped down with her. Finally, she struggled to her feet, slipping twice in the standing water and slick mud.

She could hear them laugh faintly, but the sounds were muffled, traveling from far away down into the dark.

She was trapped.

CHAPTER

SIXTY-THREE

FEE

Marcus shoved Fee inside an empty tent. He landed on his wounded shoulder and hissed.

The tent was close to his father's opulent tent but markedly different—no food and beds for them, only a few blankets for traitors and magical experiments that did little to pad the hard ground. Nicanor had wanted them in a central location, and he had them under guard.

A soldier swore, and a hand struck flesh.

Fee rolled over to see the soldier shaking a hand with bloody teeth marks sunk into the flesh. Kai spat out pink liquid, a red mark on his face.

Marcus wadded up his handkerchief. "Mistake," he growled, stuffing it in Kai's mouth and tying a strip of cloth behind his head in a rude gag.

Imani fought her way out of her minder's grasp and went to her knees by Kai.

"Untie that and see what happens," the soldier said. "You won't like the consequences."

Fee glared, sick with rage. "You think you're tough, hitting children?"

Marcus hauled back and punched him. "Been waiting a long time to do that," he said with relish.

"Now, Marcus." Nicanor ducked under the tent flap.

Marcus stood aside, but his gaze promised pain.

Nicanor stared down at Fee. "As cruel as you think me, you haven't *begun* to experience what I'll do if you botch this," he said once the soldiers had left the tent. "You will do whatever you have to do to convince your little friend to light up the pavilion where the peace talks will be held when my men give you the signal. If she refuses, I will tell Marcus he can remove unnecessary parts from you and the boy. She will burn the tent until all its occupants are dead. If any escape, I'll drown the other girl in the well."

"How will you manage that?" Fee forced out. "Won't you be in the pavilion?"

"I'll have been incapacitated by the enemy enchanter, of course, barely able to use my magic store to save myself and the heir to the throne. A deep tragedy and blow, but I'll have saved at least one of the Damaslar royals. So I *will* know if any survive when they should not."

Nicanor glanced around the bare tent and sniffed. "You never should have crossed me, Fee. This would've been so much easier if you hadn't interfered." Then he swept out.

Fee pressed his face to the ground and gave in to tears.

CHAPTER

SIXTY-FOUR

EYL

It took her a while to unpick the rope from around her waist, and from the aches, she surmised she had wicked bruises around her ribs and around her legs from hitting the ground. Nothing felt broken, though.

The smallest, infinitesimal blessing, that.

But nothing got better. She couldn't sit in the muck and water, and the walls, lined with stone, were scummy and slick. She tried to climb them, digging her fingers into the cracks of the crumbling mortar, and failed. She'd only managed to dislodge a few handholds of stone and dirt. She quickly abandoned the idea. She had no desire to bury herself alive.

And besides, the light—what little of it there was—was going.

Eyl wrapped her arms around herself as the chill from the water and mud and night permeated her bones. She kept moving, pacing and moving her arms and shivering to try to stay warm, but there wasn't much room. Wells were not designed for occupancy.

The High Wizard did this to purposefully torture Fee, Eyl thought. The look on his face...it pierced her again like a sword.

Her mind turned the problem over and over again. *If Imani and the rest carry out Nicanor's plot, they'll let me out. But Nicanor is clearly untrustworthy. And I want no more deaths on Imani's conscience,* Eyl thought. *To say nothing of—*

She cut herself off rather than think it.

Eyl tilted her head back and squinted at the tiny circle of sky above her—one sliver of moon and a few tiny stars. At least they had not put the well cover back on. At least—at least—

She clenched her teeth and squeezed her eyes shut. "Why am I here?" she demanded to the silence. "What is this for? What are you doing? I went from prisoner in a tower to prisoner in a pit. I thought—for one tiny, tiny moment—things might turn out all right. I was finally free of that curse, but now I'm right back here again—trapped, and—"

Her voice cut off, strangled by frustration and despair. "How much lower can I get?" Eyl wrapped her arms around herself and let the tears come.

She had failed. She hadn't gotten home; she had failed Kai, Imani, and Fee…Fee, who had only wanted to help them. She had failed even before she'd started. She had failed her country by her absence. She couldn't even get out of this pit, an easy enough task when she had wings—

Eyl froze in place before more shivers wracked her body.

Her wings.

Kai still had his magic. He used it by will now. Fee had done the same thing for them both—released the magic to their control. Given them choices.

If she could call up her wings again, she could escape.

She shuddered, and her mouth tasted like metal. The pain of transformation flared phantom-like, as well as the horror of the in-between stuck state. The idea of going through that voluntarily made her want to retch.

It took Eyl several minutes of shaking and pacing to get her breathing under control and force the fear back. *I've got to try,* she told herself. *It's me or nothing.*

The problem was, she didn't know what to search for.

For nine years, she had dreaded daybreak because the change

had been forced on her. Eyl knew all the signs that signaled her transformation. Tingling that became a burn and pain, the ripping, twisting morph of body parts forced into a shape not its own. But she didn't know how to *start* it.

Eyl paced and strained and thought and tried, her feet sloshing through water now icy. Her toes felt like blocks of ice—when she could feel them, that was. She tried to keep wiggling them, but she was just exhausted. Each time her feet cramped, her heart jumped into her throat because the sensation was so similar to her change.

Eyl leaned against the wall and pressed her hand against it. "I don't know what to do. I don't know how to do this. I don't understand." She wiped her nose on her clammy, muddy tunic. "How can you be *silent* when I *need you*? *Where are you*? How can you let them *do this to us*? I don't understand!"

She was sobbing in the dark, clawing at the walls of the well because God wouldn't answer. "Every step has been so hard. For almost ten years, it's been terror and fear and pain and loneliness and *how could you do this to me*? I carried this curse—and finally when I thought I was free, I have to take it up again—and now I *can't*! The one thing I could do for them—even this you keep from me?"

The tears mingled with the snot on her face as she landed in the icy sludge and cried. She cried for the girl she used to be. The girl she had to become. Every moment in between. "I'm—so—angry at you. *Don't you care?*"

Eyl cried until her eyes felt like sand and her head felt floaty. Until her whole body shook with the cold and her throat ached from the tension. She stuffed her hands under her armpits, trying to force some heat back into her fingers. Her teeth chattered.

Even the last sliver of moonlight had disappeared. She couldn't see anything at all. Her own personal pit. There could be a lion two inches from her nose and she wouldn't know until it growled.

"Wouldn't that be nice? A safe, comfortable life without any tragedy

or strife." Sister Jeanetta's warm voice floated out from her memory. *"But what about the king? What about all the people?"*

Eyl hiccupped.

"That isn't fair," she told the darkness. "That's not the same." Her head ached. She rested it on the muddy stone as the silence stretched.

If Fee were here, he'd know that she had lied.

If the old man hadn't offered them up to the war effort, what would Fee have done after his father had stolen so much of his soul, forcing him to be his pet interrogator?

If she hadn't been in the tower, what would've happened to Kai and Imani?

If the old man hadn't wanted magical experiments, what horrible person might've purchased her?

If Rilen hadn't sent her to the charcoal burners' camp, would they have been able to produce proof of the murder plot?

What if she had died before he'd realized his mistake, and Lady Petronella had been allowed to get away with regicide?

What if Lady Petronella had chosen to kill her with something that left no witnesses, like poison, and succeeded?

Evil walks.

"I've seen it," she whispered. "It's here in the camp. It's evil. It's *wrong.*"

What men intend for evil, God turns to good. Every time.

Eyl forced her clenched fists open, pressing them against the slime-covered stone. "But *how?*"

"I gave you a choice," Fee said in her mind's eye. *"You can change back and forth at will."*

He'd given them a choice—given them back the control that been taken away. Imani had always been able to manipulate fire instinctively. Because the magic had been a part of her, an extension of her will.

They all had faefolk heritage. All had magic in their blood. Fee had restored what they should have been able to do all along.

Her falcon self was not a torture device. It wasn't evil inflicted on her. It wasn't a cage. Her gyrfalcon was a part of her. The magic had been hers all along.

Eyl exhaled. When she'd been a bird, she'd ruled the elements. She'd ridden the wind. She'd understood how to turn and ascend and dive in midair.

She'd loved flying.

When I swore never to change again, I thought I was fighting some adversary. Someone or something who wanted to hurt me. But that wasn't true, Eyl thought.

But the pain, her fearful heart reminded her. *The bones breaking. The in-between-ness. The terror. Stuck not quite one way or the other.*

I've survived it for nine years, Eyl reminded herself. *Day and night, night and day. I survived. And I need to save my friends. I can take some pain if that's the price.*

It was a way out when there was no other way.

What if every step of this road I've walked has come to this?

She took a long, deep breath. Was she really doing this?

Yes. She was.

Eyl began to peel off her cold, muddy clothes. She did it quickly, before the cold could slow her down anymore, shucking the muck-covered material and dropping it to the ground.

Eyl lifted her face. Far above, she could see the faintest glimmer of starlight.

Please.

She breathed in deep and slow. And then she delved deep inside herself and *reached.*

The world spun crazily for a moment, reality distorting, shifting—and then she was falling.

She opened her arms to catch herself—

Her wings gave a great flap, beating the air, keeping her aloft.

She had shifted.

She had shifted!

No pain. No long agony. No *fight.* Eyl shot out of the well into the open air.

Free.

SIXTY-FIVE

EYL

Exhilaration was a heady drug. For a minute, Eyl just circled the Damaslar encampment, reveling in the feeling of wings—*her* wings!—under her own rule. Then she had to dodge an owl going about its business. She had never flown by moonlight before. *Now what?*

It was on her fourth circle, as she was trying to identify the patterns of the camp, to pick out which tent was which from the air, that she spotted them. The furtive movements caught her sharp eyes and she banked sharply, dropping through the trees.

They'd hadn't gone? They were still here?

"It's not long enough," Corbett muttered.

"We could tie them together," the Cadruissi tracker—Nath, she thought his name was—said.

Rilen's hands moved, but he was facing away from her.

"He's right," Corbett said. "That length isn't strong enough. It's already fraying."

Eyl dropped into the brush behind a tree and dropped her bird form at the same time. It was—easy. Like a sharp exhalation. Or a burp.

She stumbled a bit regaining her feet. The men whirled and reached for their swords. "What—"

"It's me," Eyl hissed, clutching the trunk. "Throw me a tunic, somebody." Being without feathers was *cold*.

"Why?" Corbett asked automatically. Rilen was already stripping.

"She did what they thought she couldn't," Nath said in wondering tones. "Changed her shape."

Rilen passed her his tunic, and Eyl gratefully pulled it over her head. He was a large enough man that it reached her knees, and if she tightened the lacing in the front, it would be decent.

"Keep your voice down," Corbett ground out. "We do this away from the camp."

They led the way through the trees, away from lit fires and guards patrolling. Rilen put his hand on Eyl's shoulder to keep her from tripping. It was a steady, warm presence.

When they reached a dry creek bed, Corbett slithered down the bank and hunkered down on the stones. He passed Eyl his cloak. "Clothes don't come with you, I suppose."

"Unfortunately not." She was not proud enough to refuse the covering. It was still warm from his body.

"I'm sure glad you managed to escape, miss. We couldn't figure out how to get you out without attracting attention," Nath said. "We couldn't find enough rope."

"She's not a *miss*," Corbett said. "She's a *princess*."

"Apologies," Nath said, ducking his head.

"I haven't been a princess for nine years," Eyl said.

"The guilt is mine, my princess," Rilen signed. *"But I will do all I can to help you."*

Eyl lifted her head and stared at him. Everything he had done had not been from malice or evil. He had put his trust in someone who had not deserved it, and he had carried that guilt for almost a decade. "I forgive you," she heard herself say.

Rilen bowed from the waist, deep enough to nearly press his forehead into the ground. His shoulders shook silently.

With one cold hand, Eyl reached out and touched his head. "You don't have to do that. It's all right," she whispered.

Rilen raised his head, not bothering to hide the tears glimmering in his eyes. *Thank you*, he mouthed. With his hands he said, *"I am your servant, Your Highness. What would you have me do?"*

"Us do," Corbett said quietly. "I carried a grudge on behalf of my brother because I believed Altesia had wronged him—but I will follow you, princess. Apologies about—earlier." He pressed his lips together. Apparently, that was all he'd be offering.

Well, beggars could not be choosy about their allies. What *could* they do? She squared her shoulders. "The High Wizard means to assassinate his own king and the Altesian ambassador when he arrives, using my friends to do his dirty work. We can't let his plot succeed." Fee had saved them all in the tower. Now it was her turn.

"I do not know if we can rescue them and effect an escape from camp, Your Highness," Corbett said, "even with Nath. The number of soldiers around them...."

"And the Altesian ambassador and his entourage have arrived," Rilen said.

Eyl stiffened. "Already?"

He nodded, very sober. *"This evening,"* Rilen said. *"I do not know if she is with them or not."*

"That makes things more complicated," Eyl muttered. But she could find out. She *needed* to find out. "I'll scout the Altesian camp," she decided. "We need to know the arrangements for the peace talks, where and when. That is when Nicanor plans his dirty business. If we can't rescue my friends from the middle of the Damaslar camp, perhaps it will be easier right before the plot."

Corbett frowned. "Is that wise, Your Highness?"

"Me scouting?" She raised an eyebrow. "Maybe not. But I'm the one best equipped for it. And I can do without the *Your Highness*-ing, too. Since we're co-conspirators now, I think you'd better call me 'Eyl.'" She smiled at his disconcerted expression.

SIXTY-SIX

E yl followed the flags billowing in the night breeze to the Altesian encampment.

It wasn't hard to do. Damaslar and Altesia were camped on either side of the Lliore River and easily visible from the air. Flying by night filled the world with a bit of unreality. Not only was she flying towards flags with the Altesian standard—a mountain and a forest cat in relief on silver cloth—but she had shifted three times without pain. She owned her magic fully. She chose the change versus being forced to change.

Now, if only this compulsion to go north would stop, Eyl thought. But one couldn't have everything.

The Altesian guards were out in force, patrolling the lines of the camp, ever-watchful towards the river and the Damaslar troops on the other side, but they had little care for a bird swooping overhead. She flew right into the maze of tents and pavilions without issue. It was the ambassador she wanted—and she rightly assumed that the largest tent with the tallest flag signaled his presence.

The flap at the top of the tent that let out smoke was open, since the night was clear, and she perched precariously on the tentpole, peering down into the lit interior.

She could not see much, just colorful rugs and the brazier, of course, and the corner of a desk. The clink of cutlery against a dish sounded, and then there was a rustle of canvas.

"Is everything to your satisfaction, my lord?" a servant murmured.

"Yes, thank you," a man's tenor voice said.

A cleared throat, and then a light, feminine voice, its tone tight, spoke. "The *Prince of Altesia* thanks you."

"A thousand pardons—"

"No, it's quite all right," the man said. "I am not the prince, Selar; I am merely the Lord Ambassador. The meal is delicious. Please inform the cooks."

There was a tense silence as liquid was poured, and then the servant slipped out of the tent.

In the silence, Eyl reeled. Her brother's voice. For the first time in nine years.

She closed her eyes against the ache under her feathered breast.

When the rustle of canvas signaled that the servant had gone, the woman cleared her throat again. "Evander, your humility does you credit, but you *are* the prince—"

"No, Mother. I'm not the prince. The queen still has not made any official ruling as to her heir."

"Not *yet*," she said with finality.

Lady Petronella. Evander's mother. Eyl's father's mistress. Her would-be murderess.

"Maybe not ever," Evander said in a low voice. "You know the spell shows the princess is still alive."

Eyl's eyes opened, and her beak widened in a silent hiss.

"I think that faefolk woman was a charlatan," Lady Petronella sneered. "How could the princess still be alive after nine years? The fact is, if she were alive, she would have returned. That woman was a liar. I don't believe she worked any magic at all."

"I don't know anything about magic, but the fact remains that

I am not the true heir. And there still is a chance my sister is alive, however slim. How could I ever take her place, knowing that?"

Lady Petronella's voice gentled into syrupy sweetness. "Dearest, you know it was your father the king's fondest wish that you succeed him to the throne."

"Surely, not his *fondest* wish," Ev said. "He wanted the princess's safe return just as much as the queen."

Lady Petronella cleared her throat again. "Yes, but you *know* he would have preferred the crown go to you and not some distant second cousin no one has ever laid eyes on."

"That was never his decision, Mother, and you know it." Ev's voice hardened. "His title as king was only through marriage. The queen will be the one to make the decision as to who will succeed her."

Lady Petronella's voice turned petulant. "I don't understand you sometimes. How can you sit there and not grasp the opportunity before you? You have the chance to rule, to gain the crown!"

"Mother, the queen was good enough to give me a minor title and showed her faith in me by appointing me to this ambassadorship. In turn, I swore an oath of loyalty and duty to the crown of Altesia. I will hold to my oath. *If* the queen decides to name me her heir, then, I will do my best to do my duty to her and to the country. But until then I will not seek it for myself. I am only the queen's ambassador here, and I will not assume titles I have not earned or received."

"You are an ungrateful child," Lady Petronella said coldly. "After all I have suffered for you. All this was supposed to be yours."

"No, Mother, it was not," Ev said quietly. "I am sorry you feel this way, and I do know some of the hurts you have felt over the years. You loved my father very much."

"He was going to marry me. We were going to be happy, but then the queen turned her favor towards him, and he abandoned me for her. For the crown. Because of that, you were born a bastard."

"Mother, I was born three years after his marriage. There was no chance I would have been legitimate."

"He wanted *me*. He loved *me*."

"I know, Mother," Ev said kindly. "But who are you angry at, Father or the queen?"

There was a hard, brittle silence.

"I am going to bed," Lady Petronella said in a flat voice.

"Good night, Mother." Ev sighed.

With a great flap of canvas, the lady exited the tent.

Eyl lifted her head and watched her walk away. She wore a gown of deep emerald, her icy-blonde hair in braids curled around her head like snakes. Two guards peeled off from their patrols to accompany her. She carried herself ramrod straight, not looking anywhere lower than her nose.

Eyl could not see her face, and she was glad. She didn't want to see her.

She wanted to see Ev.

She dropped down through the hole in the tent inelegantly—it wasn't very big, and she was a large gyrfalcon. With a flap, she landed on the back of a chair.

Evander started with a wordless exclamation, staring at the bird of prey that had just entered his tent.

"My lord?" a guard asked, poking his head into the tent.

"No, I—I'm all right. Everything is fine, Lars." Ev waved him away. "I don't need anything else tonight."

The guard retreated without noticing the large bird in the ambassador's tent.

Eyl stared at him. Her brother was a grown man now. His long, brown hair was tied back with a silver ribbon. He was tall, just as tall as she remembered their father being, and his eyes were brown like his hair. He wore a blue-and-silver tunic over brown boots, with his shirtsleeves rolled up to his elbows. Instead of an ambassador, he looked like an off-duty man at arms, aside from the richness of the fabric. Eyl was forcibly reminded of the days she had begged him to teach her how to use a sword.

"Hello," Ev said curiously. "Where did you come from?"

She tilted her head and watched him.

"I confess I would've thought that hole too small for you," he mused, glancing up at it. "Did you smell dinner? Well, I'm sorry to say we ate most of it, but there are a few bites left, if you fancy chicken?" He rummaged amidst the dishes on the table and produced a few pieces of meat, holding them out to her.

Eyl eyed them hungrily. She hadn't eaten since this morning. She reached out and bit gently, taking the pieces of meat from his hand and swallowing.

"Are you wild, or is some falconer going to find empty mews in the morn?" He continued to feed her until the meat was gone. "You were hungry, weren't you?" He held out his hand. "Sorry. All gone."

She took two steps towards him and rubbed her head against his hand.

His hand twitched and then brushed her feathers gently.

"You know, I was hoping for some kind of sign tonight," Ev mused quietly as he stroked her feathers. "I was worried about these negotiations, worried I wouldn't make the right decisions for my queen, my country. She's ill, you know. The queen. Not many know, but that's why she isn't here herself. Maybe you're my sign, since a forest cat wouldn't be able to come so far." He smiled. "Not as much a problem with wings."

Eyl stared at him, thankful she didn't have to reply. All those years she had wondered if he had known about his mother's plot, supported or endorsed it. She had wondered if he had wanted to kill her. But he hadn't. He hoped she was still alive. He didn't want the crown.

She leaned into his hand, able for the first time in nine years to love her brother without guilt.

The rhythmic stroking of her feathers calmed her and helped her think.

Firstly, the High Wizard of Damaslar planned to use Imani's

talent to assassinate the King of Damaslar and the Altesian ambassador—Ev.

Second, should his plan succeed, she had little faith they'd all be let go. Doing an important person's dirty work rarely rewarded, as Rilen well knew. And clearly, she could not allow his plan to succeed. Ev wasn't going to die. She wouldn't let it happen.

So. What did they have at their disposal? Her, able to fly unnoticed in her falcon guise. Three trackers and soldiers—Rilen, Corbett, and Nath.

And if they were freed, Kai could summon snakes and insects. Imani controlled fire, even if she couldn't start it. And Fee—Fee could see the truth in people. And apparently, compel them to speak it.

He had never mentioned that because of its use in interrogation. She didn't blame him. But...it wasn't enough to just foil the plot. This was an extension of the larger war. They had to prove that this was Damaslar treachery at work. They needed proof. *Ev* would need proof. And much as she wanted to talk to him, to explain everything, having Lady Petronella right outside was too large a complication. She had to help Fee, Imani, and Kai first. There would be time for the past afterwards, Lord willing and the Gap passable. Time enough for everything.

Eyl blinked, lifting her head. What if the proof came from the one who'd orchestrated the plot?

Fee was the key. If they could get him and Nicanor in the same room...assuming Nicanor didn't have any protections against Fee's magic...all the participants could hear the truth for themselves.

SIXTY-SEVEN

CORBETT

"We need help," Corbett told Rilen, watching the princess fly into the night. "We need more manpower for this. What can three mercenaries and a couple of kids do?" And with time running out, too. Marcus had paid them their fee once they'd arrived, but Corbett had made noises about resting the horses from their long journey. They had been grudgingly given a tent at the camp outskirts. He could push it a day or so more, but if the three of them lingered, suspicions would mount.

"Where can we get more manpower?" Nath asked.

Corbett tilted his head back and stared at the sky. "Well, there's a big ol' camp full of mountain folks across the river."

"You want to just waltz into the Altesian camp?" Nath hooked a thumb that direction.

"Not waltz," Corbett said. "That would be hard to do over rocks and water. But we're not affiliated with the war. I'm Altesian. Don't give me that look," he told Rilen irritably. "I'm not going to announce the problem to the whole camp. I'm going to see who's there. I'll scout for any men I used to know. And I don't want to leave her on her own, just in case."

"A good idea," Rilen said. *"We will find out where the children are, and if Fee is with them."*

Corbett nodded and pulled his hood over his head. "I'll return in a while."

Corbett skirted the Damaslar patrols leaving camp and crossed the open terrain—someone had nailed some poles in place for the pavilion they wanted to erect in neutral territory—and continued on to the river. It was easy to see where men had come and gone with horses and wagons. The banks were churned over with mud. He skirted that area for a bit farther upstream where the river narrowed and waded across. Thanks to strategically placed rocks and low water levels this late in the year, only his boots got wet. Then he made for the Altesian camp.

Corbett didn't try to sneak. He pulled his hood down and let his general travel-weary demeanor speak for itself.

"Halt! Who goes?" came the call.

Leaning hard into the accent he had been born with, Corbett said, "Corbett Gar, tracker. A ways from the front, aren't you?"

Two guards split off from the perimeter and flanked him. "What business of it is yours?" one asked, shoving his face towards Corbett's.

"None." He shrugged. "Just heard about the encampment and thought I'd see what news there was from my countrymen." He hooked his thumb. "Our camp's a ways away, but during our last job, we heard about the to-do, so I came to see what the word was on the war status." All true.

"Are you some kind of turncoat?" the bristly-chin guard asked suspiciously.

"I'm a tracker for hire," Corbett said flatly. Mountain's bones, how many turncoats would say *yes*? "I don't get involved with the war. But there're always folk getting lost on marches." *Like you numpties.* "I find 'em and bring 'em in for fees."

"You'd better come with us; our sergeant can decide what to do with you," the other guard said.

"You want to let him in camp?" Bristly Chin asked. "What if he's a spy?"

"If I were a spy, you wouldn't see me at all," Corbett said. "But I don't need to go in your camp. Call your sergeant. I'll wait. I only wanted a good gossip, and any news you could share about whether the war would be over sometime before the mountains move."

Bristly Chin didn't seem to like that much, but Corbett sat down on the ground and proceeded to ignore the both of them, so the second guard sent Bristly running for their sergeant. They didn't have to say much. He saw enough right here.

The number of horses in their remuda indicated the number of riders in camp, and the size of the fresh dug latrines showed how many souls were there and how long they expected to be in the area. The flags flying above the prominent tents told him who was here as well. The ambassador—the bastard son of the king—and the Lady Petronella, his mother.

Corbett ripped up a chunk of grass and let it fall from his hand, wishing it were her neck. Hearing Rilen's story had intensified his animosity towards her. He had always hated her because she was a raging schemer and would step over anything to achieve her goals. But her callous manipulation, throwing away his brother as if he were garbage—to say nothing of treason against the crown to further her own spawn—! He ground his teeth. She was the reason they had been ousted from their country—Rilen by force, Corbett by resentment that had poisoned him.

Someday, Lady Petronella would reap everything she'd sown tenfold, and he hoped he was there to see it.

Lord willing and the Gap passable, that day would not be too far off.

Then he laughed under his breath. Look at him, invoking God when he had shoved all religion talk away for almost ten years. He wondered what Sister Jeanetta would say to that. He smiled a little.

Bristly Chin returned, looking sulky, with his sergeant in tow. Corbett lifted his head.

"Corbett Gar?" the sergeant asked, a tall man with a tight braid over his shoulder and a long moustache.

"That's me," he said, accepting the hand up from the ground.

"Mountain's bones, what a bizarre circumstance!"

He blinked. "How so?"

"You probably don't remember me," the sergeant said. "I was a green recruit nine years ago. But my little sister got lost on Queen's Crest, and you were the tracker who found her and brought her home." He clasped Corbett's hand. "I've never forgotten that. It's good to see you."

Corbett thought back, the memory niggling at him. "Kedder," he said. "Faith Kedder."

"Yes!" the sergeant exclaimed. "I'm Uzziah Kedder, sergeant first class."

"Good to see you again, sergeant."

After that, it was almost too easy. They chatted about the recent Altesian developments since he had been out of the country—all common knowledge, nothing that would get the sergeant in trouble for sharing. Corbett didn't ask to come into camp. But when conversation turned to what he had been up to in the last several years, he let his face turn hard. "Tracking here and there, staying out of the war."

"We could use a good tracker," Kedder said.

"I appreciate that, but...." Corbett's gaze drifted up towards the flags flying above the camp. "I made a deal with myself years ago to have nothing to do with that woman. Even if it was for the crown." He congratulated himself on keeping the statement mostly true.

"What've you got against the Lady Petronella?" Kedder asked. "I don't like how much she's insinuated herself into politics after the king's death, but...."

"She had my brother's tongue cut out," Corbett said flatly.

Kedder flinched.

"He was a greenie—probably your age," Corbett said. "And she got him all twisted up around her finger, but the minute he did something she didn't like, she cut his tongue out and threw him away."

"Why the *tongue*?"

"Men without tongues can't speak."

They parted ways soon after that. A troubled expression creased Kedder's face.

"Maybe I'll see you again, eh?" Corbett said, clapping him on the shoulder. "Maybe they'll accomplish something with these talks, and we'll all go home together."

"From your lips to God's ears," Kedder said.

Corbett tried not to wince. He wouldn't blame God for ignoring him after nine years of silence. But maybe if someone else invoked it, he would turn his ear to them.

"And I owe you a drink," Kedder added.

"You owe me more than that, but I'll take a drink and maybe a favor one day." Corbett laughed.

"You've got it," Kedder agreed, and Corbett took himself off towards the river, whistling in the dark.

He waited in the trees until he saw a dark shape wing overhead and then followed.

SIXTY-EIGHT

EYL

"Ev didn't know about the plot," Eyl said without preamble after landing and shrugging back into Rilen's tunic. "Something makes him believe I may still be alive. I think if I go back and bring him a note, warning him of the plot, he'll believe it."

"You'll sign it?" Rilen asked, brows drawing low.

Eyl hesitated. "No. Not until we have the more immediate threat dealt with. But he thought my gyrfalcon form was a portent. If I bring him a note, maybe he won't come to the talks."

"It's worth a try." Nath shrugged.

"And then, we'd have more time," she continued, "to see about the others. I have an idea for Fee. Did you find out where he is?"

"All three are under guard in a tent close to the High Wizard's," Nath said.

"I could fly in, pass him a note too—"

"Too risky," Rilen insisted. *"The High Wizard knows of your other form. Any sign of a bird near the tent will rouse suspicions."*

Corbett slithered down the dry creek bed and brushed himself off. "What did I miss?"

Eyl explained what she had heard in Evander's tent. "I can

send him a note not to come. Then we send Fee and the others a note, explaining our plan."

"And what *is* our plan?" Corbett frowned.

"Fee can see people's secrets, their pasts," she said. The men all flinched. She hurried to explain. "He tries to avoid it most of the time. He thought it was the only thing he could do, but he—he learned he could do more," she said hastily. She didn't want to bring up the denizens of Blackthorn Forest. "If he was able to force someone to speak their secrets...."

"What would keep witnesses from believing that he had simply magicked them to say what he wanted to say?" Corbett asked.

Eyl faltered. "Maybe...."

"If he revealed a secret only one other knew?" Nath suggested.

"*Assuming he is able to do it,*" Rilen said.

"I'll write both the notes," Eyl said. "Can you get the note to Fee?"

"If not tonight, then in the morning," Corbett said. "Cutting it close, though."

Eyl bit her lip, then threw her shoulders back. "Better than nothing at all. Who has parchment?"

Fee stared up at the lone lamp hanging from the tent post and wondered dully how things could get worse. His father might take advantage of the invitation, but he really didn't see how.

He hadn't even envisioned things getting *this* bad.

Ignoring the ache in his wounds and his face, he checked on Kai, whose face was also coming out in a bruise. He was dozing now, tired from his struggles. Imani was curled up in the corner, asleep, evidently exhausted from fear and shock.

And that didn't even take in what had happened to Eyl. The vestiges of horror still lingered in the back of Fee's mind.

I just make everything worse, Fee thought.

"Hey, you want to play dice? Any good at it?" Fee heard someone say suddenly before the rattle came of dice in a cup.

"We're on guard duty," the soldier muttered.

"They're trussed up like a couple of chickens, and sleeping, to boot. Come on. One game. I'll make it worth your while."

Wasn't that…Nath?

The cup rattled again. "Besides, we just got paid. I gotta spend a little of it or else it'll eat at me, you know?"

"Fine," the soldier said. "One game."

Nath laughed low. "That's what I'm talking about."

Fee turned away from the lamp, blinking spots away, just in time to see the shadows on the opposite side of the tent move. He stiffened as one of the tent stakes was pulled up, and a body rolled under the canvas. Fee struggled to sit up.

The man came to his knees and looked at him. It was Rilen, the scarred mercenary.

Fee jerked backwards.

Rilen held a hand up to his lips for silence. Then he began to sign, but Fee was unfamiliar with several of them. Only one thing caught his attention—three letters. E. Y. L.

It hit him like another punch to the gut. He had relived Eyl's screams from being thrown into that old well all evening.

Fee nudged Kai awake, keeping a hand on his shoulder. "Wake up," he whispered in his ear. "Rilen is here, and he's signing something about Eyl, but I don't understand." Fee, who had been shackled with his hands in front of him, thanks to his wound, unpicked the knot on Kai's gag.

Kai blinked, coming awake. He focused on Rilen, and the man repeated his message.

Kai licked his cracked lips and swallowed. "He has a message from Eyl. She got herself free of the well."

Fee choked. "What?"

"She shifted," Kai whispered in surprise.

Rilen produced a piece of parchment. Fee took it automatically, mind reeling.

Eyl had become a falcon again. Something she had sworn she'd never do.

Hope, that elusive, seductive, flicker, began to burn within him again. Even if Eyl could just escape, that would be enough. But if she could do more, then they might just have a chance.

"Why are you helping her? Helping us?" Kai demanded.

Rilen's hands moved again.

"What did he say?" Fee whispered.

"'I owe her my life and my fealty,'" Kai repeated.

Rilen nodded once, hard. His face was set and resolute.

Kai and Fee shared a confused glance. What did that mean? Fee raised his eyebrows at Kai. Did they want to risk trusting him?

Kai shrugged one shoulder, a universal "what do we have to lose?" gesture.

Fee stared at Rilen. What could Eyl have possibly done for him? He unfolded the parchment.

Fee,

I have a plan for tomorrow. If you can see secrets in someone's heart, couldn't you also reveal them? Could you make someone speak the truth? If we can get you all free—and Rilen and his party are helping us—we could prove to the king and everyone else what your father has planned. Do you think it's possible?

Please don't blame yourself for what they forced you to do. I don't think of you differently. Your father's actions are his own. And it turns out you were right—you did *give me a choice to use my wings. I was wrong to push it away. Don't push away your magic, either.*

Eyl.

P.S. If you need to make the Altesian ambassador listen, make sure you speak of the fells.

"What does she say?" Kai asked.

Imani roused, blinking sleepily in the light before her eyes widened. Kai hushed her before she made any sudden noises.

"Eyl has a plan to get us free and reveal my father's plot." Fee turned to Rilen. "There's a problem. These chains negate magic—any kind of magic. We'd have to have them removed for me to try." Or break them—but the runes inscribed in the chains would give the wearer the same kind of backlash he faced from defacing the rune in the wizard's tower.

The man nodded and handed him a charcoal pencil, along with thin strips of metal. Fee's stomach clenched.

Kai relayed, "He says, 'Can you pick locks?'"

"Well, *I* can't."

"I can. We got into every room of the tower after a time." His face hardened.

"Great." Fee turned the parchment over and wrote:

We have to remove our chains before I can use magic. Kai will pick the locks and we will see what I can do.

Fee paused, staring at the remaining space on the paper. Then he slowly wrote:

I'm sorry I never told you about what I did for the army. For so long, I was ashamed of it. It was so connected to my magic that had caused so much trouble and killed my mother. My father came along and made me into a weapon, and I was so angry that I couldn't learn healing magic, I never wanted to use it. I had never used it for anything but interrogation or secrets before. But you're right. It isn't good or evil. It just is. I'm the one who determines that.

Thank you for showing me that.

He handed the paper back to Rilen. "When should we expect things to…happen?"

"He says he doesn't know," Kai said as Rilen signed. "Just to be ready."

Be ready to deploy a talent he'd never tried to use in such a way before. Because everyone's lives and freedom depended on him.

"Great," Fee said again.

There was little sleeping after that. Rilen rolled back out of the tent. Fee couldn't hear much from the dice game anymore. Perhaps it had finished. Imani curled back into a ball, but Fee could see her eyes flickering. Kai took the metal strips and applied them to the manacles, learning their intricacies. Fee pondered how he might possibly reveal someone's secrets to a broad audience. It wouldn't be enough just to tell them what he saw. That would be simple hearsay. He had to make everyone else—the soldiers, the councilors, the *king*—believe what Nicanor had planned was the truth. Without them all being skewered for turning up at the peace talks uninvited.

He turned his mind over all the things Lady Marlaeda and

Ciurin had told him in the Heartwood, trying not to approach the problem like a wizard looking for a loophole, but a faefolk magic user who had to be strong of purpose and bend magic to their will.

Finally, with a muttered curse, Kai's manacles came apart. "Got it," he said. "Give me your hands; I know the trick now."

"You'll have to put them back on again."

"Yes, I will, to practice getting them open faster." Kai twisted the metal in the lock. "But first, you have to practice."

"On you?"

"Who else?" Kai raised an eyebrow.

They exchanged a long glance. Imani would not be up for it after her traumatic day. "That's all right with you?"

"I want to know you can do what you believe you can," Kai said, setting his jaw. "Since I cannot look at a man and know the truth in his heart."

Fee's gut tightened. "Kai, I didn't say anything because—"

"I know why. Don't apologize. Do it now." The manacles broke open. Kai stared at him with uncompromising, black eyes.

Fee shut his eyes, rolled his shoulders, and found that part of himself that he kept bottled up, now unfettered with the shackles removed. The first part was easy. That, he had always been able to do—had never been able to ignore. He took a breath and opened his eyes.

Ahhhhhh, that part of him breathed, and it drank in the light.

He took a breath and opened his eyes.

When he looked at Kai, he bumped into the haze he had always seen around Eyl and the others, the wild magic barrier instinctively pushing him away. But, using force of will, he pushed past the miasma shield that faefolk blood provided and *looked*.

Sand, burning hot. Unrelenting sunrays. No food. One canteen of water. The soles of his shoes peeling away from walking over the sand and rock. Only two more days until he reached K'nadiye, the Great Oasis. Then his ten-day-long trek through the Sarkan would be at an end and he would be on the road to adulthood, having passed the Tsailu, the desert walk. Two more days. Two more....

But over the pounding in his ears, he heard the ring of metal on stone. Horses. Shod *horses.*

Danger. Run. Hide—*but there was nowhere to hide.*

"It wasn't your fault," Fee heard himself say, still somewhere in the desert.

"What wasn't?" Kai asked, his mouth in a line.

Fee closed his eyes and shook himself free of the vision. "Your capture at the hands of the snatchers. It wasn't your fault. You know it wasn't. The number of Sarkan'ande who have disappeared on their Tsailu in recent years—not a coincidence. The snatchers knew your route. They knew—but you still feel like a failure. Because you didn't complete your walk." Fee lifted his head. "But you survived years in the old man's tower. That's a far longer and harder test of endurance than the Tsailu to me."

Kai's face was a flat, expressionless mask. "I've never told anyone how I was taken."

Fee swallowed. "I know."

"And you saw it in my eyes," he continued.

Fee looked away. "It was what you were thinking most strongly of—or at the forefront of your mind at the time. I didn't go looking for it."

Kai touched his shoulder. "I know. I thought of it deliberately, to see if you could read the one secret I have kept for years. I'm sorry."

Fee's head jerked up. "What?"

"I'm sorry. It must be a heavy burden, to see the truth in someone's face laid bare, to know the contents of someone's heart, whether you wish to or not."

Fee closed his eyes. Swallowed. "It was so terrible. Looking at my—at the High Wizard. At his wife and sons. Seeing what they thought of me. Knowing they didn't care if I saw it. Then being forced to search out someone's secrets—*while they resisted*—I stopped looking. I couldn't bear the weight of it anymore."

Kai squeezed his shoulder. "You didn't know how to shield against it?"

"Not until Lady Marlaeda told me it was possible." Fee frowned. "But I need to do more than just see. I have to make the truth known to everyone."

"Do you think you can?"

Fee sighed. "Well, I'll have to, won't I?"

SEVENTY

Eyl ducked through the smoke hole in Evander's tent and blinked to acclimate her eyes to the dim interior. The fire was banked, the lanterns extinguished. Evander had gone to bed.

She flitted to the bed and nudged the sleeper. Ev came awake with a jerk, reaching for the sword hilt propped up by the bed. "What—" he choked out before realizing who it was.

"Oh, you're back again, are you?" he said, voice foggy with sleep. "You thought the chicken was so tasty, you'd come back for more?"

He ran his fingers over her feathers. She allowed this before dropping the note into his lap. He felt for the object—then stilled.

"Well," he said in an altogether different voice before lighting a candle.

He read the note Eyl had penned, after much thought and scribbling with charcoal.

There is treachery afoot at the peace talks. An attempt will be made on your life. Do not come. I mean no harm to Altesia. I swear it by the mountain's bones. Trust those who speak of the fells. A Friend.

The fells were an ancient name for the Altesian mountain range, the Caleahanachs. One of the titles associated with the

Queen of Altesia was Lady of the Fells. It was the best signal she could think of for someone who had his best interests at heart.

Ev pondered the note a good, long time and then looked up at her. "It seems you are more than you appeared, hmm?"

Eyl fluttered her wings.

"So I must decide if I can trust this sender, who swears by the mountains. And treachery?" He frowned, running a finger through his dark, unbound hair. "But I cannot abandon my duty. I must be there."

Eyl clacked her beak unhappily.

"I must," Ev said, reaching out to stroke her feathers. "My life is not more important than the soldiers dying in pointless strife. I must do my best to make an end to this conflict. But I will take this warning to heart and remain on guard. I wonder who your 'friend' is," he murmured. "Shall I write a note back, to let them know I have received it? I'm sure my captain of the guard will be wroth with me if I do."

In the end, he marked the note and refolded it differently before tying it to her leg.

"I will not forget this," Ev said, stroking her feathers. "You were a portent of things to come. Now I shall have to do my best to convince my mother to remain here, out of danger, without telling her why." He smiled a little. "Wish me luck."

Good luck getting her to do anything she doesn't want to do, Eyl thought, but hoped he'd be successful anyway. *Only one cataclysmic problem at a time, please.*

When he opened the tent flap, Eyl winged away into the night.

SEVENTY-ONE

FEE

"Everything is going to be fine," Fee repeated, even as he inwardly stewed, staring at the flap of the wagon where they waited.

"Are you sure?" Imani asked for the seventh time. "I can't kill anyone again—I just can't. I dream about it, and I wake up and feel sick." She swallowed.

After breakfast, they had been hustled back into the wagon and taken away from the camp. They were now waiting. He wasn't sure how many soldiers they had posted as a guard, but he had to trust that Rilen and the other trackers would be able to handle the situation.

Fee refocused on her. "You're still dreaming about it?" She had been justifiably upset and disturbed after the tower had fallen, but he thought she had gotten better.

"The dreams went away in the Heartwood," she whispered, "but they came back."

"You will not have to do that wizard's wicked deeds," Kai said firmly.

"But how do you *know*?" she whispered.

"Because we won't let it happen," Fee said. He and Kai had

practiced through the night, trying different techniques, and they thought they had settled on one.

It just left a lot to chance.

Kai slipped the lockpicks into his magic-dampening shackles. They clicked open, but he left them loosely around his wrists. "Here." He turned to Imani and unlocked her restraints, then moved on to Fee. "Keep the chains on in case they check. We must be ready for the signal."

"Everything's going to be fine," Fee repeated for the eighth time. "Eyl has a plan. The trackers are with us."

"Have a little faith," Kai said grimly.

Imani clasped her hands together.

Fee tasted the unfamiliar words. Yes. Have a little faith. For so long, he hadn't had any faith at all, and it had been nearly impossible to hope for anything to change. But faith…was like a lifeline. Even the slimmest thread of it was something to grasp on to, to pull you out of the mire.

If it didn't snap.

He shut his eyes tightly and tried not to think about it.

Someone outside the wagon whistled low. Fee scanned Imani and Kai for anything out of place. Kai stuffed the lockpicks in the pocket of his breeches.

The canvas was thrust aside. A beefy soldier stuck his head in and barked, "It's time; out of the wagon," before spitting out a stream of brown tobacco juice.

"Fee?" Imani said in a shaky voice, reaching for him.

"It'll be fine," Fee said firmly, squeezing Imani's hand. *Please let it be fine.*

Kai caught his eye.

If things are not fine, be ready to unleash terror.

Fee managed not to react to the fact that he had read Kai's mind.

Fee helped Imani to her feet and exited the wagon first to help her to the ground. He found himself face to face with Marcus, who gave him an ugly grin. "Ready to win the war for us?" he rumbled. Fee turned away and lifted Imani down. Kai scrambled out after, and the soldiers prodded them forward through the woods.

"It'll be fine," Fee kept whispering as the soldiers marched them through the woods. "It'll be fine." He willed no one to look closely at their manacles. He willed the trackers to be ready. He prayed Eyl was somewhere safe. They reached a thinning of the trees. Fee could hear the river and see the flags flying over the trees.

"When we receive the signal," Marcus said, "do your fire tricks on the tent with the most flags, girl, or we gut the two of them." He grinned evilly. "So, you get two chances to get it right."

Imani looked between Fee and Kai, biting her lip.

Fee let his gaze bore into her, be some kind of steadying influence.

Abruptly, he saw Imani on a pitch-black sea, in the midst of a terrible storm. The ship pitched and flooded. Imani, smaller, frightened, clutched the mast and lifted terrified eyes to the enormous wave bearing down on the ship. She opened her mouth to scream—

Fee shook himself free of the vision. "She'll need flame," he told Marcus.

The man cuffed him on the head. Fee flinched as his ears rang. Marcus pulled a torch from a bag he carried. "Glad you're finally falling in line, boy. But don't learn me my job."

Fee kept his gaze on the ground, working his jaw.

The torch crackled to life. Marcus peered at the round disk in his hand, something Nicanor undoubtedly had given him to signal when the time was right.

Where are they? Fee wondered. Cutting it close, cutting it close. *But they'll be here. They will. Just…where* are *they?*

Marcus straightened. The disc in his hand lit up. He snapped his fingers at Imani. "Okay, light it up."

"T-The torch," Imani stammered. "I n-need—"

One of the other soldiers took the torch and struck a flint.

"Now's the time." Marcus pulled his knife and set it to Fee's throat. "Light. That. Pavilion. Up. Or this one gets a new smile." His lips pulled back from his teeth in a macabre grin. "Remember. Only two chances." He shot a look at Kai.

Fee gulped, flinching away from the knife. Where was the signal? He could throw off his manacles and try to grapple Marcus, but the bigger man would win with little effort and bellow into the bargain. Also—knife.

Imani's eyes bounced back and forth, rolling in her head like a frightened horse.

Where are *they?* he thought frantically.

Imani raised trembling hands towards the torch, her face gray and bleached of color.

A shadow fell over the group. A falcon screamed.

An arrow sprouted from Marcus's throat. He fell backwards without a sound.

Fee hit the dirt. Kai had already thrown himself at Imani and dragged her down. More arrows rained down on the other soldiers, killing blows. They uttered choked gasps and died.

A low whistle echoed through the trees, and then Nath, Rilen, and Corbett ran forward, helping them up. Eyl dove through the air to land on Fee's shoulder, wings flapping.

Fee kicked away his shackles. "What now?" he asked, reaching up to stroke Eyl's feathers. "Marcus's disc lit up. Nicanor will be worried when fire doesn't rain down like he wanted. Who knows what he'll do?!"

"Don't worry about that," Corbett said. "We've got you a direct line to the peace talks."

"WHO ARE THEY?" Fee asked, balking at the group of Altesian soldiers waiting at the perimeter.

"Some boys who owe me a favor," Corbett said. "Kedder?"

"Corbett?" the sergeant stared at their strange motley crew. "What's all this?"

"I'm calling in my favor. This boy needs to see the ambassador. Now."

"I can't interrupt the talks," Kedder said. "And, mountain's bones, Corbett, what's this all about?"

"Truth," Fee said. "Damaslar planned an assassination attempt against the Altesian party. We just foiled it."

Kedder recoiled, his hand going to his sword. "Is this true?" he demanded.

"Yes," Fee said flatly. "Because we were supposed to be the assassins. Walk us in. Keep us under guard. You'll hear the truth, just like them."

Eyl, are you going to stay a bird the whole time? he wondered as the soldiers broke into a profusion of swearing and arguing.

"Shut up!" Kedder called, silencing his men. He stared at them, Kai's arm practically holding Imani up, Fee's bandaged wounds and a huge gyrfalcon on his shoulder, Corbett and Rilen's stony faces. "Falon, Renview, with me. The rest of you, maintain perimeter."

"Look at that," Nath breathed. "An escort."

Fee couldn't stop and marvel about it. He was too focused on what lay ahead.

STEPPING into the open-air pavilion was like stepping into a live beehive. Fee could *feel* the tension, thick enough to cut with a knife. He swallowed hard, staring at the two parties. On one side of the tent sat a man in rich robes and fur to keep off the autumn chill, with a crown upon his brow. He wore the Damaslar royal colors.

That's the king, Fee thought, feeling his blood drain from his face. The King of Damaslar was here. Well, he would have been, since Nicanor had planned to kill him, but still. The *king.*

Around him sat his advisors and his councilors, looking equally puzzled and irritated—all except for Nicanor, whose lips pulled back to bare his teeth, the veins at his temples beating a sharp tattoo against his skin.

On the other side of the room sat a man in his mid-twenties with a long plait over one shoulder, wearing Altesian blue and brown and frowning at the Damaslar party. Around him stood what looked like clerks and assistants.

"What's the meaning of this?" an aide demanded as they stepped onto the scene.

Nicanor stalked up and shoved the aide aside, his face mottled with rage. His gaze flew from Fee to the bird on his shoulder and his eyes widened even further.

"What's this about, sergeant?" a more senior Altesian soldier growled, advancing on them.

"Sir, these people have information about a foiled assassination attempt." Kedder turned to Corbett.

Corbett turned to Fee.

Through his pounding heart and tightening throat, Fee opened his mouth to speak—but Nicanor announced in his loud orator's voice, "Sire, these are attackers! An Altesian plot! Damaslar, defend!" He reached for his staff behind him.

Fee reacted on instinct, throwing himself forward.

Thank you, Kai, he thought frantically as he threw out his magic and seized hold. He and Kai had practiced grapples all through the night, mental holds to keep a lock on someone magically and allow him a foothold in their mind. Kai had managed to put up a good fight. But it was nothing like trying to hold a wizard in his prime.

Fee grappled Nicanor, his father's fingers inches from the runes that would spell their doom. Nicanor's eyes flew wide when he realized what Fee was trying to do. He fought the domination tooth and nail, making Fee sweat and shake to keep hold.

Wild magic is about the will, he told himself, clenching his teeth. *I* will not *let go.*

Soldiers advanced, evidently unsure of what or who the enemy was. Corbett reached for his sword as the sweat rolled down Fee's face. The Altesians, no doubt angered at Nicanor's accusations, were getting to their feet.

But Eyl launched herself off Fee's shoulder and raked her talons down Nicanor's face. He screamed and threw up his hands to ward her off.

The break in his concentration allowed Fee to get a hold of him and freeze him in place. The tendrils of his magic sunk into his father and hung on, though Nicanor fought against the bonds.

Rilen and Kai grabbed Nicanor, forcing his arms behind him even as the lords around him exclaimed and started to rise from their seats.

Gritting his teeth to hold on to Nicanor, Fee cried, "Hear me, Your Majesty and noble lords! The High Wizard Nicanor has perpetrated crimes against this peace gathering and against his king!"

The king leaned forward. "What? Against his king? What's this?"

Nicanor hissed, "Lies, it's all li—urk."

"Tell all truth and not one lie," Fee forced out through gritted teeth.

"Are we to suffer this—this intrusion by these rough men?" a councilor shouted. "Soldiers, remove these thugs!"

"Stop."

The command made the Altesians freeze.

The Altesian ambassador stood up and held up a hand, staring at their group, and in particular the gyrfalcon that fluttered back to Fee's shoulder. "I want to hear what these…children…have to say. Though I would caution to remove hands from the High Wizard of Damaslar."

"M-My lord," Fee said. "Thank you. My friends will be happy to do so…once perhaps you take possession of his staff." He lifted a shaking hand to Eyl's feathers, her weight a steadying presence under the unified scrutiny.

The ambassador raised an eyebrow. "Is that so? I was given to understand it was a grave insult to ask that of a wizard."

Fee gulped. "Sir, I am uniquely able to speak to his capacity for betrayal. The High Wizard is my f-father."

The ambassador's eyebrows flew up, as did every other set in the pavilion.

"You ungrateful, puling whelp," Nicanor forced through his teeth, practically spitting at Fee. "Disloyal—!"

"A dog that was treated the way you treated me would have no loyalty to its master, so I have no loyalty to you," Fee said, clinging to the magical tethers with all his strength.

"Thought I knew all your children, Nicanor." King Caldair, the Damask King, leaned forward and frowned at Fee. "Who's this one?"

"Feonar Yaldson, Y-Your Majesty."

As the furious whisper of "bastard" flew through the assembled ranks, the Altesian ambassador stepped forward and plucked the staff from Nicanor's hand. "Now that the magical element has been taken care of, perhaps your friends would release your father. Then our guards would be able to take their hands off their swords, and we shall hear what you have to say."

Rilen and Kai stepped back. Nicanor threw off their hands and stalked towards Fee, blood running down his face. "You—!"

Corbett stepped in his path. "Try it," he snarled.

"Nicanor, you can't throttle the boy; isn't proper," King Caldair said reasonably. Then he sobered. "Now. What's this about crimes against me?"

"Sire, my father has plotted to use my friends' magical abilities to attack this peace gathering and kill the Altesian ambassador… and yourself, Your Majesty."

The pavilion dissolved into uproar. Men stood and shouted, pointing fingers here and there.

But the Altesian ambassador did not look shocked. "Your Majesty, my lords!" he said, raising his hands before the group.

"Please. If you permit it, I will use what skills I have, and then we will hear all in an orderly fashion."

"You won't hear anything because I did—I did—" Nicanor froze, staring at Fee.

Elation flooded him. The magical bonds had tied his tongue. "Tell all truth, and not one lie," he said again fiercely, and he remembered what Eyl had put in her note. "By the mountain fells." Eyl screeched.

Nicanor stared around at the assembled people, including a king. Then he bolted.

He didn't get more than four steps before Corbett tackled him.

"Running? From a confrontation? Nicanor, not very sporting of you," the king said, his face darkening. He waved a hand. "Yes, Lord Evander, take the lead. Let's hear what the boy has to say."

The ambassador, Lord Evander, regarded Nicanor, his length measured on the carpets laid down, and then turned to Fee. "Speak on, Feonar."

Fee swallowed hard. "My name is Feonar Yaldson. I am Nicanor Beornraed's bastard, but I have a magical talent that helps me see other people's hidden truths, secrets. The High Wizard pressed me into service as an interrogator for the Damaslar army to pry the truth out of spies. The High Wizard corresponded with a wizard conducting illegal magical experiments to try to turn the tide of war in Damaslar's favor—and then when peace seemed likely, he decided to betray the king."

"What? Experiments?" the king asked.

"Us," Kai said clearly. He gestured to himself and Imani, setting an arm around her shoulders as she shook under the scrutiny of all assembled. Eyl flapped her wings. "Your Majesty, he tried to leverage our magically manipulated abilities for the war effort. Then he decided he would have us assassinate everyone at this peace gathering instead. But you do not have to believe us, Your Majesty. Fee's talent enables him to reveal truth, a service he has performed often in the war. Let everyone at this gathering hear the truth from the High Wizard's own lips."

All eyes turned to Nicanor, who rolled his eyes like a frightened horse and struggled mightily in Corbett's grip as the tracker hauled him upright.

"Tell us, Father," Fee demanded. "Tell us, from the first to the last, your plan—and why."

Sweat rolled down Nicanor's face. He gritted his teeth, his face flushing with effort. He didn't have to speak the truth to keep the words behind his teeth.

But I can prompt him, Fee realized, feeling the magic tendrils teach him what to do. He twitched one. "No more secrets. What did you wish to accomplish, Father?"

Nicanor growled wordlessly, but he had no magic at his disposal—no wild magic, like Fee.

Now it's finally good for something, Mother.

"I—" he hissed, trying to keep the words back, but they tumbled out instead. "I corresponded with Aedelbras the Sorcerer, exiled some years ago from the capital for illegal magical experiments. He had a theory that...that he could awaken certain abilities, imbue subjects with specific magical talents."

"Why were they illegal?" a lord demanded.

"They were performed on beggars, refuse," Nicanor bit out. "But he thought that...those on the cusp of adulthood would be more receptive to the trials. The Damaslar Concordium of Magic found out and exiled him."

The assembled company turned their gazes to Eyl, Kai, and Imani.

"He continued his work," Kai said, letting a sinuous serpent slip from his mouth. "He used the flesh-peddlers of this country, the snatchers who are allowed to thrive unchecked, to find children to suit his purposes." Several men recoiled as Kai caught the garter snake in his palm and stroked it.

"He wrote me," Nicanor ground out. "Said he had three experiments work. Offered them for the war effort. If I'd lift his banishment. But my *ungrateful bastard* stole my correspondence and set out to steal them from under my nose—"

"People aren't things," Fee said flatly. "I don't think you've ever understood that."

"My men recaptured them outside Blackthorn Forest, brought them here. By then—" Nicanor stopped. He bit his tongue.

"Is it so very bad, the truth you don't wish to tell?" Fee asked quietly, feeding more energy to the magical tendrils. He tried to hide how badly his limbs wanted to shake.

Nicanor spat blood at him, but the droplets fell short. Corbett shook him like a terrier would shake a rat. "By then, the prince had come to me with a plan—to assassinate the Altesian delegation—as well as the king."

Pandemonium arose among the assembly. Lords stood and protested; the king bellowed. The young man seated beside him—the crown prince? —turned gray and jumped up, decrying the whole thing was a lie.

Soldiers rushed forward but didn't know what to do.

The Altesians were gasping but all were watching avidly.

"It's not true! He's lying!" the prince yelled. "This is a conspiracy! He's bewitched the High Wizard!"

"That's true. How can we trust that he isn't just putting words into the High Wizard's mouth?" one lord demanded. "Maybe this is an *Altesian* plot to sow discord!"

"He's got enough magic to bewitch the High Wizard of Damaslar?" another asked skeptically.

"Some kind of strange faefolk magic," someone muttered. "Unnatural."

"How do we know it's the truth?" a third yelled.

"He can put his magic on the prince and see what he says."

"He can't perform strange magic on the prince!" Someone gasped, outraged.

"My lords, please!" the ambassador said, trying to restore order.

"I cannot compel more than one person to reveal truth at a time," Fee ground out through his teeth. "And I likely...will not be able to make this effort again. My magic does not put words into his mouth. It only reveals what is already there. Ask the High Wizard whatever you like—something only you and he know."

The gathering quieted as people settled down avidly, shushing the louder, more vocal members. People glanced around the gathering, wondering who would act as inquisitor.

Then a man resplendent in fine, chestnut robes stepped forward, his eyes hard on Nicanor. He slowly removed his gloves and placed them in a pocket. "I have a question I'd like the answer to. It's one I've pondered for some time. If this assembly is agreeable, I will put the question to Lord Beornraed."

Men murmured. The general consensus was officiated by the king's waved hand. "Proceed, Lord Sherrington."

Lord Sherrington cracked his knuckles, then looked Nicanor dead in the eye. "Did you ever sleep with my wife?"

The whole pavilion went dead silent.

Nicanor's Adam's apple bobbed. A bead of sweat rolled down his temple. But Fee could feel the answer forcing its way out and knew it before his father spoke the word.

"…Yes."

Gasps echoed, then silence reigned again as Lord Sherrington braced his hands on the table between them. His broad shoulders flexed as he leaned in to stare at Nicanor. "That's what I thought." He nodded to himself. Then his stare increased in intensity, until everyone who could see his face braced for impact. "Is Jasper my son?"

No one in the room dared to breathe.

Blood dribbled out of the corner of Nicanor's mouth.

"…No."

Lord Sherrington nodded again. Then he heaved the table aside with enough force to flip it over, going for Nicanor's throat.

The pavilion erupted into shouts of shock, horror, denial—and above it all, the king booming, "Plot against me, will you? Your own father? Take him—them—both away, under heavy guard!

Make sure the wizard has no way to perform magic! I want a full investigation! I want explanations!"

An advisor from Damaslar bowed deeply to the Altesian ambassador. "We would beg a recess from Altesia and a delay of a day's time in our negotiations."

The ambassador bowed back. "Altesia grants Damaslar a day's delay."

Fee, wobbling, released the magical hold on Nicanor, who immediately started to howl the vilest vitriol and threats he could come up with. But Fee couldn't hear it. He slumped against Corbett, shaking.

It was over. They were free.

As the peace talks devolved into a lot of very influential men having hysterics, the Altesian ambassador motioned to their party of interlopers. "Sometimes retreat is the better part of valor— unless you wish to…?" He looked at Fee.

Fee shook his head emphatically.

"Understandable. I believe some of your party are Altesian," he said, looking at Corbett. "I'd be very much interested in hearing the longer version of your tale. I'd be pleased if you would accompany me back to our camp so I might hear the full tale."

"*Please*," Imani said. She looked as wrung out as a dish rag. Unanimously, everyone followed Evander and his escort away from the pavilion and across the river to the Altesian camp.

After they all had crossed the river, the ambassador slipped through the group to end up by Fee. "How did you do it?" he asked quietly.

"My lord?" Fee asked, perplexed.

"How did you know to send me the note?"

Fee stared at him. "Note?"

"The note, warning me about the plot. How did you know to say trust those who speak of the fells?"

Fee slowly shook his head. "I didn't send you a note, my lord."

The ambassador frowned at him as Eyl took off from Fee's shoulder. "But you must have—your bird brought the note to me."

"Bird?" Fee blinked. "*Oh.*" He yanked his tunic over his head.

"He didn't. It was me," Eyl said from behind a bush.

SEVENTY-TWO

EYL

Eyl took the tunic Fee had shoved in her direction, his ears bright red, and pulled it over her head. When she was decent, she eased around the bush and caught several startled epithets from the soldiers that no doubt hadn't meant to be heard. But she didn't care about that. All she could see was Ev. She viewed him with human eyes for the first time in nine years. A grown man, with the look of their father about him. His long, brown plait hung to his waist. She unconsciously grasped the shorn, white hair around her ears.

Evander's eyes widened in shock. "Oh. I suppose that does clear up a few things. Please pardon me, miss, for assuming you were simply a messenger."

Her throat closed. She pressed her lips together and tried to pry her tongue from the roof of her mouth.

He smiled kindly at her as the group continued towards the tents up ahead, flying brightly colored pendants with familiar banners on them. "I'm even more eager to hear your tale. I imagine it is worthy of a great saga."

Eyl stumbled. Fee caught her arm. "Are you all right?"

She nodded.

"Come, come. I'm sure you are tired," Evander said, ushering them towards the large tent she had found him in the night before.

Suddenly, Eyl's legs refused to move forward. She couldn't go in there—couldn't sit and eat with all her friends as if her world hadn't shifted on its axis. "It's a long tale," she said, voice cracking. "But I want to tell it."

Evander paused, waiting for her politely. A soldier opened his mouth, and out of the corner of her eye, she saw Corbett hush him.

"I've never told anybody the whole of it," she admitted, squeezing Fee's hand and shooting an apologetic look at Kai and Imani. "Even when I wanted to, more than anything. I was afraid." Her voice broke, and she sucked in a sharp breath.

Fee frowned in concern. "What is it, Eyl?"

Evander froze, his eyes locking on her face.

Unbidden, tears sprang to her eyes. "I know I look a little different," she said, not able to control the shake in her voice. "Older. The hair." Her hands jerkily motioned. "Don't you know me, Ev?"

Her brother went dead white. "What?"

She choked on a sob-laugh. "If you want me to duel you right here to prove it, I can, but I'm warning you, I'm very rusty—"

Evander took three steps forward and pulled her into his arms, crushing her to him. "*Eylinore*," he gasped, and she didn't even care that he was squeezing her too tightly to breathe. She clung just as tightly back. "Eyl, Eyl, Eyl," he said over and over. "Heaven and Earth, Eyl, you're here. You're *alive*."

"Yes," she said, and she let the tears come.

"I missed you *so much*," Ev said. She felt his tears in her hair. "*God*. I always hoped, because of the spell, but…Eyl, I admire your flair for dramatic." Ev laughed, shaking her. "But why didn't you speak to me last night? What happened to you? Where have you been? And magic?" He pulled away from her and stared at her in wonder. "I swear you haven't grown an inch."

"Thanks a whole bunch, Ev." Eyl laughed through tears.

"Eyl?" Imani said in a small voice.

She pulled back, wiping her face. "It's all right, Imani. Everything's all right."

"Eyl, you know him?" Fee asked, staring hard at Ev.

Eyl smiled and touched Fee's sleeve. "Evander is my brother." Fee's jaw dropped.

"You're the Princess of Altesia," Kai said, revelation dawning.

"Will you forgive me for not telling you all?" she asked them, but she kept her eyes on Fee, her heart in her throat.

Fee's eyes held hers. "After all we've been through together? You have to ask?"

"Princess."

Eyl turned to see the soldiers around them—including Corbett, Rilen, and Nath—all taking a knee in an ever-widening circle. The murmurs grew as the men and women in Altesian colors stared at her with raw emotion on their faces. Amazement. Awe. Hope. And the murmurs grew from whispers to exclamations.

"Princess. The princess. She's alive!"

Ev squeezed her hand, like he was afraid to let her go. "Today, we might've made history for a different reason than I initially thought." He laughed. "Eyl—"

"Evander, my son, what is it you do?"

The lady that swept towards them in wide, green skirts had a small frown line between her brows, her lips slightly pursed. But Eyl couldn't remember any other emotion on Lady Petronella's face. "I was told there was some disturbance at the peace talks. Who are these…people?" She stared at the kneeling soldiers, her eyes narrowing.

Coldness swept over Eyl. Except for a few tiny lines at the corners of her eyes and mouth, Eyl would've thought Ev's mother hadn't aged a day. Her blonde hair, braided and reaching nearly to her feet, still showed no trace of gray.

Eyl reached for Fee's hand, instinctively seeking support. He took her hand with no hesitation.

"Mother! Eylinore is alive!" Evander cried.

Shock made Lady Petronella's eyes widen. Then her brows snapped together. Her gaze raked over Eyl. "That's impossible," Lady Petronella said flatly. "The princess is dead. This is some impostor. Guards—"

"Mother," Evander said, stepping forward. "Look at her. How can you say that?"

"Because she was assured of my death."

Eyl's words produced a curious pocket of silence, the air charged with the same energy of a just-rung bell.

"What?" Ev breathed.

"What slander!" Lady Petronella gasped. "How dare you, you little—"

"I'd beware of what insults you sling about Her Royal Highness Princess Eylinore of Altesia." Corbett's voice rang out from behind Eyl like a hammer slammed on an anvil.

Eyl glanced over her shoulder. The Gar brothers had flanked her, one on her left, the other on her right.

"And who are you?" Lady Petronella hissed.

Corbett's expression made the temperature in the pavilion drop to icy levels. "I'm *his* brother," he said slowly. "And his voice, when he asks."

Rilen stepped forward and signed, *"The princess is who she says she is. I bear witness to her identity because I did not kill her when you commanded me to."* Corbett translated aloud.

Lady Petronella recoiled as if she had been slapped. "What?"

"I do not look the same," Rilen signed. *"But I was the guard you commanded to kill two girls on the slopes of Queen's Crest nine years ago."*

"Mother?" Evander paled. "What is he saying?"

Lady Petronella balled her fists in her skirts. "These are pernicious *lies*. Soldiers, I command you to have them taken away and given a taste of Altesian justice." Her voice cracked like a whip, strong, commanding.

The soldiers' heads swung between Lady Petronella and Eyl, unsure and wary.

Eyl cleared her throat. "I went on a picnic with Lisette."

The words fell from her lips in a strange cadence. The story she had never had the chance to tell anyone but herself. "A snow picnic. Silly, but I'd whined for days to be allowed to go. We packed a basket of 'winter picnic foodstuffs' and flasks of hot tea and chocolate and went up on Queen's Crest with only a few guards to accompany us. We had our picnic, and then we went on a walk. It had started to snow." She swallowed.

"You sent a man to kill me, Lady Petronella." Eyl motioned to Rilen. "This man."

"I will not stand here and listen to these spurious lies!" she spat.

"Yes, you will." Evander's face hardened. "You'll stand right here, until we hear all of it."

"Evander!" She gasped.

Rilen signed and Corbett translated, *"You commanded me to kill two maids on the slopes of Queen's Crest. Gave me descriptions of their cloaks. And because I was such a lovesick fool, twisted up with slavish devotion, the way all your guards were, I believed the story you told me and I obeyed. I went. I killed the taller of the two girls. And then God was merciful because I recognized the princess for who she was. I sent her to run and hide in the forest and found and killed a deer to bring its heart back to you, in lieu of a body."*

"How *dare* you?! Will someone shut them up?" Lady Petronella shouted, pointing towards Rilen and Corbett.

"You already tried that," Rilen said. *"You cut out my tongue."* He gestured to his mouth, where the pale scar twisted out of his dark beard.

"Nearly died from it," Corbett added.

Evander's expression slowly faded from shock to horror to agonized revulsion. "Mother," he whispered, "you plotted against the crown? You wanted my sister dead?"

Lady Petronella's face twisted, her controlled mask finally breaking. "She is *not* your sister!" she shrieked. "You are *mine*! Destined for greatness!" Her rage transformed her face into a horrible visage as she bared her teeth. "She is nothing to you!"

"All the pushing, the machinations...." Evander blanched. "Even then? You had designs on the throne. You plotted *regicide*. Did Fa—did the king know?"

"Of course not," she spat, eyes wild. "He was so enamored with his precious princess. His sweet little girl. But he was *mine* first! I gave him up because I knew he could win the crown. He would be king. But then they were unhappy—and no wonder, she was frigid and callous to him—and he turned to me for comfort. And I did. I gave him a child when she struggled. He *doted* on you. You were his firstborn. The crown was *your* birthright."

Evander said, as soft as death, "Mother, the throne descends through the queen."

Lady Petronella nodded emphatically. "And that's why she had to die!" She threw her arm out at Eyl. "If there had been no issue, Andrette would have chosen you! I was willing to give you up! Willing to let you take on her name, be named as her heir! It was for you! It was all for you!" Tears of rage ran down her face.

"Captain Amber," Evander said, addressing the soldiers' leader, "I must ask you to take Lady Petronella into custody for treason against the crown and attempted murder of the heir to the throne." His voice cracked, but his eyes radiated agonized determination. "We all stand witness to her tacit confession."

Lady Petronella stared at her son, her lips trembling. "Evander...!"

Ev shook his head. "Mother, it's best if you go quietly."

Lady Petronella stared around at the witnesses, her expression wild and frantic. "No. No. I won't let you throw this all away! I've given you everything!" She started towards Ev.

Evander flinched. "Mother—"

"You'll have it—if it's the last thing I do—!"

Lady Petronella spun on her heel, switching from Evander to Eyl. And in her hand—bright steel.

Soldiers roared. Swords rasped.

But she was too close. Eyl didn't even have time to gasp.

The blade with the greenish sheen swung.

And then Corbett stepped between Eyl and the knife.

SEVENTY-THREE

CORBETT

The knife penetrated his leather armor and sunk into flesh, but it was not a mortal wound. The stab was fueled by the strength of desperation, not skill. The problem was the afterbite, the burn Corbett felt on his skin and in his blood.

Blood soaked the ground—but it wasn't his. In front of him, Lady Petronella measured her length on the ground, her breath labored. The soldiers had eliminated the threat to their newly discovered princess.

The ambassador knelt beside his mother, holding her hand. Corbett heard him whisper, "Why did you do it?"

"You should've been king," the lady mumbled. "It would've made it right. Made it worth it. He should've stayed with me...." Her breath escaped her lips in a death rattle. The ambassador bowed his head.

Corbett's head went curiously light. He fell to one knee, pressing a hand to his ribs. The dagger that had fallen from the woman's hand glinted in the dirt. "I assume that was poisoned."

Rilen seized his shoulders and shook him, face stricken. *"Why did you do that? Why did you take the blow?"*

Corbett coughed. "Because I knew if I didn't, *you* would, idiot.

And she stole…she stole from you. I'm not going to let her kill you. Or the princess," he added belatedly.

Rilen groaned and mouthed, "Fool!"

"You're my little brother. It's my job to protect you. And I couldn't back then." He smiled. "You were always better than me. More loyal, more faithful, more devout. The best thing that could be said for me was that I was your brother."

"Not true," Rilen signed emphatically. *"You looked out for me. Raised me."*

Corbett put a hand on Rilen's shoulder. He listed to the side. "Promise me. You'll live and be happy. No guilt. No more of that."

Rilen made an anguished noise, full of grief and pain.

Fee's face swam into Corbett's view, his scar in sharp relief framed by his very red hair. "Some kind of poison? Fast acting?"

"Wouldn't put it past her," Corbett mumbled.

"Rilen, will you let me try to help? I don't know what it's doing to him, but I can try to stop it."

"Can't make it worse," Corbett slurred.

His brother gave a sharp nod. *"You will not die. You are not allowed to die."*

Corbett huffed. "Don't tell me what to do, Rye."

CHAPTER

SEVENTY-FOUR

FEE

Fee put his hands on Corbett and was pathetically grateful for the small scrap of healing he had done in the Heartwood on Eyl. He dove in on a hope and a prayer, chasing the poison licking through Corbett's veins, heading it off from his heart and vital organs, trying to contain it where he could and burn it out when he had the chance. He didn't know how long he spent, eyes shut, hunting for the inner sense of wrongness, but it finally left him gasping, hair plastered to his forehead with sweat and his heart pounding.

"He'll live," Fee told Rilen. "I don't know what side effects he might experience from the poison…but he won't die. From this. He'll still die. But later. Hopefully."

"How exciting," Corbett mumbled. He didn't look any better than Fee felt.

Rilen signed, *"Thank you."* Fee knew that one.

Evander directed soldiers to carry Corbett to the medical tent. Lady Petronella's body had already been taken away.

Eyl appeared at his side. "Are you okay? Here, drink this. Eat this food." She pressed water and a handful of dried fruit into his hands.

Fee did so automatically. He realized his stomach was scraping his backbone, he felt so hungry. "So you're really the princess?" Fee asked, after gulping down half the canteen of water. "Evander's really your brother?"

Eyl ducked her head. "Yes. I was planning to tell you when we left Blackthorn, but we got captured. I'm sorry for keeping it from you."

"You were right to keep it secret!" Fee said. "I'm the son of the High Wizard of Damaslar! I interrogated spies! I could've done incredible damage with that information."

"Even so...."

Fee shook his head. "It's all right. I know all too well the grip a secret can have on you."

Eyl slowly smiled and reached out to take his hand. "Look at us," she murmured. "Confronting our pasts all in one day."

"Who would've thought."

She grinned, then leaned forward and kissed him on the cheek. Right on top of his scar. His whole body felt full of light.

"Not me," he whispered. Not once could he have imagined something as good as this.

Evander guided them all into the large tent set aside for the ambassador's use, and there they were able to have a full meal. He excused himself when servants began to bring the dishes in. Fee watched Eyl stare after him pensively.

"You all right?" he whispered.

"I am. I don't know about Ev. I wanted...I don't know. Justice, maybe. But I didn't want her dead."

"As painful as it is, she made her choices."

"She was still his mother."

"Which is why he needs a minute."

She nodded, looking down at her plate. Then she picked up her fork. "So. Are you coming home with me?" Eyl asked them all. "We can arrange passage to wherever you'd like to go, of course, but if you want...."

Imani smiled. "I want to see your mountains."

Kai said, "I swore to go with you to see to the end of our journey. I will send a message to my family. They must believe I am dead. I must break it to them gently."

Eyl turned to Fee, her eyes wide and hopeful.

"Am I included?" he asked.

She blinked. "Yes? Why wouldn't you be? You have somewhere else to go?"

"Well...."

"You're coming. No arguments."

"But you're the princess. Of Altesia. I'm Damask."

"First, I'm the girl you rescued and freed from both a literal and metaphorical prison, and second, yes. Because I think Altesia needs a wizard."

"Ah. What?"

"We are willing to pay very competitive rates."

He started to smile. "Well, when you put it like that...."

"And I need you, too. I need your faith in me, and your resolve to do the right thing. I need your smiles. I need you."

He swallowed. "I never believed any of that was valuable before."

"So you heard it here first." Eyl nodded decisively.

When they'd scraped the last bits of food from their plates, Imani asked, "Eyl? Do you still feel that pull north?"

Eyl tilted her head to the side. "Yes."

"What do you think it is?"

"I can answer that." Evander stepped back into the pavilion and took a seat, pouring himself a glass of wine. His eyes were a little red, but nothing else betrayed his inner turmoil. "The queen never gave up looking for you. She found a magic user who tried to locate you. She couldn't confirm beyond all doubt you were still alive, but she couldn't locate your body, either. So they created a call, a beacon, that was keyed to the queen's blood, and they thought that if you were alive, the spell would guide you back home. It was a last hope."

Eyl shook her head. "And for nine years, I was tethered to the tower and couldn't come."

Evander reached across the table and took her head. "I want to hear all about those years. I also want to get you home as soon as we can. The queen isn't well, Eyl. But we have to finish these dratted talks first."

Eyl smiled. "I have some ideas about that."

CHAPTER

SEVENTY-FIVE

EYL

The peace treaty that Evander deftly crafted and negotiated surrounding the cessation of hostilities against Altesia and the smaller hill countries included a stipulation that, in restitution for the attempted treachery upon the peace talks, Damaslar must put an end to the indenture system that was rife for exploitation by snatchers, as well as make a concerted effort to hunt down snatchers within their borders and find those trapped and exploited in order to set them free.

Backed into a corner on proven treachery from their own side, Damaslar signed.

As soon as the ink was dry, Evander organized an advanced group to return to Altesia consisting of Eyl and her friends as well as three squads, leaving behind some of his subordinates to handle the wrap-up as well as most of the army. They traveled light and as fast as was feasible.

As the landscape changed, growing hillier and more forested, they caught sight of the mountains in the distance. Eyl's pull grew to a true physical pain, and some days, she changed to a gyrfalcon to be able to relieve it a little. But it was nice to introduce Fee and Kai and Imani to the look of the land.

When they crossed Taliesin's Gap between the mountains of

Watchtower and Queen's Crest, Eyl physically felt the border. She reeled on the back of her horse as a tangible welcome overwhelmed her. It was as if the country—the very *land itself*—turned to look at her. And it said, *Welcome home.*

She sobbed for a good fifteen minutes on Evander's shoulder, as her brother patted her back and held her. Then he passed her over to ride pillion with Fee, as she was wrung out.

After a few days, they entered Cruever, the capital, at dusk. Eyl's eyes sought out what landmarks she could pick out, the strange homesickness washing over her. So familiar but alien at the same time. Then they were at the castle, and Eyl's heart was in her throat.

By virtue of Evander's ambassador status, they were ushered in through many checkpoints until they reached the personal crownsguard of the queen. She didn't know what Ev said to them —the blood was rushing in her ears at that point, drowning everything out—but she passed men and women kneeling with tears in their eyes. She couldn't see anything but the hallways before her, and then the door to her mother's bedchamber.

The door swung open, and she stepped inside, the pull within her almost unbearable. She stumbled through the room that smelled like a sickroom, her vision narrowing to only the four-poster bed hung with heavy draperies and the figure within. Eyl fell to her knees amidst the plush carpeting beside the bed, and with one last painful throb, the nine-year-long pull fell away to nothing.

"Mother," Eyl whispered, taking the cool, limp hand on the bedclothes. "Mother, it's me. I have come home."

Andrette, the Queen of Altesia, opened her eyes, the same shade as Eyl's own, and squeezed her hand. She whispered, "I knew you would."

EPILOGUE

EYL

Queen Eylinore of Altesia, Lady of the Fells, turned the heavy, silver crown around in her hands. The symbol of her status was traditionally worn on top of copious amounts of hair. While her hair was growing steadily, it was not long enough to pile on her head yet. Her maids had to content themselves with curling it in ringlets and winding ribbons through tiny, thin braids until such a time as it could be put into a proper plait.

Eyl smiled sadly. She had had her mother for longer than she had expected. Fee had pored over old, forgotten volumes of lore and worked with the palace healers to augment magic to her mother's curatives and buy her more time, but her mother's illness had progressed too far to be reversed. But it had been a wonderful five months, spent almost exclusively with her mother except for select public appearances to assure the citizenry that their lost princess had indeed returned. Eyl could not get over the unabashed joy nearly everyone had shown her. But no one was more joyful than her mother, who had always believed she lived.

The five months had been full of reminiscing, yes, but also as much training in queenship as her mother could impart to her. She'd known she'd been dying, and she'd wanted to give Eyl everything she could.

Eyl had found out her mother and father *had* sent out searchers for her multiple times over the past years, but they now knew the late Lady Petronella had always thwarted them—probably with knowledge gained from pillow talk with the king.

"Please don't hate your father, dear," the queen had told her in confidence. "Whatever his other failings, he loved you. When you were missing and presumed dead, that was the only time I ever saw him weep. The mistakes and failures between us were our own. Just make sure you learn from them."

"I don't think that will be a problem," Eyl had replied as Fee had been announced. He had come to take her to lunch in the castle garden, and then for a private flight. She'd been getting more comfortable and happier transitioning to and from her second form. She'd looked up and beamed at him. Her mother had chuckled dryly and smiled.

It was as Ev had told her: Nine years ago, Eyl's mother had found a half-faefolk woman with some not-inconsiderable power, and she had not been able to find any human remains to confirm the theory of an animal attack. But by that time, Eyl had been too far away to find via magic. The absence of a body had left too many doubts unresolved. The woman had been able to put out a beacon, a call on Eyl to return. It had been renewed each year, and it had strengthened until it had become impossible to ignore.

Queen Andrette had passed peacefully in her sleep two weeks ago, Eyl holding her hand. The funeral rites had taken time—the people of Altesia deserved to mourn their queen of many years in proper fashion. Many of the loyal retainers in the castle, as well as a portion of the populace, had cut their hair, the Altesian sign of deep mourning, from the depth of love for her. But Queen Andrette had asked Eyl not to, since hers had been a grief of nine missing years.

Now it was time to get to the business of ruling, and Eyl meant to start off right.

"Eyl?"

She turned, the crown still dangling from her fingers as Fee entered the small receiving chamber looking quite splendid in a velvet-blue tunic. She smiled. Besides her brother, Fee, Imani, and Kai were the only ones who still called her "Eyl"—in private, of course. To everyone else she was "Your Majesty," or "Queen Eylinore."

It was taking some getting used to, but as long as she was still Eyl to a few, it didn't grate quite as much. Imani and Kai were settling into Altesia well, and Eyl had extended her hospitality indefinitely if they wanted it, as well as assistance in locating any of their family members. Imani didn't have much hope, but Eyl was stubborn. Kai had written a letter to be delivered to his family, but he maintained that he would stay and assist her and Imani, that they needed him. Eyl thought there was something else to it, but she'd get it out of him eventually.

"You wanted to see me?" Fee asked, brushing his red hair out of his face. He was growing it out in the Altesian fashion, but it was not quite long enough to tie back yet.

"Yes. How go things in the magical world, Queen's Wizard?"

He grinned. "You know you have a huge, fusty, old library full of manuscripts and scrolls that no one's even touched in a hundred years? It's going to take me ages to sift through it all."

"Oh. Well, in that case...."

"What?" He approached and looked down at her. He was still taller than her. Palace healers had told her it was unlikely she'd ever grow taller since so much of her growth period had been stunted by twice-daily shifts and magic. But she didn't mind. Looking up into his face—scars and all—was one of her favorite things to do.

"I wondered if I could add to your plate, a little."

"How so?"

"It's selfish of me," Eyl muttered.

"Why don't you let me be the judge of that," Fee said. "What is it?"

"There are a lot of responsibilities landing on my plate now. The coronation is in a week. And after that, I will have the official seal of approval, and everyone will start descending with problems they expect me to fix."

"You'll have the councilors to help," Fee pointed out.

"They'll help the country. But I don't have anyone to really help *me*."

"What am I, chopped liver?"

Eyl blushed. "You're the best help. That's why I feel selfish asking you for more."

"I want to give you whatever you need," Fee said, taking her hand. "What is it? Is it about the meeting today? Because we discussed—"

Eyl bit her lip. "Not for a task. Or...not really. Just to be there for me and listen when I'm having a bad day. And hold my hand when I'm scared. And share the good times as well as the bad times. Because I want us to have good times now. We deserve it."

The corner of Fee's mouth ticked up. "Are you proposing to me?"

Eyl groaned and put her head in her hands, almost braining herself with the crown. "Was it that bad? I wrote down everything I wanted to say and then it just flew right—"

Fee smiled and gathered her in his arms. "Don't worry. I liked it."

"Enough to say *yes*?" she asked hopefully.

"It was always going to be yes because I love you." He bent his head and kissed her.

Joy welled up in her, and she kissed him back. Never had she been more grateful for the Altesian custom that allowed women—and queens—to choose their own spouses. With Fee, she believed she could do anything, accomplish any task, no matter how insurmountable. Even run a country. They had already been through fire. Now it would all be worth it. After a time, she pulled back and smiled at him. "Would you have believed one day you would be a king?"

He shook his head. "No, because I won't be. I don't think Altesia needs a king, and I wouldn't marry you to be the king. I only want to be this queen's husband."

She hadn't believed she could love him more, but she found she was wrong.

After another long embrace, Eyl stepped back from Fee as the door to the chamber creaked.

The steward coughed discreetly. "Your Majesty, your afternoon appointment has arrived."

Eyl turned. "Show her in, Hussif."

Fee took the crown from her hands and put it on her head.

"I can do it, you know," she murmured.

"You always put it on crooked, and it ends up looking like it'll slide over your ear," he whispered back.

She only had time to glare at him in promise of repayment before the woman was shown into the room.

The woman with jet-black hair plaited loosely over one shoulder wore an indigo gown of dark blue. The material was fine but simple in design. She appeared roughly ten or fifteen years their senior. The lines of her face were sharp and fey, and her ears tapered up to a distinct point. She regarded Eyl levelly with dark eyes.

"Good afternoon," Eyl said, lifting her chin to the taller woman. "Mistress Obelyn?"

"Yes, Your Majesty," the woman replied respectfully but with no obsequiousness.

"It is a pleasure to meet you. I wanted to thank you for your service to my mother, Queen Andrette. I am told you are the one who crafted the spell to call me."

"Yes, Your Majesty," the woman said. "I am sorry it was not more helpful."

"It was immensely helpful," Eyl assured her. "It was a lifeline when I desperately needed one. If there is any boon the crown can grant you, I would like to hear it."

"I need no boon, Your Majesty," Mistress Obelyn said. "I did not do it to serve the crown. I helped a mother who wanted to find her child."

"It was a very powerful spell," Fee said.

Her eyes flicked to him. "So it was."

He smiled and carded a hand through his hair, sweeping it back from his pointed ears, though not as pronounced as hers were. "I would be interested in speaking with you about how you did it. Altesia isn't as widely versed on magic as Damaslar."

A flash of recognition and curiosity flashed in her eyes. She inclined her head graciously.

"Beyond that," Eyl said, "I want to talk to you, about faefolk, the Sundering…and if you believe there's any way to undo what was done." At the woman's sharp look, Eyl continued. "So much of what we experienced was a distortion of faefolk magic—and once we'd learned to truly use wild magic, we were able to use our power to free ourselves. In addition, several faefolk helped us on our journey—I don't think we'd be here without their help. And they are hindered by the limitation of magic in Karneesia. The Sundering was an imbalance perpetrated by human wizards. If there's any way to give back what was stolen from them—from us—I want to try."

Mistress Obelyn stared at her for a long time, and then her face curved in a slow, pleased smile. "Let us see what we can do."

ACKNOWLEDGMENTS

This book was determined to off me multiple times in the years since it first germinated in 2017. Thankfully, I am still here and the book is now finally here. But neither of us would have made it without several key people.

Thanks to E.C. Farrell who read the book not once but TWICE (or maybe even three times??). That first time didn't even have an ending, so you truly went above and beyond. Plus you quoted it back to me each time, which is a delightful way to realize maybe your writing isn't that bad if it can sound cool in an excerpt. You're awesome.

Thanks to Rosamund Hodge for reading this and catching some of the religion elements that needed to be fixed, plus fangirling over Rilen and inspiring his upcoming short story! You're the best.

Christina Baehr, who gave some good suggestions and pointed me towards resources to improve said religion elements—thank you! *Jesus through Medieval Eyes* was great.

Suzannah Rowntree—thank you for answering my cryptic questions about armies who meet to parley without any helpful other context and whether there are pews in a medieval church (answer: no) and should I capitalize 'you' when referring to God (a relatively new Victorian thing). You helped cut down on the historical inaccuracy. I'm sure there's still a whole bunch left, but I appreciate you winnowing it a bit!!

Thanks to my copyeditor Amy McNulty. You caught so many things and made so many great suggestions. Any lingering typos or problems are my own fault. Next book I won't do edits out of order.

To my Deaf and sign language beta sensitivity readers, Dawn Meisenheimer Lewis, Heidi J. Siebert, and Liberty Brooke: THANK you, ALL of you. Writing a book is a group effort and I am so thankful for your suggestions regarding the use of sign language in the book and your suggestions regarding the Deaf and mute characters. Your feedback improved the work and gave me much needed reassurance that I was not stumbling horribly. Thank you for your corrections and improvements. Any lingering errors are entirely my own.

To everyone else who offered to beta read for the sign language portion of the book but was ultimately not able to due to various life situations—I appreciate your willingness! Your unseen support was more life-giving than you knew.

To the Things with Feathers: I couldn't ask for a better group of writer friends. You're awesome.

Mom and Dad, I love you. I am able to write a lot of bad parents in my books because I have some really good ones. I promise the next book will have some good parents.

To the diehard readers—wow. You're so cool. The idea that anyone is excited to read my words is still just as wild as it was when I first started this publishing journey. None of this would go anywhere without you all. I hope you enjoy the adventure.

Lord—you are the Alpha and Omega, the First and the Last, the Beginning and the End. You let us exercise our free will, you mourn alongside us, and your plans will always come to pass, even if we don't understand them in the moment. And you can take it when we doubt, question, and yell.

As C.S. Lewis says in *Till We Have Faces*, "I know now, Lord, why you utter no answer. You are yourself the answer."

Soli Deo gloria.

ALSO BY CLAIRE TRELLA HILL

<u>Gothic Vampire Romance</u>

Black and Deep Desires

Parfit Gentil Knyght: an Addie and Etienne Vignette (Newsletter Exclusive)

<u>The Karneesia Chronicles</u>

The Erlking's Daughters

Mistress of Wardwood and Other Stories (Newsletter Exclusive)

The Flight of the Spellbound

The Heartwood's Choice

<u>Tales from Karneesia</u>

When a Dragon Comes Courting

Come by Water

The Shapeshifter Drives a Bargain

<u>The Lost Treasures of Peredur</u>

Aeronwy's Stolen Child (Newsletter Exclusive)

ABOUT THE AUTHOR

Claire Trella Hill will read anything, but fantasy romance and gothic fiction are her favorites. Born and raised in Houston, Texas, she still lives there because she is impervious to 100 degree weather. She also has a bad habit of making her characters in the Sims and continuing their stories. When Claire isn't writing, she can be found with her nose glued to her library app, assisting with the last tricky pieces of a puzzle, swilling Dr. Pepper, collecting vintage romance covers, or cuddling with her cat.

You can connect with her on social media or sign up for her newsletter on her website ClaireTrellaHill.com.

www.ingramcontent.com/pod-product-compliance
Lightning Source LLC
Chambersburg PA
CBHW030107310726
48970CB00004B/1181